THE TYRANT

THE TYRANT

MICHAEL CISCO

PRIME BOOKS
Canton, Ohio

THE TYRANT

Published in the United States by **Prime Books, Inc.**
P.O. Box 36503, Canton, OH 44735
www.primebooks.net

Hardcover ISBN: 1-894815-85-8
Paperback ISBN: 1-894815-86-6

". . . he drew up a line of battle on the shore of the Ocean, arranging his ballistas and other artillery; and when no one knew or could imagine what he was going to do, he suddenly bade them gather shells and fill their helmets and the folds of their clothes, calling them 'spoils from the Ocean, due to the Capitol and Palatine.' As a monument of his victory he erected a lofty tower, from which lights were to shine at night to guide the course of ships, as from the Pharos. Then promising the soldiers a gratuity of a hundred denarii each, as if he had shown unprecedented liberality, he said, 'Go your way happy; go your way rich.'"

—Suetonius, from his "Life of Gaius Caligula"

"So he was comforted and the next day drew up his army in order of battle on the sea-front: archers and slingers in front, then the auxiliary Germans armed with assegais, then the main Roman forces, with the French in the rear. The cavalry were on the wings and the siege-engines, mangonels and catapults, planted on sand-dunes. Nobody knew what on earth was going to happen. He rode forward into the sea as far as Penelope's knees and cried: 'Neptune, old enemy, defend yourself. I challenge you to a mortal fight. You treacherously wrecked my father's fleet, did you? Try your might on me, if you dare.'

". . . A little wave came rolling past. He cut at it with his sword and laughed contemptuously. Then he coolly retired and ordered the 'general engagement' to be sounded. The archers shot, the slingers slung, the javelin-men threw their javelins; the regular infantry waded into the waters as far as their arm-pits and hacked at the little waves, the cavalry charged on either flank and swam out some way, slashing with their sabres, the mangonels hurled rocks and the catapults huge javelins and iron-tipped beams.

"... Caligula finally had the rally blown and told his men to wipe the blood off their swords and gather the spoil ... The shells were then sorted and packed in boxes to be sent to Rome in proof of this unheard-of victory."

—Robert Graves

I, Claudius

"One might well say that man has at his disposal a capacity for dying that greatly and in a sense infinitely surpasses what he must have to enter into death, and that out of this excess of death he has admirably known how to make for himself a power."

—Maurice Blanchot

CHAPTER ONE

Our Ariadne has brushed by you—in every city. You need only turn aside to see her at your elbow, a plain, dark-haired girl. She sits by the door in a complicated big bundle; the other passengers give her a wider berth and some drop compassionate looks, faint and brief, scarcely aware of the partially unassembled expressions on their own faces and she, with her eyes stubbornly welded to the floor, not at all. She counts the stops.

Without warning, and before the train starts braking, our Ariadne, here called Ella, strongly rises from her seat leaning forward on the stainless crutches that fledge the ends of her two arms, and locks the hinges of her leg braces. When shrieks come from the brakes and you are all precipitated toward the front of the car, she is already braced and leaning into it, and when the doors fly open she sways onto the platform with her eyes still obstinate because this station like all stations on this line has no elevator. The vaccine readily available the disease assumed destroyed, for want of a shot she had lost the use of both of her legs when she was five, from polio. Already a precocious child, the disease passed from her and left her mind hard clear as a diamond terrifying effortless penetrating intelligence, impatient with no wasting time. Utterly defeated and mastered by their remote daughter, her parents could only wave impotent hands when she began taking undergraduate courses as a twelve year old.

Every day, she would stand at the base of the callous stairs in this station, wait a moment for a crazy impulse to spin the wheels in her shoulders bringing the ends of her two crutches up and forward onto the first step. With her crutches' feet spaced widely apart, she would lever herself off the ground and swing both her legs forward between them, settle them down and then repeat until she stood on the upper platform, all the time the crowd dashing on all sides.

Once, Ella was standing near the top of the stairs when a man in a white trenchcoat dashing for the train raced past her along the handrail buffeting her shoulders as he went, and with a sickening heave she felt her balance swing wildly upright she reached for the rail to her surprise it was already above her someone with dark glasses was coming down the stairs with rapidly tumbling steps above her without noticing her. There was a blow across her shoulders that rammed her chin into her chest—that was the landing, striking her, she had fallen—a crutch tangled with the rail post pried her shoulder from its socket and only then came loose away—her momentum carried her heavy rigid legs unable to bend over her head and she dropped for a moment in a cartwheel onto her heels. With nothing to hand she continued backwards and her heels left the step—she plummeted to the platform and her legs clattered on the lowermost steps in a striped metal V, warm damp spread over the softened back of her head, the man with the dark glasses flashed by and into the closing doors of the car to her left, where her head was turned, her eyes stuck half closed. Persons darkly streaked over. Without understanding but fixed moment by moment in her memory she could see a red trickle escaping across the concrete, gathering into a little bulging pool before pushing further, bearing a cigarette butt. She watched that stream flow into the standing yellow pool at the base of the staircase—she remembers an oblivious kick from the hard point of a woman's shoe against the soft inside of her forearm stripped of its crutch. Conscious through some of the miscellaneous activity that followed, before her eyes would finally go dim.

They didn't stay dim but sprang back bright steady and fixed gleaming from her hospital corner, against this attempt on her life. That showed she had devoured the delirium of her long recovery. Ella returned to her study of biology and passed on to the graduate faculty, exhibiting a fresh and uncanny facility with all varieties of ectoplasm, precipitating it from dissected bodies and the comatose, and even from fruit grown in cemetery soil. She would cut say an orange in half and paint the exposed flesh with her solution, press the slice against a thick glass slide and turn on the electric current, and in a moment a round flickering pool of brilliant white fluid made all of minute rolling coils would spread from beneath the halved fruit, looking like a beaded mat of tiny pearls. Now fifteen years old, she has recently published an article on ectoplasmic behavior in the "Lancet". She rides the trains with her gaze on the floor, and whenever a young man sits somewhere near, her lids are squeezed together and the concentrated light of her gaze retreats into the small crescent apertures behind the lashes as two glaring inturned beams; in her daydreams she batters a mob out of her path with her crutches. When Ella climbs the stairs she looks avidly for an oncoming commuter, ready to lash out with fast tip of a crutch. Climbing the stairs truly minatory with the forbidding brawn of her shoulders and arms, deposited over years on crutches, and the crackling blue darts of her gaze spitting under dark, heavy tresses.

From the platform to the upper level and from the upper level to the street, Ella shoulders her way to the sidewalk and ploughs into a gnawing crowd and landscape of hard surfaces, all the city's erratic, jerky motion confined to one horizontal layer close to the ground, while the air between the buildings overhead stands stagnant and oppressive as a glass slide. Ella takes every step entire, such that her body moves forward all at once on her crutches, vehemently regular and in straight lines, throwing the point of focus of her eyes far before her and above the heads of the crowd. Though the Biology Building is dwarfed and crowded, its stones clawed and mouthed at by the surrounding commercial buildings, it has not lost its expansive, mausoleum quality. Ella fixes her gaze on its doorway elevated above the level of the street by a flight of broad shallow steps almost a pleasure to climb, and pedestrians swerve and zig-zag out of her path like gnats. The ponderous romanesque arch of the Biology Building engulfs Ella in its gloom—she levers into its shadow with one swing.

The thick doors are bronze with glass panels, silent hinges, the hall is lofty and cool, padded with carpets, dark and funereal. Ella passes the drooping head of the dozing desk attendant, enters the elevator: it's the size of a closet. Leaning against the back paneling she pulls the grille shut with the end of her crutch and its rattle startles the attendant. Once enclosed in it she can smell the elevator's musty carpet and a mechanical odor of lubricating oil all its acridity worn away, a smell like pencil leads. She bobs once and pulls back the grille. The halls are empty and only dimly lit, most of the light comes from a few high windows at the terms of the broad corridors—their glass is frosted and the light they shed is wan and gleams on the waxed floors. Ella knows the building's varnished intestines ramble monotonously in every direction without much sense to their turns; she's familiar with the department. In the foyer, where the elevator stands pressed against an exposed staircase of coffee-colored wood dripping with little bulbs, spikes, other ungainly ornaments, and where all the diverse routes through the building intersect, she passes a high case of cabinets set in the wall. This is a display of animal specimens, mostly aquatic animals, most gathered long ago, burned white by formaldehyde and alcohol, crepey and little withered. Cunningly hidden lights in the paneling shine through the jars and glass slabs from behind, but their light does not penetrate the slightly dusty glass of the casement doors, topped with gothic points. Standing on graduated steps covered in crimson velvet these pale corpses of cuttlefish, held open with pins, and nudebranchs and eels, an immature leopard shark with blue eyes like crushed shells, have the look of holy relics, all with Latin tags.

In the halls, one or two persons slip past Ella with furtively whispered greetings; they are impossible to recognize in the gloom. The office is large with a number of partitioned compartments, its door standing open. Somewhere toward the back Ella can hear a muffled conversation, and by the milky glow of the distant, large frosted windows, she can make out the silhouette of a woman typing. The rosy wooden pigeonholes for student mail are all empty, including Ella's, though she peers in to make certain. Someone appears next to her.

"Ella, the Dean asked to see you."

The Dean's office is nearby, its ceilings are high and its several large rooms are paneled with darkly glowing tea-colored oak, carpeted with voluptuously red and brown rugs. The Dean's inner sanctum is lined with bookshelves, and one wall where he has his poison cabinet, like the old daguerrotypists, and a tall closet of regular square small wooden apertures, with a labeled, stoppered glass bottle standing in each. The whole affair gives the impression of eternal arrangement. The Dean is sitting behind his palatial desk, bent over a dissection. A heady chemical sourness emanates from the bare desk-top, where bits of the preserved, pallid body, some twitching, are haphazardly scattered in puddles of formaldehyde and alcohol. The Dean is known for this slovenliness with specimens; he seems to precipitate gobs of anonymous tissue wherever he goes. It's not uncommon to find, having shaken hands with him, that one comes away with some alienated bit of anatomy throbbing feebly in one's palm. Now, for a moment, he does not notice Ella, and there is no sound but the tapping of his instruments, not unlike the tapping of silverware on a dinner plate. In his reverie, his head down over his work showing only the black dot of his skull cap and the two bristles of his bushy eyebrows at the front, he sways contentedly over his work sending some particle of tissue sliding across the smooth desk-top, to come to rest at the base of a bronze and stained-glass lamp. Tilting his head up slightly, he exposes to the multicolored light the leathery creases of his face, half-hidden by his beard. He wears a jeweler's eyepiece screwed into his right eye. From time to time, in inspecting the specimen's tentacles, a livid plume of pipe-smoke oozes from between his lips—he keeps the short pipe's stem clenched in his teeth—bathing the exposed flesh of the sample in smoke as if he expected it to change color like a litmus response. The smoke came more and more often, in concentrated plumes more redolent of orange blossom and raisins than tobacco, clearing gaps in the specimen odor. Ella stands watching him certain that he is about to glance up by chance and notice her, speak in almost complete silence in a weak voice, telling her that he had not sent for her.

With a puff, Ella's vital momentum leaves her and she becomes inert, her gaze a statue's gaze, indifferent, her mind a blank. Minutes go by; the Dean's scalpel taps the glass, the little wheeze of breath sucked through the bowl of the pipe alternates with reedy whistle of air in the thickets of his nostrils. Ella's patience unexpectedly drifts up in her like falling snow. The Dean's head droops, and she can see a piston attached to a spinning flywheel down in the dark shaft beneath his skull cap, plunging and bobbing up again at regular intervals, etched with an upright gleam on its brass-colored metal, letting off gelatinous exhaust through his lips. After a moment more, the Dean tilts his head back, allowing his gaze to slide along the surface of the desk and drop from its edge. Ella knows he does not see her; his eyes rise only so far. The Dean's eyes are dark—from where she stands, Ella can't see the whites, but only the glistening metal of them and the banked-down gleams of his gaze that flicker on the thick edges of his eyelids. His hands rest loosely on their edges on either side of the desk, with the scalpel resting diagonally across his right palm. The light from the lamp gives his thick black garments, which though they are not fully cut still fall in luxurious folds, a powdery sheen. At any moment, Ella expects the Dean to address her, but though he seems ready to address her, he also clearly has not noticed her. Confused, on her guard, Ella stands motionless and watches him for any signs, but it doesn't occur to her to speak—the Dean seems as unlikely to hear as to see.

The Dean begins tapping his scalpel thoughtfully against the top of the desk. Ella begins searching the room with her eyes—for what? —for some clue, now she is certain that the Dean won't notice her or speak to her. To her left, against the wall, there is a large cabinet with many low shelves, piled high with papers—as the Dean taps, a letter near the top of one stack of papers catches Ella's eye: it hangs out of the stack suspended by its corner, and it waves. The Dean's oblivious tapping might cause it to fall. Ella moves toward it and sees at once that it is slipping loose, and immediately beneath it there is a badly burnt-down candle, its base splayed in an amorphous mass on the wooden shelf and a long spitting tongue of fire streaming from its wick; its light hidden behind two or three other heaps of paper. Ella swivels her body toward the flame and as the letter drops she plucks it out of the air at waist-level between her two fingers. The candle flame hisses. The Dean is dissecting. The letter in Ella's hand is addressed to her, in her own handwriting.

Ella blows out the candle and crosses the room to sit on a high, hard bench by the draughty, unlit fireplace. Settled there, and able to free her hands from her crutches, she reads Dr. Belhoria's letter, accepting her application alone from among hundreds, maybe many hundreds . . . Ella reads the words from beginning to end, and her eyes skip back over them—and pick out single words here and there, now not so much reading them as looking at them, suddenly become foreign words . . . presently, only shapes. Ella reads, that part of the room breaks free of the rest and the gap spreads apart with a billow in the middle to drive the parts back. She takes on a nude look because her ambition is exposed by her satisfaction in the letter, and her concentration on the satisfying letter is stripping her, gives her an autumnal feeling of wind blowing from branches down the back of her neck as if she was illuminated by stark light although the room is only getting darker. Moments like these have clear outlines and the hallmarks of a memory in advance of its recollection, for her the instant has a double border: the white edge of the page and the walls of the Dean's inner office.

The vertical eyes of the candles at the mantle's corners grow longer and fatten though the room grows darker. The Dean is barely visible at his desk despite the obvious shining of his desk lamp reflecting its light from his hands, face, and slow-moving instruments. Soon she can barely make him out. As the room's last light ebbs out, Ella knows somewhere Dr. Belhoria's lab gathers substance and takes on a light of its own, intended for her. She's been groping toward it in long sweeps of her feelers since she sent in the application and through this letter Ella touches something solid on the other end, a solid opening.

She finds her way into the hall—completely dark, a power outage. To her left she spies a very faint bleak mist of diffuse light from one of the windows, hidden around a corner. Looking briefly to the right she sees a candle pass cupped in a glowing orange hand. She moves to the left feeling with her crutch to follow the wall and its unexpected regular plunges into open doors. Passing the landing of a grand staircase she glances down at an erratically moving light; an orderly in a plaid shirt is standing backward below her lighting the way for two others with his candelabra, these others are carrying a gurney with a sheeted cadaver up the stairs, their woolen hats bobbing back and forth as they miss their footing, trying to keep the gurney level. Ella doesn't dare try the stairs for fear of tripping in the dark, and the elevators must have stopped without power. The dark empty halls go on . . . she traces them at random and from time to time looks up at an errant candle far ahead, without finding her way to one of the windows. A metal rap tells her she has found the elevator and she lightly swings the tip of her crutch against the door, is shocked when it connects with nothing—the door is open, the shaft is blackly yawning—she can feel its musty esophagus breathe on her. Leaning against the jam she peers timidly down the shaft, wondering if there were any casualties.

The shaft and halls beam as power is restored. Ella jerks her head back as if she expected to be brained by the elevator, which actually does sweep down immediately, well-lit and empty. The hundred glass doors that segment the hallway before her shudder and then with sighs swing open in slightly staggered sequence away from her, revealing a door, marked an exterior exit, at the end of the hall—an effect out of a musical, and in fact she notices soft music, although not of the kind used in musicals. Ella leaves through the pearl-windowed doors.

*

On the train, one panel of light succeeds another scanning Ella's body . . .

Starting forward unexpectedly, reading the name of the station, Ella struggles to her feet nearly toppling forwards as the train brakes. The handle of the compartment door is low enough for her to turn it easily. Like an elephant she leans forward on her extended arms, her head tilted back between her shoulders, and with one deft shift she brings her legs down onto the empty platform in scudding drifts of ragged steam. The sky overhead is pale, hard, evenly spread with faint heatless light. Ella descends to the street on a loading ramp, shouldering past the low indistinct station on her right, all horizontal bars of rust and vertical planes of oily grey.

Puffing little bursts of steam herself, Ella has to concentrate on the uneven pavement, whose stones have been pressed out of alignment by muscular roots. The trees are too tall for the narrow streets they line—they spread their canopies over the rooftops and scratch at the walls and windows with their leafy talons. Steady, sparse brooks of pedestrians thread their way in the narrow gaps between the trunks and the storefronts, keep their nondescript heads down. The street is empty of traffic at this time of day, and Ella walks along the curb to a distant intersection.

While the avenues here are broad, paved with huge stone slabs with cobblestone margins, there are no cars to make use of the traffic light—it swings unattended on its wires high above a manhole and throws incongruously festive colors at regular intervals onto the drab walls of the semi-detacheds. The sidewalks are full to the edges with silent, swiftly-moving people. Ella crosses looking both ways—in either direction the street is empty of even parked cars, vanishes in far-off white haze. She's following Dr. Belhoria's directions, enclosed with her letter.

Beyond the avenue, the streets are narrow again, angled up steep hills. Many of them have no sidewalk—the houses here have doors set directly onto the street, swinging inward so as not to be torn off by passing cars. Ella is consulting the bent, increasingly battered directions more and more often. She finds the right street without taking too long. The houses are tall and set off from the sidewalk behind rank cubicle gardens and thick stone walls. The black trees rise by the road like plumes of smoke from cold volcanic fumeroles, their fine branches fill the upper air like smoke. Everything is damp—Ella tries not to slip. The gardens she passes are more like mounds, mostly of flowers, their faces turned in every direction, and reflected in all the cloudy windows. A handful of people here and there in the street. A little girl in a pink coat steps out in front of Ella, walks a short distance in front of her, a globe in one hand and a leash in the other, tugged along by a tiny long-haired dog. The girl crosses with softly crunching feet to disappear down a lane to the left, apparently following the sound of a voice that Ella can barely hear.

Above her, Ella can see the house and gate, surmounted by a brass plaque six feet wide "DR. BELHORIA." Her house stands at the apex of a steeply-pitched V, two streets dropping down like slides and the thin wedge of the adjacent block, a triangular house topped with a circumflex of sidewalk facing Dr. Belhoria's gate off-center. Her house rises up into the air upright but recumbent on a thick mat of vegetation with a backboard of colossal trees, their outstretched fingers make a bristly frame around the walls as if they stood ready to catch the house should it happen to fall over backwards, and those throbbing branches look thick enough to hold the walls erect. Ella makes her way up to the gate, which she finds swung back and held obligingly open by clinging vines. A path lined with dark brown pebbles leads to the front porch; as she steps onto it the air seems to grow duskier, as if it were full of transparent smoke. To either side, bushes, vines, and flowers with lurid, saturated faces grow in a sort of tapestry, giving off a fresh sour smell, a peppery odor of wood, and earth as acrid as vinegar. That black earth has sucked all the water out of the trees and leaves, is black and succulent and firm as cheese.

Ella climbs the steps to the front door, standing on the top step to ring the bell. She breathes deeply, feeling the weird air ringing in her lungs with unwholesome pleasure. The bell thumps somewhere in brick bowels and within moments the door glides hastily open.

Dr. Belhoria stands framed in the narrow doorway.

"El-la!"

Her voice is warm and even purring but her diffusely inadhesive gaze hovers somewhere above Ella's head like a shimmering blue ellipse—a blind magician's gaze, although her vision is actually very acute.

Dr. Belhoria is a complete surprise, all tan gold and blonde, like a brass instrument. She recedes and Ella eagerly steps inside, stands for a moment flanked by two large urns as Dr. Belhoria shuts the door behind her. The room is small and dark, the floor is layered with many elaborate rugs that overlap each other, everything is saturated with incense although the air is clear as crystal, the light she sees around her is faint without being dim and is nearly imperceptibly tinted green as though the house were stoppered up in a high-chimneyed green bottle—the light is faint but everything is polished and richly shining metal and wood. Ella is suddenly tense and alert, her lungs and heart tingle and she looks all around avidly like a nocturnal animal. She knows the house is haunted but not exactly haunted; she's felt that before: intriguing and horrible in all this funereal comfort. The door clicks and Dr. Belhoria goes swiftly by—she is wearing a pale blouse made out of some soft light material, with a wide folded collar clasped at her throat by a broach, and a narrow grey flannel skirt. Ella has not yet been able to get a good look at her face, now Dr. Belhoria has just gone past her without a glance, swinging her arms freely, and she makes a flickering hand gesture over her right shoulder beckoning Ella to follow her down a shadowy hallway. Ella's footfalls are muffled by an endless strip of intricately-patterned carpet; shoulder-high, where the invisible paneling stops, the wallpaper is worked in an obscure pattern on a metallic green field. She passes small tables with transparent glass-green ferns in polished brass pots and waxy cocoa-colored doors, frightening mirrors at regular intervals. After her first glance at one of these she keeps her head down, she doesn't want to see her dim reflection, those doubles step through the frame and follow her. She keeps her head down, her gaze drops until she is gazing at Dr. Belhoria's legs flashing a few paces in front of her, the calves split in half by a pair of black seams, regularly oscillating one and then the other . . .

CHAPTER TWO

Dr. Belhoria's office is on the second floor—Ella is suddenly shown in. The room is large and square with a domed white ceiling of moulded plaster with a gleaming mahogany band around its circumference. Dr. Belhoria trips easily in and out among the many small tables scattered on the rugs, heaps of books, plants growing in clear glass jars of water on the tables. There are sizeable displays set into the wall opposite the door. Dr. Belhoria invites Ella to sit, gesturing to a long leather sofa against the wall.

"Would *you* like something?" she asks.

Ella shakes her head, still engaged in sitting down.

Dr. Belhoria settles lightly in a low-backed armchair on the other side of the room, in front of a large open window. She has gotten a cup of tea from somewhere and sets it on a table within reach.

"You're here for two reasons," she says. "You are as fine an expert as anyone in the field, but I wanted you in particular because you are a quick study. This work is entirely new, and easily the most important now underway"—this last with a little smile—" . . . I've done the preliminary research myself," she indicates a ledger on a table by Ella's right hand, " . . . but I don't like to go any farther without a qualified assistant. Please—" she nods as Ella reaches awkwardly for the ledger.

Their subject, according to the ledger, is an anonymous man, raised in an orphanage and transferred as an adult to a sanitarium. All his life he has been subject to unpredictable and extremely violent epileptic seizures which often left him in protracted trances. This latter detail brought him to the attention of the research society and he was subsequently tested and released into Dr. Belhoria's care.

Ella glances up. The room is lit by a pair of mantled gas lights that throw off a diffuse greenish glow. The windows open inward so as not to brush the extremely low eaves, pressed back against the heavy carmine drapes. The sun is setting and the mingling of its gold and orange light with the room's green seems to lend the heavy furnishings greater substantialness. The rays of the setting sun shine almost directly into Dr. Belhoria's tea making it glow bright amber, while the gaslights turn its steam pale green. A breeze riffles steadily from the window, fireflies are now and then blown into the room. Dr. Belhoria is very luxuriously smoking a chocolate-colored cigarette.

"He is what they call a *world-class* trance medium," she says. Ella hears something rustle behind the almost opaque black glass of one of the displays in the wall—a leathery wing flutters for a moment there. Dr. Belhoria rises to her feet. "With your help, I expect him to achieve complete separation before the end of the year. We should be able to drop him far deeper . . . " She is gesturing to Ella to stand and come with her.

"Does he have a name?" Ella asks.

"He has reserved the right to name himself, and the rest of us for that matter—it will be interesting to see what he decides to call you . . . "

"Where is he?" Ella asks.

"He is here," Dr. Belhoria says. Ella feels a sudden jolt of alarm as if she had just turned to find him hovering behind her. "You'll meet him soon. Review my findings first. Just now, I want to show you a documentary film."

Dr. Belhoria leads her into an adjacent room with no windows, not much larger than a pair of closets joined in an L. Ella laboriously seats herself on a wheeled stool at a small desk with a console immediately by the door, facing the far blank square wall, while Dr. Belhoria arranges the projector somewhere behind her. There is a screen on the console, and the projector's white patch appears both on the wall and on the console.

"This film records one of the earlier experiments—I was present, but only as an observer."

Suddenly there are two figures in front of Ella, one large on the wall, the other smaller and, to a degree, clearer, on the console, both the same. She sees a man in a black and white film seated in some sort of medical chair; the man is wearing a pale institutional outfit, his arms straight at his sides along the hind legs of the chair and restrained with broad padded straps. His feet are out of the frame but his legs seem to be bound as well, a pair of ragged bands are flapping violently on either side of his chest—Ella peers at the bands in surprise for a moment before she realizes they are two halves of a chest-restraining belt that must have torn just as the camera started.

There is a clock face projected in the lower right hand corner of the screen and a small thick glass window in the wall on the left. His convulsions have already started; his head is dropped forward and shaking erratically spattering his suit with saliva and colorless vomit—there is no sound. Small spasms ricochet up and down his body faster and faster until his limbs are sustainedly rigid, his head nods vehemently his chin hammers at his breast. Behind her, " . . . magnificent specimen—!" Dr. Belhoria says in a droll voice. Ella's eyes flick from the wall to the console her hands grip the arm-rests—at first she took the small regularly-spaced dark dots on his shaved scalp to be stress markers or some such until she sees plumes of steam erupting from them a moment later to her shock realizing they were holes bored into his skull. Those plumes rise gently in billows what must have been jets—Ella looked at the clock in the corner of the screen, the film must be in slow motion—the man's head still down he rocks back and forth hammering with his spine against the upright seat his chin streaked with tan bile filligree of broken corpuscles spreading from his winched-shut eyes in a hot blood-colored face glistening through shreds of steam. The screen goes blank—is it over?

The blankness dims at the edges, grows transparent, the light recedes to a point above and slightly off to one side of the lens—she had seen recorded there a brilliant flash of light, small flares and bursts like strings of firecrackers pop all around the chair—the man's torso whips his head slowly forward to the level of his waist leaving a long curved trail of steam—his head bobs violently once then snaps back bloody upwards again his chin rebounding from his chest and as his face comes up his eyes open and the pupils drop down out of the sockets meet hers and strike her like a physical blow a numb thud strikes her right hip and her leg kicks out violently tipping her over sideways. She lands painfully on her side thrown clear of the rattling chair her leg brace chatters explosively like a machine gun against the hard floor. Dr. Belhoria's hands take her by the shoulders and turn her onto her back, Ella's fingers twitch her hands shake. "—yes he's a dynamo isn't he and evidently a bit contagious—" looking up Ella sees his head plummeting forward again like an upended ship sinking and as it snaps down the lights in the front of his booth go out, his head recoils upward again in a second torturous nod his silhouette carves a path through a slow-roiling cloud of rear-lit steam the crescent whites of his eyes glowing in his dark streaming face, his lips pull back from his shining teeth in a horrible ecstatic smile. The image shook and throbbed as if explosions in the earth were thrumming the camera—Ella is unable to calm the shudder that runs through her and Dr. Belhoria is heaving at her shoulders trying to pull her up—the thick window to his left vanishes, the man is engulfed in a cloud of glittering dust with a few flying larger incandescent fragments of pulverized glass orbiting his chair, a gout of steam bursts from his upturned mouth—the film runs out of its spool and flaps.

Ella feels Dr. Belhoria's small, strong hands hauling her onto her feet. She numbly brings up her crutches and braces herself upright. She can feel those hands lightly brushing at her shoulders. Dr. Belhoria briskly ushers her back into the office with its green glow and settles her on the sofa. Looking up and around, Ella sees everywhere blazing eyes in a terrible head feathered all round with coils of steam. Everyone seems to emanate smoke, she thinks seeing in her mind's eye the Dean, Dr. Belhoria's chocolate-colored cigarette, now that man's steaming head—shouldn't I be smoking, too? she wonders, and actually glances down at her hands to see if there isn't an oily wisp fuming off of her skin. The ledger drops into those hands as Dr. Belhoria crosses the room; Ella notices she's freshened up her perfume and put on lipstick. By contrast, the color of her lips makes the teeth she exposes a strangely inviting grey. She is now standing in front of the sofa with her head cocked, attaching her earrings.

"Please familiarize yourself with all that," she says nodding toward the ledger. "You're welcome to stay if you like, there are some empty rooms on this floor. I don't know what food there may be—the cleaning woman leaves breakfast and I dine at my club. You will meet him tomorrow."

Ella starts. Dr. Belhoria is bent with her hand on the doorframe pulling on her right shoe—like a gazelle, she bobs her head on her long neck. Her eyes are fixed on the frame but she notices Ella's movement.

"He's benign," she says in the droll tone she'd used before. "And he can't leave the lab in any case."

A horn sounds twice in the street—Dr. Belhoria snatches a bag from the table and rushes out the door saying Goodnight.

For a while, Ella sits and reads the ledger. It is all inscribed in Dr. Belhoria's neat, 18th century fountain pen hand; the ink has already turned brown filmed with violet. Later, she finds herself drifting around the room, and over to the window with a weirdly light, disembodied feeling. Down in the garden, hemmed in by a high wall of stained grey brick, she sees a pale oblong shape wandering through the soft bracken. She only thought it might be a man for a moment—it isn't, it's an antelope.

*

. . . as she finally lies down in the bed in the room she chose for herself out of so many on the upper story, Ella is hazily aware of all the dark hallways and rooms in Dr. Belhoria's house. What number of hallways had she seen and what number of narrow, coffin-like passageways had she been through to bring her to the narrow room and the narrow bed where she is lying now? While falling asleep, she retraces them in bits and pieces, fainter, more confused, skating by like subway stations—

—in a panic she sits bolt upright—she had caught a glimpse of him floors below, down so deep she wonders is he buried? She saw him lying on his back with a shiny face far below and she was lying the same way in the bed—she had felt his lying position grip her in a cold envelope closing like a fist and as she sits now, her leg braces curled in a chair by the nightstand and her legs lying shapelessly in front of her, her alarming breathing the only sound in the quiet house as the night thickens and the room grows steadily darker . . . is *pitch black*.

*

That morning the braces fly onto her legs, Ella is dressed and heading down the stairs before she is fully awake. The house is filled with light from its many small windows, and the many small rooms and various floors break up the light. The fear that jolted her from the bed seems out of place now, although it holds itself in readiness. She finds a small parlour off one of the ground-floor hallways and steps into a stream of brilliant sun shining through windowpanes so dusty that the light makes them look creamy. There are a few small tables and chairs, and a long low sofa with some sort of machine at one end—a ponderously heavy-looking steel box bolted to the floor, something like a generator with a hemispherical upright hatch, and the sofa is brought right up beneath its lip and a little under so as to fit tightly to the body of the device, leaving no gap.

Dr. Belhoria is there, crossing the room to the machine as if she had lightly tripped out of thin air. She looks the same as yesterday, although her blouse is pinker, her skirt browner. Without glancing at Ella she begins turning knobs on the machine's control panel; the panel hums and corrugated lights the size of quarters blink above the hatch.

"Good morning, Ella," she says pertly, "I hope you slept well."

"I don't know how I slept," Ella says. "What's this?"

Dr. Belhoria points. The hatch has come open and stands straight up, "—at attention" Dr. Belhoria quips, the room is filling with a smell of ammonia and a bit of methane. Ella sees something glisten and bulge inside the hatch—she retreats. With a slick, meaty crinkling sound a rectangular prism of transparent gelatin is extruded from the hatch on a long metal tray, sliding out onto the sofa's upholstery. When the tray stops with a click, the gelatin wobbles, its sharp edges sway back and forth slightly. There is a naked man lying on his back in the gelatin block; Ella recognizes him instantly from the film. He has his hair back.

"This is our test subject, Ella," Dr. Belhoria says laying her hand on Ella's shoulder. "What do you think?"

After a moment, when Ella's mortification becomes apparent, Dr. Belhoria grins a little and pushes Ella lightly toward the sofa—"Go on, examine him, for heaven's sake he's perfectly harmless!"

Ella does look at him. Although his eyes are closed, the expression on his face appeared very obviously to be friendly.

"He isn't—aware is he?" Ella asks.

"Oh he's *aware*, my pet! Certainly more so than you or I—" Dr. Belhoria pulls a metal arm from a dentist's office out from the far side of the box; in place of the x-ray machine, there is an oversized heart-shaped planchette studded with round lettered keys, mother-of-pearl characters with brass rims arranged in two crescents. She positions the planchette above the subject, "Here—why don't you two get acquainted?"

She plunks Ella down in a chair beside the sofa, and pulls a red damask cover from a small monitor in a pewter mirror stand above the armrest. With a shock, Ella notices that the man's eyes are open, his hands rise slow as bubbles in molasses toward the planchette above him.

"I'll have your breakfast brought in to you here."

Ella looks at Dr. Belhoria with her mouth open. The doctor smiles and slips away. The man's fingers slide out from the featurelessly shining surface of the gelatin and ripple over the keys.

The screen says: * I'll call you Ariadne. *

The letters are white on a blue field, and appear all at once, not one at a time. Ella reads them again and again.

* Our Ariadne has brushed by you—in every city. *

"*Don't write that! Don't write that!*" Ella shouts and pushes the screen flailing out her hand, sending it spinning. Afraid without knowing why she fumbles for her crutches, she wants to *leave*.

The screen stops spinning and she sees that it now says: * I wish you would stay and read—don't leave me by myself. *

Ella stops fumbling and looks at his face with a pang. He is aware of her—he knows she is frightened and trying to leave. Images from the film pop in her head, she can see the holes drilled in his skull again. Now he's lying naked in this room, almost completely still, like a preserved cadaver, voicelessly addressing her. Is he as helpless as he looks? What is his threat? Looking at him, Ella gets the feeling he's suffered, is maybe suffering now, and this makes her curious and ashamed of her curiosity. He's magnetic, his presence overflows his outline and shadows the room. When she was younger, Ella had gone with her father to visit a sick relative, her uncle. Without knowing any of the details, she nevertheless had been aware that this was her father's evil brother who'd spent his life doing bad things to himself and other people and whose protracted final illness had been regarded as a judgement on him even by her father. She remembers a hollow-faced man lying propped up in bed, a darkness in the air coagulating around his eyes, his long El Greco face and veiny hands radiating a palpable aura of wickedness and dissipation. In hindsight, some years later, she had realized it was this smouldering aura that made her so well-disposed to him and that had seemed to account for her character and her dissimilarity to her parents. "So *that's* where it came from!" There was something reminiscent of her uncle's deadly room here as well.

"All right, I'll stay with you sir," she says, "—if you can hear me . . . "

* Yes I can hear you. *

After a moment it says: * I really never learned how to talk to people. I tell stories. *

"I'm simply going to have to decide to talk to him like a regular person," Ella thinks. Out loud she says self-consciously "Well I'm not going anywhere, if you want to tell me one of your stories."

* You don't want to hear any of my stories. *

"Why bring it up if you don't want to tell them?"

The screen says: * No no. *

"Don't you want to tell me your story, mister?"

An echo sheds a shadow ring around Ella, her voice travels down its slope and stretches, the consonants turn into a faint hiss and the vowels blend together. The room is still the same but it is transparent now showing through a white landscape.

* Superstitious natives had doused him in kerosene and set him on fire, not realizing then as nobody knew that Air Mail was a visitor from a far distant white world of unrelenting snow and ice. He was discovered by your reporter and party several centuries later, perfectly preserved frozen in a solid block of cubical flames that sweated sticky pearls of tacky white emerald.

* Ere Male was restored to consciousness in fabulous salt mines. Ice-lined anterooms shepherded his body deeper and deeper into freeze, and the flames abated in crinkling streams of high-volume bubbles. As long as they could stand it, they bent their ears to his blue lips and he told them about the winter-summers back home, that would erupt at random when the winds slackened. Then the blue light of the sun would blaze back into the air from the mirror-like ice that coated everything, creating a layer of warm air up to ten feet

thick from the surface, although the ice itself never warmed nor thawed. The sun was always bright when it shone, and hot and clear, and Air Male would stand next to long walls and watch his "summer" disperse in teasing little gusts of rising wind, just teased apart in gusts.

* The wind was never sharp no matter how cold it was. Air Mail would walk along the wall. His people were all there were, and they ranked among themselves according to body temperature: their word for "king" translates to "absolute zero." The king's molecules never moved, except in geologic time—his mouth was held open and the wind would whine through it, the wind served him as his voice by virtue of mental commands. Being composed mostly of water, which expands when frozen, the king who was superfrozen was enormous and sat in a transparent block of solid air where sometimes he would jerk suddenly like a pollywog in a frog's egg.

* Air Male saw only black and white and blue, and also red. He had no yellow cones in his eyes. He had spent his exaggeratedly long childhood in long blue corridors of methane ice, farming protein-rich lichen the color and texture of frost on slabs of composted plankton. He learned how to see the future in a polished ball of frozen nitrogen set spinning in midair by telekinetic oxidation reactions, this for the short-term view, and by reading the underside of the ice-sheet, swimming in the aldehyde ocean where he was born, for the long-term.

* A man preserved in flames will recover without memories the unquenchable character of any time-tested artifact and Air Mail was no exception. Without question he was hopelessly mismatched to this world. At seances Heir Male could fall into trances immediately and profit us from them with extended descriptions of his mental state. Impressed with his loneliness we would huddle up together. Ere Male is collapsed in his chair speaking out of his trance. He could remember in much greater detail the electricity geysers milked for incandescent clouds of ozone. At the moment he is telling us about days and days at the foot of a white wall with no windows; he mimicks the exhausted sighing of the wind that races itself and bundles in frigid bands around him, unimpeded by a landscape long cleared of all obstacles.

Heir Male is as still as an old photograph there in the shadows and soon rings of crumpled ectoplasm will wreathe his head in the air and shed their light on eerily calm features. He is remembering the sweet, luminous shreds of ozone hovering like ghosts in methane caves that shed their light, gathering to watch eruptions of viscous electricity write moment by moment forming titanic trees whose branches frailly brush the blue-white walls, generating a growing haze of violet foliage that bobs on needles of plasma, shining on eerily calm features. In warm wreaths of ectoplasm he descended into deep methane with pockets stretched taut-full of dried berries. In caverns as still as old photographs he uncovered prehuman remains, dried berries and preserved artifacts from the liquid crystal era, when cities were poured in salt overnight and the citizens exchanged quips in static. Huddled up together, the liquid crystal partisans were overcome by the thaw and solidified, still screaming to each other in slow waves of solid static, recognizable, still there to be read, as silver bands flickering locked in the ice. With eerily calm features Air Mail withdraws from the seance through the wall of the apartment, pausing for an ominous moment by the window hovering above the street before permitting the gale to carry him off. *

She watches the letters form like so many white flies down in a flat blue glass, captivated at this very new very old crystal gazing—the screen is like a little counterpane thrown up admitting a chilly draught into the calm room. Ella has used planchettes before in her ectoplasm research; now it occurs to her that the motion of her reading eyes is similar to the scanning of a planchette or better the barely perceptible pressure of the fingers that inexplicably direct a planchette over the board from letter to letter. They both read in the same uncanny way. Without knowing it, she has brought her face close to the screen, although the letters are not especially small—there's a physical sensation of the light of those letters written into her eyes, when she looks closely Ella can feel the light of each individual letter, polished and gleaming but not exactly giving off light—the light is reflected somehow from the substance of the letters, the substance also sinks into her eyes or coagulates at the back of her eyes throwing off plumes of gold filligree, which she can feel but not see, into the clear gelatin of her eyes.

"The Air Mail is you?"

* Yes yes. *

"That isn't *your* story though—" she blinks, absently setting his rubbery gelatin sheath shuddering with the tip of her left crutch.

Transparent figures file into the room—she sees them there around her, though her eyes remain floating over the letters on the screen.

* The two gentlemen visit the dorothydoctor—her erectly leaning house in a remote part of town, a reptilian neighborhood grey and pressed flat and each house harboring a bricked-in back garden bristling with long-sticked spiky black trees; a scarred brick house, wood paneling etc, shown in by the cleaning woman, the dorothydoctor standing in the door to her parlour. The two men sit opposite the sofa and the device which is an extremely pale shade of key lime green and smoke, drink coffee that the cleaning woman has brought and take out their notepads, goateed old man dark olive complected with specs droopy bow tie baggy suit, other anonymous pallid old man no color full head colorless hair soft features like crumpled linen, silent.

* A fly on the window outside sees her turn and in profile with one hand—the other arm still over the back of her chair—the doctor enters business on the keyboard, the wheel on the hatch spins and the hatch swings open releasing clouds of steam the windows are fogged instantly with a splatter—the fly buzzes off. From the open hatch emerges Air Male in his cube naked of course with his hands clasped on his breast and his head slightly back otherwise not moving—the dorothydoctor brings the planchette up—Err Male's hands move through the gelatin without disturbing it excessively, emerging from the end immediately before his head dry and emanating heat in the open air the hands move unerringly to the planchette and immediately they touch it they move it to YES.

That's his (old) preset.

* The goateed man does all the talking—he asks a question—the keys click slowly and decisively while the dorothydoctor briskly voices the letters—several questions are asked, there is a loud crack or report from somewhere in the room, over the men's heads—the interview is over—the dorothydoctor manipulates the control panel—Air Mail pulls in his hands and is retracted into the machine, drops down behind the closing hatch as she shepherds the men out of the room—

* Air Male descends, the two men are walking down the hall to the door—the dorothydoctor is the null point of these horizontal and

vertical axes—he slides down the shaft—the men hurry anxiously to their old car and drive off.

* For them the world going by their windows . . . the insane lights and colors, more and more brilliant, intense, smarting their eyes, the car's limpid glass and gleaming surfaces seem to emanate an optical oil that coats their eyes making them reflective and slippery, no light can penetrate but streak and slide off crinkling into the dark seams of the upholstery, the minute black crevices in the detailing and the dashboard, into their own seams and crevices—overhead the flaring white clouds apparently resolve into weird pillars and inscrutable lucid friezes that are standing still while they rush by in their car, they shiver at the unwelcome intimacy of the sky's blue color, which probes them now like a sort of devastating confession so that they must violently stop up their ears, even against the painful pressure of their curiosity—they are shaking with the upwelling force of a special self-destructive curiosity, and glancing up at the sky they feel vertigo and clutch at the armrests and at the edge of the seat—their car is gliding along a slippery slope drawn along by an exhilarating force that isn't gravity or inertia only a frictionless attraction to some nothing that's opening somewhere at this moment, which pull is palpable and even invasive in them both—

* Finally in terrified paroxysms first one, then the other reflexively convulse into themselves as a vomiting, so much fear and creeping dissolution to vomit, lightlessly to vomit cold black vomit, night vomit—horror vomit, vomiting that violently screws them back together and compacts them into their own exhausted selves. Then, blinking, they feel a gradual, limping relief and are bolted back into place—the relief of a loose cog sprung terrified into space now being calmly sutured back in place, the comforting familiar teeth engaged again, just content to tick and tock. They will have forgotten comma everything.

* Air Mail descends and emerges into the underground, where he is conveyed on his tray through heated passages of packed earth and dangling roots that brush his gelatin, beneath him is a friendly little blue stream choked with dashing white clumps of ice, bordered on either side by scintillating lichens. *

These memories come wafting over in this unnatural way, with no proper point of view.

"Where are you?" Ella asks, " . . . in all of this?"

After a few moments and no answer, she says, rubbing her eyes and smarting temples, "How are you telling me these stories? Have you hypnotized me?"

* Not in any unusual way. *

"Well but is that really *your* story?" she asks, still rubbing.

* All stories are mine. *

"You know that's not what I meant," Ella says, nudging him again with her crutch, "Tell me a *new* story, about you." After another pause, and no response, she coaches and nudges, "*I* remember . . . "

The screen, though blank, takes on a wry expression.

CHAPTER THREE

* I saw everything then with the exalted nine-dimensional vision of a young epileptic boy, sent as an orphan to the Home for Epileptic Boys, HEB. On all sides rise up lean white buildings stark against the trees, nestled in copses and connected by paved lanes, and boys running on the paths and across the grass—girls running as well. They come to visit from the Home for Epileptic Girls, situated on the other side of the hill. Visiting today with soaring skirts their hems pummeled by bony knees. HEB's male nurses, their forearms on their thighs and their hands dangling between their knees, and HEG's female nurses with crossed arms sit together here and there. I am there—maybe I was conceived on a day like this, when some of the nurses, some of the children, are nowhere to be found. These woods are dense and deep on all sides. Though they are sliced up by roads and fields, where they stand the trees are knotted thickly together, and there are many many cool hollows bowers mossy hidden banks shaded by the low-hanging boughs like a veil folded criss-crossed over and over, amorous curtains of needles and watchful black wood, soft scales of damp scabby bark crumble off the trunks when luminous pink fingers rub them. In there, and I still hear their voices in between the buildings, their matter-of-fact tone as they make up new rules as they play, responding to everything. Up and down the field, the boy running is the one you asked me to show you. Owing to the influence of my memory, he runs in fluorescent time.

* They were always encouraging us to run, to tire ourselves—we

were not to get too excited. To keep us calm, they assigned us a very scientific curriculum, administered by very old and charming teachers. From building to building with flying legs, then we would stand outside bent in half with our hands on our hips and our heads down panting steam. In the classrooms, our desks were bolted to the floor. Everywhere there were always nurses on the watch, and the moment any boy showed *signs* he was immediately enfolded in a closing blossom or sea-anemone of white-sleeved arms and shoulders, plucked up, immobilized by a firm-gripped circle, and borne away. We would see him again later that day, or perhaps the next, pale and shaken, sodden and tousled, with fragile manners, startled and dazed.

*—and after hours and hours of frenzied sleep, the prospect of the room from his bed insistently fretting his eyes and his body groans and sweats under the heavy bedding, he comes awake again. And this time, something *definite* is wrong. He is lightly stirred inside himself. And his hand, resting on the top of the covers, twitches. He is stirred more. He sits up the blankets push back and bunch he bends nearly double his back straining against the weight of the thick covers. And he stares into the black room. There's nothing to see what is wrong is *already inside*. He throws off the covers. His hands are trembling. The trembling will spread. Seeing through time he knows what is going to happen and he goes out into the hall, he starts to run—his knees swing open behind him and pull forward slowly but less and less slowly starting to bound up toward his chest and then they snap up the wide dark halls tumble around him and the broad corners where he makes sprawling flying turns bright windows in dark rooms far distant veering in curves a door rushes at him and blindly he throws his arms across his face and ploughs into it—there is a blast as the bolt snaps and the door crashes against the opposite wall—a sudden shock to his knees and ankles dropping the few steps to jar on the paved lane outside he pinwheels his arms to keep his balance and goes on, the blank of the fit seems to chase right on his heels and he can imagine it with every nerve in the back of his neck his shoulderblades and all down his back—a see-through shadow figure a little shorter so that its outstretched hands only reach his shoulders right behind him . . . outrun it, outrun it. Along the length of a high

hedge wall he runs and turns with the path into a gap in the high hedge wall into a brink on the sky the horizon a bent line not far from his feet the blue gulf of winter sky the shining circle above him, alone, now its light is blinding, his legs buckle and he curls over with his arms crossed over his stomach in his eyes lunar light brims, glints, streaks his face, he falls over, looks up from the pavement—shudders build spread thudding out of deep wells, the moon flashes his body twists, looks up, standing over him in the gap in the hedge wall, they do not block the light, the ghosts veiled in black from head to foot holding long black hammers, raise them though he begs though his mouth is cold gluey numb chattering—a hammer buzzes through the air down through his surface into him the blow lands inside—his body jackknifes his voice makes an uncontrolled sound as the air is forced from his lungs he rebounds into the air and drops back onto the stone still conscious his eyes still open to the moonlight that *flares* the hammers drop blows inside his body throwing the levers of his limbs kicking him up into the air spinning in place above the ground like a grain of rice on the rebounding skin of a drum—the light *flares*, *flares*, *flares*, in its light he sees long serrated lunar flames standing with the trees, their edges undulate faster and abruptly streamline as the flames become jets with pale cores, the buildings are petrified—their substance—wood and stone—invaded copied gone replaced with heatless fire blazing like snow—suddenly *enraged* he feels his fit direct itself at their blazing shapes throwing fierce blows that shake the ground send curtains of decomposing flame ruptured from their foundations—vast circular ripples brush the buildings and reduce them instantly to immaterial powder—the nurses run with their arms in the air shedding burning wakes heads like torches, more stand flaming in place of the ghosts. The firm grips seize him, some terse talking he can't hear, a pinprick somewhere in a remote arm, the light is suddenly gone and he is gone. When he revives he will have to be made to understand that in the last few days he's been nothing but wind and rain pebbling his windows, a rustle of footsteps in the hallway, a scraping of pencils and chairs.

* My studies resume under observation and a medical . . . he runs weightless all over campus, transparent mind and body, empty, all forgetting, light. I remember vision so clear it was as if even my eyes were out of the way of my sight, although the memories are all fog.

The girls from the HEG are brought around, I'm just an empty shape. With nothing to hinder them every feeling I have suffuses me and fills every part of me. I'm chasing little tossing heads of shining hair, watching their legs flip and one set of legs diagonally replace another, following the legs. *

—Ella sees the rhythmically oscillating seams of Dr. Belhoria's stockings and her metallic blonde calves like champagne flutes.

* Some of their faces I never saw—so let's say I chased you, Ariadne, and the dorothydoctor— *

Ella says, "I'm too young, at that age I was already crippled and couldn't run from you; and my hair was never shining."

* One replaces another, I follow the one before me, who is she, who is this new one, who is the next one? They're flashing over the grass leaving behind them in the air the irrepressibly stimulating odor of graham crackers that, if I'm not too slow, blends with their own smell of clean laundry heated and moistened by their bodies' running, and the smell of earth, saliva, and bruised grass . . . In the shadow two faces cast over one another we converse, I hear the uncanny tone of their voices especially when they talk low, when all the brassiness disappears and there is only the weirdly soft and fine child's voice speaking quietly, without even the fits and starts and sudden changes of tack, but instead steady plausible sentences.

* These amorous exercises were only minimally innocent; our still-sunrising bodies fell short of physical competence but the spirit was there. We knew that the authorized excuse, that a little satisfaction in love would help us to better observe the demand never to get too excited, was also an opportunity taken by every orderly, nurse, teacher, and administrator for ardent rendezvouses in hidden places across the campus. Sometimes we catch them or blunder across them—"sharing laps" we call it.

* Missing the girls after the buses carried them off, we are left without much interest in our usual diversions—those teeth of the girls' leave long marks and their ghostly odors and the indelible light of their hair oppress us in their absence. We looked for distractions—we discovered an ingenious wind-up model figure of a boy that simulated seizures. The staff employed it to train orderlies in the classification, study, and recognition of the various types of attacks. He wasn't used much any more and he wasn't hard to prise from his

closet in the cellar beneath our classroom—wound up in the middle of a ring of us he would roll onto his side and curl into a ball and then lash out in wild convulsions when prodded. The bakelite carapace of his forearm would rap violently against the cement floor and his back would buck and twist like a rampant fire hose. We would peel back his clothes to get a look at the frenzy of his gears and the pair of shining pistons beneath his hard, clear breast-piece. When he would now and then flip over, the sort of smile on his rubber lips sailed placidly down with a turn of his head and smacked on the floor tossing his tousled hair. Once, in his frenzy, he spun and struck against the floor at a bad angle, his right leg broke off at the knee, and we were never able to reattach it. We were so afraid we would be found out and blamed for damaging him—but naturally we didn't stop—more and more inflamed as we watched him and afraid we would begin to convulse as well, we would keep winding him back up without waiting for him to wind down, all take hold of him and one of us would clumsily push the key into the socket in his side and vehemently twist it against the resistance of the coils— *

* we idled away our time innocently raping this machine until the afternoon it gave a long piercing cry. *

. . .

* It cried once, from behind the rubber face, its clothes stripped away showing its lungless works, the shrill went on and on while we were already flying from there *

* I hear it now. *

. . .

* Do you hear it? *

Ella says no.

* You will, all will—I haven't forgotten it, I don't remember it—it is *there*, like my skull is there, in my mind but it has nothing to do with my mind or my thoughts. It and a few other impressions I won't describe, that are kinds of memories, I can find again as I would find any memory, although these memories are of places I've never been, and things I've never done, memories that don't involve me in any way.

* The figure was removed to some other place and we never saw it again, though I dreamt of it. The door to my room would open as I lay

in bed and the hall light would gleam on the brass strip at the threshold—he would run in, and stop for a moment. But what would he do, fill the room, give me an attack? Not enough. I know he still exists, and I imagine he's grown as I've grown, become more complex. He's not a double for me or for anyone—he may be a double with no original, if that's possible, or a double of a generic original, if that matters—he's better than a double, not just for being for himself, but because he was made in no uncanny way: there is a patent on his design, and he was assembled in a little foreign factory where devices of his sort are *mass produced*. I imagine they may now run the show, there at the factory—assemble themselves in ever-greater numbers. *

*

Later Ella is sitting in the sculpture garden of a local museum eating cafeteria sandwiches. The garden is bordered on two sides by a featureless curving white wall and on the other two sides by the museum's glass halls. In front of her is a broad level kidney-shaped area covered in white pebbles and metal and stone statues artfully positioned. Early afternoon, clear sky so pale as to be almost white, cold wind, brilliant cold far-away sun. The sandwiches are cold also. Ella nods and nearly drops her mouthful into her lap but catches herself in time. From here, the breeze occasionally brings her a little of the demoralized odor of the cafeteria whose doors stand open nearby. A few people loiter by the door and one or two are sitting at the wrought-iron tables, some others visible through the glass walls, stroll and stop. When Dr. Belhoria returned, she was surprised to find the two of them "conversing" still, took him down below for his feeding, and told Ella to come to her study at four. Ella had come down from Dr. Belhoria's hill to mail a letter home, walked on pavements of crunching grit looking up to see the clouds fall into low-flying shreds snagging and fraying their rag-ends on the higher spikes of the roadside trees. She saw him everywhere, at every window, seemed as if he'd been thrust through her like a peg, feet-first between her eyes, her ribs. In her mind's eye she saw him lying flat inside her like a carpenter's level measure parallel to the ground, she also saw him in what she recognized as a more conventional way, in the trees. Ella watched the ground when she walked—when her head swung up and the down again of its own accord, perhaps to help her keep her balance, she glimpsed a monkey perched at the bottom of a stone banister, part of the front stoop of a brownstone with lit candles in all of its many windows. Startled she snapped her head back level—nothing. When she stopped at the bottom step, she saw a pair of them up at the top of the banisters, crouched in the shadows at either side of the door moulding, their small hands pressed against the moulding in symmetrical mirror-gestures. They were bronze—the one on the closer banister seemed to meet her gaze with its large surprising eyes. She could not see any mouth at the end of its dog-like snout, but the eyes and ears were lifelike and prominent, its fur was as neat and even as if it were wearing a costume. The doors whose jambs the monkeys held struck through the brownstone, halls of museum offices, to the glass galleries and the sculpture garden where she is now.

Ella stands up, and as she leans forward she hears something coming underground—she laboriously kneels on the pavement, unlocking her braces, and presses her ear to the white pebbles. Down below, even though there is no lower floor or any subterranean room there, she hears a voice speak in a matter-of-fact tone, blurred by the dirt. She recognizes the tone, the buzzing of that hollow voice or voices has been with her for a while, behind the canvases and humming in the statues. "The ghosts seem to be growing," she thinks and scrapes the black soil, rubbing a clod between her fingers—a hot white ectoplasm with fine silver grids in it oozes out. Kneading her tingling hand she peers right and left, then gets upright leaning on her chair. A voice speaks unintelligibly behind her. Turning so hastily she nearly falls Ella sees behind her pebbles, statues, earth, trees, walls, windows, clouds, sky, and beyond the sky, stars—and presumably endless space.

*

Dr. Belhoria's laboratory is an elaborate underground complex beneath the house. They stand together at the bottom of a resonating iron elevator shaft whose grill-works open onto a large hub room reminiscent of a Roman bath. The far wall to the left projects out from the foundations into the open air, its rock is pierced at regular intervals with small square bright deep-set windows. Their lower sills are long stone ramps angling down to capacious sinks carved from solid granite blocks, streaked with rust from goose-necked spigots. This rough wall is in striking contrast to the elegant black-and-white diagonally-checked polished and gleaming floor. The room is vast, shaped like a number of trunks with curved lids pushed together or the bellows of a squeezebox with curved peaks, or an oblate honeycomb, and in each of the humped vaults of the ceiling a mummified crocodile is suspended, the length of the lab spans beneath precambrian claws. High lab tables faced and topped with black marble line the other three walls. The table opposite the elevator is so far away it appears hazy. Some of the tables have recessed sinks with whalebone basins and elegant fixtures of solid gold. A number of instruments and electronic devices are there; Dr. Belhoria shows Ella the computers—cubes of smokey resin with a single switch and a single blue beryl light, pale blue screens in applique frames, and keyboards with amber keys, such that beneath every bright white letter there's a dark spot, an ancient insect preserved in each key.

Ella has been describing this morning's interview, "I saw him having another attack, and with that, combined with the footage you first showed me, there seem to be some anomalies . . . I mean I don't think he's a proper epileptic."

"No, you're quite right—I think he's been consistently misdiagnosed, although I know I haven't the faintest idea what his actual condition is—" she turns her grin on Ella practically licking her chops—"Did you notice that he remains conscious during his seizures . . . ? —Isn't that *obscene?*"

When Ella flinches and looks uncomfortable at the question Dr. Belhoria turns with a twisted mouth, searches through the charts on the counter.

Ella shifts back and forth on her crutches. "Do you know he has his own name for everyone?"

Dr. Belhoria is working the switches on a wall-mounted control box, "Oh he never gives anyone their proper name . . . I'd be interested to know what he calls *you.*"

"Ariadne."

"—Well that's better than mine," her thumb is tamped firmly down on an unmarked concave button.

"Do you think he means anything by it?"

"I'm sure."

Ella leans back against a counter taking a little of the weight off her arms, diffident " . . . What does dorothydoctor mean?"

"That's his joke on me—because he knows Dorothy is a name I've always *detested*."

"So—what is your first name?"

Dr. Belhoria smiles. "Annabel Lee." She clamps down a second switch—somewhere there's a whirr of hydraulic machines.

"Oh uh I'm not certain this means anything but this afternoon at lunch I precipitated ectoplasm from a bit of soil—using only my own magnetic field."

"Caa-pital."

"—Well I mean I shouldn't be able to *do* that—"

Dr. Belhoria waves her toward an arched opening in the wall by the control box, "I'm going to show you why—come in here."

The passage is a solid shaft shaped like a pointed arch, small wall sconces drop faint pools of light on a spongy crimson carpet, a basement smell mingles with the threads of Dr. Belhoria's perfume. The path is short and straight, forming the stem of an angular Y embracing a small chamber; there are panels with brass and ceramic knobs and polished wooden fixtures, needle gauges lit with tiny lights, rising from the floor to a height of about three feet, which wrap around the chamber in a U. Above the panels, the chamber walls are thick panes of ultramarine glass. Dr. Belhoria sits on a rolling chair and Ella settles herself awkwardly after a few moments. The strip of space between the panels and the black stone walls is cramped, and the curved ceiling oppressively low. While it is confining, Ella has an oddly exhilarating feeling of being safely hidden away; the basement lab and this room in particular are both strange and unthreatening at once, like an amusement park.

Dr. Belhoria's manipulations of the control box were evidently connected to bringing the subject, wherever he might have been, up into the chamber. As she settles Ella starts, a barn-shaped hatch dropped open and the "air male" is gliding into view on a moving belt. As he comes into position, moveable banks of glowing red coils arrange themselves in a semi-cylinder around him, leaving him exposed only on Dr. Belhoria's side.

"The heat keeps him calm," she explains complacently. "Yoo-hoo," Dr. Belhoria says as she leans into the microphone on the console, flicking its button—she says it half-distracted, Ella sees at once that this is the usual greeting. She's never seen how the two of them talk to each other—" . . . show Ella what you can do, my fine boy."

Ella might mention she's seen what he can do; she says nothing.

He opens with a crowd-warming trick—his hand slickly glides out from the side of his prism and takes up a pair of thick metal bars. He grips them in one fist so that they cross each other in an X and holds them up, motionless except for a momentary flickering contraction of his facial features he somehow causes the ends of these bars to blur like fan blades in four vertical arcs each at its own compass point—a buzz traveling up his arm and conducted down the rods, which are vibrating, not spinning—Ella can hear the deep burr they make and feels the floor hum beneath her feet.

"Keep it interesting, you old ham," Dr. Belhoria leans in with her eyes diagonal on the gauges. She sits primly up and pushes the chair back against the wall; her gaze disengages all contact as she chooses her words.

Sunset light filters through the glass, gold-orange mist with glinting pink beams flat and horizontal as boards, bronzing Dr. Belhoria in her chair by the black wall. As she talks, sanguine rays ebb to a clinging reddish haze, the faded glass starts glowing silver, flakes of snow tumble in all directions, circle and jostle each other. Ella can even hear them pitter on the window.

"As you know, when life is extinguished or converted, ectoplasm is generated as a latent charge in the freshly vacated space—those who die slowly generate a great deal around themselves hence the increasing vagueness about them, as their image bleeds into absorbent space. Your successes yesterday at the museum were a direct result of your prolonged contact with our subject, who, as we have said, is a special case. His syndrome, which I will continue to call 'epilepsy' although it is clearly not that, is a condition of superabundant vitality, with therefore a corresponding surplus capacity for death. While in operation as a medium, he oscillates between life and death and thus creates a static charge in space, which potential was to a small degree transferred to you.

"Oscillation allows him to be neither dead nor alive but puts him into another category of life altogether, which I will call potential life. His medium state is a reduction to pure potentiality of life—I mean he is only possibly alive or possibly dead under those circumstances, a quality he shares with seeds, for example. Unlike a seed, which enters into the regular order of life upon germination, he is able, as a serial being, to shift in both directions, from static to active and from active to static. You may imagine an analogy between this and the conversion of potential to kinetic energy in mechanics. When our subject goes static, the life in him is not lost but only converted, and a certain amount of surplus is thrown off in the field of living things—hence the charge you brought away with you yesterday, and which, as you observed, was ectoplasmically expressed.

"During his trances, he can act as something like a human time-lapse recorder, certainly his relation to time seems to change although it is not yet clear how. This may or may not be related to his ability as a medium to enter the underworld, which is the object of our research here."

The room is dim, the snow haloes dark trees buried in the glass—Dr. Belhoria, starkly lit from somewhere below, and seeming to loom very high, takes on the look of a brass sphinx, her exposed collarbone in particular seems as if it were cast in burnished metal, she gives an impression of wings outspread.

"Clearly there is a need to penetrate death, which equally clearly must fail—it isn't possible, it is constantly attempted—the Grim Reaper has no eyes to see, no ears to hear, no heart, no mind . . . it is only life's skeletal anchor, the structure, the underlying brittle hardness. You cannot make yourself death's confidante. He is only a friend to those he animates.

"We come closest to apprehending death at least from the outside in nightmares or other sorts of dreams. As you know, I have cured many diseases previously assumed to be uncurable by inducing certain types of dreams in my patients. These dream-cures led me to the next logical step, of escaping from dreams downward instead of upward—but for that, a medium was required. The medium is able to enter the field of images by becoming literally a still-life. The reduction to the static condition generates ectoplasm, and, as you have established, ectoplasm is the elemental substance of image.

"The image, the part that survives in the mind as memory and in space as ghost, which is not the same as but is mutually exclusive with life as we know it, but which is also, as the Egyptians knew, the posthumous libido, the life of the image on the wall or carved image, the presence on the receiving end of their idolatry—they called it 'ba'—

("Really, I can't see how the Egyptians managed to take themselves seriously with that baby-talk language of theirs," she says, dropping for a moment into a conversational tone.)

"—a kind of soul that animates images and objects, an extension or emissary of the underworld, which is populated, as we currently postulate, by linguistic elementals. There is nothing inconsistent in the notion that such beings may be self-conscious since self-consciousness in itself changes nothing. The ghost, like the medium, is not an expired life but a different sort of life, a serial being; in some cases, we have ghosts unborn in this life, beings who were born ghosts—"

Dr. Belhoria's eyes take on a subdued heated glow the color of very fresh magma. Thin headstones glow blackly in snow flurries—no horizon, the scene swims with white powder, swept overhead by brilliant phantoms, gauzy shreds of mist pass over ground where nothing stands, and above those shreds Ella can see shadowy masts and rigging, against looming icy cliffs of blazing fog.

"—conversely, normally living persons may also be ghosts without having properly died, like our subject. Life is not simply that which is additional to a lifeless thing—our subject will be induced to contact death in several varieties and then we will examine his recordings. Just as certain South Sea islanders tether the oldest house in the village to the oldest grave by means of an artificial umbilical cord, thus relating a certain kind of original loss to a certain kind of original foundation or lasting form, so we will send Mr. Bathyscape here down from the laboratory into the grave on a retractable umbilical.

"The figures we read in figures of speech, their life is the life of words. No one who is in history for us lives but that their life is living on the page, and we are no different, and live as we are, or will be, *paged through*, in a written history."

Dr. Belhoria's whole body seems suffused, her substance like transparent glass of bronze, showing an interior of space of drifting gold spangles suspended in a thick fluid dark cobalt black and blue, like cold flowing undersea glass oozing from volcanic fissures. Her eyes narrow to black crescents that seem to spit beautiful pearl-shaped gobs of blackly-blue obsidian gelatin. Light from the window spears her collarbone and prismatically splinters against it, shedding into a radiant burst of infrared beams. There is a blue-black river cut into the snow, its water crinkles over invisible wafers of ice. A duck paddles into view; Ella snickers—she's just seen a living whim. All the same she wonders if this witty duck is aware of the cadavers lying just within the bank to its left, as if it could see levelly through the dirt to the dead bodies resting like rows of machines in their graves. Immediately in front of the window, there is a peep of disclosed color—is it a low brick post? It may have been, there is no post there now, only she sees something ruby, gleaming like a ball of sticky blood. Now she sees what it is it's a cherry, really beautiful against the star-colored snow.

Dr. Belhoria runs her hands along the undersides of the words you are reading now like she's idly stroking a bead curtain. "So Ella, we're going to help our friend here break things open for us . . . "

* Now let me show myself nakeder, Ella— *

* Just beyond view of the antiseptical star-colored buildings of the Home, over the shoulders of the dips and hollows carpeted with dead leaves and voluptuous moss, our boy is clambering on the boulders. Now he's stopped short, his breath cuts off, his insides drop out like a plummeting elevator, his hands quake and go clammy, the few rays of sun that fall on him feel scalding hot on his blanched skin, his hair stands stiff in frigid waves, his cheeks bunch up baring his teeth as if he'd stepped in an electrified puddle. Across a small covered glade, opposite him where the trees thicken again, there the deeper shades make figures that move back and forth behind the trees. He glimpses them where patches of light hang between the trunks, mounted on dark bucks, figures under black veils that don't billow but hang straight from the crowns of their heads, black hosed legs grasp the flanks, one long-gloved hand pinches the pelt at the nape the other holds up a black hammer like a sledgehammer. The bucks move in long weightless bounds slow in congealed, limpid air, and where he

sees them, in the light patches, they come down, head and shoulders plunge forward the riders flex backwards at the waist in a languidly stretching angle, the hammers' weight pulls the arm up—silent, they rise and fall in low curves, this way and that behind, the trees like noiseless waves—

* The boy's chest begins to heave, he panics, he slaps the rock with the palms of his hands as though he is fumbling for something while he turns staring on his knees. He runs, his feet thump hollowly on the elastic forest floor. Out through the bracken onto the cleared slope, he turns to look—they all veer in his direction at once like a banking school of fish, cloudy streaks from the treeline following him. His legs seem to ramble randomly under him, then all at once he suddenly intuits how to sprint, he brings his knees up with each stride and flies nearly plummets down the slope grass blades twigs rocks and ground race all around him in streaks and beneath his spinning legs. The stags pursue him with slow lazy bounds zigzagging back and forth in an undulating file almost on top of him. The boy runs, his hands blaze and smear across his eyes, a kind of light is throwing its haze around him—the clouds tear open, the blue there is black, stars coming out, in the center is the moon, swelling—he can't take his brimming eyes from it, from behind a hammer buffets him face-down on a slab of rock and the bucks race past on either side making a pelting torrent. He twists and lashes the ground, like a fist grinding itself into his stomach there's a pressure that steadily pushes a weak despairing moan out, body twitches thrashes stiffens under blows of circling figures' high hammers batter him against the rock and he springs up into the air on flailing arms and legs, foam hangs from his mouth and a new froth drops in threads from his thighs—his right hand suddenly snaps in midair blindly closing on the shaft of a hammer streaking by on his right, his grip holds and the rider and buck are wrenched around, tumble spinning lengthwise along the ground, the figure spinning inside his veil, vanish in kicked-up dust—the boy turns and another rider is on top of him, he breaks the other's hammer with his own and hits out at the rider's hip sending him or her crashing to the ground, the buck kicks free—the veil rides up along the downed rider's side exposing naked ribs—at the sight the boy smashes them howling with bestial rage stepping on and crushing the veiled head—he runs to the high spot on the rock and holds the others at bay, turning quickly

around with the hammer—the silence broken only by the boy's howls the riders float about his feet and ankles in rings, like the choreography of ritual combat, and rearing high above the trees he knocks them to one side and another like toy soldiers, roaring in the clouds and stamping his colossal feet. *

*

Ella finds Dr. Belhoria, who had apparently left the room the moment she had finished speaking, leaning against one of the counters in the lab, rubbing her eyes. The full weight of her own tiredness and overloaded understanding seems to land on her shoulders with a palpable thump.

" . . . How much of that was you and how much was him?" she asks.

Still rubbing her eyes, with a sighing tone, "I couldn't say. The man's as mad as a hatter."

And, a little later, Ella asks, "He'll be risking his life, won't he?"

"Naturally."

"What if you fail?"

Dr. Belhoria is fully alert all at once, "I have never failed." Her voice is flat; she states it as a fact. A moment later, she takes from her pocket a stick of some chocolate-colored material, breaks off a length, lights it, puffs out a plume of snow-white smoke. The windows are dark. She starts crossing toward the elevator.

" . . . He didn't really say, 'You will—all will'?"

"That's what he said."

"What a ham!"

Ella glances apprehensively at the man lying naked in the lights at the end of the passage, "Say was he, ever . . . ?"

"What?"—and then her eyes widen, " . . . m-my *sweetheart*?!" she gurgles with incredulous delight, her shoulders rise as she laughs. Her surprising laughter is mellifluous; Ella had expected a harsher sound. The smokey peals of Dr. Belhoria's laughs ring like bells against the exposed teeth of the crocodiles.

CHAPTER FOUR

Ella is on the subway again, with barely a memory of the steps she had taken in the street, crowds traffic stairs and turnstile platform doors and seating herself all reduced to static, a fabric of racket and moving shapes. Now she sits by the door—her parents had telephoned, shanghaied her into attending a family dinner, where, as though played out in advance, she sees herself bunched up behind her place at the table with her eyes on her plate or sitting as far out of the way as possible accounting for herself to all her relatives, lining up her dodges and evasions so as not to have to explain the project, Dr. Belhoria.

When Ella was thirteen, she realized she was going to die, and for a month she lay awake every night in terror, flat on her back afraid she might vomit, rigid, nodding and starting nearly jolting herself out of bed, finally she would fall asleep. Now she sleeps better but with no warning she is sometimes ambushed and paralyzed with terror of death . . . Looking around the car, she can see each of these faces in its casket, grey flesh limp, eyes fallen in, nightmare caverns of stiff nostrils black as pitch, sagging ears, slack cheeks drooping away from a wired jaw and permanently sealed, livid mouth . . . The opposite bench is empty, in the black pane of the window above it there's a wan dewy frowse, Ella, and above all she can see *that* face in its casket, purple-black bruises make a wide ring around her eyes, her hair dry as hay, weirdly friable and clumsily gathered on the stiff cushion—"just fucking *burn* me" she says with cold lips sutured shut. In her mind's eye she's searing, melting and shriveling in the flames, locks of hair flap here and there in gusts of fiery wind—and that would be something like life, it would be a decision—as if she had set the fire—instead of that passive acquiescence to rot away in a wet hole. Surely her body only, and so no concern of hers—but Ella understands she will see it *all*.

Sitting and watching, she would see him flash by again and again instead of these vile sodium lights, in his element under a glass as black and cold as a patch of deep space. Glancing around herself Ella feels a sort of human pang, shared mortality with these others, and she thinks that nothing would be too much to ask, if death's cut-off point could be penetrated some way, and something made of it—letting alone, as one must, the fantasy of death's defeat and immortality, something like a sun in the imagination or in dreams, where one never sees the sun . . . What in all things would be better than that?

Ella answers herself the next moment, "Immortality *without them*," she glances around her, "yes yes, that *would* be better." She can feel a smile stretching out her face and she glances across the aisle and diagonally, catches the eye of a man in a suit and short overcoat standing by the door. Caught unaware and unsure how to respond he smiles back anxiously with a slight contraction of his brow—all his reserves of urban aloofness fail him, disarmed by this crippled girl smiling at him. He glances at her leg-braces with a flicker of shock like an antelope registering a bit of movement in the tall grass.

Ella's smile widens. "Aww," she thinks, "aww . . . " She pins him in place with a fixed stare of concentrated malevolence and that riddling grin, "Take a good look, sailor," she thinks. He keeps trying to break the connection, looking away with badly feigned nonchalance as though he were only idly scanning the contents of the car. She can see the strain as he reads the advertisements. Now and then he glances at her to see if she is still staring and his eyes flick away and back frantically. He glances at her like some people compulsively pick at scabs. He stews for three stops and clears the car in two steps cutting off an old lady and crossing the platform with obvious relief.

"heeyyy immortality isn't for *everybody*" Ella thinks. The train is moving, an alien light glows on concrete pillars shining sideways, and in a moment they are rising above ground. The sky all at once is overhead dim and grey, puzzle of blocks sprawl, their own horizon; the city looks like a cemetery full of weak daylight, cool and a little wrong, making Ella feel put-upon, like leap-year day—nothing in itself, but a nudge jostling every other day. The other passengers are lifeless, give no impression, come and go leaving no mark of shape color or tone, no mark in the air or the memory. As if the world were already over, no future, bottled up in the present and picking it over picking it over—blocked up as if to say this was all a mistake, but what mistake, whose, and how to undo it? A vast white warehouse stands by itself in the distance, behind a broad moat of brown railroad tracks, dingy broken windows sooty and bruised no windows at all and boarded-up windows . . . She sails past enormous bridges—a vast murky river gives way to derelict railyards, acres of identical truck cars standing in colorless dead vegetation—ditches along the tracks, brown-yellow water standing in ditches—dead weeds and litter indistinguishably compressed into one big mat. The embankment slope is a fibrous face of crushed bracken—streams of trash leaking down from the street—desultory sticks and branches bring to mind forested slopes devastated by a volcanic eruption. Unremitting grey, black bricks. Through the struts of a bridge she sees an island in the distance, a hump on the horizon bristling with upright trees and terminating in an enormous bulb of rock—everywhere waste and desolation, an overcast landscape. Isolation without solitude, anxious. The tracks run through an open slough, the world seems already over. After a while Ella's eye fails for sheer monotony—the spirit parches and deflates at the sight, resignation and gloomy spirits maybe but the spirit flares with impotent loathing of humanity, exhausting disappointed and overwhelmed right from the start.

On the platform, the wind raises her hair. On the street though she's late she won't hail one of the many cabs, the traffic almost all cabs—she walks with her crutches through her parent's neighborhood, a gentrified island in town. The sun is setting and it's getting dark, the streetlights are popping on, Ella stands on a corner waiting to cross, mesmerized by a long white plume of concrete banister softly rolling in on itself at the end in a frothy danish spiral, white as taffy against dull red brick—and above the narrow flights of steps all in a line along the sidewalk are stained and varnished wooden doors with brass and iron fittings, rings and knobs. As Ella passes down the street toward her block, identical with these she passes, each dining-room window appears in its turn like a crash of cymbals, a modest crystal fixture hanging squarely in each and beneath each is a table indistinguishable from the one at which she will any moment be sitting. She thinks this isn't worth all the dire trash and faulty machinery she's just passed through and why doesn't she see him behind one of those windows hovering on his back in a purposeless room with no fixtures, a house with no floors or rooms, a shell to shade and cover him? What businesslike people she's passing, who professionally dodge to one side or fold a little to edge past with a simper, like to condole her . . . "How will I fit into all this?" she thinks, her face bunching around her eyes—"What does this have to do with the experiments? . . . and how are we going to tell *these people* what we find?" Ella imagines the blithe summaries in popular magazines, the passers-by turn to each other and work him, and Dr. Belhoria, and herself, into their small-talk—"Have you read about . . . "—no, it doesn't seem possible. She glances up surprised at her own windows, buttery glow of the ground floor curtains, at the top of the steps she dazedly brushes the door or the bell, and presently the door opens and she's admitted.

*

Ella works her way back into Dr. Belhoria's house with the feeling of edging past and squeezing through tight spaces. She has to maneuver a while before hitting on the right rhythm of her step to carry her any distance. Approaching the house again, especially in the dark, she had been hesitant to go inside; climbing to the front door she had fought an urge to return home. The threshold exposed by the door as it swung open had alarmed her with the prospect of what she would have to be in order to cross it naturally. But she had crossed it, and after this period of readjustment elapses Ella readily finds her room.

The next morning she surprises a sheepish-looking man in the kitchen. With a smile distorted into a grimace by embarrassment he stuffs some fruit into the pockets of the bathrobe he is wearing and quickly pads up a narrow flight of steps on bare feet. Ella sits down at the table and gazes out the window while the room fills with smoke from burning toast. Later she meets Dr. Belhoria in the basement lab; their first experiment, a "test flight," is today.

"When did he leave the Home?" Ella asks.

Dr. Belhoria raises her eyebrows, "I seem to recall . . . a little past his thirteenth birthday he was transferred to a State mental institution. —And I brought him from there."

" . . . I thought he was older."

"He was there for *years*. No one wanted him."

"Even with his ability?"

"Well he's fine in there—" she flicks her thumb over her shoulder . . . behind her, he's lying behind the glass in cones of intensely brilliant light, "—the heat soothes him and the gelatin frankly sedates him. Under normal circumstances, he was actually found to emit a continuous, inaudible low frequency repellent to people. And animals.

"—You've had conversations with him—"

"Well only sort of—"

"—Can you imagine what it would be like, sitting in a restaurant let's say and he comes in and takes a seat? He'd be minding his own business and humming away, and curdle every stomach in the place . . . The staff at the institution was no less susceptible—they kept him tranquilized most of the time and so he generally wasn't all that presentable even. Took me months to flush their rubbish out of him."

Ella follows Dr. Belhoria down the short passage. He floats into view behind her silhouette. Ella looks at him lying there and feels no peculiar disgust. His skin is smooth and pale as wax and in places the flesh is clear milky haze around faintly-glowing blue-green veins.

A hydraulic boom swings out from the wall above him positioning a round crystal plate in a polished bone ring—fused cranial bones it looks like—directly over his face at a distance of several feet. Identically-fashioned bone needles float in a thin layer of glycerine coating the top of the plate, and he is able to see them from below.

"Is that some sort of trance-inducing device?" Ella asks.

"No, our boy is wholly self-inducing," Dr. Belhoria replies, " . . . you can't see them from here, but there are micro-electromagnets spaced along the inside of the ring. Those cranial-bone needles were magnetized in the course of the process of their extraction—"

"They're from *his* skull?"

"—of course, for sympathy. The ring however is from a donor.

Anyway the magnets are shut on and off at varying degrees of attractiveness as certain of his monitored nerve connections fire, drawing the needles this way and that. By taking up some of the burden of his physical-response consciousness, it serves as something like a prosthetic brain-stem, making it easier for him to forget his physical condition during seizure and concentrate on transmitting."

Dr. Belhoria indicates a chair and Ella awkwardly seats herself at her station. There are a number of monitors in front of her, and a conspicuously large upright wooden semicircular console with a panel of knobs, sprouting a square tower with a narrow glass window the size of a postage stamp, facing Ella. The window has an eyepiece around it.

"What's this?"

"Oh well he's going to be too preoccupied to type—through that, you'll see what he sees."

She takes her position behind a new bank of sensitive equipment—" . . . I'll be keeping track of his condition, watch the recordings later—give us the test, sonny . . . "

Ella watches the needles gather in a roseate pattern on the plate. Dr. Belhoria sets instruments.

"In your own time," she speaks into the microphone.

For a while, Ella sits anxiously shifting her gaze from him to her monitors to Dr. Belhoria—then his body rises uniformly by about an inch, the monitors reflect a slow steady even-paced change, the roseate pattern comes apart and the needles start traveling around. Ella leans forward. She narrows the gaze of her left eye and fits it into the upright slot of the eyepiece like a length of supple thread—inside is racing darkness, no light, but movement is apparent to her somehow. Gradually, she sees what appears to be a passage burrowed in the earth—dark, but she can make out the dirt, roots, loose stones rushing past at a high rate of speed. The needles spin round once in place like the second-hands of clocks—from the center of the field of view the ocean spreads from horizon to horizon white under falling snow, the waves shuttling by "below." He climbs in regular upsurging pulses, like a kite. The needles move out from the center of the plate turning like rolling pins cutting grooves in the thin glycerine—now the ocean is overhead, the black sky below, the moon is dropping into view from above an exaggeratedly-curved horizon.

Leaning backward his feet out ahead of him framed by the moon, his head still nearly brushes the surface of the water—the moonlight throws a round patch on Ella's face—it slides under his feet—the needles pivot and dive inward clicking together at the center of the plate—his body jerks and blurs in one compressed convulsion deforming the gelatin cube clouding it with minute bubbles, his form dim inside, twisted—the moon alone in space centered in the window—he thrashes a second time and the needles bounce in place, the edges of the cube are ragged and drooping—

"Shouldn't we stop?"

Dr. Belhoria tense over her consoles and flaring like a brass sphinx doesn't glance in Ella's direction—"He can handle it!"

—the moon hurtles forward its horizon engulfs the edges of Ella's window and as he spasms again spattering the gelatin the needles buzz against the plate and the moon's surface flies by—for a moment swinging out past the horizon confronted by nothing but empty space the stars glared out by the blazing moon—another moment and the equilibrium shifts, plunges headlong toward the surface it races into view like she were focussing a telescope deeper and deeper, a surface like frozen snow-covered waves. The needles slide to the furthest extremity of the ring and slide back lengthwise in a random formation—diving through the dust, the blinding-white field—below the surface, no burrow or tunnel this time, passing through solid layers of red and blue stone, a mass of ice with milky impurities and suspended flecks of soot, alloy-veins of what appear to be steel and maybe platinum, clouds of salt in symmetrical blocks—a titan cavern gapes for hundreds of miles to an interior horizon lost in glowing white haze, rippling crests and ridges stalactites and stalagmites like gobs of wax drop past as, rising, a higher apartment comes in view. Ella is pushed back into her seat by a force like a great soft hand. The needles stand straight up on squealing tips spinning against the crystal—before her are mammoth walls and towers mounting up to either side, a gaping arch dead ahead cut into walls of mile-thick marble flickering leprous white veined with pulsating green-black capillaries—the arch engulfs—buildings on mountainous scale large enough to encase whole cities streak past, and on high suspended causeways bridges shelves dotted with pallid forested gardens drifting greenish lamps show where shadowed figures move by the doors—

—needles trace lazy circles in clouded gelatin. The trance breaks and the room fills with a smell of wet cement, ozone. The window goes dark and Ella slouches exhausted in her chair pink spots swimming in her eyes.

*

"The first was to test for distance; this time we are testing for intensity."

They are back in the u-shaped room, seated at a table bisected by the glass partition, half on their side, half on his. The table is covered in a padded heat-retardant burgundy damask. Behind the glass, he has been maneuvered into an upright position on a metal plinth and situated at the table as if he too were sitting there; slowly he has extended his hands out of the gelatin and rests them on the table, where they turn red. Rubber gloves are fitted into portholes in the glass so that Ella and Dr. Belhoria may join hands with him.

Dr. Belhoria dims the lamps and lights incense. "Let's get started."

Ella takes his hand. Veils diaphanous and impalpably thin as crepe of air drape her in gathering layers.

She now can barely see or hear.

As though, right away, or however long ago, she was brought across one moment, brought far.

As she sits, holding his hand, hot and dry in her own, she feels it throb a little, regularly, with his pulse. She is keenly aware of his hand clasping hers. She becomes aware of her own answering pulse. Her heart is beating. It beats in regular strokes, like a pendulum. Now she is too aware of her heart, like the motionless warm hand holding hers. She hears the strokes, a fleshly, non-sound. Fear of death draws breath in her. A little flame-headed shadow in her spacious insides gazes up at her heart. She can feel the gaze. Any moment, she expects her heart to race, pound wildly. All rigid gelatin, shuddering with each pulse, her heart will pump faster, its rhythm falling apart, until each chamber, autonomously, will palpitate at random, wobbling like a balloon filled with water. The flame-headed shadow caresses her heart's bulges with the tips of its fingers. The fact of her pulse is like the fact of his hand, which still holds hers. She still sits at the table. As if she has come loose from her body, she turns this way and that without moving, a figure to either side of her as static as she is. They sit around the table like propped-up dummies, and though she listens down into the fluttering pit in her chest, Ella shrinks as time stops, as flat and stark as a glass slide. Frozen—if they freeze—Ella shrinking into a convulsing hole in her chest. Fear of death siphons in . . . an anti-breath that stops her breathing, detaches her from her heartbeat in a soft disembodied jolt like the tug of a train getting underway; it is a shaft of anti-light shining down into her body. This shaft has an architecture; it is complex. Its edges and surfaces are palpable but impossible to picture, and it turns slightly, this way and that. Her disembodied hand still glows in his grip. She is pressed against a fear of death wall.

A sense too, then, of lightness and intangibility, hovering in empty houses twilight or the pre-dawn glow in the windows, stark lines where ceiling and floor meet wall, all white, here and there scraps, all plain and blank—the absences she's felt in herself—now in slanting halls and evacuated cubes of empty rooms, in the spaces, black closets, musty open places in the walls, and also here, where inky shadows underline each board and shingle, in those contrasts and where objects only partially emerge into the light, in the wires swinging in the air, the weeds and dirt everywhere around the foundations and impossible to picture precisely—exactly in the insuperable vagueness of weeds and dirt, dust, the grain of wood in doors and floorboards, in the details—in mounds of banked-up time drifted in invisible colorless silt behind doors and against walls—in unnoticed inimitable sounds of creaking wood and sighing joints, memorable smells that can't be named or described—now something is there—there are things there. What is there walks. There are steps. There are gazes. A transparent figure steps out into a hallway. A gown climbs the stairs. There on the table are lightless hands like holes in space pressing into the damask rattling and violent—there behind her—the sound of clanking chains.

"Now let's try precipitating objects."

Impalpable and unnoticed until this moment, Dr. Belhoria's hand withdraws from Ella's grip; she loudly rings a triangle with a metal wand. The air in every part of the room becomes animated—directionless wind. The air in the room freshens and becomes cool. Unseen mist falls on Ella's face and hands leaving her chilled and awake, like the bubble pops. Glassy, membraneous skulls float in the corners of the ceiling their edges gleaming lavender and green, and Dr. Belhoria's assortment of brown toothless skulls heaped on a shelf emit a dull slimy tone like resonating chambers for bass flutes; humming in the old bone, the honeycomb cavities between the layers, the sinuses full of brittle curtains of bone—a revolting sound, as familiar as the interior booming of her own voice heard from within, but placed in the outer air in the viscous tone of a carrion voice. Blonde candle flames the color of fat slide by all on a level, as though dotting a passing riverbank.

"He'll run through the whole prop catalog before he's through," Dr. Belhoria says out of the corner of her mouth.

With a clunk, a heavy sea bird alights in the center of the table bringing with it a charnel reek of rotting meat, sharpened and made bitter, intensified—steadily more and more like the smell of copper. Ella's throat closes and she recoils nearly retching her hand still caught in his grasp. The bird shakes round drops of grease from its wings and takes a step or two toward Dr. Belhoria leaving marks on the damask with its rancid feet. Tiny pellets of grease sequin the table; they unfold; they're clear worms their spines a seam of orange pinprick lights down their backs, like luminous gold dust. As they writhe in toward the center of the table their spines, while they do not grow visibly brighter, still fill the room with orange light. The bird utters a few broken charps rattling in its spear-shaped beak, and gives Dr. Belhoria a knowing look, as though it were a distant relative. Dr. Belhoria returns the gaze of the bird with heavy distaste. Ruffling, its cold filthy plumage exhales chlorine.

*

Ella spends the afternoon composing her report to the Dean. When she enters her room, a quartered square of dim sunlight shines against one of lower corners of the door to the room standing open at the end of the hall; when she leaves again, moonlight is throwing a sort of vertebrate stutter against the opposite corner of that door, a soft segmented gleam.

A note on a table informs her that Dr. Belhoria is out. Ella has dinner at a Polish place in town. The lights are dim, everything is covered with white tile, she sits opposite a big blue fish tank. She is sitting in an alcove recessed into the wall, above her there are two little windows with sliding wooden shutters, each opening onto one half of the kitchen which is partitioned roughly down the middle due to the unusual floor plan. Every few moments the shutters bang open and someone barks something across to the other window, another bang following.

On the street again feeling odd after her meal, Ella is passing a nondescript building of scorched sooty brick when her glance snags on the sandwich-board sign loitering in front of the door as it were with its hands in its pockets. The sign says "Morfine" in elegant antique characters; beneath it there is a small statuesque figure in gauze, with rosy cheeks and long flowing hair, modestly padding through a field of poppies in her bare feet, pointing to the entrance offhandedly with an inclination of her wrist. Ella recognizes the name and image from one of Dr. Belhoria's matchbooks. There is a sizeable window brimming with a velvet curtain but from the edge of one of the window's lower panes Ella can peer past the curtain's edge, catching sight of Dr. Belhoria almost at once. Dr. Belhoria reclines, at the back of the room, on a tall heap of cushions, in a patch of mild golden light. She has changed into a filmy white gown; her head is tilted slightly back, a smoke-jellyfish trailing from her lips and nostrils, rising sluggishly in the air a smoke man-of-war full of light. Her date, sitting beside her but leaning forward with his hands clasped between ungainly knees, is a vividly pale, striking young man with a narrow fox's face and morose expression. They sit together as still as a picture, the smoke curling from her lips and nostrils, her suddenly very long-seeming eyelashes fluttering.

Ella pulls back from the window and gazes without seeing, stunned for a moment. And now she finds she's been staring at a comical stone jackass, adorned with a variety of heavy ornaments, standing along the mouldy brick wall beside the door. Not knowing what to think she looks up at the slate roof. As she pulled away, she had noticed some movement in a corner of the room, a narrow door opening and closing quickly on many pairs of legs kicking on a thin staircase against blood-red wallpaper. Now she sees there are rooms over the bar or whatever it is—opium den—some of the draped windows glow blood-red. Ella tilts her gaze further up, overhead clouds race by like rent tissues nearly sweeping the roofs—for a moment they are blood-red, but as Ella blinks the color from her eyes they are lambent pearly grey. The street is inky black, the air is maniacally clear and smells of water. Ella goes back to Dr. Belhoria's house.

The house is dark, and the flying clouds throw shadows on the walls, moving blots on the faint light from the street. It's silent, too. Ella rattles from one room to another angrily snapping on lights—she's not willing to postpone the experiment. She finds the room Dr. Belhoria had shown her before, and identified as the one she had selected for the experiment. A twin to the doctor's office, with pitchy wainscoting and dark wallpaper in a deep-sea motif on a shiny metallic background of honeydew green, plants in brass pots, porcelain figurines, marble fireplace. Ella yanks open the closet door and pushes back the coats exposing several sizeable geared levers. Planting her feet carefully and shifting her weight down the first lever, she opens the catch and pulls it forward. All over the floor panels covered by rugs drop down a few inches and slide back—Ella pulls the second lever and monitors fill the room. The third lever brings up Dr. Belhoria's special instruments, which she refers to collectively as "the Metaphors", designed and built for this experiment, but not yet operating. Almost completely invisible, and only partially real, they have barely the outline of a transparent object, visible here and there, powdery as though marked out with lead dust. Each sprouts a clearly visible brass bulb, however, the size of a cantaloupe with rigid vents and snaking s-shaped connecting metal tubes. Though turned off, the Metaphors give off a high quiet sound, something like ringing in the ears.

Meanwhile, Ella studies some of Dr. Belhoria's schematics involving the subject. Drawings show him centered in the room inside a metal frame, oriented with converging dotted lines. Ella pulls the struts of the frame from the top shelf of the closet with one crutch and begins laboriously screwing them into sockets in the floor, where the armature hides. Sweat wiggles at the tip of her nose, and the rolling chair in which she sits creaks rhythmically. After completing the cube-frame and setting it against the marks drawn on the floor,

Ella pulls the last lever. There's a whirr down below; a chute standing in the middle of the floor drops open a familiar-looking hatch, and extrudes him lying on his back on a long polished metal tongue—the room floods with ammonia chlorine reek. Locking into place with a click, the gelatin ripples and its corners wobble with a faint smacking sound. He is aligned inside the frame.

As Ella swivels, Dr. Belhoria enters through a wide-swinging door with an air of reckless decision her olive's toothpick rattling in an empty martini glass. Framed in the doorway a puff of white smoke; Lalique cigarette holder sweeps down to an ashtray in which a lightfooted bronze Hermes steps; Dr. Belhoria claps a radiation suit over her evening gown and covers her long satin gloves with shiny rubber ones.

"You're late," Ella says sourly.

"Nothing starts without *me,* my girl," she brightly says. Her eyes are glassy and a bit staring. She begins arranging herself at her console with an alarming air of precipitousness, prematurity. For a moment, she struggles with something down out of view, then produces a pair of mink garters yet glowing from her thighs and deftly horseshoes them around Hermes' neck. As she puts all her devices in readiness Dr. Belhoria's face takes on a particolored look, the console's colored lights chime against her brassy skin. Placing it primly on her lap she opens her green alligator bag and withdraws from its cheek a beautiful shining ingot.

"The machines will not work without gold," she beams, puts the small ingot on a black octagonal plate in the console; the ingot puts out shiny green snailhorns of milky vapor from its base. They spin round slowly and regularly as they grow and drape down to the floor like vines or trails of partially congealed wax, giving off a cool humid odor—a little sour and fleshy like the smell of bruised petals. The gold is covered in dewy frost . . . loses its sheen. The chamber is suddenly filled with whirring boxes. A pair of yoked bells burr on Ella's console and Dr. Belhoria adjusts her brass cranks and wooden levers tipped with ceramic knobs. The instruments, some of them invisible or partially invisible yet palpable as a draught across the finger tips, shudder and groan.

As the wall sconces are extinguished, Ella feels the strident alchemical excitement of a human being about to exercise control over something natural of which there is only an approximate conception. It's arcing back and forth between them—she can see Dr. Belhoria's stretched nostrils and the brilliant avidity of her eyes. "The Metaphors" glow. In the new dark, Ella can see their outlines pressed into the black glycerine of the room's air that billows from the open windows and sets the curtains wafting. A thick unbroken sheet of grey and black clouds uncannily lit someway slides by behind the trees; the air from the clouds and from behind them slides through the trees and transparently siphons in through the window. Prismatic lights twinkle above "the Metaphors," stretch and hang in space in knotted ribbons—these are the readouts, analogous to the green-illuminated dials on their substantial bases. Three-dimensional ampersands and treble clefs of light-tissue, reminiscent of Giesler tubes, turn to and fro as if they were gently agitated by the wind; their soft radiance dims out any visible trace of the machines that project them. "The Metaphors" still give off a tooth-jarring whine, however, and so are detectable in the dark. Laced all around them are arabesques and icicles of hollow glass, filling now with lavender electric mist, and dribbling long fibrous strands of translucent colored syrups. Unconsciously chortling with pure pleasure, Dr. Belhoria causes a number of iron antennas to rise up on either side of him in rows—"Whenever you're ready my boy," she says.

As Ella watches him curiously foreshortened from her point of view, overlapped crown of head shoulders and upright feet, he sinks an inch in the gelatin his hands remaining in place. In the room, the air grows smoky and shivers into flapping rags—she hears a sigh. The floorboards groan and utter punctuating cracks. He sighs and cloudy ribbons of color seep from his eyes and ears trailing slowly through the gelatin and streaming stretched hair-thin to the floor behind his head.

"Chromatic ectoplasm!" Ella's never seen it before.

His body color changes to greying blue filtered light to washed-out vermilion to yellow . . . through black-green waves Ella sees his body throb against its outlines, the room cooling, its dark walls seem to open out on deep haunted tableaux, animated by pale green will-o-the-wisps that passingly gleam on its faces, drums, trumpets, and hooded figures, all the panoply of seances . . . Shaded rows of dead audiences sit still in distant groups, Sunday school class photographs beneath spidery boughs, and a high soft pale silver horizon veiled by the transparent shadow of the wall. Ella feels a lethargy like two shining ghost hands weighing her head down, her eyes darken and her chin droops but she keeps her gaze fixed on his sinking body, and throws a sequence of levers. A terrifying misgiving gropes at her and she leans forward instantly intoxicated—she can barely move, she wants to lunge at him and pull him out somehow because she suddenly does not want this to happen but her body burdens like a sack of wet cement, slowed . . . cocooned in his swollen image, a snowy haze, he shudders, she can hear his heart pound from across the room—Dr. Belhoria is oblivious.

"That's it . . . " she says.

Rattle of drums, discordant keening blast of trumpets below the hills, airborne rivers of bats rustle high overhead—tubes of light draw streaks in the air—shotlike knocks erupt at random throughout the room . . . The air all at once seems to turn to glass and flip sides, the blackness of the room glistens clear. A hum slashes through the room in tattered waves vibrating into her teeth setting her ears ringing and her hair bristling, drunkenly she slumps in her seat her hands leave thick streaks of ectoplasm on her console, tone hums down into the space beneath her brain like the flutter of a fly's wing vastly amplified, and as the sound crescendoes something—an ascending crackle rakes her up and down with its claws and suddenly stops, as if the static electricity of the room were equalizing like air pressure. Blearily Ella sees tiny coruscations burst little expanding rings up and down his body each with a faint whistle dropping glissando and geysering thin plumes of dark blue smoke, green ocean phosphorescence invades the sundials of his eyes, his image slips—a few inches.

Ella can hear Dr. Belhoria gaily wish him Bon Voyage miles behind her. Ella can see him dropping from his body on a coiled vapor trail, his face all gleaming planes on the table his grey lips slack, below that he shrinks as he descends, falls in every direction—lights against the far wall show the pipes of a titan shrieking theatre organ, a piercing chord so searing and shrill that the brass of its pipes melts around the half-moon mouths and runs down the sides like candle drippings—the chord drops from octave to octave until the foundations of the house rumble against the cloudburst lashing the chattering unlatched shutters—then returns to the first highest notes as he dwindles, as he becomes neither fainter nor brighter but all the time more obscure, so much is he already a part of the surrounding darkness. He vanishes, a whole empty cosmos drops in between them like a slamming gate.

The room has its original aspect again, the lights come on. Dr. Belhoria and Ella remain sitting where they were, listening to the heartbeat. The man on the table is dead. A disembodied heartbeat pulses in the room, and now booms like thunder.

*

Chased from the room by that blasting heartbeat that knocked pictures from the walls and seemed on the verge of tearing down the house, Dr. Belhoria and Ella took refuge in the basement. When it abates, they cautiously reenter the room.

He's dead gone.

Drawing off her gloves, Dr. Belhoria says "The instruments will alert us when he begins to send us his impressions—He will most likely be sinking for a long time, I imagine, between ten and thirty-six days." She strides from the room as if she's already forgotten about it.

That night, Ella lies in bed, gazing impotently at the dark ceiling and walls whose stillness harbors gales of fear of death. She idles at the edge of painful sleep, half on and half off a sharp lip, precarious, poised to fall forever. Somewhere near her, springing up again and again, an abrupt black spot, something like a well, an eternal fall in darkness, and also an opaque unyielding wall. And he sinks in there, right now, sinking back, ghostly, lying on his back in infinite black—not on the other side but in the gap—and aware, the whole time . . . not identical with his body anymore, with its one place and set dimensions, he is anywhere, present here, like the presence of a conscious but unresponding corpse. He falls the length of every street, and every hall; he passes through every room, and sinks through every bed . . . along beaches, treelines, down museum aisles, down rails, bridges, paths in parks, library stacks . . . he falls through every unlit night-time . . . in the dark spaces between stars, and even though he sees the stars spin past in brilliant night or shadowy clouds and bright shadow sunshine float by made dull by a colorless gloom that screens him, he is always also steadily falling down and shrinking into unbroken infinite darkness.

Ella saw him on two occasions in the following ten days: the first, while she was sitting again in the same alcove seat in the Polish restaurant. She's fishing a bit of potato out of her soup and she catches sight of a gleam on the far wall, thinking for a moment it might be a swinging reflection from a closing door—she sees him, smaller than her index finger, falling up along the crease where two walls meet, his position unchanged but upside-down, he steams off an envelope of pearly light. Ella follows him with her eyes—he falls to a point just below the ceiling and his angle changes, he's hovering in the corner, head up, and minutely shrinking as she watches. He's falling toward the inside point of the corner, she realizes. After a few moments he seems to hover there like a greenish candle flame, sad fading weak face like a saint's, radiating waves of serenity and horror—she gestures to him distractedly . . . he dwindles into the point and vanishes, whether he returned her gesture is impossible to tell.

*

She spends the next day with Dr. Belhoria, sees another documentary in the little room adjoining her study:

To all appearances, the same lab as in the first film. Still with a full head of hair, he is given a bowl of some porridge-like stuff and a marker with green dye—he diligently marks spots on the surface of the porridge—the porridge is boiled and the bubbles break the surface only at those points where he had left his marks. A chart is shown giving relative probability of such predictions in scientific notation.

Now a lean old man with wiry grey hair, who seems to be the manager of the project, shows him the bowl and tells him about the results. The subject is delighted, and seems very eager to *help*.

*

The second time, a week after the first, Ella catches sight of his light again as she passes a municipal graveyard. She reverses direction with difficulty on the crowded street and slips in through the chain-link gate. The cemetery is squeezed into some open spaces between buildings—she stands in a bulbous yellowing plot of grass and bare trees with black trunks, tilting little headstones. Through the dwarfed willow and cypress trees the cemetery extends down a narrow alley between two tall office buildings . . . he ebbs somewhere at the far end. Ella navigates the alley dodging many surprisingly large monuments, some with lifesized angels or mammoth urns. Breathing hard she dodges in and out through them and heavy chains covered in rust, heaps of liquefying wreaths her heart in her mouth—falling in all this time, shrinking . . . dying. In the restaurant frozen over her bowl of soup she'd been so shocked to see his image appear she'd been touched only by the neutral fact that he had passed—had he seen her then? She hurries to catch up with him and offer him the sight of her, some sort of respite for him no matter how wretched a sight she is. The alley debouches into a tenement well, where the graves are protected by a sloping net suspended just above the highest boughs of the dead trees. The net catches the rain of rubbish tumbling down from high windows and channels it down its incline into symmetrical piles on either side, the bilious discharge of overflowing garbage chutes. The path is well tended and cuts across the ragged brown grass. She catches a glimpse out of the corner of her eye, he is gliding down a radiating alley on the far side, just slipping from view.

Ella struggles after him bruising herself against headstones and the edges of raised tombs—a dry gust rattles dead plumes of grass, the alley ahead is floored in bulging grave-mounds and she lopes over them barely upright. The mounds are high enough that they form a waving horizon, he's falling below its level, his weak dead beams of blue light waver along the walls like underwater shafts, recede . . . Frantic with effort Ella shouts after him her voice sapped and torn because she's panting with the exertion. The beams shudder and die down—Ella rushes—a scarred brick wall veers into her path like an iceberg and she somehow rounds it—his apparition.

She sees him falling away from her. He falls as if he were standing upright a few feet above the ground, throwing grey-white smudges of light in the reflections of the windows, shedding silence and space. "He looks," Ella thinks, "as though the world falls past stationary him—and seeing him again . . . after I've been watching for him the whole time . . . "

Hobbling after him . . . his eyes are two dark crescents, an expression of pain.

"Can he see me?"

* Yes. *

"Where are you now?"

He speaks wan worn tones, muffle of hospital rooms and funeral homes, powdery yawn of dead rooms bare walls still floors, glaring hushed mornings. Hollow, shadow voice rustles and strains with no force. Slack features smeared by the paltry light they give shine benevolently empty down on her in calm horror.

Her voice is made uneven by the irregularity of the terrain and baffled by the memorials—"Can't you stay a while—please? This alley is so cozy and seductive—and private—and we *understand* each other so well—and *I'm* not made of stone—" Dr. Belhoria, or her haunt, the Dr. Belhoria within, eavesdrops on this speech with a wry grin—and Ella sees her old classmates' wry looks, hears the all-presuming commentary already written in asides after class among themselves, and in classroom light how shameful would it sound to her as well? But in the moonlight would they feel the same? Foundering in graves—the same mean laughs then? Now her mouth is clogging with thick bubbles of ectoplasm and she can't wipe her lips without disengaging her hand from her crutches which would cause her to lose balance and fall, so she resorts to spitting right and left moistening her face, avoiding her clothes and the stones. "Please stay a while—can you?" her voice aims at divine lips, where the air streams through the part in his mouth it comes away perfumed with the smell of soot, dead leaves.

A muddy, dark spot swallows him. He dwindles into it.

Ella lurches to a dead stop, her crutches cross, their ends barnacled with clumps of grass and dirt. After a moment she casts around on all sides—which grave is his? She reads the stones. He doesn't have a name, so what does it matter any one will do, choose one that looks plausible—by now she is already clawing up handfuls of dirt, propped painfully on her knees—he's with all of them now anyhow, if

I don't find him the one I do find can show me where—

She had been making her way back to Dr. Belhoria's house—now a lurch in all directions at once as she drops out of focus, snaps in focus, eyes and head swimming with patterned wallpaper, brass fittings in Dr. Belhoria's guest room . . . a feeling as though the needle had been lifted up out of one groove and dropped down into another and she rode with it. But in between a blast of abominable cold: he's given her a lift home . . . she doesn't bother to get up from the floor. From where she sprawls upright twilight's shadows fall across her—but why should she feel bad? It's not as if he's gone anywhere, his *dead body* is still downstairs . . .

*

The passing days have no definition, less and less. Certainly she's no more aware of them, now and then glancing up as she walks in pain beneath the city skyline with a vague sense . . . The dark strobe of missing days and their names . . . More haunted than ever, black against wan grey sunsets the devouring outline of Dr. Belhoria's house threatens to eat the world and she won't go near it, though she must if there is to be any hope at all. She checks in at random, usually receives a brisk "no change my girl."

In the meantime, lightless wind ravage her mind, ambling slower and slower her hands grubby from the crutch-handles that emboss her palms with their painful creases, and her clothes are full of her own sour humidity, her feet fall like blocks of wood. Now the thought of glimpsing his spectre again fills her with terror and she wonders how she had been able to bear it the first two times. What would he look like after *falling all this time*? She keeps her head bent and sees nothing at all. Ella's not even hanging around, something less than that, haunting her own time. And any moment the phantom could appear again from around any corner out of any doorway or down the hall receding in front of her, or above the bed as she lies awake terrified, and one look from those eyes and she would be driven insane forever.

On cobblestone street, the wind turns cool and she hears rain start to patter in the distance behind her, and barely moving though still at least acting as if she were walking, Ella hears its inexorable sweep catching up with her—next moment, upon her—

Dr. Belhoria met her in the entrance hall, clutched at her forearms regardless they were sopping, her eyes lit the room like blue jets, held Ella up and spoke with tautness and a sort of evil joy: "He's started sending pictures."

CHAPTER FIVE

Ella folds her gaze and introduces it through the narrow aperture of the boxy wooden periscope—she can hear Dr. Belhoria operating the controls behind her. Her other eye goes numb, she sees only through the one, pressed against the eyepiece boring long plumbing shafts into a fathomless glistening dark. She waits.

"He says he's found a street," she says not knowing why.

"A street!" Dr. Belhoria says behind her.

Cold drapes Ella's shoulders, a street etched there thrusts away into the dark. Between the blocky pavements the star-lit street is almost invisible, nothing shines out of the drooping smudgy street lamp she sees. Ella doesn't dare crane her neck to peer up at the sky she already knows is a void—the street seems to appear in a circular opening in the dark all around—it's black, not dark.

The street moves by. The glass bulbs of the street lamps are all fringed with spikes sticking out like wildly irregular crowns of silver glass—the crowns turn to follow as the street goes past—Ella realizes that the lamps are lit and that the spikes she sees are their beams, pale as shadows themselves, but brighter than the black pavement, the filmy walls.

Arches span the street at regular intervals. They sport life-sized bas-reliefs of the sort that adorn cathedral doors, colossal figures three-quarters relieved from the flat stone backing loom out precariously overhead, gathered around a robed form in the center sitting or standing, emanating stone rays. The pillars that support these arches are coiled round with stone lianas.

On a smaller street: the buildings are a nearly invisible black-grey against the clear darkness. They are dusted by a soft powdery bluish glow that moves with the view, like a feeble follow-spot. Their bricks have perfect edges, their outlines are like blades. Some of the buildings appear to be under construction, though it is like new construction of old buildings. They are all older than the oldest existing buildings—Ella can see some pass by with open walls and the flickering view inside suggests exposed wooden skeleton I's and N's where the partitions will be . . . on the pavement are neat stacks of shadowy bricks like hard-edged pitchy diamonds.

Around a corner, little incline swings the view round on a severe narrow building, brought up short for a moment before it—a figure in the window—Ella goes rigid her breath cut off she starts back from the eyepiece claps her hands over her eyes sending her crutches slipping to the floor—

Dr. Belhoria's hand on her shoulder—"It was only his reflection, my girl,"—and when Ella shudders and her breathing see-saws uncontrollably the hand tightens, "Get a grip on yourself!" That hand seems to want to guide her back to the eyepiece.

"—I can't! —I can't!"

"Don't you know he hears everything we say?" Dr. Belhoria hisses, waving at his body, all its gelatin turning grey, lying cold glistening and pale at the far end of the room. Ella has only just seen him—she is suddenly staring at his ears—he hears.

"Don't worry, he won't allow any *further* images of himself to get through."

Presently Ella puts her eye up to the eyepiece again, jerkily as though it might be searing hot. Barely visible buildings floating by, just outlines travelling in her eye as though a bright light has just been shut off and the shapes haven't entirely faded yet, or she were seeing only the faint glow that outlines give off just before the eye closes, glimpsed through the eyelashes. The regular walls are pierced by cold panes cut from interstellar space . . . bare rooms with glowing walls . . . in some the open doors show long vertigo-inducing successions of open doors . . . in others the doors are shut with deep white crosses . . . The room fills with the smell of dust and linseed oil, there are all new unused rooms there standing ready . . . Ella can imagine a dark narrow bed pushed into a far corner, a figure there on top of the covers, soft dark fibrous suit luminous collar bisected by the tie; lie in total quiet, open eyes gazing at the glowing ceiling, maybe peripherally noticing her face passing the windows in the street, peering in . . .

A light dusting of silvery ash . . . the buildings pass and her angle is lower and lower, looking up at the ground floor—swoon out. Fall back from the eyepiece as dark clay seizes up heavy gripping her buried body as it congeals . . . or perhaps down a long hallway, dim light dimming, into a gathering darkness darker than lack of light, dark of a lack of all . . . end of time . . .

*

Through her eyepiece—

As she peers into the dark, a slightly flexed horizontal band of faint light spanning the sky overhead sweeps away from her to the horizon. Beneath it, rolling heath, dark bare hills, nearby a treeline, shadows of branches slide around the roots as the band goes by aloft, the leaves reflect brightly and the spaces in between the boughs are clots of black . . . Scattered cemeteries surrounded by low stone walls on the heath, a few obelisks and flat black stone . . . There a gibbet . . . The band winks out at the horizon—then, it rolls back, nothing in the sky to obscure. Ella watches the band sweep toward her and away from her like a visible sonar ping, gradually becomes aware that there is a slow drift in the view toward the woods, the gaps between the trees like dark halls . . .

. . . a long white figure issues from them with weightless curving strides—

Ella shrieking pitches backwards and while Dr. Belhoria is admonishing her—"*El*-la! You can't keep going off like this!"—both of them are interrupted as the dead figure lying opposite them says—

* Stay away from those dead woods . . . from them, even ghosts never can come back. *

*

The band stayed at the horizon and became a haze there. The hills pass. Now black waves roll where the hills were. Where there were burial grounds there are luminous icebergs, outlines shining down below the black surface—no land at all.

Ella takes in what she sees neutrally—so that's how it is on the other side—with the deflated feeling that comes with discoveries as all other possibilities are discarded and only the one remains, and that is no longer a possibility either but only a flat fact—and she is looking flatly through the eyepiece—dark landscapes, so that's it.

* Is that so? *

Ella's view is caused to close in on an iceberg's contour that lingers like a bit of lightning enfolded in a black thunderhead as everything else fades away. Fingers close on it, a kinked thread of smoke, grip it like a pen, snowy page throws soft light onto the circle of writing thumb and forefinger—a line of writing stretches off beneath the mountains' level to the horizon traced by a moving wisp of smoke held by invisible fingers, that and the writing too blow through all the spaces and periods of the world like a feeling veil . . .

A familiar boy points to a gap in the rock where a spring welling up from underground makes a small mound of clear water that breaks and spills down a narrow channel at one end. He says, "That's its source."

Alone, Ella sees spring up beside her a park, a floating mat of grass and vegetation and dirt swirling on a flat surface of icy black water, throwing out spiral-galaxy arms of pointed grass banks and sprouting trees like plumes out of star-estuaries moist leaves dry and barky trunks, concrete paths. The air here is still, but higher there's a strong wind carrying vast low-sailing clouds like whole landscapes or the debris of exploded landscapes rolling past. The park solidifies and Ella walks in—

This is Hiding Boy Park or Reading Boy Park or Running Boy Park or Dead Boy Park or simply Boy Park . . . Hollow bushes bunched up against the skirts of the park-house, rustling and opening for wiseass eyes to peer out at her. She will see a boy running in fluorescent time.

* Were you a witness to my boyhood adventures, Ella? *

Ella has the sensation of running, something she hasn't felt in a long time—running low to the ground, in and out of gaps in railings and beneath overhanging shrubs—

* Feel how cold that is? *

The air is cold, wonderful, blows straight through her light head.

The air is spicy on her face in her lungs; she also remembers that *spiciness*: the spice is acrid, peppery wood and vinegary earth and a smell moist smoke on soft chilled air that spice makes your lungs ring in dusky light—smell of cold bacony smoke—black earth has sucked all the water out of the trees and leaves, is black and succulent and firm as cheese. Scents of sweet alyssum, jasmine, sage, wisteria, orange blossom, magnolia, loquat, rosemary, vanilla . . .

Overhead the sky is clear velvetty blue darker and darker but the color does not turn to black. Night's machines are just rolling out, just late enough so as not to be clearly seen, where the sunrise would allow a glimpse of their last few rotations and their rolling back again. The air turns to night air loosening and moistening, everything partially dematerializes; with less light things seem less diluted.

She sees what must be him sucking on a drinking fountain and goes over to him. While they talk he does not move, his mouth made a little red smear on a rubbery, clear column of water through which he speaks without distortion. Every now and then she can hear a slurp, the fountain emits a steady pipe-hiss of escaping water.

He nods against the stream, "I got killed off a long time ago when things started taking their course, but I still crop up in the ol' intervals." A nasal wiseacre voice he rolls his words around a little in his mouth like old vaudeville. "Of course what's *really* funny is—" he pants in midsentence like many children do when they fumble for words, "that you don't understand this because you're not older—" pant, "and because you're not as young as me."

"I decided things early," Ella says.

"Get over with it fast, and that way, you won't suffer for so long." A tide of cricket-chirping rolls in like fog—"Give my memories to the insects to keep," he says.

One more time she is running down park streets and on dusty hill paths her nostrils sipping young air.

*

Dr. Belhoria is leaning back in a full-length fur coat, elbow on the arm of the lounge one finger resting on the bridge of her nose and another on her forehead in a gesture of fatigue. Her other drooping hand seems about to begin toying with the miniature urns and fronds in the wallpaper. Outside mist falls in curtains past the window.

Ella looks around suddenly aware again. She came back smoothly and gradually as though there were a hypnotist counting down, fading her up to the level of a daydream and fading the daydream. She glances over at Dr. Belhoria, who seems tired and headached, settled in her chair. The experiment is now as much a presence in the house, and over them, as the presence of his cadaver, has been joined to it. That mutely eloquent shadow lies all around in a gaseous state, like an atomized face holding both of them with its expression.

"Are you there yet Ella?"

"I'm here."

"How do you feel?"

"I'm fine."

"Are you tired?"

"—No not at all," Ella shakes her head.

Dr. Belhoria leans forward interested—"Really? Can you describe how you feel?"

" . . . I feel alert, a little excited—"

"Anxious?"

"I'm not *worried* . . . "

"More like you're expecting something?"

"Y-yes, yes that's right."

"And not at all tired?"

"No, I feel mildly exhilarated actually."

"Describe how."

"I don't know."

"Exhilarated like after a good scare?"

"More like—after some vigorous exercise."

Dr. Belhoria gets up looking brisk again—"I want to examine you—just stay where you are."

After a brief efficient physical—Dr. Belhoria's hand on the back of the chair leaning down to look Ella in the eye—"It's just as I thought—homeopathic exposure to death. You feel as though you've just exercised because you have, you've been running with him."

"Is that what we've come for?" Ella tilts her head as Dr. Belhoria unbends.

"It may be—or there may be more cropping up as he goes along."

"I didn't physically—"

"Go anywhere? Certainly not, and you didn't run with him as such either. —There's a reason it's the three of us here. He is the best subject because he is the most alive, with surplus life as a matter of fact, so he has a superior capacity to die—but he also is in a superior category of desire, and so are we. We're more ardent, because we want the part of everything that always gets away."

"... If it *always* gets away then what is he going to find for us?"

Dr. Belhoria is puttering around behind her. Ella does not turn her chair.

"He's going to find us a way to run after it *forever*."

" ... Won't that get boring?"

"Keeping it interesting is part of the way he'll find."

Why not? Ella thinks.

Dr. Belhoria crosses in front of her with fresh makeup, "Instead of catching it—we try to remain in the umbrella of its presence, by chasing after. Faces *move*, masks *don't* ... The challenge now—" she is fixing her earrings, "—is, that he will keep going deeper. Neither you nor I have any sense of the real extent of his power, which will only increase as he goes on. The task at hand is to keep him interested enough in the experiments to tell *us* what's going on. (Now I have an appointment)."

Alone, Ella gazes out the window at the dismal, beautiful fog in the streets. The city is always most alive when it's most dead, most visible for what it is, a great exciting night full of architecture. She can see them running forever, the part of each thing surrounding her, the backdrop, and especially the part of her and of him that get away, and for that matter the part of Ella that gets away from Ella, all open a little vacuum, cool suction moving air around her like a reverse wind teasing her in, run with light feet down the halls of an infinite childhood home. Dr. Belhoria is going out, Ella thinks, she'll throw her arms around some figure in the scene out there and be embraced into it by a man or woman—or cadaver for that matter she'll contact it. Ella wishes she could go out to embrace something man woman or cadaver. She could go, she turns musing and there he is still dead white as fog on the table across the room—No *not there*!

*

Black waves . . . icebergs . . . fathoms below, the ocean floor is colder than ice and no sunlight reaches so far down, but here black plumes sprout from small volcanic fumeroles, rich with the minerals that nourish mats of bacteria and great beards of brine shrimp sun or no sun, beneath tons of icy water . . . The black ooze of the ocean floor stirred up by their feet flows up to the surface in oily veins and creeps up feelers black as pitch against glowing white ice, feeling for the surface.

Now Ella can see a stone vault in a catacomb. A low, wide stone arch, opening onto a passage with other crypts and passages opening onto it, and so on. There are slabs and shelves, carcasses lying on every one. Ella can gradually make out their pale slack faces, the features dark pits and slashes. Many of the bodies seem unseasonably young, and all still have their shape and flesh. She is looking down on them from some sort of gallery, a little above the level of the floor, with a stone railing. No time, nothing stirs, silence.

There is a round drain in the floor, surrounded by a sloping area. Suddenly something dark and glistening bulges there—frigid water laden with deep-sea ooze is backing up from the drain. Shadowy patches and rills on the flags of the passage outside flow forward to meet the welling blob shouldering out of the drain. In moments the whole catacomb is flooded, on the waves, the hair of the cadavers drifts around their heads, their faces rock back and forth, their hands float. The water stops short of lifting them from their places.

"He's up to something," Ella tells Dr. Belhoria, describing the scene hastily. Dr. Belhoria comes up beside her.

An ectoplasmic froth is bubbling from the dead mouths nostrils eyes ears and skin building in thick webs especially around the hands and eyes.

"You know what that is, Ella?" Dr. Belhoria asks.

"No, ma'am."

"That's the substance of all their sensations, my girl—and stuff I've been trying to condense for years."

"You mean it's their *sense-memory*?"

"That stuff's better'n *memory*, dear, that's the real unlost feeling, the physical residue of a lifetime's sensations . . . What does he know that I don't?" The light from the consoles gathers in the appetitive creases around her eyes as she listens to Ella's descriptions.

The froth is borne up on inky waves and gradually gathers together in one great conglomerative mass spinning directly above the drain. The bubbles are laced through with fine black threads of sea-bottom ooze, like rotted blood. The mass folds in on itself, and gradually forms three horizontal layers that tumble over and over, the bubbles shrinking finer and finer. A body is forming cell by cell in frigid oleaginous fronds of undulant blood.

"He is *not* making tissue—" Ella hears Dr. Belhoria say in disbelief.

The first layer forms the alimentary canal and the second layer folds around it. Partially transparent it is coagulating into grey bone muscle veins and arteries. The third hovers at the surface over the first two, a flat clear manta-ray shape enveloping erratically flickering strands of shining beads. Now as the mass below takes on a more determined shape, the upper layer looking like a man o'war drops beaded tendrils down to thread them through the spine and enweb the flesh, the clear paper of the man o'war's hood engulfs the whole body, here and there the flickering of nerve webs is still visible as fitful lightning flashes in pale grey clouds of tissue—sporadic flares in the extremities but along the spine and around the newly-formed brain and heart are what look like fragmented waves and pinprick sparks. As Ella watches, these random firings jolt together and the body jerks and thrashes the water in something like an epileptic fit, the sparks shatter up and down the limbs and gothic arches pop from the spine throwing down elaborate smaller structures to either side and the head and chest are snow-flurries of cold sparks—another jolt and the pattern is regular, the body leaves its spot above the drain and slides out of sight floating on the surface, apparently exhausted, but with all the self-sustaining processes of life in synchronous action.

Now Ella can see him sitting against a wall, water sucking at the stone by his feet, and somewhere above there is an opening that admits what appears to be moonlight. He is cut across by a diagonal shadow and he wonderingly holds his arm, with tissues still clear as glass, out in front of him. It's a dark greenish-purple color. She sees his abdomen rise as he takes a breath—a brilliant red percolates through his arm as the oxygen circulates, then ebbs out as it is absorbed. His flesh is becoming opaque. He takes another breath, a brief percolation and his arm glows with ruby arteries . . . ebbs to dusky veins . . .

*

She sees colossal swells of black water, hills valleys and terrifying mountains dotted with dwarfed icebergs. The gale stirring the waves somehow does not create spray, as though the water were too heavy, or made gelatin. There's no horizon, no froth on the waves despite the wind, the pale icebergs are the only source of light—Ella catches sight of him swept up along the backside of a steeply-pitched swell, only his arms are visible and occasionally the sole of a foot. His dark streaming head bobs between his shoulders horribly pale. He's clawing at the water trying to keep from being dragged under. Having caught sight of him she is nearer to him, sees the ocean drop away as the wave sweeps him up, then he is plummeting down the wall of a canyon of water with a sickening plunge he falls below the level of the surface. The walls soar up around him hundreds of feet, any deeper and the wave will expose the ocean bottom—a lurch and he is staring up a thin shaft of air at a shrinking edge of sky—only the whites of his eyes are visible—the edges of the waves above tilt in toward each other a moment more and they will meet, the canyon will collapse and a mile of water will thunder down on him, but the edges stop and fall away, she sees his eyes wink and bob as he thrashes. He shoots into the sky just under the peak of the wave the wind blowing water from his face, and as the wave slows and stops he flailingly pulls himself up onto its peak which is ten feet across and nearly flat.

In the same moment both he and Ella catch sight of a blacker patch in the distance and now one end of it flares and sweeps the water with a brilliant beam of light. Hastily he starts pushing back from the top of the wave as it begins to drop because closer to land it will curl in on itself and tuck him deep inside. Like the shoulder of a huge waterfall the surface in front of him bows forward, he claws backwards—the wave rolls toward land. Ella sees a vast iceberg the size of a city block sweep up the wave's oncoming curve and hurtle end-over-end down its back throwing up water in tall sheets that slap down on his shoulders. He slips over the top of the curl and drops through the air his hands and feet making little white gouges where they lash at the wave—the curl drops—he vanishes in black froth—

—pops out the top on a long sheet of water sliding along the surface—catches sight of the lighthouse beam and his arms and legs churn. To either side of him waves surge and plunge—she sees his icy pale limbs glow pushing through heavy water and flipping up into the air. Above him she can see cliffs and the lighthouse looming on a promontory—he crazily hacks at the water—she can see his face in the lighthouse passes, it's scoured and crazed. The cliffs hover at a regular distance before the waves—now all at once they loom over head bristling with burning trees and he tries to evade the rocks. Swept into a channel he flies past jumbled boulders and ragged outcrops and tears his fingers trying to latch on but the swell carries him too fast. Then he's got hold but is dragged back—he seizes again and pulls himself up, the swell bunching around his waist sucks at him, he slips but keeps hold of the rock, the tension of the wave relaxes a moment and he scrambles up as though released from a grip. Veering headlong on slimy rocks up the slope out of the reach of the water that still snatches at his feet. Atop the rocks there is a wall of crumbling earth topped with shaggy grass and though the bank disintegrates with his clawing he gets a purchase on a root and hauls himself up . . . pitch forward onto the bank, over onto his back, lie in tufts of grass like a white beam.

He gets to his feet, alert. Puffs of wind cold with spray come up out of the dark grey air dusting him with tingling drops, the air intensifies the sensation of cold in his hair and stirs the loose locks, billows in a steady current through all his open senses. Overhead the lighthouse beam spins like a pair of long cones of white mist yoked together. The lighthouse rises from a basalt outcrop to his right, its foundation just above him, a dark grey door dimly visible atop a nearly vertical groove in the rock with dried blood colored iron rungs regularly spaced.

Weeds and tall grass hiss around him. He can see the edge of the cliff across from him outlined in shining white spray—tufts of grass, here and there the remains of a collapsing wrought-iron fence, stone crosses and headstones. To his left, a blazing copse of tall trees. Their long shadowy hands hold aloft the flames, like black roads on the surface of red globes. Above the roar of the waves are audible the roar of the flames and percussive cracks of black boughs that are burning but imperishable. He walks in the cool dewy grass around their roots and no cinders sparks or fruits of flame drop from those perfect fires.

Now the fires are behind him. Through gaps in trees with dark purple foliage an entire continent can be seen, and a track is there lined on either side with dingy brass rails half engulfed in bracken. He takes to the track with bounding strides his exhaustion melts in his muscles and joints delicious aching and weightless. To either side the track is lined with trees that bear dark fruit with thick spongy skin, the color of wine lees purple—thick spongy skin with a hard heart of deep amber hued candy; the fruit of the dead who eat it the dead are all sucking sweets their teeth gleam glassily sheathed in a clear glaze of brittle candy that splinters when they gnash—he's peeled one of the fruits and looks down panting over his palm where the skin of the fruit is peeled back in regular petal-shaped swatches. Inside is a ruby of red candy that opens in sections with a click, each section is encased in a translucent white-veined brittle glaze that comes apart in flakes—he lifts it to his nose and sniffs at the white glaze, convulsively he crams the wedges into his mouth their edges and ends jab painfully at his cheeks

—sometimes, for certain peelers, this fruit peels to expose a heart of odorless clotted sinew sectioned in puckered wedges of sooty skin—torn open the pale sinews shred in frayed knots that make a fibrous popping sound as they are pulled apart, a sound that groans in the gums like dry cotton gagging between the teeth—

he batters the candy apart with his teeth with a thunderous open-jawed crunching and grinding noise like any others there unseen in the forest, cracking bitter candy skulls their jaws dropping a fragrance a mandible all of dark wine candy polished bitter and fragrant, a click of glass lips of purple death mouth.

Ella watches, her hands gripping the edge of the table her eye pressed to the eyepiece, and inside the eyepiece he eats the candy of the underworld in the shadows of the trees, his gnashing teeth lit by candy sparks and slivers caught in between, and by rising coils of blinking fireflies like greenish bubbles in a shadowy fluid of trees and bracken. Cloudy spots of green light drift up his body and face—most clearly she can see the white gnashing of his teeth bared in a wolfish grin and watching them she has a feeling of vertigo again as though she was about to fall. A disembodied pleasure seeps in a cool pulse from the eyepiece, her mind seizes asthmatically and she reflexively pulls back her eyes cool and raw-nerved as though she had mint in her eyes and the feeling is spreading. Inside the eyepiece a foot from her eye but still clearly visible in some perverse optic trick he cracks candy in his jaws dribbling sparks from his lips—and although his face is now as bright as the sun, darkness gathers around Ella.

Dr. Belhoria looks up in alarm to see Ella slump forward and start to slide toward the floor. She scrambles around her console and seizes Ella beneath her shoulders hefting her back into her seat. "Ella! Listen to me!" Dr. Belhoria says urgently, but she can think of nothing more to say—what possible reason could she give to this crippled girl to convince her to return to her body? She peels back the eyelids and takes the pulse—concludes that Ella is in danger of her life and may fall through the eyepiece in which a piece of positive blackness ebbs and bleeds. What do I say to her—you have so much to live for? Still despite her doubts the doctor does feel a distant, custodial concern for her girl and besides the project depends on Ella.

"Ella, there'll be plenty of time for that later on!"

Ella moans as though she were suffocating. Her soul is ravishing from her body at the sight of that unearthly candy jaws and teeth . . .

"Don't you want to know how it all comes out?" Dr. Belhoria asks impatiently as she tugs a drooping Ella back into the seat.

Holding Ella upright she senses a strange, chilly tingle across her palms. Her vision dims as though shaded by a dark wing. The familiar objects of her study suddenly seem to break off and lose their names, become alien, obscure, as though she stood in the muck of the ocean floor staring at dreaming coral ramparts and towers through frigid black water dense as iron. Disoriented, Dr. Belhoria keeps hold of Ella, whose green face shimmers before her with firefly light.

Nearby, in a glass case, is Dr. Belhoria's prize fly; a breeding experiment that supplied interesting data for this case. She had manipulated its simple genes, and when the maggot pupated—or whatever they do—she was rewarded with a fly whose heavy head bulged with seven large eyes or one or two eyes asymmetrically segmented. The body had an additional thorax which slotted into the first with a slight overlap. This second thorax had its own pair of legs, giving the fly four pairs, and a pair of upward-folding wings which joined the normal pair and a redundant pair on the first thorax. When it flew these wings would beat in perfect time each one flashing into the space vacated by the other only a moment before and vacating it in turn for the next wing, so that its head and abdomen appeared to emerge out of a whirring grey ball of wings. Now this fly hovers a few feet away from Dr. Belhoria. It hangs in space perfectly motionless and the distinctive whine of its wings swells to become a booming drone, though not painful. The fly passes easily through the glass pane of its case which dimples and ripples like a sheet of water.

Dr. Belhoria watches it fly back and forth before her and she understands what she is being told or shown—the cold gelatinous life of the carrion-fed insect like the icy ooze of the ocean floor, a different sort of life altogether. Its syrupy entrails encased in a hard shell it lives mutates survives changes bodies feeds on carrion and throughout its primary goal is to reproduce and thereby cheat death if not of itself then of its species. But this particular fly had been bred to live indefinitely, a fairly simple alteration—so it could breed indefinitely and fill up the world with others like itself.

"Yes, I follow," she says, turning inadvertently to the body lying nearby. Ella's face swings with her and seems to look through its eyes in reverse, seeing through the back of her head even in her trance. Standing beside his soft body there appears the upright hard shell of a bronze statue. Feeble light plays over murky seabottom scene, on a statuary *tableau mort* of the tyrant frozen in a characteristic gesture: implacably ordering a frivolous execution. Look at the stern, outraged cast of his features:

* I'm asking you, doctor, with a look in my streaming eyes that are too full and dark to see you—do you see him? *

"Whatever *are* you getting at?"

* Myself, as I appear in the dark. He will disguise himself in me, wear me, step into me like a suit of clothes. A flabby, flaccid envelope, and beneath, the cold, hard, bronze, cruel tyrant. He may already demand your submission, ordering you out of his way. Exhaling death and orders, his order is chaos even for himself. Even in his sleep his breath rustles through and sets shuddering an impenetrably complex web of threats and counter-threats, spun and constantly respun by him. My heart—a mammoth, sooty metal heart bulging with straining rivets, filling a vast lightless nowhere with the roaring of its pulse—do you hear that? *

The eyes that glare back at her are dark spots in two brilliant white ovals fixed in a familiar bronze face. Shreds of protein and feathery wisps of glassy bacteria flap lazily in the fluid between the two of them.

* I will change forever, if you don't choose to end the experiment now. *

"Really. Am I supposed to be Frankenstein or Don Juan—or maybe I'm both? . . . In any event, there is no way to recall you or to affect the course of the experiment from this end, as you're well aware. What you do is no responsibility of mine, I am simply an observer."

The bronze index finger points at the cadaver's chest.

* This is the point from which I am suspended. Sever that, and all is ended. *

"Would you like me to stake it for you?" No reply. The finger continues to point. He will not warn her again. Dr. Belhoria leans forward and decisively says, "No."

*

A brief pause for smelling salts . . . Ella, looking as if she's lost a pint of blood, sits at her eyepiece, her lips parted, white . . .

—everywhere there is a blue light . . . stronger than strong moonlight, but diffused everywhere, glowing blue white off the snow . . . and all around are black rocks, black trunks, black roots. His skin blue white, and pale as snow. He is plodding arduously along on a compacted icy track so as not to stray into the woods . . . Silent vultures black as oil make blots in the higher branches though none fly . . . and snow is caked on everything though none falls. A blanketed meadow floats up alongside the path. Off in a far corner near the treeline and some boulders lies a dead horse nearly buried in snow. Instantly he rushes out to investigate, bounding knee-deep with blue legs and feet. He already looks different.

It's a huge black clydesdale, lying on its side, its neck outstretched. The lips are pulled back frozen from the long evil-looking teeth, the mouth framed with iced froth, the staring eye its pupil a great white dot framed in clear ice. He kneels down and begins to speak like she's never heard. A voice, for the first time. The orphic words bubble out in a torrent bursting from his chest like a sustained gush of heart's blood. He raves at the dead horse seizing it by its ears and dragging its head back and forth a few inches on its brittle neck, he circles around it shouting orders bare limbs flailing pink and dun against the snow, commanding it to get up, awake life in this mound of dead matter insulting, cajoling, tantrumming, raving and barking like a rabid drill sergeant, his words racketing off trees and shivering into scattered shards among the boughs. He plods around the body for hours tirelessly repeating . . . the horse's ears flutter in the breeze, open and defenseless against this onslaught, passively hearing all with dead but open ears . . . Then with a sound like tearing cloth there is an inrush of breath, and the horse rolls onto its stomach, its massive head recoiling jerkily. Still shouting he marches straight at it vehemently spitting out syllables—the horse snorts at him its eyes showing white all around the pupils in a horrified rage.

"Wake up get the lead out get on your damn feet get up up UP—!"

The clydesdale pummels the ground with his front hoofs and stands up mountainously; his body trembles and steams, legs stiff. Then, stronger, he holds himself steady and motionless as a statue, the long jet aprons of black hair drape around his hoofs and make four commas in the snow.

The tirade stops, and suddenly the Tyrant's eyes flood with tears—and she sees he is the Tyrant, that's what she heard in his voice. He drops to his knees before this horse he has just seen restored to life from death, at his call. He balls up his fists and presses them to either side of the base of the horse's neck. He looks up at the giant face looming over, set against a motionless grey-white sky. He can feel the burning breath, with a smell of soot and ash, on his face. The clydesdale drops its head down and turns its right eye toward him—like being stared at by a wall—he takes the forelock in his hands and presses his face up eye-to-eye so that the pupils almost touch.

His voice tight and choked with ardent emotion, the tyrant says to the horse "you will serve"—it is both a command and an oracle. And the next moment, he is mounted, and they disappear together.

CHAPTER SIX

Ella at the eyepiece, and deep within, trees whir by—here is the Tyrant flying down the narrow way. He has equipped himself and his horse from all the battlefields, with a saddle and bridle pulled from the snow, and he is resplendent bare-headed in a sober high-collared uniform with boots gauntlets black braid and a high tight white neck-cloth sabre and pistol all cloaked in a voluminous ebony cape that billows in the cool soft silky air of the underworld—he has also found a pair of steel wire-rims. Ella records it all on a clipboard.

Dr. Belhoria makes a wry face over Ella's shoulder as she scans her written description.

"—Like a Puritan Napoleon!" she says.

*

His first stop, a mortuary lumber-room, cadavers lying draped in sheets on tables in a basement spangled with shadows from the ivy-covered windows. With the great strength customary among maniacal enthusiasts, he wrenches the bolt from the door and wanders in among the bodies, which lie at all angles; and the moment he crosses the threshold the ranting words march from his lips. He stands more or less in the midst of them all stamping the concrete floor with his boots, pacing up and down turning and turning again, so that they all at one time or another are shaded beneath his flying cape, and in that shade their faces and hands shine with black outlines. The Tyrant claws the air and balls his fists haranguing—"Get up! Get up! On your feet! No rest for you! No peace for you!"—he bellows words with terrible violence, the sounds of thundering hoof-beats, rumble down into ears open and helpless. Dead ears hear everything everywhere said, but his words are *stirring* words—they *stir* even what is dead.

The bodies start and shudder, they sit up trembling and panting. Now their eyes glimmer ecstatically. Their teeth glimmer in glimmering grins that glitter against the dark of the room. Still hurling his orders the Tyrant is through the door with these fresh recruits close behind. They ransack the adjacent rooms for clothes, men and women donning suits and dresses dresses and suits indiscriminately. In the columbarium they tear cinerary urns from their niches and smash them to the floor. The Tyrant on horseback paces back and forth the length of the building howling at the grey mounds and scattered grey streaks of ash on the floor his horse's hooves splitting the marble tiles —these heaps of ash coagulate and writhe on the split white tiles like writing; bodies shudder together filling the air with moans and laments and agonized fingers. The Tyrant shouts insults over the groans and screams. One by one these heavy twisted bodies suddenly bound up from the floor light as balloons, the cries of pain dwindle on all sides as reconstituted forms grow light and whole, spring to their feet with blazing eyes and grinning teeth.

The Tyrant leads a motley-dressed shouting mob in an attack on the graveyard. Wheeling his clydesdale spins in place and kicks the gates with its hind legs—a tooth-jarring report—the gates fly open ineffectually waving the ends of a severed chain and the riot storms through. Those who are further from the gate waste no time in getting there, they charge the wrought-iron fence and tear the bars their hands boiling with weird power.

The mausoleums were hit first. "I lived my life in and for the bank," said one vulturine old man on his death bed, "and by cracky I want to be buried in one!" Stately granite columns and ponderous metal doors hide stored up the cadaverous safety-deposits . . . a distant booming swells in nearly an instant to a deafening roar that cracks its whip on all sides. Stones bricks and broken-off bits of tomb ornaments crash through tasteful stained-glass windows, fists batter and tear at bronze doors with bas-relief wreaths, the doors fly open like shutters in a cyclone banging against the walls, and shadowy figures blast through shattering slabs breaking open the coffins dragging the bodies out into the lanes where the Tyrant races up and down his voice raging like a tornado his words pelting down like hailstones—

"Isn't that just like a man—" Dr. Belhoria was saying, "he can bring out the dead, but not without turning it into a Krystallnacht!"

Groaning anguished cadavers flinch and feebly paw the grass coughing dust and cobwebs. They look up. The Tyrant looms above them on a wild-eyed staring dark horse and raves against the dark sky—up and down the lanes saliva spraying everywhere—and the word passes up and down along the lanes and graves:

"The Tyrant will deny the living their lives and the dead their deaths."

"The Tyrant will deny the living their lives and the dead their deaths."

The ranks ripen. Groundskeepers' sheds are pounded apart in a frenzied search for shovels, picks, spades, trowels, hedge clippers, even fence pickets. Everywhere the stillness is undone by the choughing of shovels in dirt. Dirt flies on all sides, corpses are hauled screaming from gaping holes. Soon there are hundreds racing in a great wind beneath willow boughs through duck ponds and reflecting pools trampling tulip borders and toppling tombstones and obelisks—this wind with limbs hands and glinting grins. Knots gather at each unopened grave—the occupant lies as he has since his interment, and now there is a dull thudding, louder a scrabble and scuffling on the lid which splinters apart dozens of hands thrust inside seizing arms legs lapels—the body is swept into the air shrieking with the anguish of a mouth filled with earth, lungs dead and dusty as attics, joints seized and locked with grit, shriveled eyes like raisins rattling in the sockets, shrunken heart flipping behind the ribcage like a hunk of cured meat, dry veins and arteries crying wind through tunnels of tortured thirst and the pins and needles of rigored muscles all pummeled and hammered by this relentless, impossibly violent voice—but this passes. One by one the bodies go supple, light, sparkling inside, the eyes flood and flare with evil joy, the legs flash beneath and now they are buoyed up by that strident drumbeat voice, one by one they join the wind stirred up by that tattoo voice . . .

*

As the experiment continues over the next few days, it is agreed that Ella's account of the Tyrant's campaign is beginning to suggest a pattern . . .

"Now that he has picked up a considerable number of the deceased, such as we will call the Indifferently Disposed . . . " Dr. Belhoria dictates as Ella types up the report.

Calling all the world's lost, he rides round and round the empty spaces of the underworld with a skipping army behind him. The Tyrant speaks—his eyes are a different color with almost every word. They come sounding off: crossroads, mass graves, and unmarked suicides' graves—mad ribbons sluice from asylum walls, the inmates recover all their colors from out of the grey haze; only the Tyrant is afflicted with black and white, with one light eye and one dark. Shapes ooze from the walls of convalescent and old age homes spitting venom. Ghosts musically pop out of windows twisting into fantastic delicate shapes before they alight *en point* among the ranks, and some drag themselves from the drained swimming pools of derelict theatrical hotels as though kicking off the last coils of an oppressive night's sleep. They glide from the gashed sides of shipwrecks in elongated green ropes, and every human sacrifice in history appears at the head of the columns in officers' uniforms.

Here and there they would encounter small villages and towns of enervated and monotonized spirits. These invariably disclosed small powder magazines and armories where uniforms, weapons, horses and other equipment could be acquired.

"The work of life is short, but the work of the dead is *long*," the Tyrant took time to quip to a reporter at the scene (there are *underground* journals in circulation, so to speak). And Dr. Belhoria noted, "The dead made unparalleled soldiers—after years of lying in cemetery rank and file, staying in formation comes to them as second nature; their morale is *superb*."

Eyes blazing like gobs of molten metal in transcendent rage and evil joy, they blacken the horizon in dancing battalions. Ella witnesses one of the first great battles in a grey valley lined with groaning trees. Where the bases of two opposing hills meet, a modest river flows; and the equally modest underworld city raises its walls around a fork where the river forms a little delta. They've had advanced warning enough to call out their defenders, and a force of cavalry and infantry have taken positions on one of the ridges, while several more units fortify the town. The Tyrant's army plunges into the valley and at the opportune moment the fighters on the ridge charge them—the Tyrant's forces moving with blinding speed cover the bottom of the canyon and surge up the ridge right into the oncoming defenders. Ella finds her view restricted closely to the area around the Tyrant, but she can follow his view as he stares down from his command post. One of his charging infantryman is cut down in the instant he's cut down his image detaches still charging —she can see the black gape of his silently roaring jaws glint of his sabre in the air blinding glare of his eyes in dark sockets. The air is torn by repeated fusillades of musket fire and the battlefield is quickly obscured by plumes of smoke.

Riderless horses wearing defender colors stagger up the ridge, below there is a continual ebb and flow of forces—

"How can dead soldiers kill each other?" Ella is peering this way and that, looking to see if they fall. Slowly she begins to understand—to be sliced with that icy sabre or penetrated by cold shot, she would fall though showing no physical wound, fall in convulsions choking out her life in stuttering gags, and then—in a moment her heart stills, and wind blows through it, her blood turns into a spiced wind, something is changing inside her, she is buoyed to her feet by colossal strength—as if cut there, the characteristic grin of all his soldiers would split her face and she would rise—her legs snap back and forth beneath her like cracking whips the earth blurs beneath her tumbler's feet as if with each stride she were causing it to spin . . . Ella watches the defenders fall, then rise to join the regiment of their own casualties now forming on the Tyrant's flank. Within moments, where there were two armies there is now one larger army, battering open the gates to the town. The Tyrant howls orders waving his arms in the air apparently infuriated by the resistance of the gates. He shrieks to them to redouble their efforts—she can see the vision he sees—gates burst apart, the soldiers storm in. Smiling soldiers prowl the streets bayonets lowered, picking off the inhabitants who moments later spring up into their ranks—sardonic phantoms prowling cowering streets with sharky, superior grins glowing on their faces . . . Look at the Tyrant, the spirit that seems to respire in his open throat—open in an ecstatic shout and his cheeks streaming with ecstatic tears as his enemy falls, brandishing his arms in a gesture of bestial joy. She looks, even as he shouts the enemy soldiers hacked down by his troops rise again to their feet with leers to swell the ranks that dash like black froth of waves against the city walls . . . He seems to clutch the city like a hot gem in his hand.

"MALE-o-drama," says Dr. Belhoria, rolling her eyes up and then to one side. Ella understands what she means. She sees the Tyrant's wild ecstasy, and Dr. Belhoria's wry, unimpressed penetration all at once; and she wonders, will I ever be big enough to contain both of these admirable qualities in myself?

*

As the campaign unfolds she watches monasteries and lamaseries blown open by the Tyrant's army. The swollen ranks congeal out of nowhere in a single spot like a tornado of men and horses—stone blocks tumble to the ground, heavy doors evaporate. Everywhere the closeted quietists and hermits are hauled from their cells and those who will not fight are heaved into the air and devoured by the soldiers, without a scream, without a change in their calm facial expressions, or a drop of blood; their flesh turns to smoke in soldiers' jaws and is swallowed all the same. Weeds engulf stone abbeys—prayer wheels rattle in the wind—shrines charged with centuries of chant-rays are drained for black powder.

Rumors circulate everywhere like shreds of smoke in the wind, smell of smoke, flashes of heat lightning or artillery on the horizon. The Tyrant's army, always on the move, dancing along on feet lighter than air, has acquired the funeral train of a former head of state—its black plume can be seen underlining the horizon moments before the sudden rush and percussive blast of wind, the piercing whistle and then the cavalry pour down like gargoyles plunging from their alcoves.

Ella once sees them in a strange city of titanic spires, perfectly squared-off and white, glowing brighter than a white wall in a full moon's light but not as bright as it would in the light of the sun, which never shines down there. Towers with no windows or doors, walls with no openings, and broad white glowing streets sloping steeply down. The shadows are grey like shapes painted with dust-paint. The only black is the figure of the Tyrant as he walks down one of those streets, and in the far distance, she can see the masses of his army boiling like a shade margin just below the walls.

She sees him in another town riding along what looks like the high street, lined with screaming crowds. Soldiers two deep form a human chain to hold them back and they surge against the barriers holding out their arms and screaming with tears in their eyes, all soldiers. The Tyrant is riding in the midst of his officers past enormous multiple gallows, flung up by his engineers in a matter of minutes on the sites of razed houses, each one can hang twenty-five men. He passes one of these after another, and the trapdoors to each all drop as he passes. The dancing bodies on those ropes will be cut down moments later and join newly forming battalions whose uniforms and muskets already stand by waiting for them. The dead are killed back into life, into active service. The Tyrant rides by without seeing, though his eyes start from his sockets, his horse and uniform soaked in gore of his own wounds and others', his face still paler, his mouth open, his arms at his sides holding by their broken poles the grisly standards of the enemy defeated only after a long battle, while the crowds moan and sob and claw the air shouting for him, and the hanged victims bounce and jerk on their lines . . .

Vampires of the world, staggering on rickety stiff legs flopping out from motheaten shrouds and caskets caked with dust—their victims stir within, in response to distant bugling . . . Muttering on a molecular level rises to a low roar, they take to the streets of withered tarry old arteries, straining the sinews demanding release and redress; and what happens next? Well . . . acrid clouds of vampire dust blow out to sea on the wind, issuing in hissing streams from shabby tuxedoes, brittle capes rattle against street corners, pounded into dead leaves by flying hoofs, a compost of monacles medallions collars cufflinks silk hats and crumbling shoes all powder and mold among tree roots, brooms sweep mounds out of the street, choking gutters eventually drain into the sea . . . These fragmentary scenes blink in and out of view like dream excerpts.

A barricaded city, forewarned by the rumors. The walls surrounded in a matter of minutes, the gates barely closed before a hail of shot spatters the wood and stone—no warning, no terms offered. Inside the walls, they can hear the soldiers roar and the popping of muskets, it sounds like crackling fire or splintering wood. From the walls they see the locomotive hurtling toward the gates its whistle howling—the stokers shift from coal fuel to a special mixture of smashed coffin wood and tombstone, shoveling it in: brass handles silk lining granite urn marble angel's head and all. The engine glows black-hot and the smoke from its funnel deepens to impenetrable black. The smoke billows thickly forward over the walls, poisonous, lethal at a single breath. The city's valiant defenders and scurrying citizens alike breathe and fall shaking, dying. The locomotive shoots on like a comet and barrels into the blocked gate blasting it to smithereens, sending deadly shards of wood flying in all directions—and the smoke casualties are already rising again to their feet showing their teeth in the characteristic grin . . .

As the train careens down the main drag the doors to the many cars it hauls behind it roll back and soldiers leap out landing square on their feet guns level at hip without collisions—cavalry bounding from the cars landing like mammoth javelins forehoofs-first on city guards in the streets, chopping down police, guards and citizens alike with hissing sabres. Within minutes the streets teem with soldiers marching in waves abreast, the foremost sweep the streets before them and the succeeding waves have already started the house-to-house. A black banner with skull and crossbones is unfurled overhead and muskets and sabres are brandished in the air.

The train has passed out through the city and returned again through the ruined front gate. It pulls to a stop in a large centrally-located square, where prisoners are corralled. The caboose, still adorned with black wreaths, opens, and the Tyrant emerges on his prancing horse, riding up and down, stopping here and there with the clydesdale dancing and buttocking in place, excited even when he stands still, his bulging muscles tensing and untensing audibly with a sound like creaking leather. The Tyrant, however, remains motionless. The captives are drawn out in lines and shot—rise moments later all smiles, receive their marching orders . . .

Those sardonic looks . . . nothing prevents his soldiers from turning that grin back on the Tyrant himself . . . not at all a mindless smile . . . and it is a happy smiling that he does not and cannot reciprocate.

*

"It looks like he's taking revenge . . . although I don't know what for . . . " Ella says.

"I imagine he has something else planned . . . "

"Well, he does seem to have some plan . . . maybe your plan."

"He's not taking orders from *me*."

"Well, it's like you both hate people, and you want to let us know it." Ella is pleased to see that Belhoria seems nonplussed by her observation.

" . . . Could be," she says finally. " . . . but if we hate all humanity, we hate with *love*, dear."

Ella doesn't know what to make of this or how to reply. Dr. Belhoria goes on a moment later, "Humanity for a good time, at least for me."

"Ah-huh . . . what about for him?"

"For him I don't know. It makes a splendid spectacle, whatever he's up to."

"You talk about this—" she's pointing to the flickering viewfinder beside her, where the Tyrant is riding in a colorless frame like a range rider in a western serial—"as though it were all an illusion."

Dr. Belhoria shakes her head slowly, to show she's serious despite her smile, "Oh no . . . it's happening *now*."

*

The Tyrant considers the dead his people—"How dare they punish *my people*?" Sabres drawn; we're on our way.

Hell comes up slowly out of a horizonless blank; as one draws closer the farthest-flung outbuildings and derelict plantations come into view—the Tyrant's army is upon them with blinding speed, two locomotives plunging in parallel lines two dozen yards apart, and the cavalry thundering in between. No sentries are posted—Hell expects no invasion for some time; only here and there the occasional prospector or hollow-eyed eremite, or the last few handfulls of a once-prominent infernal family in their final tatters of finery. All onlookers and bystanders are target practice for ten thousand muskets.

Many of the Tyrant's soldiers have passed through Hell's

unconfining outskirts before, and can supply reliable reconnaissance information. The first target is an isolated fort just within the skimpily-held picket line. The sentries there are caught napping—the line is torn wide open. The Tyrant's forces speed like a cyclone for the fort—demons erupt from caves and crags. Demons are by no means indestructible, but, while they may be killed, their number is infinite. Fortunately spatial considerations prohibit their concentration, at least in an open fight, in infinite numbers in any particular spot. A vast flapping mob races out to meet the Tyrant's army like a spreading oil slick. The locomotive engineers change to all grave-wreck fuel, shattered coffins and stone markers, the smoke-stacks belch pitchy cemetery-smoke that absorbs light. Its coils reach the foe and choking demons fall in heaps. Their line spreads only to discover itself flanked on either side by two more of the

Tyrant's war trains. The boxcar doors slide open and musketfire throws demons back in a recoiling wave, their ineffectual tongs flails tridents and darts clatter on the baked soil. In a hail of fire they break and run for the caves. The rout boils into a low canyon, trampling their line officers whose warnings are drowned out. The walls of the canyon are topped by musketeers muzzles and bayonets bristling like porcupine quills angled down. Bottled up only a few hundred yards from the caves, the demons are reduced in seconds to a homogenous mass of mangled flesh. The Tyrant's laughing cavalry whistles through the remains after the smoke clears, dispatching the survivors.

The soldiers know what to expect—"They won't be joining us," the Tyrant had explained, "they're mortal but they're not human."

Wasting no time, they turn their attention to the fort beyond the canyon. Its gate, fashioned from the black cedars of Hell, is splintered by cannon—lethal black smoke washes over the garrison atop the wall, sending waves of dead crashing to the ground. The cavalry are already inside—the Tyrant cuts the cord on the flagpole sending Hell's crimson banner with motheaten pentacle off on the wind in a flutter, like a pair of wounded wings. His skull and crossbones now flies in its place. On the brink of Hell flaps an alien standard. The Tyrant surveys the grisly scene—contemptuously trotting his mount among the heaps of dead demons. "Infernal dogs!" he sniffs.

With great celerity, soldiers winch the heavy guns to the top of the wall and turn them down toward the next canyon, while others are set up along the ridge where the infantry digs in. From the long-neglected lookout post, the distant glimmer of colossal brass is visible through the sulfurous haze. Hell is old, and, being built to the scale of foot and hoof traffic, is geographically concentrated. The capital is not far from the border for those equipped with trains.

The alarm goes up on all sides now as news of the invasion spreads. With horrifying speed, demon regiments form a shadowy skirmish line on the ridge opposite the fort. Muskets flash from the fort and from about half of the entrenchments on the hill crest—obscure shapes tumble down the opposite ridge. With the exception of a few blunderbusses loaded with gravel and bits of chain, there are no black powder weapons of any kind on Hell's side—darts and bolts rain down from the devil line, falling short or bouncing harmlessly off fortifications and stone walls. Among the infernal line officers the situation is deteriorating—orders from "on high" forbid retreat, or strategic containment: they must retake the fort. Meanwhile invading muskets pepper the front line, casualties are heavy—if they're dying anyway, they might as well charge the hill.

The line overflows the ridge and boils into the canyon. They reach the bottom unopposed and surge up toward the fort. Now the remaining half of the Tyrant's muskets pop up shooting. His cannons break their silence, their sights on the middle of the opposite slope—a line of explosions rips through the charging masses parallel to the ridge, cuts the demon ranks in half. Initial explosive rounds are replaced with special canisters packed with grapeshot, designed to fly apart in midcourse—trapped between the cannon fire-line and the fort's ridge the demon regiments meet the concentrated fire of the muskets, and as they collapse in a haze of smoke and flying ears fingers arms teeth eyes wing-leather, the Tyrant's cavalry plunges down among and through them. In a moment, there is nothing but mutilated remains separating them from the other ridge—the cavalry closes the gap and dives into the confused masses thrown back from the ridge-crest. The fort's cannons throw shells over their heads into the routed demon troops. The infantry is close behind the riders. In short order, the war trains are brought round; the Tyrant's army advances at top speed into retreating demon ranks . . .

"Where is he now?"

Ella squints into the eyepiece and manipulates her knobs—she sees flames and black crags, writhous mobs of grotesquely distorted figures seething under a pitching sky. Flickering red and jaundiced light plays on her features as she describes it.

"That's not Hell, is it?"

"I don't see what else it could be—" she picks out a few among the more readily visible forms, describes wings horns tails and tusks—

"Quaint," says Dr. Belhoria.

The thrown-back front liners meet the advancing reinforcements and regroup instantly, turning round to face the Tyrant in a scorched waste of precarious bluffs and undulating hills riddled with caves. The two cavalries meet and shatter into skirmishing pockets—the Tyrant's trains race up and down belching venomous smoke, his gunners are already stationing cannon on the bluffs.

The caves are filled with damned souls. Here's a naked old man up to his neck in boiling water. A long chain links his collar to a staple in the rock wall. He is only one of many in a colossal tank, and the devils saunter on catwalks above, prodding them with their forks and the same infinite jokes about being "done", pissing and shitting down on them from time to time. But this old man is at one end of the tank, closest the cave mouth—and outside he hears commotion, screaming, he feels the walls shake, with a pang of nostalgia he hears cannons: now sees a form on a horse spring past the cave mouth, demons being cut down, and above all a black and white flag, the skull and crossbones, wave over massacred legions of devils . . . DEATH! DEATH! Outside, the Tyrant's words ripple through the ranks of his army "How dare—how dare—how dare!" The mark that has so long disfigured the old man's forehead fades. His gnarled hands seize the length of chain and the staple, now covered with rust, groans and snaps. The others in the tank watch the devils break off their idle torture and run to investigate . . . bobbing in place but no longer screaming they see a roaring figure set upon these devils, see a length of chain snap tridents . . . here and there, brow-marks fade . . . Suddenly staples all over the caverns tear apart, naked figures stream onto the catwalks swinging lengths of chain, the moment they appear the devil guards are immediately engulfed borne up in the air hands tearing and clawing—the cry goes up the roar swells into a tornado—

"What are you in for?"

"Aw I cheated on my old man . . . "

"WHAT?! ETERNAL PUNISHMENT for *THAT!?*"

"I was one of the murderers of Julius Caesar . . . "

"WHAT?! ETERNAL PUNISHMENT for treason to an EARTHLY STATE!? Like HELL . . . "

"I killed a guard in order to escape the plantation . . . "

"WHAT?!"

"I wanted to raise a little cash selling indulgences . . . "

"WHAT?!"

"I didn't see why this new foreign religion should prevent me from keeping up with the old usual practices . . . "

"WHAT?!"

"This guy ruined my life and I ended up cracking his head . . . "

All over Hell—

"WHAT?!"

"WHAT?!"

"*WHAT!!*"

And—

"How dare . . . "

"HOW DARE . . . "

"*HOW DARE* . . . "

From caves everywhere belch naked streams of howling souls—their demon captors, already on short numbers owing to the sudden call for personnel to repel the invaders, stand nevertheless confident they can contain the riot. Unfortunately for them they have failed to recognize that the negligible, bartered strength of the damned, with which they have been accustomed to deal, is nothing at all like the strength of the recently *ex*-damned. The rioters blast from the cave mouths like water from a fire-hose preceded by a dozen feet of singing lengths of chain. The demon riot-guards are pulped where they stand the mob taking no more notice of them in their eruption than would a speeding freight-train. They pour onto the field from all sides and see the gigantic Tyrant lead charge after charge over the trembling ground, his cape flaps behind him like an arc of black sky, his sabre glows black with demon ichor and his pistol spits brilliant flashes from a barrel red as a hot coal. From the cannon-sprouting hills comes an ear-splitting wail of bagpipes with a sound like searing breath—on all sides the ex-damned fall on their tormentors raving

"DEATH! DEATH!" and "TYRANT! TYRANT!"

Again Hell's legions turn and run. Meanwhile the war trains rush alongside skipping mobs of naked ex-damned drenched in devil ichor. The boxcar doors slide back and laughing soldiers toss crates of muskets and uniforms to them, while the flashing fingers of the lieutenants appoint officers from among them on the fly. A new sound is heard all over Hell—popping chains.

In the heart of Dis, a shining figure appears on his spacious balcony to survey firsthand the smoking, roaring ruin approaching the city walls at fantastic speed.

"Is that who I think it is?" Dr. Belhoria asks.

"If you mean Satan I suppose yes—" Ella does not take her eye from the eyepiece, but describes the statuesque, golden-Apollonian personage she sees.

"Hmm—not bad . . . "

The rag-ends of the failed defenders of Hell's hills meet and are absorbed by the elite Pandaemonium Guard of Dis itself marching from the city gates. A wall of droning pipes seems to throw forward the Tyrant's army like a frolicking tidal wave. Already they have pushed to the capital. The war trains circle the walls, cutting off all avenues of escape, and the black smoke begins to trickle over the ramparts. Those devils as have wings are sent to fan the waves of black smoke back, but these quickly succumb to inhalation themselves.

The demon ranks pour out of the city walls and spread into wider lines as the gates hastily draw shut behind them. Two masses form and race forward only to be met by a wave of musket fire. Already in position, the infantry fire in three-rank rotations, one line kneels and fires then stands and immediately commences to reload while the next steps forward kneels and fires, and then the next; by the time the third group has fired the first will have finished reloading and will step forward to fire again. Under this continuous barrage the right flank of the army of Dis shivers apart as though run headlong into a colossal threshing machine. On the left, demon phalanxes are overwhelmed from behind by surprise legions of the newly de-damned . . . Devils are thrown aloft and torn to shreds by naked mobs. The demons gibber and flail the air running in all directions but the former tormentors do not get far—"Seems to me like *they* been having all the fun around here well guess who's turn it is *now*??" The elite Pandaemonians hack at their rebellious charges but their weapons batter uselessly against rocks and gouge up the stiff earth, while savage switches of lengths of broken chain lash their gory flanks; they vanish under a sea of rending hands.

The cannons open fire at the walls and the gate to the blistering keen of pipes and the Tyrant has added an innovation of his own—dozens of smiths batter incandescent chains into sabres and bayonets on every hilltop so that the air resounds with ringing anvils. Steadily more cannon are brought up, perched on two low hills close to the gates—nearly nine hundred guns on one hilltop and more than six hundred on the other they fire nearly in unison the ground shudders and the air shakes compressed in hammering waves the air turns cloudy and the outlines of the guns on the hills waver as though they were underwater. The fire concentrates on the vast gate, although many guns shoot directly at the crenelations and knock off titanic blocks that plummet to the streets crushing whole regiments and mobs of howling citizens. Still other guns lob balls and grapeshot canisters over the walls into the city blowing apart buildings streets citizens. The bursts of the cannons bludgeons the ear until the outer funnel will tear and fall away from the head and a crater is driven in. But the Tyrant's gunners howl over the shot to shoot louder and louder and the ringing of the anvils and the shrieking of the pipes is met and amplified by pealing bells raised all round on every high strong spot that can hold them—guns muskets pipes anvils howling soldiers the war-trains' shrills and the clapping of deep-toned bells up all in a wave of sound to crash down on the arrogant wall and the gates that rebound in their places with their first terror. The hail of cannonballs on the gate is so dense that nothing can be seen of it but smoke and flying fragments while on the other side hysterical uncomprehending faces flinch back as splinters the size of telegraph poles spin out in all directions from the hastily-barred gate.

A moan goes up as the doors sag off-kilter on their hinges and then moments later like a sinking ship they turn grossly and collapse. Cannonballs hurtle through the gap for only a moment so quickly is their fire redirected to the tops of the walls which suddenly bristle and bloom with round clouds of dust from pulverized ramparts and parts of bodies hail like cinders. In the brief gap as the guns are retargeted the shout of the Tyrant's charge howls down every street—he is the first to soar over the rubble of the gate through the curtain of smoke and dust rising from it, his face unimaginably convulsed flanked in train by eight huge black bulls and the cavalry close on behind their sabres raised over their heads. The devils rush forward the Tyrant wades into them slashing and shooting. His horse crushes their heads in its jaws and worries them in the air, the bulls charge gore trample and toss clearing wide swaths. In a moment the Tyrant and his evil-eyed bulls have cut through along with several dozen of the most vehement cavalry with fire gleaming on their grins. The Tyrant leads them headlong to a vast colossus-straddled square and from there directly up the wide straight way toward the palace.

Back at the gate the cavalry sluices through pouring like vitriol up the streets steadily eating away at clots of Pandaemonians and militia. A staging area is quickly established just inside the gates in an open space. The infantry subdivide readily into smaller skirmish and search-and-destroy groups—some will penetrate further into the city to support the cavalry and the Tyrant if possible—others will clear the ramparts—while the rest will commence the house-to-house. The cannons are inside the gates—the legions of ex-damned assist in hauling them to the top of the wall with their chains. Small bundles of cannon are already on top of the walls, training their sites further into the city, cooling their ruddy barrels with the ample ichor of the many casualties. Here and there, knots of regrouped defenders are visible on the sloping streets toward the middle ring of Dis. They are pounded to rags by grapeshot canisters from the walls. The flashes of the muskets spread and multiply along the tops of the walls, the inner streets are a-dance with whinging bullets . . .

Now the cannons are bombarding en masse—the whole city shudders like the head of a drum. Obelisks statues columns pagodas spires walls of steel and glass bridges gardens balconies fly apart fall collapsing or succumb to gaping rents. Meanwhile demonic sycophants and functionaries cringe in their heaving estates with their few pampered damned slaves—a stray bullet pings through a roof tile or a leaded window, a slave falls unnoticed and rises a moment later with a new unservile smile and a now former master feels the crushing bar of a forearm against his throat, feels fingers seal her windpipe, feels tearing hands . . .

The Tyrant's contingent, heedless of the falling cannonballs on all sides, are turned into the side streets by a toppling tower in the middle of the main avenue. Here they race straight into and through a skimpy barricade manned by a squadron of palace guards—dispatched in an instant by flickering shot and heavy sabres. The guns are all on the walls now, they pound the interior of the city in concussive waves and rings—ahead there is the golden palace of Hell. The bridge has not been cut though the door is sealed—deliberately weakened the bridge's pilings shear underneath them and give way but the Tyrant and his contingent are blindingly fast already within the thick wall, where huge clumsy guards lunge forward and are thrust back or sent flying. The bulls charge the door and send it hurtling back on its hinges and the Tyrant erupts into the midst of the palace guard mustered on the other side. His horse pivots on its front hoofs spins its enormous body cracking like a whip its hind hoofs lash out too quickly to see and three guards drop in place their breastplates deeply dented and laced with oozing red cracks blood clunks out of their faces and they fall dead. The horse is still pivoting and kicking, its neck snakes out and its long vile teeth sink into a shoulder tear the body open like a rag with one sideways jerk or pull out an arm. Mounted on his back the Tyrant swings his blade it cuts the air and even a nick with the very tip is like a shot from a gun. His pistol cracks points cracks—guards crumple guards drop—the bulls are charging around goring throwing trampling biting, and the handful of cavalry beam and slice and hack—and now more horsemen are sailing through the ruined door, they have jumped the half-ruined bridge. Outside as winged posses drop from the sky and from the higher golden spires of the palace, nests of musketeers suddenly erupt like bundles of tubeworms with white gouts of smoke. The airborne demons fidget in the air as the bullets hit, gaps open in their fleshy wings, they fall to the ground in bits.

The Tyrant and his contingent have cut their way through to the great spiral ramp of pressed platinum leaves that winds up to the throne room. The palace reels and lists as cannonballs tossed from the crenelations gouge great plastic rents in the soft golden walls. They are taking potshots, some of them, at the proud golden pentacle that stands upright atop the palace. Spinning up the ramp now Geryon appears to block their way his heavy fist nearly flattens the Tyrant—unfazed the Tyrant swings at the recoiling fist. A finger the size of a rolled-up rug plops and slides down the ramp—the Tyrant fearlessly presses forward slashing and firing—Geryon awkwardly swings and swats and fingers drop, he is bleeding. The Tyrant shoots his left eye out and Geryon kneads his face with what's left of his hands in a panic he rambles backwards and dives out an open window. Grinning bayonets run to meet him on the boulevard below . . . Now as the bells rise over the walls and the pipes wail bellows in through the gates the Tyrant wades through acres of billowing white satin where Dis' most prized concubines and catamites, pale and doughy or red and shiny or bruised blue and oily or any one of any number of any combinations of alluring venom, lounge and loll, not at all so beautiful when their glistening entrails make floating wreaths in white fountains . . .

A precipitous flight up the ramp corkscrewing in wider circles through raving shades and routing guards to the high towering spot with the balcony and inlaid lava beds of molten gold under a clear quartz floor. Guards fled, devils fled—now the Tyrant, drenched in ichor his black clothes sodden and dripping with his own blood that gushes from countless wounds, appears alone in this high domed chamber. At once a gigantic shadow and figure soars down at him like a javelin from the roof where it perched and the Tyrant is obscured in the shadow of dark wings. Now there he sees as it comes the burnished golden breastplate, the brilliant yellow curls, the ivory face . . . The Satan's hopeless blade breaks on the Tyrant's shimmering sabre which arcs up as the golden wings drop past him to one side and shears off the crown of the Satan's skull. He lands skidding spilling blood and brains on the quartz floor. The Tyrant, still mounted, watches as he slides to a stop. His gore slops out from his uncrowned head as he jerkily puts his palms to the flags, staggers gallantly to his feet, and with impossible effort raises the sword he still clutches. The Tyrant fires three times punching inky holes in the Satan's splendid breastplate. Clutching his chest, with a melodramatic gesture of despair, the Satan swoons, clatters bloodily to the floor . . . the Tyrant is by him now—he dispatches the Satan with his sword, cuts off his wings.

Back on his horse, the Tyrant surveys the body a moment. Now, one of his revenants (pronounced like "lieutenants") enters the room on foot and stops, looking first at the body, then, with the same grin, at the Tyrant.

The Tyrant says, "Plenty more where that came from."

"Are there?" the other asks.

Now the Tyrant exhales and looks tired. His blood drips on the floor. Sighing again he says, "There'll be another soon enough . . . which is all the same. His shoes won't stand unfilled for long."

The revenant seems to think for a moment, tracing little shy circles on the floor with the ensanguined point of his boot . . . "You think you're the next one, boss?"

The Tyrant fires pointblank into the other's chest with a little toss of his hand which does not leave the saddlehorn. The revenant's smile widens. The Tyrant's playful mood passes and his grave face becomes graver.

"Governor of a penal colony? No, soldier brave," he says, sighing again, "I have much bigger plans than that."

With a look that says, "well, back to it," the Tyrant pulls from under his cape a bundle of dynamite and lights the fuse from the green flames of a perfumed brazier. Riding out onto the balcony he lobs it up onto the roof directly overhead.

All throughout the city the report is heard. Those who were watching saw the colossal golden pentacle atop the Satan's palace blown to smithereens.

*

Misty transit. Now the legions of ex-damned have undergone their baptism by the noose. The war-trains hurtle through space at top speed—they drive upward at forty-five degree angles. Inside the troops are resting; the Tyrant is in his casket tilted up on a plinth at a forty-five degree angle, in the center of his private car adorned with black wreaths. He lies where the light from the windows can sweep over him, with his eyes open and fixed on the point many cars ahead where the stokers shovel grave rubble that burns white. The grey dwindles out of the air as they climb through milky layers, more and more light. In the cars, the cannons jostle, the horses paw the floor, the Tyrant's clydesdale whickers to itself and drops its nose back into a feedbag filled with undertaker's hatbands. The cloud-fringed circle of Ella's eyepiece discloses the whirling pistons—she listens to the blacksmiths' hammers fall, strike the anvils, she glimpses a hammer beating out a hot edge. They're making sabres.

No one before has ever made it here by *main force*. The Tyrant leans forward in his coffin frothing into pneumatic voice tubes that carry his words to all trains—

"Stoke! Stoke!"

The clouds tear away on either side revealing spacious depths carved into the clouds—the stars the moon the sun begin to come out in such a dark blue-black sky, not burning light, radioactive white brilliants.

After a few moments Ella begins describing a scene of rolling shining white clouds congealed here and there into diverse landscapes, small towns, a hazy city nested in colossal blazing beams.

"Oooooh," says Ella, catching on, "he must be in the *other* place now!"

"Our boy certainly touches all his bases doesn't he?"

"It looks smaller than Hell . . . " Ella turns her head toward Dr. Belhoria in a few thoughtful jerks—"He isn't going to *attack*, is he?" The question takes her by surprise, she spoke it as the thought occurred to her.

Dr. Belhoria shrugs and Ella is astonished.

*

In Heaven, the first observable signs: blotchy grey discolorations in the white fields of undulating cloud. Moments later a black ribbon streaks the white, laying down a stripe whose leading edge races toward the border of the woods. Other stripes in parallel courses appear on either side of the first, all close by, more or less in a row . . .

The first black streak—its leading edge rises on a smokestack, the Tyrant's black war train emerges through the white—locomotive first its whistle screaming—and the others rise steadily into view. In their midst several cavalry divisions emerge dark against the clouds the arcs of their sabres held high over their heads. The trains reach the treeline and some, including the Tyrant's own—that's the one with the funeral wreaths—pound straight through. The others peel off with the agility of fighter planes and circle round like gargantuan vipers belching black smoke the wind carries through the trees.

All the trains begin to disgorge their troops from the boxcars. Cavalry bound through the trees their sabres in the air their mounts dancing over boulders and stumps the cavalrymen flex backward from the waist as their mounts bound forward and the motion carries their sabres up a little into the air. The infantrymen whisper through the trees like ghosts . . .

Parts of Heaven are dreamy and vague, others are surprisingly stark, where knife-edge-outlined people touch each other with a sound like a bowed saw or the whine of a metal saw—and they have a beleaguered, slightly anxious look, like colonists catching snatches of war-drums between gusts of wind. But here they hover in cool groves and fragrant meadows. Now the Tyrant's trains roar by throwing them this way and that blocking out the light with waves of black smoke. Black smoke prowls through the trees all throughout the woods. Here the forests are not forbidden as they are elsewhere, or rather they have different guardians. But the saved choke and strangle on the smoke. Where they fall, they drop through the cloud floor and can be seen by those troops stationed below on the ground as spread-eagled asterisk-like silhouettes. One by one they begin to rain down on the spongy field beneath, around the edges of which the Tyrant's troops stand ready.

A group of lustrous figures is walking together down this path. They stop and stare as a band of infantry slinks around the bend, frozen there while the soldiers kneel and fire, rise for the next wave to kneel and fire and rise. Gunned down where they stood, these pedestrians sink from view through the cloud floor, drop to the field below.

Small villages, meadow gatherings, groups at the feet of huge snowy columns, suddenly black smoke grimes the light, suddenly there are horses and soldiers everywhere—from everywhere howls of pain despair—"Not *again*!" Memories of slaughter come back all the more horrible for the betrayal that they would happen *here*, massacres *here*! But the Tyrant's army is shouting too, catching up the Tyrant's cries grow from a mutter that rose from the earth with the trains—"Who dares to judge my people—carrot-and-stick *my people*! Who dares to *buy off* my people—*buy off* my soldiers—*Retire* my people—*make children* of my people! Who dares set up *my* people to *laugh* at the damned in Hell like a cloud-cuckoo peanut-gallery?" Everywhere among the soldiers the mutter is "carrot-and-stick!—carrot-and-stick!" and grim "DEATH DEATH DEATH!"

The Tyrant's troops stay mobile, the cannons fire from moving trains raking hillsides with grapeshot. Cartwheeling bodies rain down from the clouds. And in the streets and gardens everywhere there are desperate souls crying "Where are the angels?!"

The angels spiral down from their celestial rookeries.

*

Angels, unlike demons, are finite in number; but, also unlike demons, they are indestructible, even by impossibility itself . . . Such that, even if "the Master," in all persons and guises, should somehow be extinguished—even if the whole of the universe were to disappear—they would endure. They would go on singing their songs of praise . . . even with no one to listen to them. Waiting in utter darkness . . . because they have more patience than even the Most High.

It may be that the angels have already passed through one, perhaps several, such periods; when they, and their songs of praise, were all that existed. In otherwise total nothingness they waited, still, singing for eons, until a Divine Light reappeared. And they, with terrible, calm faces, turned without joy without relief without expression to the new, but familiar, object presented to them.

*

Now an angel is there in one of the meadows, between the panicking mobs of the saved and grinning purposeful lithe ranks of soldiers with spitting level muskets. With one sweep the angel batters dozens to the ground—they will be back on their feet soon. The angel turns to face the rest, their razory grins meet his plain, blank, moveable but unmoving face. The crowd on the other side is pinned down against a wall, they cannot retreat without running along the line of fire. The angel's outspread pinions nearly span the meadow, bullets thump against the plumage and drop into the grass at his feet.

One of the trains erupts from one side of the meadow—rams the angel sending him flying his wings recoil around him. The train slows the car doors slide back and the guns shower the screaming huddle . . .

That group was not reached in time.

Elsewhere however the angels come down in greater numbers. Here in this shady park they surround a knot of terrified souls with a solid cordon of impervious bodies. Bullets whinge from their armor. They cannot counterattack without breaking the protecting circle and exposing their charges to harm. But now the Tyrant has added new units of grenadiers, mostly ex-damned . . . They try to lob grenades over the angels' heads into the center of the knot. The angels speedily intercept them but not without moving a bit too much. The muskets fire into the gaps, and souls must collapse. The angels drop down again to screen the victims and those in back must look to the grenades but in the shuffle one gets through and the circle perceptibly expands, then greatly contracts . . . Now another angel hangs in the air over the circle his wings lowered like a roof—they respond quickly—but the black smoke slithers round their feet and more are dying of inhalation at the edges. The angels beat their wings and the smoke sails down the slope toward the soldiers who are naturally immune. The flapping of the wings opens intermittent gaps and more bullets dart through, more souls fall on the other side. The grenadiers now toss their grenades—some go high and are batted away, but these are distractions—several burst at the angels' feet, knocking the line asunder—more bullets and black smoke sluice through before the line is closed again. The circle is shrinking steadily, soldiers gather on all sides cackling like hyenas . . .

And at the celestial city—the gates and walls are pocked and torn, cannonfire tears at them and their substance flies away in plumes of white vapor. Grinning soldiers already overrun the streets, grenades in every window, souls of all kinds in the houses in the gardens, grandmothers children and rare warm-hearted genuinely humanitarian priests and doctors, shot down, bayoneted. Cavalry of wind and smoke on all sides, the whistling invisible sabre cuts like the wind, the victims plummet to earth through the cloud floor.

But now all the angels are fighting. The Tyrant's forces are operating hit-and-run. The angels don't waste time trying to kill dead soldiers, they attack only to buy time, or possibly to knock them out of the clouds. Otherwise they put themselves and their force between the troops and the souls in their charge and those who make it into their circle, something only singleminded fanatical will wholly independent of physical strength could achieve, are generally safe.

Now the *archangels* are on the field; Gabriel pushes back all the trains. In a clear spot between towns the Tyrant has paused a moment to give instructions, when he turns to go on, Michael is in his path.

The Tyrant is not really a skillful fighter. His talent for strategy is above average, but in these direct confrontations he has only anger fear desperation, wildness. Michael is there in his path monumentally impassive. He will not attack first—angels never do unless the safety of someone else is involved.

The Tyrant raises his sabre and charges—blows too swift to see wrench him from the saddle onto the ground, pain shoots up the arm he lands on, his sword arm. A transparent shadow looms over him and he barely raises the sword frantically battering away the blows that rain down they crash against his sabre and jar up the length of his searing arm. These blows should shatter his sabre apart but his sabre does not break, he deflects the blows. Somehow he lunges forward whirling the blade feeling one two blows smash against it and deflect, the tip grazes Michael's breastplate harmlessly. Michael's sword arm rises and falls his sword one long white flame its hammer-blows barely stopped by the Tyrant's sabre struck this way and that like a reed in a gale. The Tyrant clumsily overswings and is off balance leaning forward Michael's slashing blow clangs against the blade knocking him backward sending his arm up his sabre too high he can't bring it down fast enough to parry Michael's sword is one thrust from his heart the Tyrant's left hand suddenly thrusts his pistol an inch from Michael's face and fires. The angel flinches, and swings again. The Tyrant is faltering, he staggers back parrying, he fires once again into Michael's side—the angel presses harder—two bouldering blows knock him to his knees he accidentally jackknifes forward on his waist and Michael's blade hacks a furrow across his back. The Tyrant groans and empties his gun—Michael flinches at the shots. The gun falls empty, the Tyrant tries to rise and falls backward dropping his sabre his fingers vanish from the end of his hand—he sees them but does not feel them . . .

Michael will not kill him, would not dispatch him on the ground. He turns and surveys the Tyrant's forces ravaging here and there like a forest fire. He springs into the air spreading his wings and falls back to earth a weight suddenly pressed on his shoulders—the Tyrant's hands are locked around his chest. With fingers like stone, Michael pries the arms loose. The Tyrant suddenly lets go and flings his arms again around Michael's waist. When he looks up, Michael's fist clubs his face. A tooth goes spinning and he droops slack, slumps to the ground his face streaming blood. Michael lifts off—but arms frantically grapple his leg, drag him down. Michael seizes a handful of the Tyrant's cape pulls him to his knees, with a fist like marble he strikes the Tyrant's face, strikes again, again, again, the face is bloody, tearing, ruins. It hits the ground with a juicy smack when Michael releases him.

But the arms cling to him when Michael turns to go. The Tyrant holds on white-knuckled to Michael's ankle, ruined face upturned—he is buying time. Michael can hear the distant screams. He draws back his foot and kicks once twice, again . . . The weight at his belt stops him again, he turns and strikes the Tyrant's face knocking him flat—no, the Tyrant has locked his legs around Michael's knee—Michael draws him up again by the cape and raises his fist. Without expression, he looks down at the Tyrant from on high—the Tyrant's eyes white and livid stare back from grisly pulp. Michael lowers his hand to his side. He opens his other hand, releases the cape, and the Tyrant falls senseless through the cloud floor.

*

The Tyrant's army withdraws from Heaven instantly, pursued by the angels. Below, in the fields where they have been falling, the celestial casualties revive . . . They look around and see actual trees earth streams sky for the first time in *how long*? How exciting to be back . . . They smell death and danger like smoke in the air . . . Beautiful mixed all-in-one landscape greater than they are. Many are grateful to be back—how much we missed this, without knowing!

The Tyrant's soldiers slip through their ranks—"So, how does it feel to be born again?" . . . and the mutter starts to stir through their number—"carrot-and-stick . . . carrot-and-stick . . . who said I wanted to spend eternity in a retirement home? who said I wanted your old rewards and penalties routine anyway? who said who said who said?" They're starting to queue up for muskets, uniforms . . .

The Tyrant's army swift-descending rushes all about them with the angels led by Michael and Gabriel on a retrieval mission, in pursuit. Bullets crack and ricochet off their impermeable armor their adamant wings and flesh; they stand solemnly in airy ranks with flak breaking all around them, and they might stand there forever . . . But now the recently de-saved raise forests of muskets, they alone are firing at the angels, who stop, the bullets of those who recently were their charges thudding against them. "Go back where you came from!" "Get out!"

On the field, there are a few who refuse to join the Tyrant's army . . . These are swiftly gathered up by a handful of angels, who do their work unmolested. Then the angels stand beneath the clouds in hail of flak and bullets, sad-eyed gaze from impassive faces drop down upon the Tyrant's newest recruits. He is there, somewhere among their number, possibly crippled. The angels turn around and their wings lock together in a solid wall spanning the heavens from horizon to horizon. The escapees have been locked out.

CHAPTER SEVEN

He has dropped out of sight. Ella sits up long hours by the wooden eyepiece of her console-periscope; days succeed days. From time to time she allows her head to fall forward onto her arms, or she will sit back in her chair and stare at the dim carcass across the room, until the illuminated surfaces of chest face arms legs become hollow, glazed shells of light the wan hue of dead flesh—scud and stutter beneath her eyelids like dips of sunlight dropped between trees.

Weeks pass and the viewer shows sometimes a dead void, sometimes a bumpy fabric of very dim steady or flickering brown iridescence—the underside of a cloud? But on occasion she will catch at a rattle of rooks' wings, a flinty rag of yellow sky disclosed by a boiling rend in a cloud's boll already sealing, a subterranean animal whine . . .

Ella is still sitting at her viewer, too tired to look. Her gaze becomes diffusely inadhesive, like Dr. Belhoria's. She is pale, even to her lips, and there are faint purple circles pressed into the flesh under her eyes, just two delicate round indentations above her cheeks. It seems her visual attention focuses from within her eyes—she homes in on objects without moving head or eye in the least. Just now, she is blankly regarding some gauzy bits of white cloth caught in the bare black branches of the tree outside the window.

And that night, an intuition jars her awake. With difficulty she reels down the stairs in the dark to the parlor and loudly drops into her seat. The darkness in the viewer is shivering. A colorless, murky scene filters through . . . Blobs of smoke undulate and scatter before an icy sky, the horizon is mounded up with shadows—hills? trees? —but she can see by the dim brown-yellow glints on faces and shiny bayonets, horses' coats, buttons, buckles, spurs, badges, fingernails, teeth, kepis—the Tyrant's army withdrawing, without a sound. His dark standards flap on poles carried here and there, and in one spot there seem to be a great many flags collected together but she can't see through them—they are too far, too many things stand in her way. Is he there? She doesn't see. She searches the blurry faces of the soldiers—nothing about them seems to have changed, nothing tells her anything. They don't seem to be giving up—where are they going?

The viewer is dark.

*

To Dr. Belhoria's mounting concern, Ella loyally posts herself at her station and, despite the recorders, doesn't dare to budge. Nothing new—and she has watched for days. The effort grows hateful; dully, halting and distracted, she fills out forms and crossword puzzles, peering into the eyepiece at intervals. The viewer is always the same, always dark. The Tyrant, if he still exists, and his army, have gone somewhere beyond the bounds of their extended vision. Ella is dying to know what they're doing there, where they are—dying too, to know that they have not permanently passed from view.

Now her hope is sickening, the life in her dwindles in searing ebbs.

After a week has passed, Dr. Belhoria tells Ella that she is planning to discontinue the experiment, is considering an autopsy on the remains. She wants to move him downstairs into the lab, arrange storage for him. Ella listens helplessly; the news eats a shaft down her throat into her heart and entrails like a cold, viscous ball of acid. The time will be soon—and, the experiment ended, she will have to *return home*.

"May I come visit him, sometimes?" she asks miserably.

"My girl, what for?"

*

Ella is climbing the hill to Dr. Belhoria's house. She has just mailed her final report to the department; the last line: "The experiment was concluded on 13 October."

She stops, breathing hard, and looks up at the slate-grey sky and trees blown naked of leaves. The wind lifts her heavy tresses around her head, and its cold bites with special vehemence into her cheeks. Surprised, she disengages her hand from her crutch and rubs her right cheek, bringing away wet fingers that she stares at incredulously. With an inner spasm causing her to sway a little on her one crutch, her brows bunch down onto her eyes as though tugged firmly on a wire. Ella feels bright-hot streaks instantly chilled on her cheeks and looks back up at the sky and trees with angry sorrow.

*

Her last visit. Dr. Belhoria has requested her assistance putting his cadaver in storage. The house and the day are relieved somberly against each other. Dr. Belhoria admits her to the house grimly; her stern face and figure are a silent admonition to Ella.

Dr. Belhoria enters the parlor first. The moment the door opens, Ella is aware of a dark, massed presence waiting for them in the room, like a weight in the air. Dr. Belhoria stops short at the sight of them and Ella has to angle herself around her back awkwardly . . . Three persons in mourning are sitting by the open windows, in the corner next to his body. Hindmost is an old smooth-headed man holding his top hat in his lap. He has the sort of small eyes that show no whites, seem to be all iris and pupil. Sitting in front of him and to his left—a lean, frail woman with her veil raised, full dry lips, large slightly sunken eyes that seem a little red and wet, reedy elongated hands in her lap. She and the old man are only sitting and staring . . . but the other meets their gaze directly, raises his chin, smiles broadly, without showing his teeth . . . This one is an alarmingly large, sallow man with wide shoulders shrouded in an opera cape—wide smile stretches his lips thin on a big face—bullish, ponderous head, topped with a soft black fez. His long-fingered hands in their gloves are knit complacently over his solar plexus. While they are not looking at the body lying nearby, Ella feels an inner knell: they aren't looking at him because they are already certainly in possession of him.

Aback, Dr. Belhoria stares incredulously at them for a moment—but Ella can see livid, fierce lights pop like so many flashes in the skin of her face—"What is the meaning of this—"

Nothing changes. The old man, and the woman, remain impassive, the other smiles and his eyes gleam greenly.

"*Well* who are you?" Dr. Belhoria takes a step forward.

"We are mad hallucinations," the smiling man says in a horrible voice delighted and unctuous rising from his seat—his cape falls back as he opens his hands—Ella can see as the cape parts that from his right knee down he stands on a wooden peg with a cracked ivory tip, and this peg is fractionally longer than his left leg so that he bobs up and down as he flowingly draws near. Ella suddenly pivots and plunges out of the room in a panic—rushes across the landing and brings herself up short in a doorway—turns and sees Dr. Belhoria backing out of the room. His bulk blacks out the doorway before her—he steps out into the hallway . . .

Ella's breath races. The expression on his face is awful for the expression it veils and which seems at any moment liable to emerge. The prospect keeps forcing itself on her, she can almost see his features bundle and warp as the obscenity leers through.

He stands just beyond the threshold of the parlor, facing Dr. Belhoria. Ella knows she is looking at someone who is capable of *anything*. Although he is doing nothing more than standing containedly in place the sense that he might explode at any moment seems to hold her at bay like a physical barrier, such that her spine bends backwards away from him. Dr. Belhoria stands with her head a little lowered, glaring at him, seeming to want to speak but not speaking. The man's grin widens yet and his eyes widen. Ella is irrelevantly reminded of silent movie villains but she isn't staring him directly in the face as Dr. Belhoria is. When the doctor tries to speak again Ella glances in her direction and sees there the reflected change in the man's expression that moment and out of the corner of her eye she sees him hold out open arms—

Dr. Belhoria reels backward at the sight of him and screams, screams again as he comes toward her—Ella can't see his face—he screams aping Dr. Belhoria's screams—now Dr. Belhoria is crouching by one of the tables in the hallway—under his mocks her face abruptly twists and snarls and with a furious shriek she rushes up from the floor shoving him backwards traveling with him striking crazily at his chest and face—he raises his outstretched arms and roars, the laughter booms from a crooked-toothed grin that grows wider and wider . . .

Exhausted and giddy, Dr. Belhoria steps back, turns away, brushes some stray hair out of her eyes, leans against the banister. Ella steps toward her and stops. He is standing in the parlor, framed by the door, smiling at them.

"What is this?" Dr. Belhoria asks without looking, resting her elbow on the banister and her forehead in her hand.

"My employer is interested in this body," the large man says.

"No one can have any claim on that body—" Dr. Belhoria is saying without looking up; Ella takes an inadvertent step toward the door.

"Your employer—?"

He doesn't seem to hear. After a moment he says, "We're here to see it receives proper treatment."

"This is ridiculous, I don't have to share anything with you," Dr. Belhoria mutters. "You're not even a doctor."

He indicates the old man in the corner—"He is our coroner," he points to the woman, "and she is his nurse."

"And you?"

"I am a judge," he stands straight and still, like an abominable black nail sticking up out of the floor, draped in his cloak, hands hanging invisible, "I am here to settle questions of the Law."

"I don't want these people in my house," Dr. Belhoria growls under her breath.

"We'll be in and out," he says mock-reassuringly.

The nurse in the meantime has begun to fuss around the body. She produces a length of wire with wooden handles at either end and uses this to shear off the upper layer of gelatin, which drops to the floor landing edgewise without splattering. Ella watches from just outside the doorway, while Dr. Belhoria paces the hall. Despite her apparent frailty, the nurse's motions are brisk and businesslike. She plunges her hands into the gelatin and effortlessly removes the body, transferring it to a gurney she pulls out from behind the curtains. After deftly collecting the few clinging gobbets of gelatin from his skin, she then unfolds a white linen sheet and flings it over him with a crisp snap. One, two, three, four stops punctuating her orbit of the gurney, as she tucks him in without wasted movements. She covers his face and returns to her seat.

After a moment, Ella asks, looking at the body, not the judge, "Is he alive?"

She knows the judge beams all the same, a threatening, cryptic smile, "Yes. In the sense that he will die."

His voice makes her grip the jam of the door. "Where did he go?"

"It's a secret," he says, "He's indisposed, and very busy, and we are here to look after his body for him."

With that, he takes hold of the door by the edge and gently closes it between them, his fingers sliding audibly back from the shrinking gap. Ella drifts backward all at once seared and numb. The latch clicks; the door is shut. Dr. Belhoria slumps onto a chair; her head droops; her legs slide out in front of her. The elastic, implacable engine of her body that could crack like a whip, flags. She chews her lower lip and looks into space. The door's closing has shut them up in a whole world vacuum. It's silent. Ella can hear Dr. Belhoria's breathing—long inhale short painful exhale.

Ella has the eerie-numb feeling she no longer exists. She tries to imagine the world beyond the room from which she's just been pushed and it's all phantom pictures. Dr. Belhoria has lost all her power, and Ella never had any. She's watching the panels of that door swell as she dwindles. Ella lowers her head.

*

From that time on, the door is usually kept shut. *They* keep it closed. Dr. Belhoria goes about her business with an air of futile, dogged endurance, and does not exchange words at all with Ella. Given the altered circumstances, Ella has not gone back home, but usually remains in her room.

What is she waiting for? She doesn't know—is everything over? Will she see him again—what will become of things—does anyone anywhere know what this pain is, that I feel it—who knows that I suffer? . . . she thinks.

The others are "in and out" as Judge Daisie had expressed it. Ella discovered his name from the mail that's been coming for him. Dr. Belhoria won't touch it. On the chance she might catch a glimpse of *him*, Ella sifts the judge's mail out of the post everyday and slips it beneath the door, often feeling it snatched away on the other side.

When she stands by the mail-slot pulling out Daisie's letters, long white plank-like and hand-addressed with no return, each bearing crisp-edged black unmarked stamps which on close inspection sometimes seem to conceal a pale shape or a portrait varnished over with webs on webs of black, she is naturally tempted to open them. She doesn't dare; but she will toy with the flaps, which are always thoroughly sealed, and heft the thick stiff letter in her hand, so obviously filled with heavy-bond sheets just the size of the envelope and perfectly folded in so as to leave no spaces. Are these letters from *him*?

*

Ella sits in her room, by the window, gazing out on the garden behind Dr. Belhoria's house. The judge steps out from behind a bush, straightening up, turning toward the house . . .

"I don't want to see the expression on your face!" Ella shouts, clapping the shutters closed. She puts her hands over her ears because she knows that he will be chuckling his chuckle all liquid clink of throat and guts . . . She doesn't want to see the outlines of his white face and ungloved hands turn cloudy against the dusk while the black of his clothes turns invisible or see the incrumbling of his eyes . . . And already she can feel that unheard laugh drumming in the siding-boards of the house.

*

Two weeks later, Ella is bringing up the judge's letters when she finds the door flung back. This is the first glimpse she's had within the threshold since Daisie shut the door in her face. The room has somehow grown larger—the opposite wall is thirty feet away. The furniture is jumbled in one corner while the coroner and his nurse remain seated where they were. The window has become a french window, standing ajar on a wrought-iron balcony, shrouded by long translucent white hotel curtains that ebb and billow a little in the draughts. The ceiling has receded as well, completely shadowed. A lurid emerald underwater light hangs in the air, weakly illuminates the scene. Judge Daisie is not there—Ella leaves his letters in a stack on the floor and goes over to *him* where he lies in the near corner. She wants to pull back the sheet. The nurse stares at her like a sphinx. Ella can't pull back the sheet. But, she stands beside him, and rests her hands on the gurney an inch from his side.

*

And time just goes by, and they remain, generally unseen but impossible to get used to like remembered loved ones that existed only in our dreams. Ella will see the three of them sometimes returning from town together, without having been aware that they were gone, and Judge Daisie will stop before Dr. Belhoria's gate with the enormous brass nameplate and raise his arms in that same embracing gesture, throw back his head rejoicingly as though he would gather up the whole place between his hands. It was horrible to feel the tiny shudders that went through the house as they entered—the sharpest were the raps of the judge's wooden leg on the stairs.

"To think one of my experiments should end like this. I give that ingrate a lifetime's opportunity and he sends his gargoyles to keep me away from him!"

"We're *all* his gargoyles."

Dr. Belhoria laughs curtly, "That's good."

Ella wants to put Dr. Belhoria into a more combative frame of mind, but within a few moments they are reduced to staring, silent dummies, as before. Then, Dr. Belhoria rises irritably and crosses the room nearly tripping herself up on Ella's crutches.

"Ella you are terribly *underfoot*," she snaps. She looks ready to say something more—Ella knows what she means to say—but Dr. Belhoria says nothing, turns and goes. Much as she wants her to leave, Dr. Belhoria won't expel Ella from the house.

*

Then Ella finds one day the door is ajar and going in she sees that the two chairs by the french window are empty . . . Judge Daisie has pulled back the sheet and is half-crouched over his side, his left hand on the ribs and his right on the top of the thigh, his face pressed to the side into the cavity he chews—his jaw muscles work around his temples and he wrenches his head right and left with these tearing bites—he doesn't notice her at first, but when he does he merely raises his head a little with a long yellow grin smeared across his cheeks and chin, and the scarlet tip of his nose, the skin of his face gobbeted with shreds of flesh he says to her, "My services aren't *free*—!"

In a panic, Ella rushes upstairs to find Dr. Belhoria. She finds her typing in the attic looks up angry at being interrupted but the expression on Ella's face alone is enough to wipe her anger away—a few words Dr. Belhoria flies down the stairs—the parlor door is closed—Dr. Belhoria beats and shoulders at it with fury—Ella appears on the landing above and diagonal to the door—Dr. Belhoria cudgels the door with her shoulder her hand on the knob the hinges rattle like teeth the heavy door jumps and buckles long splinters flying and Dr. Belhoria bludgeons the door into pieces rushing into the room as Ella arrives so that they see at the same time that it's empty—

Dr. Belhoria rushes to the french window and onto the balcony looking "That's *my property*!" she screams "You fucking thieves!"

"You're wasting *time*!" Ella shouts from the door.

Without hesitation the doctor turns and races from the room, Ella is panting and in confusion leans a moment against a door. Dr. Belhoria marches grimly past holding a rifle and Ella jerks astonished at the sight of it.

Lit in brass light from the sunset she steps through the curtains onto the balcony raises the rifle aims and fires drops it to her waist levering another round and raises the gun again. A black train slithers on the horizon and in a moment it will disappear behind a hill. The sun's last beams blaze her lava-colored eyes Dr. Belhoria aims fires lowers the gun levering in another raises aims fires again fires again fires again as they get away fires again fires again lowers the gun a scream of rage erupts from her mouth as she levers her lips close again as she raises the gun aims fires the last round—

—In his compartment, Judge Daisie is reaching for something when a spot of sunlight the size of a silver dollar appears in the outer wall, high by the window, and at the same time he feels a stinging buffet tug at his hand. He sees the ring finger of his right hand write a red and white spiral in the air, bounce on the carpet. The judge stares in amazement at his bleeding, four-fingered right hand.

CHAPTER EIGHT

Now Ella is sitting in the middle of an empty wooden bench in the train station, and looks out across the floor. Her gaze goes out from her head unfocused on any thing, so that she sees abstractly the motion of the forms of the people who pass before her, ever vaguer and more unreal.

She is thinking, "I used to think that no matter what my outward circumstances were I would always be able to retire into my imagination, however much its geography and contents might change . . . In every real landscape there is always some bit or other that opens onto a corresponding spot in my imagination. Now, I'm losing my hold on that other world, and as a result of that I'm losing this one, too.

" . . . So there is only the one.

" . . . Or none."

The kidnapping . . . or body-snatching . . . happened over a week ago. In its aftermath, Dr. Belhoria hardened and seethed and became very active. She was coming and going, telephoning offices and contacting authorities and informants, corresponding with acquaintances around the globe. Ella would see her more often around town than at the house, always at a distance, storming hat—and coat-less up and down the street in bad weather like a human icebreaker. Her face hissed steaming frost; Ella sees there frozen ether poured on a mask of hot ceramic.

Then, after three or four days, the doctor was gone. Ella discovered a spare note on lavender-scented stationary leaning against the salt shaker on the breakfast table that morning. It informed her of Dr. Belhoria's departure for an indefinite but most likely prolonged period of time, and advised her to return home. The cleaning lady was due to close up the house. The note ended:

"I regret that our enjoyable work together has ended like this, and that I am unable to say goodbye to you in person. I valued your assistance in the experiment most highly, and have left in the attached envelope a sealed letter of recommendation. Rest assured that you will be among the first to be informed if I manage to recover our subject's remains. Until then, I would not expect anything further to come of this, if I were you.

Best wishes,
A.L.B."

As Ella left the house for the last time, the furniture in most of the rooms, including the parlour—which had returned to its original shape and appearance—was already sheeted, and she could hear the thuds and soft bangs as the cleaning lady shut and locked the windows on the second floor.

*

Now the doldrums settle in . . . raining down like gelatin settles around and on every pebble in the museum's rock garden and on the bowl of soup Ella eats at the Polish restaurant and through which all kinds of people flash on the sidewalks—between the cars—in the windows and reflected in the shop windows—and their voices and sounds spread shimmer hiss and chatter in sequences of gelatin frames standing in the cold streets and around the dank houses. From the rock garden and the long galleries with their successions of frames and figures now Ella passes up and down long streets with their successions of windowpanes and figures, cemetery walls monuments mausoleum doors and stone figures, regular boundaries of wrought-iron, regular streets, regular succession of backyards with ranks of walls like steps on a staircase . . . Water-darkened coffee-colored concrete walls with lumpy tops showing the broken ends of bottles pushed in like currants on a bun, every kind of green growing at their bases and all water-freshed shine brilliant solar green here and there are needles on the black branches of the trees that are as silky and dark as seaweed.

Ella sits at her old window in pale white waves of this afternoon's washed-out light. She gazes out through the glass at a landscape raw and somehow dead . . . Irradiated with haunting beams. Opaque dead backyards and the back ends of houses shot through with haunting shafts like fine electric threads tossed and curling on the mild wind just idly brushing the yeasty black dirt the clammy grass the lush fronds of the bushes and trees with fine thready shock-bearing fingers that will barb you through with one touch.

And suddenly Ella splits and she's standing alongside herself staring open-mouthed in astonishment and somehow watching as her face crumples in agony and her hands flimsily bunch against the glass—and from her mouth comes, of all things:

"*Oh my love!—Oh my love!*"

in a changed voice. Astonished Ella sees boil over feelings she hadn't thought herself capable of, and had even been counting on that—*my beloved Tyrant*—a cripple like her, she's been hiding this from herself—she sees these new feelings and sees too how she has been taxing herself shell-gaming this love out of sight, and now in her breast it all blossoms into view at once like a mass of flowers so large she can't believe it and each tightly-closed blossom is relentlessly opening. She won't be able to stop them from all opening every one so that she is being overcome with fierce weakness and the crumpling soft burden of all the dark-cultivated light-blooming flowers—all too late. As long as the body had been present there had been some kind of hope . . . that he might mysteriously return to it, but now that even the body is gone, there is no hope.

She could have been alone with him. Lovers alone together they would have punched apart dead opaque closed landscapes like the view from this primeval window she cries against.

The infinite stern self-hiding of this ugly crippled girl the Tyrant called Ariadne—she's always known she was an ugly crippled girl and she was offended to find in herself any shred of self-pity or concern for the good opinion of anyone else. Ella has always been better than this and she knows it, but she's not better and she knows she's not better . . . Drowned out in her under waves of such colossal power are sentences 'I wish I was desirable.' 'I wish I was whole.' . . . They don't wear down, and they are barely silenced. She's done everything she could to kill her own heart, and had torn and devoured every feeling, admired and tried to imitate Dr. Belhoria's apparent coldness. She wishes she could be that way because she knows that she is not and never will be—and every movement of her heart that she plucked at and ground to powder—caused herself all that pain—was a branch or stem of a root that stayed and grew deeper into her—because her heart owned the greater part of her will all along.

*

Echoing streets melt into dark autumn rooms—melt to black plastic bags inflated by the wind and spinning on playground blacktop like free-floating punctuation . . . The horizon is just a line and past it there's only black dark . . . that rolls toward her as she walks in its direction . . . Smooth-worn wooden chairs at the bakery where Ella sits tea on the table in front of her, it's getting dark but the girl behind the counter hasn't turned on a single light yet . . . Ella animal-staring into the street: "Did I ever even touch him?"

*

She walks around the old neighborhood—her parents are out of town, she's alone. Ella has been asked to put together a presentation for the School . . .

She starkly sees her inanimate future blocked out before her right through to her own end—without him . . .

. . . and worst of all she knows she will be *asked* about him and be called upon to talk about him and tell the story again and again . . . her jaws will work without end with all that talking her jaws will chew up the ravel of all her remaining life, telling the same story until it becomes bare and alien and something blunt to her; more the belonging of other people and no longer hers.

Now she has to live ordinarily . . . She's going to have to numb herself if she's going to go on—no going on from this point without getting numb.

"He's gone away from me, and now me isn't anywhere I want to be."

She wants to throw herself into her work and bury herself in her work, but he *was* her work—had been for a long time. She toys weakly with the idea of some kind of ectoplasmic paper but abandons the idea within the moment. He stopped being her work a long time ago.

And now she walks down the old streets without seeing, dazed and vacant except for those moments when she painfully remembers again that she's forgotten she has nowhere to go.

*

A dream: Ella walks anxiously up and down a green lawn without limits at the base of a low hill browed over with bright houses and buildings. She walks along a barbed wrought-iron fence nearly twice her height and as she walks back and forth her attention is repeatedly drawn to the street on the other side. Grey rust-streaked sagging facades and house fronts with drooping gables; in the distance something like a house with a peaked tile roof on her side of street . . . a crude arch or punctured wall joins it to a huge prison-like warehouse-like edifice that's hard to make out. The arch shades and obscures the rest of the street and what she is looking for will emerge from that arch.

A procession is going by, officers on horses. Now she is below the level of the street in a damp grassy depression and a few feet from her face the horses' legs dance and strike the ground like pistons as they go bobbing by. Ella walks up and down more anxiously, searching and constantly losing her footing—a dark shape blots out the arch from behind and passes through in the next instant like ghostly smoke and a chill runs through her so violently she nearly falls again. Ella flings herself on the fence and begs her arms to be strong enough to bend them but of course they don't budge. She searches the chaotic procession, heads and banners swirl and superimpose—

She shouts when she sees him there in the middle like the black iron heart of this parade of wicked officers. He holds the reins in his left hand and a bloody sabre in his right, the point down by his right stirrup. His bare head is sternly lowered and frowning and his eyes are blinding points of light like two murderous stars. Ella calls out to him as he passes but of course he passes oblivious while Ella searches up and down the fence for a gate, addressing him internally all the while as though she had already caught up to him, was spilling her heart to him, "I want to be equal to and part of *that.*" She sees herself lifted up and joyously calm like someone who sits complacently at the window while a hurricane convulses outside, knowing she is completely safe in her fortified house, and that the storm is now as much her *protection* as are the walls and the doors. How she wants to come under or get behind his eyes' light and receive his gaze as his friend . . . knowing in advance that her efforts are all wasted.

*

Murderous stars . . . murderous—lying in bed this brings her up short . . . Ella's grown accustomed to thinking of him like this, but he's never murdered anyone—has he?

He's no killer—for her, if anything he gives life . . . life is what she sees in him—appetite . . . but doesn't he murder *something* . . . Doesn't he want to murder the whole world—? To make way for another? Ella doesn't want a world made for her this world is too "made" as it is—

You don't want to destroy these people, do you Ella? Don't you really want to *show* them?

Show them *what*?

*

Now Ella sits on the bench in the train station. Her parents have been out of town, visiting her grandfather. Ella was called up to join them not long after, and lacking the veto, she was forced to spend a few days at his house in a damp, bricky suburb. Now, returning several days ahead of her parents, she is waiting for the next train. The station is vast-roofed, and presents to the eye in every direction nothing but an antiseptically white and featureless marble expanse.

"The judge said he was a mad hallucination—I can make nothing of that." Ella knows what the judge was—she knows she's seen a demon. "But he's massacred demons, and had the audacity to fail to outfox an archangel. Even on this side, how can this one get the better of him?

"—It's all a question of *whose* demon Daisie is . . . *His* demon, from within not from without.

"So where's his angel? He can't not have one can he?

"So I may be his angel."

She stops, and her brows contract.

"Yeah so *I* might fucking *be* his angel! For all I know! Am I?

"I know Dr. Belhoria is *not* going to find him.

"If the story ends here, then he is gone forever . . . and then it all comes to an end . . . ends *here* . . . Up to now I've been just a bystander—but it will be up to me to keep the story going if I don't want it to stop *here*—" she looks around at the tramping feet and discarded wrappers, newspaper leaves, stained paper coffee cup, "which is the *wrong place* . . .

. . .

" . . . wrong because *I* know and *I* say it's wrong."

*

Weeks of brain-wracking, turning over and over the same thought that haunts and chases Ella monomaniacally . . . but with that repeated turning, something of an idea begins to accumulate. In a flash of inspiration, Ella finds the key to the maze and holes up in her room upstairs.

For someone who is not readily able to use her legs, everyday business becomes an intolerable bore. Each routine operation, from making the bed to preparing breakfast to bringing her tray up to her room to bringing her tray down from her room, is a problem and she must plan her moves in advance so as to economize her energies as much as possible. Everything must be done in two trips, and once she has settled in one spot she had better have everything she needs not only in the room but within reach if she's going to be able to work steadily without constant lengthy interruptions. What's more, something as simple as carrying is out of the question, her hands are not free. So Ella must bring what she needs up and down the floors by means of a dumbwaiter, and for everything else of manageable size she has a cloth bag.

Now, Ella to's and fro's heedless of the effort, busily, abstractedly jumbling all manner of junk into the dumbwaiter, clumping up and down the stairs with labored breath. She had insisted on a room upstairs, with a view of the rooftops. Within a few days she has put together a prototype; something she calls "the oracle's gorge" . . . "gorge of the oracle" . . .

It sits on her desk, where the sun shines cold. A brass cup lined with ceramic, set on a motorized base that can be made to spin round at a high rate of speed. Its circular edge remains perfectly level the white and brass make two alternating halos. This device is manipulated by the fingertips, the fingers brush the edges with potters' caresses which do in fact cause perfectly symmetrical alterations in the shape of the silently spinning cup—although when the motion ceases the enigmatic cup seems not to have changed shape after all. There is a hollow in the base between the motor and the cup; the hollow was made out of a pewter napkin ring—its contents:

. . . Ella makes several visits to a Portuguese neighborhood in town, all bachelors, many are Jewish. She's seen them in the streets their high-waisted trousers suspenders pull them up to the breastbone, sodden white hats, short broad thin silk ties faded patterns . . . They tend to have a slow tired walk, their movements are gentle and resigned. After a few sorties, Ella discovers the best place to observe them closely—at the wine bar.

The wine bar has no wall on the street. Structurally speaking, it's little more than a converted garage: a rude counter and a room full of tremendous barrels with burned-in names . . . Here she hides by the counter and collects specimens—dreamy tired middle-aged bachelors, tonight's dinner in a paper bag in the hand, have some drinks with no small talk and when they do speak they wince with embarrassment as if they were stepping out naked from their changing closets at the public baths. Ashamed, and ashamed of their shame, and working with perspiration against both . . . Every one of these bachelors will plod on to some staircase and a dingy apartment; and gradually rediscover the minarets of their imaginary empires there, realer than the walls the floor and the ceiling . . . They will hover there, rapt or lost, or bitterly edgy, or anguishedly distractible especially when it comes to street noise. From their tweedy jackets and even from their exposed stockings Ella. armed with a pair of nail scissors, stealthily cuts off samples redolent of cigarettes and musty male bodies and resignation, desperate filmy otherworldly odor. Sometimes she catches one coming in from a really good walk—they're all big walkers—bearing on his face a transcendent rejoicing look, exhilarated gestures. He saw fog sluice between the headstones at the cemetery or he climbed the cathedral dome or he found an ancient decayed unchanged part of town, a real version of some dream—and the clippings she gets from these exalted ones are damper, cooler, more acid in odor, but also fresher, the fibers are covered in ethereal citrus sweat.

A concentrated mixture of male extracts brewed from the swatches Ella recovers is treated with magnetic fields and powdered onto patches of tweed wool fibers and pulverised elastic granules from all kinds of underwear and then packed into the pewter chamber between the cup and the motor.

Her first attempts ended in complete failure. Hours would pass, and Ella would insistently work her fingers up and down the sides of the spinning cup until, even with repeated moistening from a finger-bowl, her fingertips threaten to blister. At the brink of chucking the whole thing out the window in frustration she recalls in a flash Dr. Belhoria's stipulation: "it will not work without gold."

Worth a try. No gold to be found tonight, but the next day she winds a length of golden links around the cup's base. Results start to come through right away. Unfortunately, she is unable to raise more than the occasional subterranean echo, which rises from the mouth into the dark room . . . husks of sound, brittle crusts of overtones—no clear information. Trial and error finds the older the gold the better and that, beyond a certain point, quantity of gold ceases to be a factor.

A more continuous static is an improvement . . . A rush of faint noise like the whistling of the wind, coming in more sharply the darker the room is. Now and then, a voice, speaking unintelligibly . . . Now faint, now booming but hollow. No matter how loud, the sounds are not completely present, and never ring or grate on the ear, nor do they cause any palpable vibration in the air or in solid objects. The sounds are intangible. Ella pores over the cup incessantly, forgetting to eat, growing stiff and unconsciously famished, her mouth getting crackingly dry unnoticed. Apart from purely necessary distractions, she is always hovering over the gorge. One problem: she has to keep stopping the machine to clear it of cold webs of ectoplasm.

*

Here is Ella working her machine, as though she were exquisitely fondled by some torture—sways, her fists open and close, and then she reaches again to touch the whirling cup. As time stretches her movements are alternately vehement and then weary. Now her hands hang limp by the edges, sweat drips from her nose.

This time, there is a new element in the experiment: Ella has set up her electric plate so that it is suspended above the gorge. In a small gold cup set in the middle of the plate, she has placed a drop of his albumen, drawn from samples taken by Dr. Belhoria, and which Ella brought away with her. A low current is passing through the plate and the cup and is mildly shocking Ella so that her fingers are racked with painful cramps. Rocking back and forth she doggedly runs her fingers up and down the gorge, and its shape flattens and narrows and grows round again in regular oscillations. Ella pours it on; and now she's gasping and giving brief exhausted groans.

Suddenly she opens her mouth—nearly invisible ectoplasmic filaments begin to whir out of her jaws. They are fine as gossamer, float down attracted to the electric plate and the golden cup. The threads come out in tiny bursts like fireworks, sending down curling streamers. They begin to wind into the bowl of the golden cup, bundling the droplet of albumen. As the bundle grows to the size of a pea, Ella suddenly pushes the plate down onto the gorge, setting it spinning. The ectoplasmic threads braid in the air as they flutter from her mouth and bunch around the growing mass in the bowl, like the unwinding of a silkworm's cocoon shown in reverse. When it is the size of a large chestnut, Ella begins to mould it with her fingers as it spins, like a lump of clay on a potter's wheel, while the fibres still shoot from her mouth. Over her open mouth, Ella's eyes pounce madly on the little mass she is forming.

The ectoplasm is no longer coming, and Ella stops the gorge and shuts off the current to the electric plate. She drops back in her seat, sopping with sweat, her fingers raw and smarting, her eyes glazed, a weak grin on her face. In the bowl on the electric plate in front of her, a fibrous white homoncular figure sits with its knees drawn up to its chin.

This poppet looking back up at her is the sympathetic image of his form in space—that it took shape affirms that his form endures in space. Now she knows that he is alive, is somewhere, and this little figure is her link and guide to him. Knowing this and this only, she will set on the world.

*

Ella has been busy working up her grant proposal. For two days she had agonized about matters of ways and means, seeing no way before her but to become a runaway—visions of cold rain-swept streets, rancid alleyways, box-cars and minatory hobo jungles . . . Would she set off into the whole world after him with only her own slender resources? She saw in advance the slow winding-down of hope as worldly trash cakes up around her feet, the gradual and inevitable bog-down still humiliatingly close to home, no nearer to him than when she set out . . . She ransacked her brains—sell all her possessions patent an invention anything to get at the ways and means! Then it came to her in a flash of inspiration joyous smile of fortune.

She approaches the school and proposes a sweeping and I mean *very ambitious* survey project, to sample and analyze ectoplasm from all the country's greatest necropoli. The proposal nearly assembles itself—working her way toward him is as easy as working without him is impossible. The response is ready. It is common knowledge that, in addition to the excellent qualifications to which her school records testify, she had been the only protege of the nearly legendary Dr. Belhoria. The grant is unconscionably large. Everybody wants to be seen making generous contributions to foster the burgeoning career of this handicapped young prodigy—to manure the roots of this promising young shoot. And suddenly travel and accommodations are within her means and enough left over to furnish her with "top eats" as she puts it.

With references from the department, she orders some portable instruments to be made exactly to her specifications. When these are ready and lying on the gleaming teakwood table in her hotel suite, all polished wood, porcelain, brass, and gold, she packs them away in boxy leather cases. She gets a very basic satisfaction from putting these pleasing shapes snugly in place—each one in a contoured velvet impression—closing the cases and hefting them. They don't even rattle.

Ella is hunting for the Tyrant. During their interviews, now as luridly off-color and out-of-focus as an old home movie, hadn't he said that he was "a serial being"? What does this mean? By Ella's reckoning, this means that the Tyrant's existence is punctual, not continuous; it is only apparently continuous owing to the rapidity of the periods, in the same way that a film presents only the appearance of continuous motion. The Tyrant's life strobes "against a backdrop" of death.

Now, given the evidence, this strobing is not only temporal, but spatial, too. What we have seen, Ella thinks, suggests that neither the fragments of time nor space occupied by the Tyrant need be continuous, or at least are not part of the same continuum common to so-called ordinary mortals. The point of all this: though he may flicker through the cosmos, the Tyrant will always have to be *somewhere* at any given time. Even his kidnappers will have to travel as he travels, through fragments of space. The Tyrant's second body is confined to another world—the dead world she had peered at through her eyepiece, and to which she now listens through the Oracle's Gorge. Ella does not expect to pick up any trace of that body until such time as she has located the first; it makes sense to assume that the original controls or limits the destiny of the copy.

Basing her survey on the assumption that his presence in a spot would not go unattended by strange and inexplicable phenomena, every morning Ella has a heap of newspapers delivered to her door. She sits in the bathtub with her elbows propped on her breakfast tray, scouring the pages while the bathwater goes cold—eventually reports start trickling in, very curious little stories, usually. Usually tucked away in the more unpopular, less professional newspapers. There are occasional exceptions; in fact, weirdly exceptional exceptions: reputedly true-life ghost stories in reputable high-brow magazines, published in no sensational way but with a more unsettling meditative and measured style. Who's writing these things? Well after a while Ella begins to notice the new unfamiliar names associated with these articles cropping up all over . . .

Ella clips the stories, little fragments of paper drop down into the remains of her scrambled eggs, and after extricating herself from the bathtub she makes copies of them for her scrapbook. The originals are ground into powder and then chemically reduced into a black paste, which is her poppet's food.

The poppet, which she keeps in a burgundy-colored ring box, is her bloodhound. After an episode is reported in such and such a place she will procure a map of the area involved and set the poppet upon it. The poppet crawls over the map and sometimes it stops with a little shudder painful to watch. When it hits a hot spot it will first tap the map with the edges of its hands, momentarily fall onto its side in convulsions and then she knows *he* was *there*, recently. Unfortunately, the poppet cannot speak to tell her what she wants to know—when was he there, where were they heading, etc.—and she will learn nothing unless she selects the correct map for it.

Knowing where the Tyrant has been is only so much tantalization. When he crops up somewhere within a day's travel she resignedly sets out knowing that there will be no trace or clue by the time she arrives, sets out anyway on a slim hope . . .

Then a minor breakthrough—a series of almost regular hits in the same area—little northern town on the coast. If they may be counted on to continue at least for a time, she might be able to anticipate, be present at the next appearance. Graveyards and mortuaries are favored spots, as are some haunted houses.

On the train—this is Ella's first trip north—despite the stiffening of her neck she doesn't take her eyes from the window. The city opens gradually and rolls back away from the eye—she's now and then in the country. The grey capillaries of the forest grow, more and more a presence, grey shoulders above the buildings, more obstreperous, more forward, braver and more alive. The landscape and buildings conjure an agreeable fear in her . . . Everywhere on the banks different greys and browns rust rock mud and exposed earth, gravel mounds of brittle vegetation clumped and matted, heaped over everything like dry dead hair, and russet carpet of dead leaves . . . Brown fields like sopping slabs of bread . . . Graffiti on living rock . . . Dead shrouded trees . . . A hill in the distance shaped like a spoonful of sucked ice cream . . . Trees bristle on the spines of great rocky promontories like the stiff hairs on a boar's back . . . The fields of tall grass, soft and undulating, like the tops of clouds. At times, the embankment rises, looking down at the tree-tops feels more natural after a while. Looking over the treetops she sometimes sees derricks cranes spires and smokestacks . . . then come blocks and blocks of utterly empty warehouses, brick warehouses with dingy small-paned windows and no windows at all and boarded-up windows, slate roofs green with verdigris . . . Rows of identical, slouching houses sprouting back stairways . . . Avast mound of sooty black earth . . . Concrete pillars . . . A school bus yard . . . A parking lot sectioned in cracks, with bushy manes of grass bulging in the fissures . . . The intersection of Railroad Ave and Organ Street . . . A cindery grey house, all the paint flaked away, and through the open upstairs window she can see inside, constellations of streaks in the interior darkness show the gaps in the planking . . . Derelict switching houses like miniature towers, slightly diagonal metal catwalk, a grey door hanging on one hinge . . . A warped grid of tall naked pier-pilings their outlines zigzag in the water . . . Red pagodalike Victorian exterminator's house in tall weeds, large sign out front . . . Heaps of rusting spray paint cans by the tracks, and rusting cylindrical tanks behind the chain-link fencing are like blown-up versions of the cans . . . Everywhere concrete streaked with livid rust . . . Galaxies of broken panes . . . Brick walls webbed over with dead brown vines, looking like creases in wet brown paper . . . And once, when they glide through a narrow stone passage, a buried alive feeling—the stone wall, hanging with moss and waving cold fronds, closing out the watery sunlight.

Ella emerges onto the platform, looks up at the second horizon of the trees, to a black and crimson sky, belfry sable against a Halloween-orange sunset . . . where there are buildings, the skyline is dotted with urns.

*

Sometimes, when she had been working very hard, Ella liked to daydream about little towns like these. She imagined elegiac days lying on the grass . . . Thoughts of death fraternize with the sunset . . . and with the trees reflected in stagnant ponds . . . and with the trees themselves and the breezes that brush them . . .

A small insect flies out with Ella as she hastily lowers herself down onto the platform. She moves quickly to preempt any assistance from the conductor, who, at the sight of her, has already started forward with his arms out before him as though he were about to bend over and pick up a heavy trunk. Happy to disappoint him, looking away so as to avoid even having to acknowledge his good intentions, she sets her eyes on the doors of the small station house.

Now she steps out onto the nearly deserted streets, the air saturated with darkness already . . . not knowing where to look. Pausing for a moment on a bench in front of the station, she reaches into her bag and, without producing it, stealthily opens the red ring box. Inside, the poppet glimmers like a snowflake, lying on its side on the padding, one trembling arm extended points towards the edge of town.

When Ella reaches the end of the last block, where the street becomes a road and ambles off into the dusky woods, she again surreptitiously checks her compass. It points her to a packed dirt path threaded in through the trees. With great misgivings, Ella sees the black boughs knit together over her head, tunneling her there in the cold mossy air between the trunks. Her hearing becomes sensibly more acute. She can hear the wind stir and the nervous sound of birds, the ringing in her own ears.

The path opens to the left onto meadow with a dilapidated barn drooping into shambles at the near end. The grass here groups together in shaggy pads leaving patches of exposed muddy soil black as tar. There, after a diligent search, and in total silence that hushed even the wind, she found a massive hoofprint in the black mud.

Was this unfamiliar field somehow the same field she had seen through the eyepiece? Did it somehow overlap with the spot where the Tyrant found his horse?

*

There seemed to be no end of defunct farms in the area. Ella made a survey of these commonly haunted spots and saw many old farmhouses and barns, abandoned to rot on the shores of weedy meadows or fields somehow reduced to naked mud sores, fringed by oddly reticent trees. Sometimes, when the mood takes her, and while standing well away, she gives these places the onceover with her custom-made ghost goggles—a layer of ectoplasm sandwiched between two panes of magnetized glass, clamped together with brass wingnuts and fixed to the front of the head by an ungainly mess of straps.

More than once, there will be a figure in an upstairs window, gazing.

*

After nearly a week's survey, Ella packs it in and returns to the city. While bitterly disappointed, she has collected numerous samples and made good on some of her ostensible research objectives . . .

Trains give way to more trains and Ella finds herself standing very tired on the elevated platform of the station nearest her hotel. She resolves to hire a car. For a few moments, she stands still, her eyes closed, the wind playing in her hair. She waits for the other passengers to empty out the station, clear the stairwell for her to make her tedious and painstaking way. And she wants to be away from them all for a moment. She is basking a little now that the burden of so many staring eyes has been taken off.

When she opens her eyes and looks out over the night-lit city, she is alone. A blue, egg-shaped spot of light drops in the sky and disappears behind a long low cloud.

Ella jolts. She stares, but there is nothing more there to see, she knows that somehow. She looks around—no one else there to see, did anyone else see? What did *she* see?

Ella knows she saw no hallucination—the audible drumming of the poppet in its box, and its immediate cessation on the disappearance of the light, is proof of that; and proof of some connection between what she's just seen and the Tyrant.

She's been trying to follow him as he skips from place to place . . . But isn't there something far greater and more sweeping going on? The Tyrant disappeared, both here and there—and until now she has thought only about him and given no thought to his army—*they* disappeared, too. Like him, they must be somewhere. Where are they now?

They have paid their respects everywhere but one place.

CHAPTER NINE

Hiring a car and driver: Ella is underage and not physically able to operate a car. She lightly brushes her planchette with the fingers of her left hand, confident the story will provide, and, with one deliberate motion the planchette rustles over the pages of the want ads and stops.

Homey little cobbled street. The address is neatly painted with black paint. The few houses on this short street are all brilliant white plaster with rounded edges more folded than angled and tapering inward as they rise. Thick walls continuous with the walls of the houses enfold the patios. Her planchette-selected address presents a pretty blank face to the street, only a few mole-eyed windows. An enormous tree grows by the driveway, far out-towering the modest houses and spanning the street with its boughs. A stately old dark-green Packard is parked in front, an occasional leaf drops from the tree and slides along its rounded fenders.

The only door seems to be in the side of the house, up the driveway. The sun is setting, Ella is brought up short by a sudden ambush of surprising pink light. When she called earlier, the soft accented voice told her to come round and knock, not to ring. It turns out she does neither. He comes into the shaded drive to meet her: stolid old German driver named Carl straight from central casting. He doesn't smell like cabbage and he doesn't call her *gnadige fraulein*; he shakes her hand cordially; they discuss terms briefly. He is not especially talkative, still handsome but getting heavy and thin up top, only a little taller than she is, probably called "strapping" when he was a young man, beefy and rosy, with incongruously delicate hands, florid coloring . . . he could be the source of all this salubrious pink light. They talk quietly and she takes a shine to him. That pinkness is also a sign that night is coming on, blue behind the veils of startlingly pink cloud now going purple. Soon all color would be leeched away except for the hard glints of the murderous stars. As they part, their arrangements made, the air around her is blue and brown, though the sky is still bright.

*

Always a quick study Ella rapidly gets to where she can sense it . . . Come into a town—even in the middle of January—there's an evil spiciness in the air that feels just like Halloween . . . Mournful and fiendish, abounding liveliness stimulated by an overburdening presence of death, or its denial—something she associates with the Tyrant, who, standing still, oscillates life and death so rapidly as to permit a bullet to pass through his body, not without bleeding and pain but without dying. The Janus head has a mourning face and a fiendish face, and they oscillate atop the Janus body that oscillates mournfully and fiendishly dead, and fiendishly and mournfully alive. She comes to think of it in shorthand as the "mood"—a makeshift name, inadvertently the reverse of "doom", that steadily gains currency with her. Alchemic breaths of that mood sail in the winds' folds. A little embarrassed Ella snuffs the air, imbibes a mysterious airy vein that acts on her body someway, makes her flesh fizz with peppery static. Then she'll certainly turn this way or that and catch sight of jack'o'lanterns on front porches, low dancing orange face lit from within. Then she knows this lead is really hot . . . In some places she finds herself stepping into a crime scene photograph—Ella grew up with the cheap true-crime murder books in the supermarket book racks big type and newsprint and the middle insert of glossy cardstock with the photos patinaed in magnetic soot on grey antique mirror—wonderful rotten photos fairly reeking of ectoplasm . . .

Her electroplate bubbles with ectoplasm at the hot spots. She takes samples away with her and later exposes the poppet to them under controlled circumstances. Ella dabs the poppet with ectoplasm using a delicate brush of cadaver eyelashes and generally nothing spectacular happens. The poppet undergoes this indignity with good spirits and the occasional twitch. Other times, however, on application of the brush, her poppet will suddenly drop and curl into a shivering ball, its body jerks and lunges violently in a fit, and Ella knows she's pulled a trace-sample this time. Neutralizing the poppet's fit with a few strokes from an amber rod, Ella makes note of a definite hit. Unfortunately, although this allows her to trace the Tyrant's appearances on this side, she derives from it no special advantage in anticipating his next pop-up.

She expands her search. She visits a secluded religious community in the mountains who have their own version of the Roman Capuchin chapel on the grounds of their meeting house. The door is flanked by a pair of skulls recessed into the jam at head level in Gallic fashion. Inside there is a small chamber which appears dimly at first to be decorated with bits of broken crockery. On closer inspection these bits prove to be human bones, a low arch of pelvises cemented together opposite the door and de-mandibled skulls in neat rows against the two flanking walls up to the ceiling, parting here and there for a few alcoves. There is a door to one side whose clicking bead curtain is all teeth. A mummified cleric nestles in an alcove with his head up like someone fighting nausea; apart from their discoloration, his hands are still beautifully preserved, clasped over his collapsed stomach and bearing a plain iron ring. His fingernails can still be observed. Ella has brought with her a sizeable battery-powered electric coil, copper and brass on a dazzling ceramic plate. With permission, she turns it on and the bones ooze long opaque strands of ectoplasm; the tooth-curtain is a single, delicate sheet of ectoplasm, like a flattened soap-bubble. Working feverishly, her hair twinkling with sparks, Ella takes her samples. As they pull out onto the highway, she sees a stream of shadows issuing from a red barn—gone by the time they return to inspect the site.

Her maps take on a secretive look . . . Ella flexes her fingers over them like a safe-cracker. Nothing conclusive from the chapel of bones—she has plenty of leads left. Along with the daily bale of newspapers, Ella's hotel room is now flooded with boxes of occult books delivered every day. Godwin's *Lives of the Necromancers*, *The Annihilation of the Rose*, Null's *Fornicati Demonorum*, du Fresnoy's *History of Hermetic Philosophy*, *The Secret Commonwealth* by Kirk, Horst's *Magic Library*, James of Voragine's *Golden Legend*, the *Silent Poems* of Helen Lee Flask, Sykes' *History of Persia* and a daily raft of unspeakable rubbish far beneath her notice.

The topographical equivalents of these hopeless books are far more terrible. Dead ends and dead soul depots, turning up a null reading on the gauges . . . parched and blasted, spiritless, ashy, without tension, razed like the object of infinitely concentrated attention . . .

These places have their opposite counterparts as well—the needles of her gauges flick to the top of the scale. Too active, too much noise . . . something comes over her in an old railyard, rusty tracks, uriney train station, disembodied voice loudspeaking numbers times and place names . . . A gap pulled up in the chainlink with a depression hollowed out in the dirt beneath it—that aperture sizzles with residual force.

Her leg braces get her access everywhere; they have a way of opening doors for her. She learns to case new places from the street. For example, she could go into this bar over here and know she'd be left alone . . . She is too formidable-looking for that . . . But if she started getting pushy she could cause them to close ranks against her, tell her nothing. Would those jaundiced types have anything at all to tell her? Ella also learns how to tell the good eggs from the bad eggs. Compare the upright polite types, with their self-contained correctness, their kind of seriousness: tightly wound, cordial, impersonal, easily alarmed, flighty . . . Now compare that picture mentally with this young Mexican man playing piano by the tables just under the awning. His gums come down low on his teeth, he's soft-spoken, long blithe fingers, beautifully shy: that's a good egg. He meets his friends—all young men with threadbare moustaches and wolfman haircuts and they swagger a little when they're walking around but when they sit down together they sit close and touching, speaking quietly, smile at each other shyly . . . They know how and why to keep a secret.

That was one of the hardest lessons—asking herself, "If I shot someone dead in the street and X saw me, would X report me to the police?"—answer is emphatically YES . . . Pass on, place no trust in this X person . . . Given the sort of thing she's mixed up in who knows what she'll be called upon to do and she is prepared to do *anything*.

Gradually, Ella works her way out west and back again. Here, in an antiseptic, glaring necropolis in the desert, the brilliant white of the tombs and stones smarts in the eyes and leaves ghost-inscriptions hovering on her retinas. Ella takes the final readings of her cemetery survey. He has visited one cemetery after another and the readings everywhere are low to nil . . . He has hit them *all*—they are *all* out.

*

This time the poppet's fit was so fierce it tore holes in the map. Stroking it with the amber rod, Ella felt frantic waves of urgency emanating from it and she knew this was the strongest and most promising indication yet.

That brought her here to a sprawling hotel not many stories but spread out along a ridge overlooking the town. From the window in her room (Carl down the hall—the desk clerk had glanced up at him and asked her, "And for your father?") she commands a far view of rolling black land spotted with lights and illuminated buildings. After bolting her dinner, and impatiently waiting for the place to settle, she shuts off the lights and pulls the drapes wide open.

The window is a large, single pane of thick glass roughly eight feet wide and three feet high. Ella is unpacking her instruments, setting them on the narrow rectangular table she has placed parallel to the window, two feet from the wall. The table is narrower than the window by three feet—the gap is entirely on the left, the right hand edge of the table is perpendicular to the right edge of the window.

Ella sits facing the window with the table in between. One of her instrument cases rests on the floor beside her. She puts the tip of one of her crutches into the case and fits it into a spiral hose with a nozzle that clicks firmly onto the end of her crutch. Producing a sort of a trigger on a long rod, Ella fits the end of the rod into a socket on the nozzle's ring and attaches the trigger to the shaft of her crutch next to her hand. This done, she raises her crutch with its nozzle tip to the upper edge of the windowpane and squeezes the trigger; with a sound a little like tearing cloth a blob of insulator foam blossoms from the nozzle. Ella carefully traces the outline of the window until it has an unbroken insulated border. She removes the spray apparatus from her crutch.

Lunging forward with a few unladylike grunts as she bends at the waist, Ella plugs one of her tabletop devices into the wall outlet. From this device trail a pair of wires with adhesive pads at the ends. She sticks these to the window, leaning over the table which wobbles unsteadily under her weight.

Ella drops back into her seat and pulls the oracle's gorge from its case, plugs it into the device, which she switches on and spends a moment or two calibrating. Current charges the windowpane. Ella starts the oracle's gorge spinning . . . gazes out the window for a moment . . . the lights wink and shimmer in the cold wind she does not feel, the black patches between the lights titter and smoke, the many brilliant stars conjure grey-brown inaudibly cackling clouds that turn the sky blue and glowing . . . She gradually lowers her gaze to the gorge, and places her fingers on it. With her eyes closed, she rocks back and forth in her chair, her fingers slide on the whirling cup. Some time later, when she opens her eyes, she is hearing a sound—when she is able, she begins to make it out, like far-away pan pipes' wailing reeds. Ella looks woozily at the window and sees ectoplasm precipitate out onto the glass in zonate patterns, circular prisms travel on the glass like clouds, the town and stars distort through them, buildings lights stars and clouds seem to lunge drunkenly forward and roll big and lazy by, shrink away again. The prisms slide in both directions, pushing through a reed curtain of long ectoplasmic strings. You may have noticed that Ella has a real knack for clairvoyance. By this means she can observe even you even as you read.

Ella pulls firmly at the lip of the gorge and blinks biting her lip trying to wake herself further, trying to bring the whine of those pipes closer. When she looks again at the window, the ectoplasm congeals in a single spot and forms a lens.

By holding the gorge in her right hand, and jerking her chair sideways, Ella is able to move to the left, toward the lens, and bring the gorge with her. Moving it to the edge of the table, she maneuvers the chair forward. Impatiently she levers herself upright and locks her braces, keeping her right hand always on the rim of the gorge.

The ectoplasm lens magnifies a large building hidden behind several stories of scaffolding. Ella has seen this building before, they passed it several times earlier in the day. It's an enormous old library currently closed for renovations. After some trial and error, Ella finds that by manipulating the shaft and the cup of the gorge with her free hand she causes the ectoplasm lens to flex, altering its focus. Contracting the lens causes the focal point to roll forward jerkily. Ella is having trouble keeping it steady, the contractions cause the lens to bunch up and grow denser, making it more likely to rebound outward. All this zooming in and out is making her sick. Ella tries manipulating the gorge further down on its surface, and this seems to steady the perspective. Pressing the focal point forward, Ella gasps as it effortlessly breaches the outer wall of the library.

She is now looking through the walls into the building. The focal point gravitates forward now of its own accord, drawing her view up through the building to the high small apartments on the far side, beneath the attic and the decorative towers. Walls part in front of her like fog.

Now the lens finds its room; a pale, unlit windowless nighttime room, illuminated for her by invisible radiation from the lens, oblique shafts of light making elastic squares on the floor. It's one of the reserve rooms, plain tile floors, white walls, dense rows of book-shelves crowded together and shrouded in plastic. There are ladders and paint buckets. They've been rewiring the walls. There is a jagged hole torn in the plaster, plaster dust settling everywhere on the tarps.

Something catches her eye. She looks closer. Now here in the plaster dust there is a track, a footprint that alternates on one side with a large dot . . . Looking at these marks she receives an audible impression as well: the report of the peg leg like a drumstick striking a tom-tom . . .

Now Ella hears a rattle—the burgundy-colored ring box is tumbling on the table. Propping herself on the chair so as to dispense with one of her crutches and still remain upright, she picks up and holds the gorge in her left hand, opens the box and offers the palm of her right hand to the shivering poppet. It feebly climbs into her hand, its touch cold and electric. Ella raises it to the level of the lens. The poppet recoils in pain and writhes in her palm like a worm. Ella looks again, adjusting the focus to scan through the room, bookshelves flashing by without substance like massive curtains of seaweed. There, between two shelves—the poppet flails on her palm—there is a big wicker basket, a sort of a hamper. Moving in: from the marks in the dust, she can see that the hamper had at one time been set against the wall. From there, it had later been abruptly dragged forward, and its lid flung open with such violence as nearly to tear it off. Something dark inside, glistening in the light from the blazing sunbeam lying diagonally across her field of vision. What sun? The hotel room flashes as she goes through the beam and angles her point of view down into the hamper and sees bloodstains. The poppet contorts and seems almost to scream.

Ella holds out her right hand to the lens. The poppet's convulsions become even more extreme so that its body is distorting. The distortions come faster and strobe, its pain seems actually to diminish, if it can be called pain that is. Its form melts and blurs apart, it sinks into a puddle in her palm.

The puddle expands, sliding over and under the surface of her hand. She feels a tongue of cold electric tissue ooze around the base of her thumb and rejoin the mass in her palm. The stuff spreads and sticks and forms a glove. Ella reaches for the lens. There is a mild shock as she touches it with the gloved hand. She feels something breaking loose in her like cargo in a storm-tossed ship and for a moment she nearly panics. Panting and trying to steady herself, ardor and fear fight inside her.

Still terrified, Ella forces her gloved hand into the lens and forward. The glass yields like gelatin . . . She seems to stand before the window extending a truncated arm, ghost limb hand drawn into nothing, but from her point of view her phosphorescent hand shines in the reserve room over the open hamper . . .

Ella touches the little puddle of cold blood. A jolt races the length of her arm. The glove froths. No doubt, the blood is *his*.

Ella withdraws her hand . . . What happened here?

She peers again into the lens, and sees something she'd missed: a thread of fine powder fitfully catching the light as the motes turn confined orbits in place . . . This line extends from a diffuse, nearly dissipated cone of particles over the bloodstain, down into the wall and through the building.

With improved skill Ella tracks the line through solid walls and vast echoing rooms . . .

Now she is in a small room just off the loading dock in the rear of the building, nearly the furthest point in the library from the reserve room, and nearly the closest point in the library to her hotel room. The dock's sliding up-and-down door is at half-mast. There is a tinkling fountain on the concrete dock for some reason. Past the stairs to a long hallway, into a little room off that hallway. The thread trickles out—on the floor, a few beads of dark blood . . . With her heart in her throat Ella pushes her hand again through the lens . . . Lightly with her fingertips she brushes the droplets of blood without breaking their surface tension, and leaves each drop crowned with a tiny wreath of froth . . . *His* as well.

What happened here?

The room glows with disembodied sunlight. A modest windowless office with bare walls, a filing cabinet, metal desk and desk chair, green office lamp . . . Gleaming heap of powder about the size of a pink eraser lying on the desk, the fine particles that made up the gleaming line linking this room with the reserve room. Ella draws in closer to be sure but the sunlight has already shown her what that powder is that has precisely the hue and light of sunlight—gold dust. Now Ella leans forward nearly exhausted but feverishly intent searching every corner. She finds one final clue—forgetting her fear she reaches through the lens once again and draws it out into the hotel room. It is a dark brown cigarette end, chocolate-scented. There are indentations in the filter showing where it had been secured in a cigarette holder.

*

The ringing in her ear of unanswered phone calls makes long ellipses in her days . . . . Dr. Belhoria is gone, no, no one knows where she is or how to contact her and you've already left her five messages as it is . . . In the meantime, wherever Ella is she is forever breaking away to place another call back to her hotel and never a message waiting . . .

Finally resigning herself to Dr. Belhoria's hopefully temporary incommunicado, Ella returns to her own search with her entire attention. The errant stories in the newspapers and magazines and other media are growing in frequency and taking on an ominous tone. Mass hysteria reports from three widely separated areas, and some of the diverse persons who follow these sorts of things are beginning to mutter about a wave of traceless disappearances, and a cryptically-defined trend involving an increase in the number of claims people are making with regard to ghosts . . .

As usual she grinds these stories up after copying them and feeds them to her poppet. As for his droppings well, for a while, she with mild distaste had collected and discarded them, but recently, just to see what would happen, Ella has been using them to manure an apple seed she keeps in a small pot. It sprouts rapidly; its leaves are black and white. In just under two weeks it produces papery white blossoms with shiny black hairs that give off a bizarre perfume—a bit like soot and raisins. Ten days later those blossoms have mostly given way to brilliant vermillion fruits with a woody flesh and a smell like candy syrup.

*

Around dusk on a thundery day, Ella visits the aquarium. She takes up watch around at the back of the place, waiting for closing time, while alarmingly black clouds mass overhead, the sky's oceanic skeletons . . . Her hair and clothes are fairly sizzling with electricity when lock-up starts. Ella sneaks in and conceals herself in one of the cavernous ladies' rooms, Ella's version of the old stand on the toilet routine: she sits on the lid, her crutches in the air and her legs propped on the stall frame. Unnecessary in this case—no one checks. The smell of ammonia and detergent means the place has already been swabbed out for the night.

When she is certain she has the place to herself, Ella makes her way first to the cafeteria, just down the hall from the bathrooms, treats herself to a short pink lemonade, sitting at one of the long tables in the murky remnant of the day's light.

From there to the atrium. This aquarium has a dome the size of the Roman Pantheon, painted all over with archaic representations of dolphins krakens leviathans and such. The floor is one vast mosaic with coiling, patterned paths, lined and lit by old four-pane Parisian gaslights left burning all night—saves them the trouble of lighting them all every morning. Perhaps they shouldn't be allowed to burn, but no one here is too concerned about fire hazards in an aquarium.

Her crutches and brace-stirruped feet make loud reports on the hard floor, and the sounds hum in the dome losing every moment their distinctive outlines, merging into a faint roar. Ella wanders into one of the galleries. The poppet in its box rides in her bag; she waits to feel its rattle.

Now here are cases and cases of preserved specimens under glass . . . like *him*. Worms and simple tubular creatures flattened in glass bricks or bleaching in jars. Pausing in front of a horizontal cylinder filled with creamy spermaceti, "that's the way it is," she thinks, "whenever you deal with knowledge you always find yourself surrounded by death, preserved death. Specimens, dead wood, dust . . . Dr. Belhoria's alchemical stuffed crocodile or was it an alligator . . . "

And in the galleries that follow, polished seamless black floors like whaleskin, panes of night lined up on either side, the exhibits seem to glide levelly by as though she were on wheels. Clammy exhalations of the glass chilly mist her face. On either side of her are living brightly colored ribbons and bows. Gaslights throw strange shadows into the water of the tanks, the flames are coldly doubled in the glass. Here they have a display of marvellous otters—the water level falls short of the top of the tank, where there are exposed rocks and plants. When they see her, a pair of otters sluice face-first into the water and scoot back and forth looking at her. They palm the pane with their small canny hands.

Here in the darkest rooms are her favorites—luminous gelatin animals from the greatest depths. They resemble the paramecea and other single celled things that she sometimes can see floating in space—when the light is at the right angle and against a ground of certain colors—adrift in the gelatin of her own eyes. Some of these fish are little more than floating eyes, floating skeletons. She withdraws her hand from her crutch and leans momentarily against the glass. Five little ellipses of fog appear around her fingertips like haloes. A tiny dark spot darts over the surface of the glass and Ella recoils. With a start she recognizes Dr. Belhoria's seven-eyed fly . . .

cold living carrion . . . flies away in the next instant . . . out of sight, but not gone. The acoustics of the hall disembody and amplify the whirr of its wings, the sound comes from everywhere . . .

. . . If empty skulls have thoughts then that is their sound . . .

She knows Dr. Belhoria has not been here . . . What does it mean? The poppet is tapping a little. As she advances the tapping grows more insistent.

A long broad gallery, with benches. The fly's whirring is still audible in irregular pulses far behind her.

Here at the end, a huge bank of glass, the deep brine tank. The poppet bangs in its box.

She sees nothing, not even the rear wall of the tank. She might be gazing out at the open ocean. Ella leans forward and looks down. The tank is terrifyingly deep . . .

Something is stirring down in the depths of the tank . . . Ella seems to feel the water rustling past the glass as it rises. Looking down at an angle she sees nothing yet . . .

Then, a sinuous line, darker against the black. Presently a pair of lines . . . swell wider . . . then a fine sprinkling of faint illumination in the middle depth exposes a massive shield-shaped back, flanked by swimming triangle wings—the sinuous lines. Ella steps back. It rises into view, filling the window, nearly twenty feet across . . . an ancient manta ray. Chinless, faceless face trailing a hoary beard of seething remoras—his court. His eyes glisten like faceted globes of black oil, the wide wall-eyed gaze takes her in without focussing on her—diffusely inadhesive, like the gaze of Dr. Belhoria at first . . .

He hovers, his wings stir making small adjustments. The remoras detach, fly about him like birds around a steeple, then reattach themselves to his underside, or inadvertently to each other, forming long chains. He is oblivious to them; his lozenge-shaped toothless mouth opens on a ribbed dome, pulls rhythmically at the water, as though he were in a trance.

Leaning on one crutch, Ella puts her hand on the pounding box in her purse—can it be *him*? She has her instruments with her but she can't very well electrify the glass without shocking the inhabitants. But it is a thundery day, and there may be static enough locked in her hair—she most likely could do it simply by touching the glass . . .

Ella gingerly presses her palm to the glass, her hair crackles faintly;

the fly whirrs somewhere farther and farther away behind her. The glass pane like the window in the hotel room is suddenly beaded with small glycerine droplets. The lemonade she had earlier seems to make her more conductive. The glass oozes ectoplasm streaked with ropes of pitchy primordial slime from the sea bottom. After a moment's concentration it has all resolved into a concave lens, a ridgy circle of ectoplasm condensed to the consistency of cartilage hems in a flat bowl of the clearest plasm—immediately before the winged face of the ray.

Again she holds up the poppet in the palm of her hand and again it sways on all fours, trembles and then yields up its shape, becoming once more a glove for her hand. Something in her strenuously opposes her thrusting that hand into the circle, through the glass into the tank and nearly into the mouth of this awful primeval beast.

She reaches into the tank. Her hand is engulfed in shocking cold. It has vanished as though cut away—but she knows it is *inside* the ray. She can feel his staggering age rumble down the length of her arm. His gaze hangs fixed in the air like a canopy, like the surface of the water. Ella reels a little and for a terrific moment she wonders if she is going to faint. She works her stiffening fingers uncertainly in the cold. She pinches with her fingertips something round and hard . . . with a shock she wrenches her shoulder and hauls her numb hand from the glass. It drops to her side and hangs immovable as though it had been petrified—something drops from her fingers and strikes the floor with a dull ringing sound. The poppet coagulates again into its regular form and stands looking strangely confident with its feet on the inner folds of her knuckles.

Ella plucks it up and replaces it in its box, where it curls contentedly on the dimpled cushion. Leaning against the wall, she kneads some sensation back into her prickling hand.

She recovers. The ray has not moved. Unlocking her braces, Ella now searches the floor for what fell. She sees something grey . . . a small iron ring.

With an inscription on the inside that reads: "APOCALYPSE."

Very far away now and perhaps at the top of the dome the fly whirrs. Ella looks up again at the ray. She seems to close her eyes only momentarily, and allow her head slightly to fall back, something inside her goes slack. When she next opens her eyes, she is standing braces locked in the doorway at the opposite end of the hall. But for its lambent white underside, the ray is indistinguishable from the dark water, hovering in its tank like a shadow lit from below . . . watching her still, across that great distance.

*

Strange reports are now appearing even in the big city newspapers. Her scrapbooks are thickening nicely.

Mysterious plumes of smoke spotted and photographed in the mountains by an amateur . . . the best picture shows a high snowy peak shot from somewhere down in the valley, a tall python-shaped coil of black smoke runs nearly horizontally across its face, sheltered from the wind. This smoke line bends abruptly to earth at one end disappearing behind a ridge—the reporter investigates the likely spot sometime later and finds no trace of fire. A campfire? Producing that much smoke? A bonfire? Leaving no trace? A fire that big is not so easily cleaned up; the surrounding terrain is rocky and barren, far above the treeline. Who's going to haul a great load of fuel up there? So this reporter consults seismologists and geologists and draws a blank, there's no volcanic activity there and never has been. The investigation is left open and—we may never know, he says . . . But Ella knows the moment she sets eyes on the photograph because she's seen that plume before, and before that, trailing from the stacks of the Tyrant's trains.

Sailors off the coast of Greece hear a great cry of many voices,

—"Pan!"—

—"Pan!"—

—not from the shore nor the sea . . . as they in shock turn to look in each other's faces—they are the source. They fall drunk and raving to the deck . . . Picked up later and brought into shore, hospitalized for observation—and none with any past record official or otherwise of any crazy behavior, none acting unusual in the hospital . . .

The pictures beaming in from the dish of a satellite conducting a photosurvey of the Martian surface shows straight dark lines criss-crossing the surface roughly approximating the apparent canal network on Lowell's maps. On closer inspection the lines prove to be train tracks, steel rails gleaming and new in shallow drifts of red dust . . . Dreaming heads jerk awake—no sign of the tracks, the smoke, just red dust slithering over black stones . . .

The trees in a landscape hanging on the wall of a South African home rustle audibly in the wind.

The wind from the vast and empty Pacific carries the sound of gunshots to numerous witnesses on Easter Island.

These events draw some small notice and it is not long before a few interested parties start looking for connections, a common cause, explanations. In a bewilderingly short time, Ella finds herself part of a growing pack of discredited and uncertain investigators. Although her privileged position and special means of gathering information set her well ahead of the rest, she finds herself doing a lot of looking over her shoulder. She does not want to become an object of investigation herself.

Meanwhile, whatever is happening seems to be gathering steam steadily. Every day Ella can feel it a little more strongly, floating around her an uncanny presence—light . . . lighter than air, lighter than light, cold and rare—drawing close to the vacuum at the edge of the air . . . airless, lightless, heatless, fresh . . . The edge of the world sometimes draws immediately near, perhaps just a step away.

Ella follows the traces west. Chapparal landscape, old low hills, trees on top of ridges like fan-shaped paint brushes, against the western sky their silhouettes are wiry black scribbles at the sky's lower margin. Telephone poles tilted a bit this way and that—cold western scene. Setting sun's light red on brown leaves yellow on green leaves like soupy haze. A secretive mood is part of the weather. The hills are stoically mute, the trees aloof, the scrub and the animals furtive. Everything secretive every house a potential murder house haunted house mad house. The oddly silent, motionless pauses that can come over a modestly busy street all at once like a mood swing . . .

Ella turns slowly in place with her goggles on. Telluric hum of the hills against the sky at dusk, smell of wet wood and acrid dirt. A whole landscape in dreams with invisible traits, hidden animals . . . rustle of dirt sliding down the slope with a faint hiss, what's up there? She sees only an unruffled screen of branches.

There are spots here that look like murder sites, veil themselves in a black and white crime scene photograph with all their menacing blankness. While they present no palpable obstacle these cold spots are psychic cul-de-sacs—there is no passing them. They have no future to pass into. There Ella reads abundant ectoplasm even hanging in the wind like invisible spanish moss. She finds herself looking around as though she had reason to expect an ambush. This isn't ordinary silence; the land here is hushed, it listens to her. Her footsteps, the rustle of her garments are so loud she winces at the sound. Above, the setting sun's rays shine on trees high on the ridge—surprising patches of copper like dabs of paint lurk in the dimming green branches, not always at the crown. The sky pales out from clear blue to silver . . . the silver beads of Ella's ambient detector shine in the dark attracting and accreting the dissolved light out of invisible suspension in the air. Her hands smell a bit like dirt even though she hasn't handled anything but her scrupulously clean instruments . . .

The hills lie flat against the darkening western sky. As the light fails, they cease to be prominances. They grow concave—shadows hiding—? . . . Thundering cavalry charges?

*

Still no word from Dr. Belhoria, and nothing more regarding either the judge or the Tyrant. Ella has momentarily stalled out in a western suburb where she is staying with some relatives. At first she had planned a hotel stay as usual but the moment she set foot in the lobby and smelled the institutional cleanser and air conditioned air and old food she realized she could no more bear to stay in another hotel for another night than to put up in a stale aircraft cabin. Vile spiritless places that deaden the breath, depress and enervate the blood.

Her relatives, maternal cousins, live in an old suburb in a little arroyo with wood frame houses, big trees, cradled together in the palm of the low rustling hills. Soft nights of fragrant air, yelping coyotes, little deer tiptoeing in the streets sometimes. Ella keeps a few monitors running on her windowsill, every few hours she changes the electric slide in its amber frame hanging just below the window screens. The slides always come back in with a bubble of ectoplasm about the size of an eyeglass lens.

As the moon clears the horizon Ella starts awake from where she had been dozing over one of Cotton Mather's infinite supply of monotonous witch stories. In a daze, and unsure entirely where she is, it takes her hours to reach the window, by which time the haloed moon is high overhead. She takes up her binoculars and stares at it. With an avidity that surprises her she moongazes thirstily, squinting shutting first this then that eye, trying to focus until her eyes get tired and she has to look away, returning to the eyepiece again and again like someone taking draughts of almost unbearably cold water. The halo seemed more or less to swell a little, only just so much and no more, in response to her gaze. Seeing it now she feels it shining on her and remembers his vision, running along the hedges and turning the corner finding it hovering gigantically there. Blast of wind rush up and down in between houses between hours stutter in her face, a storm hits out of a clear sky without clouds or rain the air turns to frigid slush and the light near the ground flickers out. The moon's light is the only light and it brings with it a crazed wind from space.

Ella's cousins are asleep. With grim resolve she fights her way from the front door into the empty street—overhead the moon is a nest of songbirds, a footprint, a footstep, a whirring fan blade, a coin, a beating heart, a top, a switch, a drum, a maze, a pearl, an ex libris, a nerve, a stage, a skeleton, an island, a gargoyle, a trophy, an oath, a canal, a nude, an urn, a hedge, a commonplace book, a palm, a country house, an oracle, a censor, a flue, a grave, medicine—shadows in the moonlight . . . The Tyrant's army is *here* and—*here* and—*here*. Ghosts spin around the houses like leaves in the wind—the whole giddy air spins like a top. Ella rushes back into the house slamming the door just ahead of the ghost attack. Outside the atmosphere is filled with swatting cats' paws—draughts stab in under the doors—the dead army smells like clean laundry—a maternal odor, perhaps as a sign of the maternal love of the earth in which they had once rested. Peering through the rattling windows out at empty streets—something flashes by an elongated black shadow about a yard long several feet above the ground—a disembodied horse's head. Now a general flickering attracts her attention and she begins to notice dark shapes reflected in the windows of the other houses—the images of flying horses and riders invisible in the streets reflected in the windows. Responding to a cry from toward the rear of the house she makes her way in the dark to the bedroom of her cousins' young son, who is awake and standing at his window shaking. Through the window they both see them bounding silently fast and yet slow over the yard wall eyes blazing in the dark—one after the other. The boy is whimpering and sobbing in growing panic, he notices Ella and looks to her. She smells his urine and hurriedly ushers him away from the window with her crutches. She can see his round head bob along at waist level in front of her—his parents still seem to be sleeping obliviously.

Ella cleans him up in the bathroom, setting him on the counter by the sink and leaning against the wall herself, the house booming and shuddering all around them. Then the whole place rocks violently as if swatted by a great hand, the jolt nearly throws Ella down. The boy lunges forward and grabs her shoulders and she holds on to him. Hurriedly she rights herself. The naked boy climbs down and throws his arms around her waist. Ella awkwardly drags a towel from the rack and flings it about his shoulders. She looks to the door and then to the crown of his head where he is pressing his face into her stomach—then to the door again—if it wasn't for this boy she would be able to see——

—they were insubstantial, not entirely here after all, not yet———

—In less than half an hour there is nothing to hear. When he is calmer, Ella disappointedly escorts the boy back to his room and sits by him while he falls into an exhausted, limp trance. Wide awake, she sits with his hand in hers grumbling.

*

Certain things suddenly click into place for Ella later on as she travels east again, back the way she came. They had stopped over for the night in a little resort town high in the mountains, taken two rooms in an A-frame rooming house. Now Ella sits out on the deck alone overlooking black and white speckled peaks and pine forests; dazzling sunlight, wind steady and cold. In a fur coat and sunglasses, with a scarf around her head, Ella looks rather like a starlet incognita, and for the hell of it she completed the ensemble with black satin gloves and a heavy golden bracelet on her right wrist. Ella wonders how anyone can stand to wear such colossal baubles, banging against everything with a noise as loud as a gunshot, dragging her arm down, and forever catching on things tangling with things. The efficiency of her right hand is grossly reduced by this preposterous thing. Exasperated, she pulls it off and slams it down on the table in front of her. Herd a pack of these glamour types into close enough proximity with one another and, she imagines, they'll lock together in a Gordian mass of inextricable golden links.

Carl had risen early, eaten quickly, and is now taking a bracing walk. Ella hates hotel breakfasts. They take too long and leave you with a taste in your mouth like some kind of alien bacteria. You can throw your whole day off just digesting that mess. Over greasy muffins and coffee she idly thumbs through one of her old historical books sampling passages at random, and she runs across a reference to sappers. These were medieval engineers employed in besieging castles; while the attacking army laid down covering fire or created a distraction, the sappers would hustle up to the base of the castle wall, usually in a covered wagon, and hastily erect a shelter for themselves flush with the wall. Once they were in position, there wasn't much the defenders could do to stop them; in relative safety the sappers would begin the arduous process of tunneling down beneath the foundations of the wall, in much the same way one would dig a mine shaft. After burrowing nearly to the other side, the sappers would fill their tunnel with fuel, evacuate personnel, and put it to the torch. The fire would burn out the timber supports causing the shaft to collapse, hopefully taking a part of the castle wall down with it—and the attacking army would then invade through the new breach.

With a flash of realization, Ella just now glances at the heap of newspapers on the seat next to her. On top of the heap weighted down with the salt shaker is her list of byline names, the few dozen amateurs who write most of the relevant stories: *sappers*. Writers, propagandists, working on this side to breach the wall and let the Tyrant's army through . . .

They are engaged in a reciprocal arrangement with the Tyrant's army. Reporting and embroidering on each appearance sowing flickers of credulity everywhere and this greater credulousness somehow makes—what? Facilitates further appearances, more substantial manifestations—? Somehow Ella knows that can't be right. The Tyrant's army does not really need that kind of assistance, they will come through sooner or later regardless . . . But these sappers all the same are working together taking the necessary steps to prepare. They spread propaganda, they will be or already are speaking for the Tyrant's army. Does the Tyrant speak through them? Or is this writing some kind of by-product? So the sappers work toward the Tyrant's ends: *get them through*—and *get the message across*.

Here in the papers are the latest words and images—entranced teenagers hold sweat lodges in their garages dressed in nothing but old cereal boxes, drum on boxes and chant—

—Headline shrieks SUICIDE CULT: videotape found in an abandoned tract house shows more than fifty people sitting in crosslegged circles in the backyard happily drinking poison and dying in convulsions. Photo of the police milling around in the matted grass in and out among irregular white sheets, litter of paper cups crushed into the dirt. The bodies will disappear from the morgue without a trace . . .

—And here's a schoolbus lying on its side in a ditch—a class trip from which no one returned—

She realizes there must be branches all over the country—reading these newspaper stories . . . Somebody somewhere is writing all this. Maybe somewhere ahead the future lies already written all in rank and file of words like soldiers in formation or graveyard plots pages ahead, words on ensuing pages, the time passes at the rate of a reader's eye . . . but only her arrival on the scene will bring them sense . . . ardent *love*.

Ella struggles to her feet. Her hostess, who had been doing something in the kitchen, emerges and asks her if she needs anything.

"May I use your telephone?" Ella asks, a list of numbers culled from newspapers and journals in her hand.

*

Packard on a two-lane prairie highway, Ella on the verge of carsickness in the back, list of numbers with a newly-marked address bent in her hand. Outside the land rises and falls like open ocean, tall russet and green grass, dotted with copses. She's here to find the only sapper whose address she was able to wrangle from the papers. The man at the hotel desk—dry-voiced spare old bright-eyed man—tells her where to find him, just off the highway a few miles from town.

Ella catches sight of a cluster of cars parked along the road. The wind whips round her as she climbs out, thrusts her head up into a sky of torn and mashed-together rags of clouds from horizon to horizon, hurtling by unbroken. She leaves Carl with the Packard. A few hundred yards off the empty road she catches sight of them: a group of a dozen or so men around a bonfire in a ring cleared of grass.

They wear tailcoats and petticoats, their hair sleeked back and shining, faces painted white as bleached skulls, kohl smeared around their eyes and on their upper lips, and some have a dot of kohl on each cheek. Though their faces are for the most part plain their rapturous composure makes them beautiful. They are all physically ungainly in one way or another, and this starkly offsets the exquisite grace and precision of their motions. No one notices her. They twirl to no music and brandish their sabres over their heads, parry and return each other's nearly lethal blows rotating and revolving in a circle these warlocks form a warlike living clock the click of their sabres ticks off the seconds—their movements and the wind alike rifle the hems of their skirts. They are the wind; and for as long as they dance, they are time.

The clouds break admitting a deluge of sunlight—naked brilliant swords of sunlight stand upright on the grass and strike needle-like rays from the leaves of the trees. The illuminated sappers are their own shadows—brightest of all is the patch that shines down in the center of their circle and transfuses into the flames some of its snowy whiteness and lightness its likeness and transparency. In its brilliance which is not glaring or hurtful to the eye, Ella perceives for the first time a crystal skull in the middle of the fire: it has two real human eyes sealed into its eyesockets, which are closed vessels filled with limpid and utterly clear tearlike preservative gelatin. The eyes are green . . . The sunlight that shines vertically across their irises lightens their color nearly to white, the pale unnamed color of dried grass. The sunlight alchemically transfigures the whole landscape from horizon to horizon making it gleam like a naked body, and it gazes bodilessly back at them like an idol in a shrine all clouded with incense.

There is a pause in the proceedings. The head man comes huffing over to meet her at once.

She finds she is addressing the head sapper, a burly man redolent of brylcreme and with an exalted expression. When she asks him about the articles, he indicates the others.

"We are all writers," he says. He goes on to explain the dance, telling her sometimes they find themselves in the midst of a churning mob of ghostly horses, everywhere a smell of gunpowder . . .

When he catches sight of her iron ring his eyes nearly dart from his head. Hastily, trying to distract him for reasons she doesn't fully comprehend herself, Ella asks "Where're the women?"

The head man points to a mound-shaped hill in the distance behind her—grove and meadow at the bottom of the slope—and figures rushing in and out of the trees zig-zagging through the meadow.

Ella tells him she'll be right back and makes her way toward the grove. She approaches through snatches of song—fragrant air between the trees under the leaves damp and cool, fresh as the vacuum of space—everywhere all of a sudden women zoom like comets tailed with hair. They are wearing loose homespun dresses similar to those worn by Mennonite women, but as one dashes by Ella sees threads of gold woven in with the coarser black fibres. Their faces and hands are painted bright red and throb like arterial blood against the fleshy green grass, cyan upper lips and eyesockets blue as the sky, their hands they keep at waist-level . . . The left hand is empty, palm out, the right holds a sabre upright in the queen of spades posture. The whites of their eyes shine like clouds lit from behind in their dusky red faces. They streak effortlessly by like fireflies, occasionally thrusting their sabres straight up in the air. One woman runs up the hillside, her legs stiff, just kicking out behind her, her small pointed feet only skimming the ground, her hair ripples, her skirt fills with wind behind her taking the shape of a Chinese bell. She returns down the slope at another place—how did she get over there?—holding a torch in her left hand, and soon all the women are holding torches. The flames stream back from the heads of the torches like hair and braid themselves into the unburning locks of the women, weaving into their dark hair like the threads of gold woven into their dark homespun dresses. They whir spin race dart shedding flakes of gold into the grass.

As the sun sets the trees split the light like prisms, holding the color in their branches and throwing zonate patches of dazzling color on the grass. Color exhales from the trees and drifts over the meadow in hazy blobs, the women streak through them and set the bands of color kaleiding; they reflect off feathers of gold dropped from the torches . . .

They are all going up the hill with their backs to her. The whole scene's been so frantic, Ella hasn't had a chance to talk to them, not one ever paused or took notice of her. Now they ascend the slope together in a line, taking little scissoring steps with rigid legs their feet just kicking out behind them, and now in one weightless bound they disappear over the top of the hill . . .

*

One of the sappers had mentioned reading news of the Tyrant in a journal called "The Cemetery Partisan"—a scrap of doggerel which included the phrase "flesh of ether" or it might have been "flesh of either". Ella makes the rounds of the newsstands and libraries, no one has ever heard of "The Cemetery Partisan", but shortly after her meeting with the sappers she observes a copy in a dream, lying conspicuously on a table. She notices different editions everywhere in her dreams—they look like regular newspapers, with murky engravings instead of photographs—but they are frustratingly elusive. One may be lying within reach, a tantalizing-looking, upside-down banner headline magnetically draws her eye, but a leaden drag on her arms and hands somehow prevents her from picking it up. She will sit fuming and stuck, only glaring at what she is powerless to read.

Ella avoids the sappers, almost in revenge for this newspaper teasing, but also to spare herself their questions. How can she expect them to understand . . . or how can she make it clear to them . . . that she does not *remember* him . . . and it pains her even to try . . . because he is still always present to her . . . *now*. She pursues him, but her mind holds no image of him; rather she lives towards him, follows him because, where he is, she is able to breathe and feel fully alive. To talk about memory *here* would be like suggesting the diver rushing back up to the surface for his next breath of air does so out of a kind of nostalgia for breathing, remembering back to the good old days of his most recent breath.

Everywhere now there is a new air, something alarming, quickening, brightening, sharpening. Depending on where you are you will see on every third, or every other face, the same interrogative look: something's going on—what's going on? Usually, it's a sulky, resentful, betrayed look: they want to know why it can't all just be like it was, why should they have to change all their plans—and after all it's hard to blame them; they didn't ask to have their imaginations ground or beaten out of them. Many others are fearful, they look around—and especially up—with trepidation; they're confused, troubled, saddened a bit more by each flickering and uncertain day. They feel benighted, they look to each other and shrug their shoulders in a sort of despair of understanding, shrink from reflecting. However, on some faces, Ella will see a fleeting look of happy apprehension, or a glimmer of amazement with a freshly woken-up look; with some of them, it was as if they expected very soon to be able to reveal a long—and painfully-kept secret. When this feeling had its greatest ascendance in them, their eyes were hard and ferocious and vivid, a fierce sunrise would seem to steal into their features from behind.

She's beginning to understand what life as a fugitive is like. They fly from place to place with an oddly directionless presentiment of escape, of thrown-off constraints. An unintentional haste invades her surveying, and shows itself even in her offhanded mannerisms; she hates to spend more than one night in the same spot, and resorts to rotating hotels in the same town where possible. And more than by any pursuer Ella is hounded by the realization that despite her efforts her discoveries her encounters, she is still no closer to finding the Tyrant. If he appears soon, as she expects he will, she may be among the first to know and the first to see, but she will still be, for him, one of a crowd . . . and may be held back from him by that crowd. That is an *intolerable* thought.

*

They are heading south following a new lead when one of Ella's instruments starts giving readings. She always leaves at least one of her counters going at all times, so as to be ready to jump if the opportunity arises. Their new course diverts them into a region of grassy crags, roundly creased landscape like a scooted-up tablecloth, the hills are gentle risings above shallow gullies that slither in and out. After half a dozen stops and a number of confusing and unpromising readings, they pause for lunch out in the open. Ella takes shelter in a little hollow with her thermos and sandwiches. The taste of juice and bread reminds her of sack lunches out on the benches behind the Montessori school when she was a girl.

Suddenly *it's* in the air, she gets up sniffing. The wind slides over her face and through her hair in thick gobs. After a moment she points with her crutch toward the inverted ogival mouth of a gulch a few hundred yards away—"There! There!" They take the car off the road bouncing and jerking, Ella braces herself steady in the back seat with her crutches against the frame. Carl dextrously steers the Packard around the dimples and dips in the ground, but their way to the mouth of the gulch is blocked by a broad field of large stones lying in the grass like dozing cows. Ella urges Carl on with incoherent commands—she can feel it rising everywhere like dark weather. Their course takes them up the side to the top of the ridge. With Carl's help Ella disengages herself hurriedly from the car and peers down into the gulch below.

At first glance she sees nothing out of the ordinary—a deep, shaggy-walled gulch with rocks flanking the bed of a glittering stream . . . glittering—while passing through the shadow of the far slope, on a lowering day of thick unbroken overcast? Through her binoculars Ella sees that what she initially mistook for a stream is a floating ribbon of raised and bobbing sabres brandished by invisible cavalry. The blades are nearly invisible themselves, they appear only where they glint in the brilliant light of another sun, in a different day than this . . .

Now the sabres are gone. Ella can sense them slipping away . . . and now they are somewhere behind her. With a harried look, Ella laboriously clambers back into the back seat and directs Carl to head for the hollow again. Her arms ache as she braces herself against the tossing of the car.

Now at the hollow—she steps out into the tall grass every sense alert. The wind, the temperature, the smell, the great booming, transparent space all around her tell her *they* are near. She hears the drumming of their hoofs on all sides as though she stood in a Persian circle of horses—she turns this way and that trying to follow the huge shapes that dart at the edge of her vision but they are too fast—all around her she knows there are upraised swords muskets bayonets trooping feet drumming hoofs—is *he* here? They are gone.

. . . Feeling abandoned, Ella waits a long time before returning to town. The buildings appear seemingly out of the ground on either side of the road; and in the distance a field is burning . . . giant ruby red tongues of flame rayed through with black, tawny smoke, over blonde flames with black hearts, dissolve into the tallow-colored sky.

*

Ella's eyes are smudged with shadows the following morning. Through the window on rising she sees it is a magical, cloudy day—quality of light, seems everything is lit from within. The pale green spring leaves on the trees, straw-colored summer dust on the road, autumn clouds between the winter rooftops that loom in a narrow, precarious circle around her window. She chokes down a bite or two and then goes to find Carl in the lobby. Fresh readings during the night, and again—only a short while ago. Below a dirty white sheet of unbroken, featureless cloud, littler clouds scud by at fantastic speed. When she steps out into the bracing wind and heads for the Packard, she watches a cloud pace along with her. From her vantage point it looks as if the cloud were skulking along the roof of the hotel, tracking her like a sniper.

Rolling land, stands of trees, sudden gulches and dips. The road follows the train tracks, which now fall away down an incline into a gully, while the road continues on level with the horizon. The tracks disappear into a tunnel—the car passes by. Ella gasps and tells Carl to turn back. They stop at the roadside and she gets out and she makes for the chain-link fence along the margin, peers down at the tunnel mouth fifty feet away. There are telegraph poles running along the fence. The tracks look old, but there is no reason to run them through this dip in the ground, and no reason for this tunnel—in fact, this tunnel didn't appear to have an other side, nor had she seen any tracks further along.

Carl is asking her something Ella holds up her hand her body rigid as she sees wisps of black smoke creep from the apex of the tunnel mouth. Ella starts to hyperventilate—the smoke gathers and becomes a steady billow, the ground rumbles and deep within she hears a howl, strident, bearing down. She feels it coming on like a fit or an avalanche—the smoke vomits from the tunnel mouth with an earsplitting bellow a mammoth black locomotive roars through the smoke the ground shudders nearly throwing Ella off her feet. She cries out—she has seen the black wreath on the front of the locomotive. The cars flash past showered in dense black tendrils—though she knows the smoke is lethal she is not afraid, it hangs low, close to the tracks as though hemmed in a net. The last car blinks by and Ella can see sabres dancing in the thick smoke. The tunnel mouth has swollen now to cavernous size, and they emerge with incredibly long, graceful bounds as though gazelles and not horses were their mounts. She sees the sabres flash, and the dark arms and shoulders, the pale and terribly grinning faces, the undulating horses' heads, and the air reels with nightmarish cheers. Ella shakes and falls forward clawing at the bowing chainlinks the shock of seeing the hoofs of that dead cavalry maul the living earth the black plumes on their heads and plumes of mist from their muzzles dance in the living air that she is breathing. Their black standards half-blended with the pitchy smoke flap heavily in the air. She sees the banner-bearers riding four in a square, and a rider in the middle—and one of the standards marked DEATH flaps lazily up, and out, and screaming she sees his face just like her dream his eyes like murderous stars his chin grimly down his wounds darker patches on his dark uniform. Exhaustion and ardent desire tear loose and she falls forward in convulsions her leg lashes out and shears one of the poles of the chainlink fence in two with a chiming clang it whines and the fence deforms drunkenly falling in on itself.

Now Carl is beside her holding her shoulders. She seizes his arm and pulls him down like a sack of potatoes growling her jaws streaked with yellow bile "Help me up!" Frightened he somehow automatically obeys. She lunges to the car and with a cry hurls herself into the back seat with loud bangs "Go after them!" she shouts. As though her ardent commands banished any hesitation he immediately pulls onto the road and together they run in pursuit. Their quarry now are smoke shadows still riding in a black cloud—"Roll up the windows!" Ella shouts hoarsely. The smoke skids all around them, Carl tries to keep his speed but he can barely see where he's driving. Trees line the road and darken the sky. Suddenly there are *horses* all around . . . they seem to flow like dark blobs of ink in water . . . soldiers everywhere . . . bobbing and diving turn and spin on horses, bayonets tilt and sabres scythe the air cavalry men in kepies bolt upright in their saddles like exclamation points. Most hold their sabres low, like croquet mallets, so as to bring them up with all the horses' momentum. The sabres and bayonets of the Tyrant's army won't break—"The infantry must be in the trains!" Ella shouts at random. The horses bob and dance. A ponderous black banner, heavier than sailcloth, wafts over them slower and slower . . . In agony Ella looks from window to window as darkness congeals.

Light skips by, broken into wheeling flakes by the trees. Shadows gone, horses gone, all gone. Ella groans and seems to deflate against the back seat. Carl's eyes concerned and creased in the rear-view mirror. She lies there, slack and yet shivering head to toe, her lips white . . .

*

Lying in her bed, Ella is calm enough now to think again, and admit some thoughts of her own into her head . . . Down her cheeks stream tears of pure joy—shared glory shared victory—hundreds of years ago Holderlin writes

" . . . *I waited, and I saw it come,*

and what I saw, the holy be my word . . . "

now tears of internal sunrise run down and she happily allows them to drop onto the blanket . . . *They* have broken through finally altogether they are *here* . . . More than she ever dreamed to wait for she has seen and expects to receive. He had spoken kindly and with such warmth to her, she can hear him still . . . What will he do with his old body . . . does it matter any more? What are they doing now? She has been sitting up trying repeatedly to scan them in, to no success—she doesn't care, it is all happening and will happen the words ring again and again round her flying head like a laurel wreath . . . her body shatters in ethereal fragments, shafts of tearful illumination. This wretched hotel room with crispy cigarette-smelling sheets—those evil breakfasts—the slouching tired streets—even her clumsy armored stegosaurian legs. Now she can stand them all she is going to meet her lover, buoyed up by his triumph . . . She loves this inhuman Air Male, and she dreams of climbing into a little egg with him, to be inside alone with him where the two of them can just be together. No one can blame Ella for being unaware of the painful burden of her malice and her own yearning to put it off if only for him.

*

In dreams, new cities and towns appear in coils of pale blue mist—the wall is breached—the Tyrant's army has broken through—sluicing in like an infusion of fresh blood in everyone's type . . .

In Ella's hotel rooms, maps are spread out and dotted over with pins. Every day, new places seem to appear on the map, and soon even its contours are changing. Where ocean only should be, sailors and pilots are brought up short by smiling green breasts of new land, gone the next instant. Other regions on approach seem to exhale a weird, transparent white-blue haze, and closer still they seem to have grown oddly flat and dark, and closer still the salt air buffets the face and dazed onlookers gape at rolling waves where a city had been. Floods creep across the face of Europe.

Dream towns unfurl across a seamless tissue of sleepers extending from coast to coast. Spectral horses and glittering steel crescents, a massive blue-black horse with mad eyes and long knotted locks streaming from its hoofs . . . An atmosphere of electric gaiety and danger . . . There will always be someone dreaming somewhere, at any time, and these are the pilings on which our dream towns are founded. Dreams have behavior, and some are more aggressive, more urgent, than others. There are disappearances, and troubling reappearances, all smiles.

Meanwhile, these new spots on the dream map are launching

dream expeditions of their own. Small bands of persons known to have been gunned down by police make daring noonday sorties. Turning a corner in a squad car, or walking the beat, certain officers suddenly find themselves confronting oddly familiar faces they had never expected to see again, let alone see smile . . . Behind closed eyes the Tyrant's soldiers playfully ring around the police precinct house their muskets firing through windows and open doors at random. A police officer drops to the floor twitching and the soldier who shot him sings out "Oops! It was a accident!"—hail of bullets streams in through shattering glass splintering doors even through the walls in puffs of plaster and brick dust—"Oops! . . . Oops! . . . Oops! . . . . . . Oops-Oops-Oops-Oops-Oops-Oops-Oops! . . . It was a accident!" Dead police stir and jerk to their feet like marionettes smiling wildly they join enthusiastically in *recruiting* their fellow officers . . . When the street empties of its shadows, people peer out from their blasted windows and doorways, beneath the covers . . . The street is littered with shells, shredded police hats, mangled badges, buckshotted and overturned prowl cars, all ruined in an instant, and without a sound . . . They see the empty and half-demolished precinct house and, scarcely knowing what to think, they nevertheless find themselves heaving sighs of bewildered relief.

In the larger cities, sleepwalking administrators wearing uncanny grins quite out of character for them address the precincts: "I'm afraid we have no further use for you. Regrettably, circumstances compel us to hand you over to the crowd for mass beatings. Please accept our sincerest apologies—it was a accident."

People are disappearing, people are acting strangely. Authorities are concerned—mass hysteria, and riot season descend. Now Ella doesn't want to be caught up in any checkpoints. What's this equipment? Where are your parents? She doesn't need to be stopped somewhere and interrogated. But these fresh spots on the map are sprouting up all the time, drawn there by her poppet's inky palms. Ella needs to get in and out of one of these new dream towns before the ensuing hysteria makes travel in the area too difficult. She is certain she will be able to wring some information about the Tyrant's whereabouts from the "citizens"—perhaps they have some way of communicating with each other, a special radio network or courier service between towns.

In the meantime, the journalists don't know what or how much to say . . . the country is getting lost in dreams, often *shared* dreams. Most spectacular of all these mass visions—across from Ella's own city there appears facing it, another island . . . A mirror-image, but instead of skyscrapers there are colossal obelisks. Instead of buildings there are gargantuan tombs . . . and vast headstones, wrought-iron fences, huge urns . . . Instead of public parks, there are mammoth wreaths and mounds of flowers. In the squares and streets, instead of pigeons there are evil-smelling armies of crawling bats that fly up in creaking, leathery clouds when anyone draws near. Most are small, mouse-sized creatures, but there are larger varieties . . . "Flying *foxes*?!" one exhausted dreamer fresh from the ghostly streets of this new city cries with his eyes wide, "—more like flying *wolverines*—flying *bears*!" But most terrible of all are the dreaded flying polar bears. Perfectly round black lemur-like eyes that reflect light like limpid balls of oil—and at the right angle they shine blue like the hearts of ice caves . . . Sure it's a majestic sight to see one of them explode from the shore's ice-caked waters into the night air. Despite their enormous size these bears are as silent as owls in flight, swoop down without warning. They can pluck a full-grown man off the street with astonishing speed, often the victim is out of sight before he can utter a sound. Standing by the river's edge, one will now and then see a long, sleek head slide out of the water, nictating membranes slide back to expose the naked eye while sluicing frosty river water down the muzzle. Or you may see them swimming by sometimes, their bent-back wing-arms patiently plod the water, magnificently graceful they amble along without disturbing the surface. Adventurous nocturnal gourmets aver that their flesh is excellent.

Naturally, all windows in this new city, even on the upper stories, are barred, or must be strongly shuttered at night. Unfortunately, most of the buildings have capacious ledges—and obviously the dropping problem is extreme . . . As for the *sewers*—while there are no alligators, there are fantastic nudebranchs ranging in size from six inches to as long as a city block, their bodies ablaze with discordant colors and bristling with snailhorn spines, feathery gills on tree-like trunks, chitinous feelers, bioluminescent structures glowing white or yellow or violet or green at the tips . . . all over seething with venom.

These share the city's intestines with tremendous snakes . . . every now and then, a manhole slides silently back and a triangular head edges out on a sinuous, gleaming trunk—strike at blinding speed that nearly cracks the air like a lightning bolt, and a dog or an unlucky pedestrian is gone. The young of these big snakes, and their normal sized-cousins, gather in writhing knots at storm-drains and sewer grates; after frequent torrential rains the deeper puddles nearly froth with snakes and eels.

And legions of penguins gather along the boulevards and on the riverbank. Sometimes a heckling crowd of males will gather on a major artery in a ring maybe twenty yards in diameter, slowly turning, each with an egg balanced on his feet. All traffic stopped indefinitely until they disperse. You will see them soldiering down the sidewalks in single-file, unconsciously parodying weary commuters. Herds of wild horses roam freely up and down the avenues, kick and scream and wheel and whinny, indavertantly bashing in store fronts and damaging cars with their antics, savagely biting people as they emerge from the subway. Trees grow from the cornerstones of buildings and shred sidewalks with their muscular roots. Thick boughs span the streets. If you were to press your ear to the trunk of one of these trees, you would hear a regular driving pulse, a sound like a hundred muffled double basses. Legions of squirrels live in these trees, but they keep themselves well out of sight. They are never seen; the only evidence of their continued presence are heaps of crushed nutshells, and peculiar markings they've taken to scratching into the bark, which have all the appearance of primitive writing. Unnaturally large cats, weasels, otters, leap from roof to roof, creep along the ledges and stare in through windows with uncannily glowing red eyes.

And at night, the sky overhead is criss-crossed by rapidly-moving shapes of colored light . . . The clouds above the towers take on nearly human shapes, and seem to gesture. The stores are all stocked with cheap imitations and although the food is excellent, no matter what you order in the restaurants or buy at the grocers', it all has a faintly sweetish flavor—even the tap water, which is also mildly alcoholic.

The city even has its own variety of "little people," apparently. Small figures are sometimes to be seen, dressed in loose-fitting black clothes, their heads round and pale as cue-balls, long hands and feet, long fingers and toes. They are most often sighted jumping from building to building like monkeys. They run along roofs and ledges, alternate shoulders rolling—their arms and legs outstretched looking like a cross between an X and an H . . . they jump alone or in groups of up to half a dozen or so, silently falling sliding through the air and suddenly stopping with a jerk as their long fingers seize and wrap round a hanging cable or a vine growing on the side of a building. No one knows what they eat, or where they sleep. No one has ever seen one of these up close, or gotten a good look at their features, but they can be heard calling to each other with long sighing cries, equally melancholy and blissful . . . Sometimes chorusing reverently together, sad and moving hymns from the roofs and fire escapes.

The entire city is haunted, every building, possibly every apartment. At night the streets are absolutely silent, except for the sound of rattling chains, disembodied groans, and the howl of the wind. The payphones whisper and bark with remote voices, rendering them generally unusable. During thunderstorms whole choruses of wailing and chittering voices can be heard. Dream immigration to the new city, however, is like nothing before seen. People of all walks of life are fleeing in droves to take up residence in the unnamed "city across the water." Disappearance statistics climb.

This exodus notwithstanding, there is some feeling in the ranks of the Tyrant's army that an added incentive is lacking. Waves of shadowy wind cataracts in the public squares of the living city, crashing waves of darkness crest in the streets sprouting snarling horses' heads cavalry men upright strong and flexible as rapiers flying banners and among them in the heart of them the Tyrant's face pale as a skull eyes blazing . . . Ghostly figures race and twine keening in the streets laugh hysterically or curse like furies directly in the faces of the populace nearly insane with fear.

In the massive central train station, from out of the tunnels come a rush of thunder. Antique locomotives fill the cavernous underground switching yard with lethal black smoke, erupt along the platforms as cavalry race along the dark tracks intermittently lit by the yellow sodium lights, charge onto the platforms slashing gleefully on all sides. Howling crowds belch from the tunnels into the main concourse, mounted men and infantry hot behind them. The huge vaulted ceiling rebounds with screams and fills quickly with white gunsmoke—horses wheel dicking divots in the marble floor with their hoofs, the infantry set up in the galleries over the main floor shooting down heedless. Their bullets will pass harmlessly through their mounted comrades. One of them decapitates the information kiosk sending its bulbous clock smashing to the floor, planting a ponderous black banner there instead. The cavalry billows from all tunnel mouths, races up the ramps to the doors and explodes in cascades of shattering glass onto the sidewalks and into the street. Dream horses pivot on their front hoofs spin and lash out with their rear hoofs knocking cars and cabs over onto their sides with one blow as their riders twist firing pistols hacking with their sabres. Sirens keen on all blocks. Traffic balls up and slowly moves aside to admit streams of police cars which buckle and cartwheel in all directions under a volley of cannonballs from the station roof. Shouted orders to reload while the police scramble from their stricken vehicles. Shrieking cannonballs rend the facades of buildings plunge through the hoods of police cars and shatter the engine blocks sending flechettes of sharp metal and hot machine parts back into the cabin. The cavalry sweep the avenues—knots of infantry advance kneel fire rise reload advance, each round of shots cutting swaths out of the crowd. Police are already establishing perimeters out of cannon range, or so they think. Beneath the streets subway cars suddenly lurch and veer off course into new tunnels, the lights go out and the doors fly open on either side to blasting dark wind. In the muzzle flashes horrified commuters see bayonets and dark figures a shower of bullets. The trains pull into new stations with peculiar names, with crates of uniforms and muskets standing in asterisk-like bundles waiting for them . . .

Police surveying the train station from behind their cars turn to see soldiers flood from the subway stops. They empty their guns into grinning advancing figures who do not flinch nor sway, who grin and pick their time and deliberately, unhastily bayonet them. As the police are picked off squadrons of fire children make their debut: delicate boys come skipping up to the dead cops and sprinkle them gracefully with fuel, delicate girls with fairy wings of wire and gauze follow up carrying perpetual sparklers, curtsey down as though they were picking flowers, and tap the doused bodies with their magic wands. The bodies of the police are enveloped in soft blue flames. The cavalry race on—from the subway tunnels raging locomotives claw their way into the open air and storming like dragons vomit torrents of poisonous black smoke. Meanwhile the burning cops wink out one by one their uniforms badges and gear thoroughly consumed, naked they stir and grin and rise don their new uniforms take up their muskets and race to join their new units.

The complex of buildings around city hall: mobs of people scream and scurry trying to escape the black smoke. They claw the blankets; they rush for the bank of glass doors belonging to the mayor's office building, and with great agility the police manning the lobby race forward to lock them out, blocking the doors with a desk and sticking a broom through the loops of the door handles. Anguished and horrified men women and children crush up against the glass. The police point their pistols at them from the other side. The smoke overwhelms the crowd and everywhere they are dropping. From the smoke emerge zig-zagging cavalry weightless and silent as shadows they drive among the crowd slicing and shooting. Not knowing what to do the police officers inside the lobby run to the elevators—the mayor is still upstairs—against the glass corpses slide collapse the glass cracks. On hearing the tumult, and after listening with mounting alarm and trepidation to the fragmentary reports coming from the dream street, the mayor and the police chief head for the elevators one of which opens of its own accord as they approach police bodies are heaped on its floor. The elevator adjacent opens a moment later full of grinning faces—the mayor and the police chief are seized bodily and carried back into their offices. A boy and a girl are visiting the heap of police bodies in the elevator. The mayor and the police chief are picked up and tossed back and forth by gaily laughing soldiers, hurled bodily back and forth like medicine balls over gleaming mahogany desks. Hurtling dizzily through the air and disoriented as they are they both recognize the new soldiers who enter the room a moment later still tugging on their uniforms—familiar faces, utterly unfamiliar grins. Mayor and police chief fly back and forth from hand to hand hands of all colors of course and then all at once those hands close on the folds of their clothes with a terrible strength and implacable resolve and now they are conducted faster and faster the length of the building, and now they are in the air. Heavy plate glass shatters with a deafening sound and with a horrible shift of inertia, from forward, to down, like riding a rollercoaster, they drop like sacks of rags to the street. Hoofs churn their remains.

Every street in the city screams—gunshots, cannonballs, clattering hoofs, shattering glass, hoarsely roaring flames, banshee-wail of train whistles, dwindling sirens, laughing to make the ground tremble . . .

A jaunty revenant shouts from his horse, ". . . always said this was our kind of town!"

*

Cabaret dream—the usual showgirls are succeeded by an unannounced brigade of women in scarlet strapless dresses, from which each emerges upwards like a bouquet in a vase, exposing the shoulders, the throat, the fine bone structure, the heaving embonpoint. Dark-haired, lynx-eyed dancers whose skin is painted crimson and whose upper lips and long-lashed eye sockets are painted sky blue, hike up their skirts to expose dazzling white stockings and hard, evil black shoes. Their hair is arranged in orderly piles on top of their heads, so that their shining ruby ear-rings will show. At once and with such speed that they leave the accompaniment struggling to keep up they launch into a frenzied can-can, bounding over each other landing in splits with loud cries. The music reels after them in drunken disarray the drums thundering madly, their nostrils flare like horses' as they drop in splits and rise again without using their hands simply pushing their scissored legs together again. The boards of the stage tremble and groan beneath their maenads' feet. Now with smooth purposeful movements the white-aproned waiters are gliding through the tables their faces are white their upper lips and eye sockets are black. The music storms the drums' pounding is suddenly echoed by the dancers' feet, stamping urgently on the stage, their wild faces blast out vehement demands, the sappers disguised as waiters draw their knives from behind their aprons and spin like dervishes among the tables their eyes and knives flashing like their fixed grins. With one stroke a knife cleaves a throat nearly in two and all over the floor they are slashing fast as lightning, the guests tilt and keel their faces blank they paw the snowy white table cloths with gory hands and slide to the floor. Tables and chairs topple—the dancers shriek and stamp stamp stamp. The sappers bob and slay and glide—while some of the more agile or shall we say sensitive types hasten outside. The floor is a welter of thick blood black as ink—still pristine white the sappers' arms dart and plunge—screams and death rattles, breaking crockery—the dancers are triumphantly dancing on the tables under which people are bleeding to death sucking breath through gaping throats. The maitre d' takes advantage of the confusion to make a dash for the exit. Emerging from his hiding place behind the piano, he makes two steps, and is swept from the floor by a knot of dancers who toss him into the air and tug him screaming back and forth like a rag doll tearing him limb from limb with their crimson hands. Cool and methodical the sappers fan out into the street beaming their arms outstretched like singing waiters in an MGM musical . . .

*

Pins sprout across Ella's maps, which are saturated like sponges with ectoplasm; it wells up from every new pin prick. She can rake the map lightly with her fingernails and raise beautiful glassy ridges of ectoplasm. She rubs a little between her fingers and it sizzles and tingles on her flesh like topical cocaine—cool flames of pleasure flicker up the length of her arm.

Of course, not everyone elects to remain in these reclaimed areas, with their plague of dreams and disappearances. Old towns empty out in days, police trying to hem in the ensuing looting only provoke riots. Roadblocks appear everywhere, and it's hard to get to the hot spots. On a back road she encounters a solitary man, the bed of his pickup truck loaded with a hastily assembled heap of belongings. He is kicking a flat tire in frustration when they pull up and offer him a lift. Later, they stop for a meal, and Ella interrogates him in a back booth. After her first few questions, he seems to get offended and makes to get up and leave. Ella reaches over, plants the tip of her crutch against his chest and shoves him bodily back down in his seat. He slumps back open-mouthed and aghast at the irresistible physical strength of this fifteen-year-old girl. He begins giving answers, but they are not especially helpful.

Refugee: Oh everything's changed.

Ella: Such as?

Refugee: Well . . . the land there . . . (trails off in confusion, fatigue)

Ella: What? Is the ground torn up? Fields burned?

Refugee: No, it just looks different.

Ella: I don't understand.

Refugee: I don't know how to describe it—it's like the landscape's a different *style* now.

Ella lets him off at the bus station later that evening, muttering in frustration, and returns to her search.

Her poppet typically rests in the corners of the map on relatively undisturbed patches of blue sea—and now she watches it spring to action, seize one of her pins crawl laboriously over the map and plunge it into a fresh hot spot, like an explorer planting his flag on alien sands. Ella reflexively reaches out and grasps the pin. It hums sears sparks against her fingers and she knows this is a *new* hot spot, only just appeared and nearby. If they move now, they can get there before the confusion hits, the trouble, and then the roadblocks.

They have to leave the highway and thread through a maze of country roads, many of which are not marked. The poppet sits in a little container of ectoplasm on the dash and acts as a floating compass. As the sky grows dark, Carl starts grumbling about heading back. These roads are jagged in places and completely unlit. They haven't passed a house, or so much as a telephone pole in miles, and Carl is so to speak seeing the buzzards circling. Ella adamantly refuses . . . but, if something doesn't turn up soon how can she justify going on? The poppet stands at attention—Ella shouts and points. A dirt road branches away through the low hills; a signpost stands where the road forks. Ella calls a halt and clambers out of the car to take a closer look. It's straight from a B movie, an illegible warning in white paint on a sorely weathered grey plank, rustily nailed to a post, topped with a human skull. "That was thoughtful of them," she thinks.

Carl is saying something about the dirt road. It is too uneven, the Packard will likely wreck itself. Utterly fed up with his caution, Ella turns fiercely and tells him to wait. Then, with rapturous expectation, like someone stepping at last into a storybook, she sets out on foot.

The road is uneven, with deep ruts. Ella has to keep her head down, looking carefully in the dusk so as not to catch her crutch in the ruts. In one lazy bend the road conducts her out of sight of the car. Ella smells dust and hot straw, a sunset smell. A dry stand of trees rustles by like crinolines and the road slopes upwards. The incline is not especially steep but Ella has to reduce the sweep of her step to keep her balance. She realizes with a bit of a jar that there is no one here to help her to her feet again if she falls. She keeps going. The brush has an oily acrid smell like turpentine, brittle branches and leaves whirr in the breeze.

And now the dark air around her fills with gold . . . A gold shine dances up from the other side of the hill . . . Ella gasps and redoubles her efforts. Starry motes like amber fireflies drift past her as though the road were a giant's route through space. With crazy endurance, Ella follows it up the increasingly steep slope her eyes fixed on the hilltop. Sweat snaps out all over her face her shoulders and chest—the top of the hill seems to hold itself tantalizingly aloof. Hate for it froths blackly in her chest and her eyes claw at it with deadly rays. Her shoulders jump in their sockets and she pounds the ground with her crutches like a couple of piledrivers as if she were going to pummel the hill down or punish it for being in her way in the first place. She pants, and her hair droops down into her face, where it brushes her brow and cheeks the touch so faint and light as to be overwhelmingly exasperating—and then she is there, the verge falls away and she is brought up short gazing down. The tawny beams sway in the air like shafts of sun below the surface of the sea, but these shafts shine up not down. The beams seem to be sticky at the ends and when they play over her she feels a mild bodiless suction what an exquisite feeling!

Suffused with this galvanic, autumnal golden light, she is looking down at a one-street western town stereotypical in every detail but one—the train station the hotel the saloon the bordello the casino all loom many stories above the street. These wood-frame skyscrapers should collapse under their own weight, and they are all slouching precariously; yet Ella knows they won't fall, or rather she isn't in the least afraid that they will. As with the familiar two-storey buildings, there are shaded porches forming a roughly continuous cloistered sidewalk on either side of the dirt main street, and these porches have balconies set atop them on every storey, stacked one atop another with slightly protruding eaves. These upper storeys also taper in a bit, giving these tall western buildings a pagodalike appearance. In the main street she sees soldiers from the Tyrant's army standing in small knots here and there, talking inanimatedly, if at all, hands at their sides, still dressed as Hussars and Uhlans, but there are a number of clearly living persons present. All drunk—for the most part local people, truck drivers and farmers, but with some exotics as well: a man leaning against the post of one of the bordello's higher balconies hollers down into the street in Russian. A whisky priest sits dangling his legs from the saloon's porch puffing a cigar complacently . . . Ella nearly floats from the earth . . . her heart blazing, she can hear the creak of her leg braces as she seems to swell—a soft grey barrier there, like trying to wake up, trying to remember where you are, recognize the room after waking from a nightmare . . . She is down in the streets, golden light sifting all around her.

CHAPTER TEN

Here dead and alive both stroll up and down on the street's glowing dirt . . . and Ella is with them . . . She is submerged in the street with flames in her breast. She stands on the street in triumph as though she had just trampled her enemies into its dust.

The town seems much larger seen from down here than it did seen from above. She looks up for the ridge somewhere overhead behind her right shoulder but the glare of the lights is too dazzling. She sees nothing much past the rooftops but a handful of stars. There are quite a few living people around and all of them seem to be drunk or someway intoxicated . . . A carnival atmosphere . . . The dead ones are part of it but they do not partake of it, the air and the light, the threads of music insinuated everywhere, the webs of voices and miscellaneous noises, all seething with violence, and yet Ella feels safe . . .

The street is lined with hotels, saloons, casinos—here's a jeweller's barred window full of crimson silk, on which glinting eggs webbed with gold and studded with gems are sporting around a diademmed electroplated skull. Now a pet store with gambolling kittens and bats; now an open shop front with sumptuous bolts of rich Turkish rugs slopping out onto the boardwalk. Here's an example of that sort of bordello which identifies itself not with a red light, but with a stuffed wolf's head on the wall of an otherwise ordinary, lamplit parlour . . . a sturdy leg in seamed hose kicks a pump into the air from the second floor balcony overhead. And here's what appears to be a reading room: dirty, loose-rattling floorboards, the tables are long planks laid across sawhorses, the walls lined with luxurious calfleather-bound volumes so satisfying to handle. Dazzling golden candles sit in bubbles of light on enormous pewter stands studded with pearls—scholarly- and rabbinical-looking citizens sit and pore over the pages . . .

Standing between two buildings, almost completely invisible in their shade, an enormous equestrian statue of the Tyrant rests on a cyclopean basalt base. All cast in dark greenish bronze the color of seaweed, except for the flaring whites of his eyes white as chalk in a face that is nearly obscured, showing only in the brow's stern furrows that seem to grip the eye sockets fiercely . . . One upstretched arm vanishes in shadow where it brandishes an unseen sabre, the other points its pistol across the street over her head. The legs clamp the horse's sides, he steers with his knees, the reins hang down from the mane in two crescents. His horse rears ferocious on its hind legs, its forelegs just a foot or so off the pedestal, hoofs draped with bronze locks streaming like thick froth from the hoofs of a sea-bounding kelpie . . . Ella brushes the illegible inscription with her eyes—this isn't the last time she will stand looking up at yet another version of him: she can see again in her mind the underwater statue he had shown them when the experiment began, the crazily implacable pointing finger.

A group of soldiers come into view. They stand together as though they were conversing pleasantly with one another, but they are silent. While they are oblivious to everyone else—they stare directly at her—her ring has drawn their attention: it is clearly an important token of some kind. She wants to address them, but she stands only throbbing in place, her spirit quailing, unable to approach. They stand together cooler and cooler, smiling. They glance now and again in her direction, and then turn back to each other and their silence. They are not looking at anything, their gazes join with the air in their midst and they seem blind. With a bit of inner browbeating Ella forces herself to move toward them, where they are standing half in the shade. She keeps her eyes lowered . . . They silently observe her coming. Unable to look directly at any one of them she tosses her question in among them—

"Where is the Tyrant?"

She is blunt—she doesn't want to stand and babble at them . . . when they know all there is to know . . . She is unafraid, but a self-exerted pressure bubble forces her back away from them like magnetic repulsion. It makes standing in their presence an effort.

Their smiles widen, and that is their only reply.

Their smiles seem to say, you'll have to find him yourself.

Ella wonders—are they mocking her, or encouraging her? A cold exhilarating deadness issues from them . . . She feels light . . . She turns and plants her crutches on the soil of the street with new purposefulness . . .

*

. . . The ebb and flow of golden light seem to come in surges. She follows it, with the idea she might trace its current to the source. Gold is important. Buildings swim by like card houses on a turntable . . . She hears carny music—a fairground . . .

She walks freely onto the grounds, feeling oddly relaxed and at home. She watches the swirling lights circulating like luminous blood . . . A line of elephants scuds by tails in trunks—a couple of serious looking young tall men in thick sweaters march by their noses stuck in their books.

The carnival has been set up in a natural stone bowl, its sides striped with red and brown clay layers. Here and there on ledges and outcrops all around the circumference, steaming ice sculptures of all descriptions have been set up and lit from below or behind. They are like shapes frosted into the dark air. There is a rampant, ribbon-like Chinese dragon—gargoyles—a huge grouper with a rather wacky expression—an ice-jellyfish with icicle tentacles draped all down the side of the canyon bowl—a bat creeping along on all fours like a mummified heart rendered in ice—an eel-like leopard shark in a spiralling posture making a coil, all blonde and cloudy ice dotted with brown spots—a great horned owl with piercing aquamarine eyes stands guard over a clutch of perfect ice-eggs—a stunning ice tree with tinted emerald leaves and a snowy trunk . . . as the stems evaporate in the dry night air, blood red ice-fruits fall with a thud and melt into the soil—a colossus of ice strikes a triathalonic pose in the center of the carnival grounds . . . it was quiescently frozen in layers so that the carmine muscle groups shine through transparent ice skin and flesh—a creamy ice moon with a cold lantern nested inside it—and of course, at the very back of the bowl and high up nearly out of sight, another equestrian statue of the Tyrant in oily black ice, this executed in a rough and faceted Soviet style unlike the naturalistic renderings of the other statues . . . He is all black except for the whites of his eyes, and from below, where he looms overhead against the night sky, those whites may easily be at first glance mistaken for stars.

Most of the people she passes are living—and drunk—but occasionally she catches sight of a few soldiers in the distance moving along so elegant and beautiful, their faces are lit from within like cold lanterns . . .

Ella passes a snake charmer, who provokes his cobra with the occasional tap of his finger or bat with his pan pipes. And they are hawking sugar skulls here of course —Ella picks out one with her name on it but when she starts fumbling for change the vendors take one look at her iron ring and say "No, no", smilingly push the skull toward her over the counter—they won't take her money. Ella tries to thank them as graciously as she can, and moves off feeling a little embarrassed.

She sits on a log crunching her candy skull contentedly, watches as a voluptuous line of showgirls in pretty brief outfits, consisting mainly of feathers, bustles through a tent flap like an embattled flock of hens. Mascara and talcum smells mix in with the frosting taste of her skull. Ella visited fairs once and a while as a child, when people felt sorry for her and wanted to show her a good time; mainly she resented her benefactors' good intentions, but she did enjoy herself then. She remembers those vulgar and braying fairs; their crassness was exciting, everywhere people were getting sick—sickness, mainly from the food and drink, was the great lurking threat of those fairs—grown-ups acting their worst. This fair, on the other hand, is quiet and decorous in its own way. She is sure that she will not be disturbed here.

Ella looks around some more. She knows she is neglecting something maybe or someone, but she stalls that thought off for a moment. She allows her thoughts to remain a bit in disarray. Now she passes through an arcade of gorgeous cyan ice. The light wafts up around her like in an ice cave, and here and there niches and alcoves are carved in the ice-blocks and glass or ceramic sculptures are set in them, lit with brilliant orange and red lights—the contrast is breathtaking. Her eyes thrill with pleasure. Looking down she sees herself luxuriously spangled with colored light. To either side, people sit on benches in the blue, dreamily sipping laudanum ices from ponderous brass vessels.

She emerges from the arcade into a place of blonde light, and there's a teacup ride whirling within its wrought-iron enclosure. She goes up to the fence just as the cups are spinning to a stop. One of them halts practically beside her she gives as start so violent as nearly to totter her off her feet when she recognizes Dr. Belhoria as its occupant.

Reclining in a full-length fur coat, her cigarette holder between her thumb and forefinger like an ember-tipped pen, Dr. Belhoria allows to stream from her nostrils two jets of perfectly white smoke. Beside her sits the sad-looking fox-faced man of long ago, and there's a half-empty bottle on the seat between them—the moment the doctor's eyes meet Ella's she snaps into focus out of a haze of dissipation.

"El-la!" she beams, holding out both her hands although of course Ella can't take them—"Ella how perfectly ecstatic I am to see you again! How on *earth* did you get here!?"

Ella sort of shrugs and Dr. Belhoria cheerfully offers her the bottle—"Won't you have some? It's older than *you* are, my treasure."

Still recovering from her surprise Ella politely declines. Dr. Belhoria looks at her a moment.

"Well—! I can't imagine how you found your way here. You must have made extraordinary strides on your own—I hope you're enjoying yourself—they are very partial to outsiders here—" she waves vaguely around with her cigarette holder, "Sort of a flimsy-looking town, isn't it? The buildings don't collapse only because they don't have any substance, no matter. Who knows but that in a day or two it won't all just blow away . . . I came here to meet Allan."

"Hello," the fox-faced man gives a disengaged two-fingered wave.

—This is all irrelevant, Ella thinks,—she's actually nattering at me! It may just be the drink, but Ella suspects Dr. Belhoria is putting her off. The wind seems to blow through the gaps in the conversation like the rushing of empty space . . . it makes Ella feel alone . . .

"Well, I made it this far myself, aren't you going to tell me anything? What happened at the library?"

"Oooohh I'm *so* tired of the story really—not tonight . . . " Dr. Belhoria replies in a lamenting tone. "My dear I'll happily answer all of your questions some other time—I assure you the old boy is fine—I just can't *bear* going over everything once more. I feel like I've been explaining myself for months—those sappers are just such pests! . . . I came here to *enjoy* myself . . . "

Ella can only blink at her.

"Oh for heaven's sake—" Dr. Belhoria thrusts a visiting card at her—Ella gradually takes it, a white rectangle. "—I've just taken a place in Venefy—that's the provisional capital—I'll meet you there sometime in the next few days and explain everything at positively *disgusting* length then, all right?"

Ella looks at the card—

DR. BELHORIA, M.D., death science, Street of Wax VENEFY

She looks at it and then at Dr. Belhoria.

" . . . Will he be there?"

"As far as I know—yes."

"Where is Venefy?" Ella suddenly feels tired and lightheaded, as though her blood were all sunk into her feet.

"It's in the mountains. I assure you you'll have no difficulty finding it."

"Won't the roads be blocked?"

"My dear *we're* most likely in a blocked-off area by now—"

"Well then how are any of us supposed to get out?!" Ella's voice rises in frustration but there's little force behind it. She has no energy.

Dr. Belhoria smiles . . .

"—for us, there is free travel between these towns—using *his* roads. One need only follow the signs . . . How did you get here?"

Quiet again, Ella replies, "I have a driver."

"Excellent, Ella! Where is he now?"

Where is this heading? "He's waiting by the signpost—he couldn't chance the car on the road . . . "

"You should get him into town before he's picked up. You will find there's a better road further along the route—I'll fetch you a cab—"

Dr. Belhoria only cocks her hand in the air and a hansom cab pulls up from between two tents . . . the buttocking, plumed horse reminds Ella of the showgirls.

Dr. Belhoria points with her finger at Ella's ring smiling. "Trust in *that* to get you there."

Ella purses her lips and looks around in confusion—surprise has disoriented her and she is unsure what is best.

"Well? Don't just stand there!" Dr. Belhoria teases, her face a mask of carnival lights.

Ella is reluctant to part company with her. Dr. Belhoria smiles at her with unusual warmth.

"Don't worry you'll see me very soon . . . and while you're here I encourage you to make the *most* of the place—for heaven's sake you look dreadful!"

Ella reluctantly turns and the driver is already at her side to assist her. He puts his arms firmly under her arms with such assurance she is somehow not offended. With astonishing strength he hoists her into the cab. She pivots and drops heavily into the seat. Looking to one side she sees the teacups have started spinning again, Dr. Belhoria shuttles away from her, on the right, then on the left, on the right, then on the left, the cup dances off into the dark as the reins clap and the cab lurches forward.

*

The road takes her behind the buildings of the main street and slopes gently between extended hummocks of brush heaped up like hedgerows. All light from the town blinks out and now there are only a pair of dim pale spots flashing over the leaves, shining from the cab's two kerosene lamps. Dry wind in her face, constellations over her head unmarred by any cloud, these two rows of heaped brush on either side of the road like the edges of the world. They turn out onto the main road; Carl is still in the front seat of the Packard flicking his fingers on the wheel with apparent anxiety. Ella waves to him and the cab stops. The driver nimbly alights and with the same effortless strength bears her down onto her feet. A moment later he is in his seat. "Can we follow you back in?" she asks with a sudden dream-fear the buggy will disappear, the roads will disappear, the town will disappear.

But the driver nods and slowly turns the buggy around.

The car is somewhat wider than the cab and its wheels straddle the more level part of the road; it yaws and dips like a boat on choppy water while the cab seems to hover before it. Pulling around onto the main street, seeing the buildings and the passersby from the front seat of the car, the whole scene strikes Ella as utterly unreal. Another billow of euphoria. Carl parks the car in the alley by the hotel. Ella rushes out looking for the cabby—"What do I owe you?"—but the cab is already strolling away. The driver glances in her direction and his only reply to her question is a vague gesture . . . he taps his ring finger, then points to her.

After locking her equipment in the trunk of the car, Ella and Carl check into the hotel—regular hollow thud of their feet on the steps and the wide veranda—rustle of potted palms flanking the door. They ring a shrill bell at the front desk, which is something like a toll-booth set into the wall, banks of pigeonholes, a rack of hooks with little swinging keys, in the corner behind the flap in the desk a mysterious narrow red door with brass hinges opens onto the tiny office. A young woman in a beefy cream-colored sweater with a long snaky red braid and freckles on the backs of her transparent hands sleepily takes down two keys with brass tags and turns the ledger round for them to sign. Carl signs them both in on crisp new white pages covered with brown antique signatures and, picking up their two small bags, motions Ella to go first. Fortunately for her arms, their rooms are only on the second floor.

The whole place is banged together from unpainted planks, smells faintly of lumber and creosote. The stairs and halls are four feet wide—Ella is able to brace her crutches in the crooks of the floor. The strip of paper-thin carpet that runs the length of the upstairs hall is so badly worn as to be nearly colorless but here and there there are patches that have been unaccountably spared, rich scarlet and green as vivid as rose petals and leaves. The room numbers are carved into the doors—Carl opens Ella's and sets her bag down in the room, asks her if she needs him for anything else. She notices how tired he is and gratefully excuses him. He shuts the door decorously and Ella listens to his footsteps pass away.

She's standing in a wallpapered box; two shutter windows without sills or curtains, just square holes cut into the single-plank walls.

There's a beautiful amber-brown cherrywood dresser, pitted oval mirror above it, marble-topped nightstand with a lacquered metal bowl and pitcher, iron frame bed, and a framed engraving of a storm-tossed ship on the wall by the door. After locking the door and drawing the bolt, Ella undresses laboriously. Sitting on the bed in her nightgown she for the first time notices that the even, mellow light in the room has no source—no bulb in the ceiling, no gas jets, not even a kerosene lamp. Nor does she now recall any sconces or lamps in the halls or lobby—with this even light settled on the place how is she going to get any sleep?

Too tired to bother looking, Ella draws herself into the bed under the quilt. The mattress is little more than a tightly-packed bag of feathers and Ella sinks into it with extraordinary pleasure, relief for her aching arms. Sighing, she closes her eyes. The room is dark when she opens them again—a faint glow from the line under the door.

"Well I'll be . . . "

Ella lies there for a while abandoned by her thoughts. They have locked her out and are conferring privately together . . . in some partition of her mind her conversation with Dr. Belhoria is playing over and over again, and somewhere beyond even that shines the dark figure of the Tyrant that she yearns so much to see . . . Thoughts she has that afford her no access . . . After such a prolonged and relentless pursuit she is happy to be able to stop driving herself for a moment.

Though there are random enigmatic noises, woody thuds and clicks mostly, the hotel seems wonderfully still. From her pillow Ella looks directly through the window at the sky, diagonally bordered by the upper balcony. The sky was dark when she arrived, now it is sheeted over with crumpled glowing clouds the color of mossy stones. She lies awake looking, not nervous or exhausted. Sometimes she hears hollow footsteps somewhere on the verandah outside. They never approach her window, and she intuitively knows they won't. From time to time the whole building sways gently; it feels a bit like lying in a hammock.

Just boards hanging together in the air, the hotel is like a stringless wooden mobile, as much made of wind as wood.

*

She wakes in the morning to find herself down at breakfast. She is seated at a table, alone, the room is missing two of its walls, the edges of the floor are already engulfed by the dry yellow-grey soil of the encroaching desert, weedy tufts rustle in the breeze. The sky is overcast as usual, the daylight is slatey and the air is cold. Ella spreads an unidentified preserve she takes from a clay pot onto small spongy rolls. The jam is plum-black with intriguing inky whorls down in it; it has a weirdly familiar raisin-fig taste with a sort of ethereal strawberry fleshyness and tartness, the bouquet blooms inside her nose like musk and she wonders if there isn't some opium in this stuff. Dreamily she enjoys her speckled tin cup of decent coffee and two crumbling strips of slightly overcooked, heavily-smoked bacon . . . and fugitive volutes of black smoke trail by, nearly invisible in the air outside against the palely glaring clouds.

Rows of old brownstones stand among the dunes further off; she can see them with their windows open, and the curtains wave out from the open windows like cloth flippers. Someone emerges from one of the brownstones and heads off to the right—an old timer with a stiff-legged, self-jostling walk—apparently making for town on a path she can't see from here.

These things happen without seeming to happen and Ella's chair and table drift in space, bearing her along.

Some time later she looks up—a deer has put its head in through the window nearest her . . .

When Carl comes asking for her, she staggers after him to the front desk. Her ring waives payment for the room—the young woman with the copper braid down her back taps her ring finger wordlessly and disappears into the office again. Out on the plank verandah, they see a knot of five or six thrushes making a startling amount of noise over a handfull of seed, jostling and dodging in and out.

*

Carl busies himself with the Packard's engine while Ella asks around town for directions. Condors spread out in the air a mile or more overhead, casting microscopic shadows on the ground. A small group of people crouch in the sand just on the margin of the main street. When Ella comes closer she sees they are holding a race between a black and a red ant, and taking bets. She inquires of a few of these sports and generally gets listless and incoherent replies, they all seem drugged. No help there. For a while she contemplates each of the passers by in turn—a group of immaculately-groomed Egyptian men, a few young people with the shabby nondescript hollow-contentious look of stereotypical university students, Korean man bustling a drum with brass rivets, a plainclothes showgirl, some lonely tribesmen of the prosthetic limbs . . . slow forearm travels towards her and away from her . . . the man passes on by . . . She watches them all pass, in self-conscious paralysis. But no one here seems to pay much attention to anyone else, they seem to have no curiosity about each other, or about her. Finally she crosses the street and asks a bunch of bright-eyed bowery boys throwing dice against the bordello's clapboards.

"How should I know, lady? Ask Mr. Earl—" one of them points a few doors up.

The place is a pharmacy. A fat waiter in a white apron stands to one side of the wide-open storefront like a cigar-store indian impassively taking in the street. Ella goes inside. Though the day is dim and the light aloof she gets the impression of having just come in out of the dazzling sun into a shady refuge. Pausing under the ceiling fan she is delighted to find a marble-topped soda counter against the wall to her left. The prospect of that counter makes her mouth water. She goes over, nimbly levers herself onto a stool, and presses her palms against the cool marble slab, pitted and veined like a petrified cheese. The soda jerk appears a moment later in his paper pillbox hat—rather old for the job he seems, shaved head, transparent stubble still faintly tinged with red on his cheeks, and beautiful indigo eyes. She orders a float, and while he prepares it for her she notices the pitting in the marble is actually engraving, worn letters . . . Tracing them with her fingers she realizes with a frisson of grim pleasure that she is sitting at a tombstone. With the calm self-containment of a Buddhist monk he makes her soda in a heavy bottle-green sundae glass and places it on the counter in front of her with a glassy click. The float is miraculous—the ice cream is dense and fine-grained and crusted with frozen sasparilla, delicate as sherbet, not gummy at all. It melts away without clogging her throat. A man in a sailor's uniform sits down at the other end of the slab and orders an absinthe float.

"I wish I'd known they served those when I came in—" Ella thinks.

In the corner, to the immediate right of the door, there are a number of plush chairs and divans surrounding a round table draped in a low-hanging red silk cloth with long gold fringes. The floor and walls there in that corner are thick-swaddled in rich Persian rugs, and the dragonfly-ornamented blue-shaded tiffany lamp in the center of the table throws off a field of indigo light. A number of elegant persons sit around this table nodding placidly to the music on the gramophone . . . Trickling strands of incense rise from the snouts of burning braziers and lose themselves in the shadowy ceiling, caught in thick webs woven by intoxicated and smoke-addled spiders. These nodding persons radiate a smooth sexual vibration, a subaudible tone nestled in concentric waves of dreamy magnetism. Ella knows only lightly to brush the humming flesh of their exposed faces or hands with her fingers would occasion in her a deadly pleasure of overpowering intensity.

Finishing her float, and eyeing the graceful chrome swan-necks of the soda heads ruefully, she tears herself away from the counter to talk to Mr. Earl, who still stands curving in the air like a poplar tree behind the pharmacy counter. Behind him is a wall of shelves holding all manner of labeled and priced bottles and jars. The air here at the back of the store smells like tea leaves. Mr. Earl is a lean man with surprisingly smooth, red, shiny features. Ella puts her ring hand on the counter with a metallic rap and asks him about the Tyrant's highway. With one balanced down and up glance, Mr. Earl nods and gestures with his finger—opens the flap in the counter for her.

Ella follows him to the double doors of a storm cellar set at an angle into the ground out in back of the store. He kneels, undoes a padlock, and flings the doors open. Mr. Earl stands back and looks at her.

Ella peers down through the doors—wide flight of steps, and a dark space down inside, with a few red and green lights scattered around. The lights wink and change—the highway is underground.

"And I suppose that's the only way in?"

Mr. Earl nods a little acerbically as if to say obviously.

"Well how are we supposed to get our car down there?"

Mr. Earl shrugs and walks elastically back into his store.

So Ella goes off to find Carl. He pulls the Packard up before the open cellar doors and gets out. Standing by the front fender with his arms crossed he looks down at the steps, furrowing his brow and blowing his cheeks out. Ella points to the door with what she hopes is a firm dominating expression; Carl doesn't seem to notice. He squats down before the first step and peers down, then vanishes into the cellar. A moment later he emerges and looks speculatively at the car.

"The steps fortunately are steep enough that the car won't get stuck teeter-tottering on the edge here. The passage is just wide and high enough I think for it to get through, but I'm just worrying about the suspension—" Now he looks at her thoughtfully, "—and going down at such a steep angle I don't want the car to dig into the ground at the bottom of the stairs."

"To be safe, you should wait here and then follow me down," he adds after a pause. With that, he scratches his head once with his ring finger and puts his cap on as he walks around to the driver's side door.

Carl inches the Packard forward and gently rolls it over the first step. From then on, it's stop and go, the front end dips dangerously and Ella worries the car will scrape or stick its belly on the steps, but somehow it only pivots forward and gradually waddles down the steps like a hippo. The shaft is such a tight fit that the sides of the car gouge out powdery scars of earth as it lurches first this way and that. Carl is evidently trying very hard to keep the wheels on the same steps. Finally, as Ella watches from above, the car levels out and glides away from the base of the stairs. She picks her way after it carefully—the tires have crumbled some of the packed-earth steps.

When she reaches the bottom of the steps, Carl is out of the car patiently checking the tire pressure. He then lies on his side with a flashlight surveying the underside of the Packard. Ella walks toward him knowing already that the car is all right. Beyond, in the dim red and green lights, the tunnel is dark, dry and inviting like a dark pit of sleep, and as she glides through the open passenger door her consciousness escapes in a jet of ink like an octopus . . . The earth tunnel floats around solarized yawning for the Packard green brown shady cool red and green lights . . . yellow-green soil of the encroaching desert, weedy tufts rustle . . . slatey sunlight . . . plum-black with intriguing inky whorls of ethereal strawberry . . . bouquet blooms like musk . . .

Ella dreams.

. . . One need only follow the signs . . . a stone bowl . . . How did you get here? . . . its sides striped, quiet again, red and brown Ella replies, clay layers steaming, I have a driver . . . ice sculptures . . . excellent Ella! all descriptions have been set up . . . where is he now—lit from below or behind? . . . where is this heading? Shapes frosted into the dark air—he's waiting . . . there is by the signpost a rampant ribbon-like Chinese dragon . . . he couldn't chance the gargoyles . . . you should get him an ice-jellyfish . . . tentacles before a bat creeping . . . he's picked up a mummy's heart in ice . . . eel-like there's a leopard shark . . . better road spiralling further along a coil all blonde and cloudy . . . the route spots a great horned owl . . . stunning Dr. Belhoria . . . voluptuous tree with only cocks, a snowy trunk . . . her hand, as the stems evaporate in the air and a blood red ice-hansom cab . . . fruits fall with a thud . . . pulls up from between two tents and melt into the soil . . . the buttocking triathalonic pose . . . plumed horse was quiescently frozen . . . carmine muscle-creamy showgirls . . . ice moon with a cold lantern . . . Dr. Belhoria points with her finger at the Tyrant in Ella's ring . . . oily black ice smiling "trust in *that* to get you there" . . . the whites of his eyes—looms whites easily mistaken for stars . . .

CHAPTER ELEVEN

Speeding through the tunnels—Ella is jolted awake by a burst of static from the radio.

Carl's eyes in the rear-view mirror: "There have been several bulletins already."

A voice materializes in the car speaking with sharp deliberation tacking each syllable in the air as though it were fixing them with pins onto a bulletin board . . . Outside, dark rough walls of earth and rock stream by the windows . . . Inside, voicing grainy words level, level and full of power that fill the ear while seeming to bypass it and like arrows thumping into a target the shaft vibrating from the point buried to the fletching those words thud into the brain and vibrate there along their entire length, every syllable, every voiced consonant, every unheard disembodied breath drawn.

"Flash.

"We address the people of the world. We address the population of that other half of the world, who live and breathe and who yet deny us our rights.

"We have come to take what is ours by right of death. The dead want to be *dead*: not dwindled away in your forgetfulness until we become nothing, not tools of the living, and your life's justice. We have had it with being your examples, scapegoats, memory custodians. We will not be forgotten, and we will not be your cherished memories, your monumental examples, role models, villains, excuses. We will not be reduced by you, and we will not disappear from view. We will not serve, and we will not be forgotten. Like you, we also have needs. We were history's slaves once. We built your world. We refuse to vacate the world we made. The dead want to *be* dead, not forgotten into oblivion, and not falsified by your memories and your stories, as if we became merely imaginary when we died. We are not imaginary. We *are*, dead; and that means, we are going to stay right here, with you. We will stand beside you, walk down your streets, sit with you, eat with you, wring our hands over you, laugh in your faces. We are dead and we are *free*. We are free to be here with you as we are, to enjoy *our* happiness.

"From the phantom ruins of all the demolished and destroyed cities and ghost towns of history we have assembled our own cities and towns here among you. We welcome you, everywhere. Come and visit. Go when you please. You will come to *stay* in time.

"We look forward to receiving you here."

. . . The silence that follows goes unmarked for a long time, as though the voice still spoke, or still echoed inaudibly—yes that voice is still resonating in Ella's own flesh and brain, so much so that she only gradually realizes that the road has emerged from the tunnel into the open air . . . Not the Tyrant's voice—can she remember it? She can; no, this voice is a living voice, not a stirring voice. The Tyrant's army does not speak. It must have been a sapper, an enthusiast, or someone sleeptalking into an open microphone. Replaying the announcement in her mind, Ella has the impression of isolated enthusiasm, a presumption on someone's part to speak for those who remain silent; a self-appointed ambassador, prone to exaggerate, overstate, and simplify.

Gazing out the window, gradually, she is able to relate a concatenation of impressions—of increased light, of increased depth on all sides, of airy buoyancy, of slackened oppression. She remembers the sudden boost upwards and the shocking flash of the tunnel mouth as it momentarily cut the world in two halves—dark confined underground, and dazzling infinity of white and blonde desert, lying flat and white, and black mountains in the distance thrust sharply upright. The sky is white. Ella glances fitfully at it with smarting eyes, the muscles around her eyes bunching and spasming weirdly but it is a daylight she can't get used to. She eventually hides her face in her hands. Her eyes are branded with daylight-seared car windows and flaring desert, flicker and dart back and forth like bits of film raying from a convulsing projector.

Ahead, the road lies straight and clear, an unpainted plank of blacktop, driving itself like a spear into the base of the mountains. A jolt of sudden terror at seeing horses and riders wheeling in the distance with impossible speed; but they do not approach or render any sign that they have observed the car. The ground on either side of the unbordered road is pebbly sand with moldy-looking patches of white frost . . . Bit by bit the daylight dies away, and the twilight gathers around, even though the sun is at no time visible in the white-shrouded sky.

*

The road tilts up abruptly. A voluptuous feeling as they begin to climb . . . She sinks back into her chair a little—what it must feel like to lie back with cut wrists in a warm bath, a voluptuous dwindling feeling. The car hurtles with terrifying speed. As each new curve approaches she unconsciously braces herself to be launched into space; Ella is disturbed by the volatility of her emotions, she seems to feel everything at once or in such swift succession it's as if she were babbling to herself. Not wanting to panic she holds herself rigidly together.

The peaks are sharp black and alarming. They glide and jostle in and out of different alignments; inverted stone curtains now show now hide luminous clouds. As twilight settles the white patches of snow on their slopes begin to glow, as though the mountains were black retinas flecked with blazing afterimages. Below the bare slopes, in the steep-creased canyons are spread the canopies of enormous trees, filling the gaps between the peaks with writhing nerves. First on one side then on the other murderous slopes like bared carnivorous jaws streak by the windows and then plummet to the horizon, exposing roaring vistas that seem to burst into view and stun Ella's eyes. Her gaze is relentlessly stretched and compressed by the turnings of the landscape and Ella tires quickly as though she were working an inelastic muscle, but as they climb precipitously higher the vistas are more and more infinite and there are fewer interruptions of her view. Ella feels relieved. Becoming aware for the first time of the tension in her arms she realizes she's been holding on for dear life. She relaxes her arms.

On all sides mountains roll by in awesome excavations of space. Here and there she spots towers on high peaks and promontories—some of these towers are round like cannons stuck butt-end into the ground and some are faceted like onyx anvils. As she looks at them she can feel herself growing dissociated from her own thoughts, anaesthetized—and she thinks "Oh, no—not now! Not *now* when I most want to *see* . . . " but there is something in that air and in that time that is stealthily capturing and thieving her mind and dreams intrude. Now the mountains are all around them—the road is a path through a maze. The mountains are walls with the representative presence of monuments . . . The walls of the maze are colossal black waves dotted with white foam . . . waves, walls, maze, monuments, shadows, towers, obelisks tombs and cenotaphs . . . and somewhere behind the sheet of cold white fog overhead, so difficult for her to see now, a mammoth full moon hangs like a voice in space. This road will bring her there. Ether shudders through the narrow aperture at the top of the window, the air is already mercilessly thin. In the rear view mirror, Carl's eyes are glazed and far away as the twilight robs the mountains of their definition, so it seems to be shadowing up her mind—and she wanders among soft masses of light and solid shadow mountains . . .

*

And all at once: moonlight—sky blue on the black rocks that whir by the car windows. A square bubble of moonlight across Ella's lap glinting in the metal of her leg braces—outside the smear of rock and snow. And a huge presence—gathering size in their path—and all at once blue walls flash by and she is *in*

—big square emptiness full of blue light, the air here is dry warm the light is cold air is soft still—this is *his* city. She knows at once he's here in one point in space, and suffused throughout in this air these walls towering peaks and paving stones and squares, in my breath . . .

Ella asks Carl to stop, and steps out onto the pavings of his city. Her first step on Venefy's soul—I mean *soil*, she thinks, but perhaps it's just as well. Ella looks around at the pale streets and mountain-sides—it's quiet. She feels her heart lighten breathing with her whole body becoming insubstantial as if the light and air were working such a pleasing physical change in her. Stands a moment in suspense in space as though she were only webs of dim light—an element of this night time—moonlight is light of another day, visible from tonight.

She hears singing. An old man paces up and down one edge of the square, about a hundred yards from where she's stopped, and he sings as he paces. An old man in a turban and caftan, with dark intilting eyebrows, moustache still dark though his beard is grey-white, plaintively warbles and exults in a halting, unpracticed voice, hands over his head, arms flexing in a loose diamond, back and forth in front of one of the buildings at the edge of the square. The top half of a dutch door hangs open, casting a clear-cut shadow on the wall, and inside, in the dark just behind the door, roughly a twin of the old man sits watching with what appears to be an amused expression. With a sphinxlike smile, he occasionally bears the tube of his hookah to his lips . . . the phosphorous smoke bubbles from his mouth, rises and bunches up against the upper lintel of the door like folds of fabric, then slithers up the blue wall and into the sky.

No—no dreams no distractions. As the resolution forms in her the ether around her crystallizes and drops out of the air leaving it light and cold. Ether ice powders the pavement at her feet and around the rubber tips of her crutches. She takes the poppet from her pocket. The moment she opens the case the poppet stands upright with unusual decisiveness and points. Ella plots the course in the indicated direction, visualizing a slender line of smoke in the air from the poppet's pointing homoncular finger . . . gets back into the car and gives Carl his course. Immediately the car whirs forward and the black and blue streets rush up to meet them . . . tentacle streets. On a sudden impulse—she's decided to trust them—she orders Carl to turn off the headlights . . . they drive by moonlight, without disturbing anyone with their lights.

Uneven streets buck the car in regular jolts . . . Narrow lanes, facadeless houses and buildings, balconies, vines, plaster, indigo flowers in window planters, moon bouncing metronomically from side to side of the street reflected in the unshuttered windowpanes . . . first in this window, then in the next . . . Walking figures take a single step in the time it takes them to pass by dim squares and side-streets . . . Ever ascending to the palace over the city . . . A vulture crosses their path—a shaggy blob of shadow . . . Sharp-edged shadow canyons between buildings, ceilinged over with transparent sheets of the moon's light.

Now out from among the buildings, the road cuts across a rubbly slope populated by unearthly pine trees, barely visible and furred with black clots. Evergreens, Ella thinks, stay green in winter. The branches languidly pat the air over a tan carpet of long dead needles. High above them, white walls. The Tyrant's fort, a tooth dropped by the moon. The road climbs, and they pass through a series of arches, each one supporting a great scallop or ogival carving of the sort that adorn cathedral doors. The car emerges from the trees into a level area of gardens with low hedges and sand gardens, all decorated with headstones, grave angels, obelisks and urns. The topiary is all wrought-iron cemetery fencing braided together into big cats, horses, a griffin. Beyond that, the fort sits like a dreaming head.

Again Ella asks Carl to stop, and she alights from the car among grave angels into deliciously soft air. She is feeling unusually uncumbersome, as though the gravity here were reduced, or she were even stronger. Above her, the fort looms oddly silent and dark—as though it were strange for such an enormous building not to be roaring or something with its own grandeur. The wind, the trees, the flapping of a few banners, the crickets and cicadas, all these she hears, but nothing from the vast structure in front of her.

The walls are not made of stone—somehow she understands, that is, she gets pictures in her mind . . . The Tyrant has developed a method for culturing bone: when it is still embryonic the bone is highly plastic, moldable into any shape, and is often at this point in the process lightly scented with attar of roses. As it matures the bone stiffens to adamantine hardness, presenting a smooth, unbroken, and continuous surface. The exposed works of the fort are all made of lambent bone white and creamy as soap; leafless black vines, or perhaps some sort of fungus, scribble across the white walls like black creases in snow. The outlines of the fort are vague, and it is difficult to make out where the fort begins and the mountain ends, as though it were only half-materialized. Within the outermost wall she sees domes minarets and arches all frosted with blue, and the top of what appears to be a featureless black ziggurat.

Ella gazes up at the ivory hood of the Tyrant's observatory. The poppet is gesturing animatedly—the Tyrant is certainly there. Rooks call to each other in the trees, and in the air above the walls white and horned owls and big bats are circling ominously, now and then perching among the many gargoyles. There are a few soldiers idly pacing the glacial battlements, accompanied by their spectral shadows. The night-sky gates and shutters, planed from the sky's living substance, are fast closed, salivate powdery blackness into the air . . . mingling with the blue and white motes from the walls. The soldiers and the Tyrant's standard stir dreamily. The face of the fort is anonymous and aloofly officious, like a mausoleum. Ella approaches the front gate, a tall, lean pair of iron doors fitted with gold, bas-relief wreaths, and covered with a thick coat of glossy sable paint. In Gallic fashion, skulls have been set into an alcove on either side of the door, and a third has been pressed into the lintel overhead.

Ella raps on the door with her crutch—a dull muffled sound . . . no response. A little anxious, and somehow unwilling to disrupt the general silence, as though the dark mountains all around were lightly sleeping, she has to struggle to bring herself to call out to the soldiers on the walls. No response. Even though she can see them on the parapets, it's as though nobody were there.

Rushing on headlong in a daze, now abruptly brought up short by this mausoleum wall, Ella turns this way and that as though she can't believe her eyes. With a blank animal incomprehension she seems to be searching for a way through, although there is none. She looks up at the observatory overhead. How does she know the Tyrant is there? She is intuitively certain, the way one is certain of things in a dream, but she knows she is not dreaming. How does she know she's not dreaming? Likewise, she is intuitively certain—she simply knows she's awake. The certainty that she is not dreaming is of the same variety as the certainty in dreams. She knows she is not dreaming the same way she knows he is there—and she knows too, that she will not get in to see him yet.

*

Ella returns reluctantly to the car and they descend back into the city . . . city of my sorrow, Ella is looking despondently out the windows. She fumbles out Dr. Belhoria's card and they stop to ask directions on a dimly lit street lined with tiny restaurants. The restaurants all look like chapels, lit by candles. Ella stops a waitress, white shirt, black skirt, white apron, black and white. The waitress stands half in shadow her face hidden, Ella can't see if she is laughing at her or not.

"What city is this—?" she meant to ask directions to Dr. Belhoria's street . . . her voice sounds feeble and far away.

The waitress answers readily, as though she were accustomed to the question . . . maybe everyone must ask this question first, before any others, on arriving . . . "Venefy," the waitress says benignly, "named for the chaste consort of our lady of sorrow."

*

The lamplighter, who slowly and meditatively lights the meagre gas jets along the curb, points Ella in the right direction. The address turns out to be nearby if still tricky to find. Following his meticulous directions, they arrive at a short street lined with old gables incongruously mixed in with the faintly glittering facades of nightclubs. A pair of chorus girls skip out of an alley and disappear through crystal doors.

Ella is feeling lightheaded and has difficulty reading, at least in this light. —There's the number, beside a yawning black double door. Ella dives in like someone ducking into shelter from a rain storm, head down. Looking up, she is taken aback to see herself surrounded by roulette wheels and crap and blackjack tables in a great smoky room, a lurid, dimly-illuminated bar against one wall. No one rushes up to her with any prohibitive words about her age; no one acknowledges her as she stands in the foyer.

Ella makes her way over to the bartender and asks after Dr. Belhoria.

"In the back, in the back," he says, pointing vaguely.

Ella picks a path through the tables, the mostly older men in ill-fitting suits and the glittering showgirls with their long bare legs. With a start, she notices two enormous circular platforms suspended above the casino floor; they are the two halves of a colossal balance, hanging from a pivoting beam invisible in the shadows near the extremely high ceiling. On each of the platforms she can see a man at a desk, facing the door. The one on the left is lean and tall with abundant silver-white hair and a delicate complexion; the flesh of his face is soft and rumpled, his expression is serene and benign. The other, on the right, is stocky with shiny black hair lacquered on his round head and a luxuriant moustache . . . rather Teddy Roosevelt she thinks . . . dressed in a dark suit with a cigarette in his stubby, beautifully-manicured fingers. There are ramps going up to either platform and, as Ella watches, she realizes that the fellow on the left pays out while the one on the right takes in, and as the bets are won or lost and the respective platforms take in or pay out money, so the two platforms rise or fall slightly; but evidently remaining always more or less in balance.

At the back of the casino, the ceiling is much lower, and there is a partition wall protruding out onto the floor. Nearby, there is a passage for waiters and other floor personnel to the hidden rooms further in the back. The partition wall is covered with deep scarlet paper, criss-crossed with dotted gold lines in a diamond pattern. The single door is darkly stained, black and red, with brass hinges and a bulbous knob on a long neck. Dr. Belhoria's card is tacked in the middle of the tall upper cross. Ella raps the bottom of the door with the tip of one of her crutches. A moment later the door opens and a bit of fragrance seeps out. Dr. Belhoria's face appears in the opening, looking strange lit from the side. She takes Ella in as though she had only just been startled awake.

Ella is overpoweringly tired. A wave of exhaustion breaks over her and she bows her head. Dr. Belhoria, without a word, retreats behind the swinging door, holding it open for Ella, who care barely manage to lurch over the threshold. She mumbles something about her driver and Dr. Belhoria flags down a passing waiter—"Oh Charles," bangles slide up her arm as she raises it, "this girl's driver should be waiting out front. Would you see to it he gets put up somewhere in the upstairs?"

"Sure thing, doc."

Ella hears the door shut behind her. Even though the apartment communicates with the casino—in fact, the partition wall doesn't even reach the ceiling, leaving a narrow apparently unobstructed and unscreened aperture at the top—no sound or odor of the casino penetrates into the apartment. The place looks and feels as though it were still somehow a part of Dr. Belhoria's house. Ella half-expects to see the familiar walled garden from the darkened window.

"Oh my poor thing, don't you look as exhausted as you could be."

Ella's looking around increasingly absently. Dr. Belhoria is wearing a kimono with some sort of headband, possibly to keep her hair from trailing in her facial cream. The room is softly lit, scarfs strewn everywhere and over the lampshades, silk fans in glass cases on the walls, fringed table cloth, potpourri—no sign of the foxfaced boyfriend. There are papers and files on the round central table.

"You're writing up the experiment," Ella says absently.

"Yes—I don't expect any trouble getting the journals to publish it," Dr. Belhoria looks at Ella and furrows her brow—"Are you all right?"

"I went up to the palace to see him . . . " Ella speaks as though she were in a trance.

With a look of concern, Dr. Belhoria hastily clears papers and a few bulky instruments off the sofa and takes Ella by the shoulders, guiding her over to it and settling her down on the cushions.

"Why don't you lie down here."

"Oh, I don't want to interfere with your work," Ella says earnestly, her voice faint.

"That's all right," Dr. Belhoria says, "I was finishing up for the night anyway."

"—Is there anything I can get you?" Dr. Belhoria asks a moment later, not having moved.

Ella slowly shakes her head.

"Well then, I'll say goodnight." Dr. Belhoria again takes Ella by the shoulders and pushes her down on the sofa. With surprising deftness she lifts Ella's legs onto the cushions and then draws a blanket over her. She moves swiftly through the room extinguishing the lights. Ella is asleep before Dr. Belhoria disappears into her bedroom.

*

The next morning, Ella and Dr. Belhoria thread their way to the front entrance through a dim shadowy casino lit entirely by sunlight reflecting from the sidewalk; deserted, the air rank with the grime of stale cigarette and cigar smoke. On the wall, an old mirror covered with what seem to be cobwebs—on closer inspection the "webs" are spidery signatures sportively carved into the glass by debutants with diamond rings. Overhead the two currently untenanted palettes of the balance drift in the air like spiritualist planchettes. The bartender is leaning with his elbows on the bar reading the newspaper. No sign of Carl this morning it seems. A pasty cleaning lady enveloped in a copious grey coverall swabs the tiles up in front, where the many panels, each with a glass pane the size of a full-length mirror, fold on their hinges. The casino is wide open to the street. Dr. Belhoria leads Ella across a dry patch of tiling and past the cleaning lady—her face is old but her hair is young, the streaked blonde and brown color of lightly stained wood, and glossy as though varnished.

As they step out into the sunshine of the street the city seems to explode around them—calm as it seems, everywhere there is a suppressed excitement, even a fiendish glee. The wind sheers their clothes to one side as they enter the path of its blast. Ella picks up the apprehension in her stomach, below her navel, a chevron—or badge-shaped spot. Looking up at the sun overhead, Ella feels a little watery in the knees and the ground seems to yaw slightly left and right like a swing under her feet, the whole world wobbles at the end of a string from the sun. Dr. Belhoria walks beside her. Ella glances sidelong at her and sees an armature of vigorous powerful motion like an abstract statue, all polished brass. The rays of the sun walk up and down in the street alongside them.

"You certainly came a long way," Dr. Belhoria says with a little effort, overcoming what you might call the conversational inertia involved in broaching a thorny or involved subject, or perhaps she is simply stifling boredom. "You care much more for him than I would have thought. Did you and he ever um—?"

"How *could* we—?!" Ella says with exasperation. There's something clinical in Dr. Belhoria's curiosity that she doesn't like, if only for being poorly concealed. With a pang, she ducks her head.

"Oh well you'd have to go and dash my fond dreams—"

"Why won't he see me?" Ella stops a moment and her shoulders sag.

Dr. Belhoria stops a step ahead of her and looks back, nearly silhouetted against the glare from the blazing cobblestones.

"He doesn't see anyone. It's practically impossible to get an audience *when* he holds them."

"I'm not just *anyone*—and neither are *you*!"

"My dear Ella it is certainly nothing personal. You should have learned by now, after all you've seen. I think it is very likely his presence may be dangerous to living persons at this time. Reincorporation seems to have made him highly radioactive."

"Reincorporated—has he merged his bodies?"

"Wouldn't you, if you had two?"

Dr. Belhoria starts walking again—Ella follows.

"He did it *himself*?"

"Yes."

"Well . . . do you know how?"

"That, my dear, is one of the mysteries."

"But how could that be possible?"

"That's another story or perhaps another book."

"What?"

Dr. Belhoria hustles Ella across the street just before a trolleycar and guides her down a sloping lane, off to one side.

Here and there, Ella sees slow-moving, laboring figures, pushing heavy carts, loading or unloading barrels, or bales. Once, she passes close to a team of men in caps and suspenders and heavy buckskin gloves, unloading open-topped barrels filled with skulls, which disappear into an enormous brick building with a sagging slate roof and cataracted, small-paned windows.

They pass one end of a long row of vacuous warehouses and enter into a bustling open area, women in shawls and bowler hats with long black braids down their backs, and men hatless in the streets wearing baggy suits, their faces glitter with shining coins. Around about the city, the looming mountains are stern and sharp and tall like gods inflexibly demanding human sacrifices.

They pass through a prim little square with tables on the wide pavements, multicolored umbrellas, waiters in pea-green jackets, and Dr. Belhoria neatly alights on the narrow, high steps of a bakery perched on one of the steeply angled corners. Ella thrusts her way in and drops with a thud into a chair by the window. This bakery has rather a small space for customers given the apparently cavernous kitchen behind the glass counters. Painted and candy-shellacked cakes sit in smug rows on their trays like quaint little cottages in a tourist trap hamlet. Dr. Belhoria suavely takes Ella's order up to the front. There are only a few other nondescript types sitting around looking strangely oblivious, or even frankly entranced. The two aproned girls behind the counter serve them dreamily.

"Is everybody in here drugged?" Ella sotto voces when Dr. Belhoria returns.

"Almost all livers are intoxicated here," Dr. Belhoria says matter-of-factly in a normal tone of voice, "—I mean given the circumstances who could blame them? They haven't had the benefit of our dead exposure. The dead ones, on the other hand, are always sober . . . I'll put it to you this way—when they're *not* sober, it's really time for *concern* . . . "

Ella is having coffee and a Portuguese muffin—a bit like an English muffin but larger, breadier, and sweeter, very delicious with a little butter. Now and then someone will drift by the windows . . . an old man . . . a pair of grandmotherly women . . . a young woman with flowing blonde hair, dressed in a tennis outfit . . . all with the same eerie, unfeeling smiles on their faces, and Ella nearly gags on her breakfast.

"Try not to notice, dear."

*

Now to the loose ends. "How were you able to track him?"

"When I shot him from the balcony, the wound established a bond of hatred between us. This hate-bond can register on the electro-magnetic spectrum through a converter of my own design. I suspect that you enjoyed a similar bond, a love-bond, with 'Air Mail'."

Ella can still hear the quotation marks around the name. She had been referring to him—and not to the Judge, as Dr. Belhoria assumed—when she first spoke. The love-bond angle is news to her.

"Actually, I created an ectoplasmic poppet from a drop of his albumen, from your sample archive. The poppet formed a three-dimensional echo of his form in space. I have it here, see?"

Ella produces the ring box from her bag and opens it. The poppet is resting on the cushion with its head on its hands.

Dr. Belhoria takes the box and studies the poppet this way and that with undisguised admiration—"My goodness, Ella—he's *marvellous*!" Handing it back, "Wonderful!"

Ella actually blushes slightly. It's a frank compliment that she feels. "This poppet acted as a sort of a compass and tracking guide. Actually, it led me to the library where, I suspect, you took him back."

"Yes, precisely. Allan and I were after Daisie for months, or what felt like months. As you probably experienced yourself, our chief difficulty was in getting to the next site of appearance in time. It was dumb luck—or fate—that brought us to the library something like twenty minutes before the Judge made his appearance there. At first we were jumping to conclusions and just positive we had missed them as usual, but I could find no trace of him anywhere else and our 'readings' were only getting stronger . . . and eventually we had to face our good fortune. I triangulated his place of materialization, and then set up within line of conductance in that small room—"

"I've been there."

"—and then, using a portable 'metaphor', we were able to pinch his body from Daisie's basket and spirit him away."

"I found traces of his blood there."

Dr. Belhoria nods—"Yes, well, Daisie had been gnawing on him a bit."

The scene flashes in Ella's eyes—"My services aren't *free*!" foul from the grisly lips and fangs.

"Don't worry; I examined him myself in the car as we fled the scene—he was still mostly intact. I think that their serialization in time and space would have necessitated constant adaptation to new circumstances, and this may have denied the Judge opportunities to feed. Or perhaps their time was abbreviated relative to ours. Anyway, I have it on good authority that his reincorporation has more or less made him whole once more."

"That tallies with my own hypothesis. Since the poppet's body remained whole, I assumed the original was as well."

"That poppet really is splendid."

"So all that bit about the Law, and Daisie's employer—?"

"Hot air."

"—But I'm puzzled . . . He sort of disappeared after the fight with the angel, and I thought something might have happened to him. Then his body vanished and so on; yet the manifestations began again before you retrieved his body. Can you explain to me the sequence of events?"

"Yes. You saw how badly that last fight went for him personally, if not for his cause . . . "

"Was he healing during that time?"

Dr. Belhoria smiles wanly and barely shakes her head. "He does not *heal*. No, during that period of vanished time he and his army were undergoing translation from that world—the one in the viewer—into this."

"And were the sappers doing the translating from this end?"

"Well, no. Translation is a notoriously difficult problem, and ultimately he had to do it all himself, you know how it is. The sappers were more like his scouts, and publicists. Like most propagandists, they rather misstate the case."

"Yes, I think I've heard one of their radio broadcasts."

"Oh they go on like that all the time. But, in their own fashion and no doubt for their own reasons, they opened the field in which he would appear. They are still opening it now, everywhere."

"So . . . his apparent failure in the other world really had nothing to do with the theft of his body?"

"Not as far as I know. He was temporarily 'lost in translation', but that would have happened in any event. The manifestations on this side were initially random, as he and his forces collected themselves after their translation was in the main complete. Then, as you might imagine, things got more and more purposeful."

"And now he's set up this parallel kingdom—?"

"You could say that. The dead are deader for being so close to the living. No pole without its other and all that—at least, that's how the sappers put it. This Venefy is merely a provisional capitol—as it can only be . . . Things have to keep moving. I'm just glad the dead favor these high mountain places—" Dr. Belhoria sighs "—I am utterly fed up with the sea!"

*

"People come dreaming in from all over the globe," Dr. Belhoria is saying, back in the wind and sun, smell of wet pavement and wood smoke, "digging up their lost loved ones. They're slowed, usually, by the suspicion that perhaps they don't want to see their whozits anymore after all . . . The recently bereaved persevere the most heartily and some of them actually make it through—and this leads to some surprising scenes. Astral youngsters paying their respects to some venerable old deceased ancestor who sits smiling at them like a looney bin, grinning at the whole world . . . Who knows what their reverence looks like to him? It's not uncommon to see one dead, one alive at table, the live one speaking very animatedly while the silent dead one grins wider and wider staring nodding . . .

"The dead and their invincible happiness . . . and that's what Venefy means—*invincible joy.*"

" . . . but how do all these living ones come to be here?"

"Some already have more disassociated relations with the dead, mostly former sappers, or persons who attached themselves to sapper groups—hangers-on . . . they're known as the sappers' "aura" . . . And some melancholic or morbid types. I've encountered many people who simply found themselves here. They remain, I think, because of the happiness of this place. There is joy here of course if you want it—you have only to *breathe* it in my dear. But I'd be careful if I were you—you can end up giving yourself to it, and then you'll never leave, nor remember why you came—nor would you care . . . and why after all should you?"

"—But you don't *breathe* it in, do you?"

"No," Dr. Belhoria smiles a little ruefully, "for better or for worse I am wedded to my work. I shouldn't like to forget that just yet . . . "

*

Venefy is a very different place during the daytime than it is at night . . . Blazing icy sunlight everywhere . . . Great masses of air moving around the city all the time. All the while, her face is sterilized by the cleanest air she's ever breathed blowing always over her face like vaporized silk, the satiny air whistling over her sliding cool antiseptic, chemically or elementally pure . . .

. . . city of my sorrow, city of invincible joy, magpie city, city of the Oracle King, city of autumn . . . Rifled and petted and startled by a ragged wind out of old horror movies . . . in the mountains, arroganting overhead, is the Tyrant's fort, and the Tyrant's observatory, from which he does not appear to stir. In his observatory the Tyrant is the telescope, he is the eye.

They pass a man in faded sweater vest and flapping loose trousers, flopping sandals the size of snowshoes, and sloppy turban piled atop his head, and all the dusty tan color of his wan skin. Crossing a vast square bordered on one side with ornate vertical European facades of flesh-colored stone. Wrought iron basket balconies draped with weird flowers, lean windows, the line of the roofs all undulating lozenges like a Louis Quatorze bedstead, and streaked with rust. On the other side, there are several Georgian buildings with spare classical features, painted sky blue and canary yellow, trimmed in white. Beyond these latter public-looking buildings is an area of little rises and low hills covered with brown grass. Boxy, barnlike sixteenth-century houses are scattered over these rises at all angles to each other, with considerable room in between, criss-crossed by paths in the dirt. Some of these tidy little homes line the streets in that place, and are more tightly fitted together. Mostly unpainted dark wood with small many-paned windows, lacking the imposing facades of nineteenth-century homes which can only be approached by means of a separating stair. The thresholds of these older-style houses rest directly on the border of the pavement, making the whole street more like an open-air dormitory than a row of family palaces.

The air in the square is astonishing, Ella has never derived so much pleasure merely from breathing. Air with a diamond's transparency and the texture of milk. Though the sunlight blazes from every reflecting surface, it has the fading quality of the sun of Halloween day. Everywhere, even where there are no trees, even indoors, there are loose and solitary dead leaves—maple, by and large, Ella thinks—russet, or yellow as bananas, dusty odor of pepper.

Into a slalom of little roads generally sloping down . . . at the end of one street an uncanny tableau: inky cypress trees set against an azure sky. The sight has something indefinable about it—an air of menace like the house of Usher. It takes her breath away, makes her start backward, something unspeakably unnerving about those trees and the house that they shade, but as Dr. Belhoria informs her, it is only a post office. Ella stands looking aghast.

"It's as though a murder happened there—or something."

Dr. Belhoria puts her arm around Ella's shoulders and presses her forwards, "Murders happen everywhere, my girl."

*

There are cooing oros with porcelain mouths in the trees, even on streets lined with tall buildings when she looks directly overhead she sees the branches of trees passing by . . .

Jack-o-lanterns sit on elevated platforms around each street light, facing the four cardinal points.

The park is on a slope at one end of the city, though not quite at its lowest point. Opposite, there are huddled clusters of shanties strung with red blue and green electric lights, looking like a collection of beached houseboats among the great black rocks. As they descend along the lanes the great trees rise up around them. Among the trees there are the shadows of intimate confidences, tender afternoons cool quiet damp smelling spicily of dead leaves and smoke—the crooning shade and the trees rustle . . . the wind moving masses of air everywhere great and invisible slabs of blue and transparent air . . . electric. Now they pass through tree-arcades with lit jack-o-lanterns swaying on chains overhead . . . black cats dart across their path . . . in the distance, intermittent cries, laughter, voices pitched weirdly . . .

"I assume Daisie discovered the theft pretty quickly . . . "

"Yes, he was after us almost at once. We had to keep moving."

"He was able to track you as you had tracked him?"

"I have no way of knowing how he tracked us, but he was never more than a step or two behind."

"But you injured him once—couldn't you well, kill him, or incapacitate him some way?"

"Killing him is out of the question. Let alone me, the Tyrant himself couldn't kill him. It is true that I was able to wound him, and I think precisely for that reason he has chosen not to confront *me* directly again. That is I think he does not want to make himself a target again. He traced after us stealthily and incognito, and made numerous attempts to take the body back by distracting or misdirecting us."

"And this went on until—what, the Tyrant retrieved his original body from you?"

"Actually, I brought it to him—here. For a long time I was of two minds as to what to do with that body."

"Was that before, or after I met you in the fairgrounds?"

"After."

" . . . While you had them, were his remains inert, or did they revive at all?"

"I saw no signs of revival, but I really never had the opportunity to study the body as thoroughly as I wanted to. Anyway, bringing him back to the house was obviously out of the question since Daisie could no doubt find his way back there without difficulty, and hiding the body was not going to work either. I wanted to keep it, but I was frankly unable to devise a way to protect it from Daisie. So I thought it best to put it into the Tyrant's hands. Better that, than it should fall into the hands of my enemy."

"He should have allowed you to observe his reincorporation."

"Well, he gave me full citizenship here and extended his protection to me . . . and besides, I *was* present at his reincorporation, but I am rather embarrassed to admit that everyone present, including myself, lost consciousness during the transfer."

The path is leveling toward the center of the park.

"And where is Daisie now?"

"No idea."

Here is a pool in a marble basin where the groundskeepers breed miniature sperm whales—bonsai sperm whales only a foot and a half long . . . It's unnerving to watch them swim just under the surface, their tails slowly plowing the water, rising up to pipe little plumes of white froth into the air with high-pitched whistling sounds. It's as though she were a giant looking down at the ocean.

"Where's Carl?" Ella wonders—she has just seen someone who looks a little like him—but Carl is disappeared, forgotten now like part of a dream. It makes sense. The real world, the rational world, are words, like any others. All dreams, no less than the irrational world or the unreal world. The world is bigger than any mind, and mostly imagined.

They stand together for a while, listening to the whistles, and the steady churning of tails in the water. One of the little whales snaps its jaws, spurting water out to either side, then dives to the bottom with surprising speed. Dr. Belhoria moves off, waving Ella on with a look that promises something. They continue toward the center of the park. The green breasts of the lawns seem to rise and fall breathing out soul-voluptuousness breathing it into Ella. Sunshine fills the landscape, and yet always with that especially pleasing fading quality of light on Halloween day, which is fashioned from bundles of stories.

"Why is Daisie pursuing the Tyrant?"

"He is the Tyrant's demon. You said that yourself."

"I meant—do you have any idea what he wants?"

"He wants to replace the Tyrant, by devouring him. Now get a look at this."

There is a vast natural basin, its slopes carpeted with rich grass, at the center of the park. A bright lake, fringed with streaming fronds, fills the bottom of the basin. The lake is occupied by a miraculous hybrid, a cross between a sperm whale and an orchid. It has the powerful flukes, the general shape, even the narrow gangway jaw, but instead of the broad breadloaf-shaped head there is a catastrophic riot of enormous fleshy petals and stamens (which seem to serve as sense organs). At first glance, the petals seem grey blue and black like the rest of the whale, but when they catch the light they prove to be iridescent fabrics of vermillions and violet, specked with lurid blues and yellows and leprous white patches. When the light of the full moon shines down on these petals, they fluoresce and throw many-hued gleams on the grassy walls of the basin as slow strength swims them back and forth. By means of this reflected light, it is possible to see disembodied spirits flitting along the banks of the pool, or breathing in the rushes that creep and twine themselves like a ground-mist around vines of translucent thorns. Unearthly lotus-like perfume wafts over them with each jet of the whale's spout. Its motions and gestures and especially the pronounced vibration of the water between its petals give an inexplicable impression of great laughing and subtle intelligence, as though its undulating petals were the exposed lobes of a colossal brain. As Ella watches it swim back and forth, she feels a profound, faithful calm being communicated to her . . . languid, dreamy, and lucid.

"It is fed three times a day on ten barrels full of squid stuffed with earth," Dr. Belhoria is saying when Ella starts listening to her again.

"All magical places have their genius loci, and this sperm-orchid is the genie of this spot."

Languid opium-smokers recline in willow-shade or beneath sprawling parasols on the steep slopes of the lake's banks. They point at the whale from time to time with the long stems of their pipes. The smoke hangs about the smokers, haloing their slack, dazed, downcast faces; they toss back their heads and spout jets of narcotic smoke into the caressing air. Teenagers in red silk monkey-jackets dart from one parasol to another bearing little tables and pots of tea, or leaded jars of macaroons to the music of an invisible flute.

Ella looks at the whale and her heart aches in a new way. When she was younger she had read a story that described how DDT was thinning the shells of robins' eggs, and stories about the do-do and the passenger pigeon, with a feeling of impotent and horrified despair.

"He should bring back the extinct animals," Ella says.

Dr. Belhoria looks at her with surprise—she seems to think she's just caught a glimpse inside Ella. She says with some intrigue, "All in good time . . . I'm sure he'll get around to it . . .

*

They have passed on to the other side of the park, and Dr. Belhoria has parted from Ella for a moment to procure an Italian ice from a small kiosk made entirely of human pelvic bones. Ella stands on the path. She thinks again of all the trouble she went through to get here. Now, here she is, and she still hasn't seen him. She feels cruelly deprived and tantalized—come so far and through so much at such effort—and now she is here in his city, looking up at his observatory, and she is nowhere near him. Her heart thuds inside her like a bell rung by a hammer. And yet, at the same time, he is here, all around her, his presence fills the city, his words write each moment that passes. She looks at the leaves in the trees and the dark branches and the sky and the wind and the sun, and now her heart begins to swell up, and now she begins to feel as rapturous as though she were already in possession of him.

"Can he read my mind? —I'll try to call out to him—" she visualizes herself standing on the spot without her crutches as though she'd never had polio, her arms raised to the sky her face beaming, and great invisible shout somehow rising from her to the white dome of the observatory, a voice she can't hear but that she feels rise past her hair and her ears—"Will he hear what I cry without words? . . . Is it working?" She sees in her mind's eye a few random images. The interior of a white dome, a shining figure . . . but are these images a response to her call or only her imagination? Who's to say? Moving a little off the path she cries to him in her mind, glances up and gasping she sees his face—only another statue . . .

She stands before it, the black bronze almost vibrates with presence. The wild, severe expression on his face is like a wave that sweeps her up in its frenzy a turbulence forced between channels. A wing drops over her—she wants those two eyes to flare up and bend down onto her, she wants to be pierced by their rays, seized by his arms like two seething waterspouts, be pressed to his cyclone body those two eyes gazing out of the calm center. She's staring in disbelief at this astonishing face, a face that doesn't cease to be astonishing no matter how long she looks at it, that she almost can't associate with this huge dark figure—like a beautiful ogre . . . She remembers the look of beastial triumph she had seen on those features before, without fear, then or now—if anything she wants him to be more savage, *more* savage, *more* towering, *more* dark and menacing and draw all the world's power into himself only bear me up with you evil, evil man—*I love his evil*. She sees him in her mind's eye plunging headlong into a confused mass of rival cavalry and footsoldiers like an avalanche, bellowing, his body flexes back and forth in the saddle his spine straight. She remembers how her blood was just boiling as she watched him fight. Now his figure looms up before her like a dreamy centaur, dreamy and somehow vicious at once; the rearing, snarling horse brandishes his sharp hammerlike front hoofs in the air, standing on his hind legs exposes his sex and in his boiling cape the Tyrant sits erect his legs clasping the horse's knotted flanks, controlling it without reins, slashing sabre in his right hand and pointing a cocked pistol with his left hand, his head thrust up into the low-hanging branches of the oaks to either side of the path behind the statue. The head has an aloof dreamy expression, escaping like smoke into the trees . . . Ella realizes her breath is coming suddenly short . . . The air is so soft and yielding smelling of dead and dying leaves, and Dr. Belhoria's perfume, and the carnauba wax from Dr. Belhoria's lipstick. She glances to one side and Dr. Belhoria is there, observing her and grinning wolfishly at her. Dr. Belhoria says nothing but now purses her lips, closing her grin without abandoning it. *I don't care if I'm ridiculous I don't care if I'm horrible for feeling the way I do,* Ella thinks, and the thoughts seem almost to sputter from her eyes. Dr. Belhoria walks off with a loose, languid stride, swinging her arms and allowing her head to droop slightly to one side, giving Ella a diagonal look—"Coming?" she asks.

CHAPTER TWELVE

Returning from the park in the late afternoon, heading in the direction of the casino, they pass the outskirts of the Lunar Quarter. Day or night, the streets are veiled in silver shadows and the walls glow with a soft blue flame, passersby float in the streets with elongated strides or leap up onto overhanging balconies and roofs. The narcotic fragrances of Selenite creepers rise and fail just within the boundaries of the quarter.

A brief detour, back to Dr. Belhoria's rooms at the casino. The tables are just beginning to hum; the heavy, lacquered-looking man with the Theodore Roosevelt whiskers is loitering on the steps by his platform, waiting for his counterpart to appear on the other side.

"Any sign of Carl, yet?"

"I'm sure he'll turn up dear . . . "

Dr. Belhoria wants to give Ella a vaccination—"Many of the dead ones here are victims of disease and still contagious . . . " She peels off an elliptical sheet of clear adhesive plastic with a yellow-brown spot the size of a silver dollar in the center, consisting of many tiny beads of waxy vaccine. Rolling up Ella's sleeve, she wraps the sheet around Ella's arm with the spot against her skin. "The vaccine should be completely absorbed within an hour or so—now, we need to find you some lodgings . . . "

Ella passively allows herself to be conducted onto the street again . . .

"You said you were present at his 'reincorporation'?"

"Present, if not conscious, yes . . . "

"What can you remember?"

—A number of grinning bearers in uhlan uniform met them at the gate with a stretcher. They were conducted through the forecourts across to a sort of a barrier or wall emerging from the mountain, with the bearers following. Some others, mostly senior sappers, joined them there, and an officer led them to one of the corners, through a narrow door, into a confining L-shaped room; all red and soft, with thick carpets and padding under a layer of red velvet on the walls. The officer herded them all into a long slender elevator with brilliantly polished brass grillwork and fittings.

After brief upward acceleration, they emerged into open air and sunlight, on a white patio set in among big crags, towering above Venefy. Overhead, the bare edge of the Tyrant's dome was visible beyond the rock, where it stood on the wind-tossed peak. A flight of steps and through a sky-blue arch of plaited glass, into a long gallery open to the sun, where the path was flanked by rows of huge trees growing from blocks of crystal-clear ice, their roots plainly visible. The doctor's party breathed the cool air he found so stimulating. They came to a steep flight of steps in an enclosed area, to either side of them a blazing creamy blue-white tree of perfectly static electricity, supported in twin fields from which every last mote of time painstakingly had been pared. Their progress was observed by a pair of arctic foxes, a whooping crane in a stand of oblivious penguins, and a bengal tiger with icy blue eyes, who lay on a shelf high overhead and gazed superciliously down. ("If he gets any more totem animals he'll undermine the whole idea—they can't *all* be totems.") The frosted iron steps they climbed were lined with obelisks and urns.

Presently they arrived in a circular room just below and before the Tyrant's observatory, which overlapped the opposite wall with its foremost edge by a dozen or so feet. This room was filled with the most exquisite grave statues, plundered from the richest and most exclusive corners of the world's most luxurious cemeteries. Almost all were female, or androgynous, figures: melancholy, stern, or prostrated . . . Above the arched entryway a huge cowled bronze figure pored over a colossal book, the folds of its ample hood completely obscuring its face. One of the lieutenants tripped lightly before them beaming, indicating to the group with a few elegant gestures to collect in a semicircle just within the entrance, beneath the cowled bronze figure.

Before them, the floor was completely bare . . . and opposite were two enormous screws at least six feet across, running like columns from a pair of circular openings in the floor to a similar pair in the marble ceiling, set into the far end of a free-standing rectangular cut-out section. Shafts of light filtered down through the gap, outlining the separate section of the ceiling with a dim glow. The lieutenant crossed to one side of the room and pulled a ponderous-looking lever protruding from the floor. With a well-oiled whine the two screws began to turn, apparently screwing into the floor, and the ceiling section, a mammoth marble ramp, smoothly tilted down towards them . . .

—Dr. Belhoria squints and presses the heel of one hand to her temple—

. . . the ramp was a solid, hollow shaft, like an excised hallway, the underside was white the "hallway" itself black very black—someone could—would—walk from the observatory floor down this ramp-hallway and stand in the end as it dropped into this room, the room below, in which they had gathered . . . Its end would come to rest immediately before them. There was an oblong and upright box like a coffin at the end . . . the end that was descending toward them . . . and a figure—the Tyrant—stood motionless in it, shining like a comet . . . The cold light he radiated seemed to inundate the room as he descended . . .

". . . and then we, Allan and I, were sitting together in that bakery up the street from the casino."

"And that was it?"

"Yes. —No . . . no I do remember something else—the bearers came out from behind us—I remember too, the great thud as the ramp touched the floor . . . Then something I can't be certain is a memory or something imaginary, where I see two silhouettes in a bright light . . . and then I see one silhouette . . .

"—and that's all."

*

Dr. Belhoria leads her down torturous alleyways, narrow passages between white plaster walls, with catwalks and balconies overhead. Although she doesn't see them, Ella gets the impression that people, mostly women and children, are rapidly withdrawing at their approach. They pass an open doorway—just inside a handsome Ethiopian man glances up as they go by—what was he doing? He was mending the sole of a shoe.

Now the alley opens onto an irregularly-shaped street, narrow at one extremity and curving around growing bulbous as it swerves, then narrowing again at the other end. Some of the modest houses lining the street are immaculate as little French cakes, others are only shells whose windows open onto rubble. Dr. Belhoria conducts Ella to a lanky, lean house painted white, with a generous porch of loose planks. The door is rounded at the top and hangs open, covered only by a pair of long brown drapes that waft. Dr. Belhoria pulls the bell rope—either the bell is silent, or perhaps that very faint and unplaceable noise was the bell.

"This will put you close to the Master Square—he delivers all his speeches there."

"Oh . . . "

"Rents in this area are usually at a premium—"

"Aren't there any hotels?"

"*No hotels*," says Dr. Belhoria in tone of official decree.

. . . and thinking of all the lousy times she's had lately in hotels, Ella can't blame the ban . . . Yeah to hell with hotels.

From the hall behind the drapes, a sound of footsteps, firm tread, but dragging slippers. Ella sees the feet step into a smear of reflected light on the polished wooden floor, and the drape is pulled open by a heavyset man in his late thirties with a bush of curly brown hair, dressed in a black silk nightshirt and grey sweat pants and pointed-toed black slippers. He regards them with the glassy blank goggle-eyed gaze of the habitual absinthe drinker. Dingy half-moon spectacles perch on his stub nose.

Later, when the arrangements have been made, and a very low rent fixed, Ella stands in the front parlour of the house. Dr. Belhoria is outside hiring a porter to bring Ella's luggage round from the casino. Screen, the landlord, sits there at a rough wooden table, vacuously peeling the foil off of chocolate Easter eggs and setting them one by one in a row on the table before him, nestled in foil cradles.

Dr. Belhoria returns—"Well, that's that. I will take my leave of you now. You can call on me at any time if you have any more questions."

"I don't know anyone else here—can I see you tomorrow?" What is she going to do now?

"Yes we can meet for breakfast if you like—but there's one more thing . . . are you still wearing the ring he gave you?"

"Yes," Ella can feel its weight on her ring finger, and against her skin the letters of APOCALYPSE.

"Good—make sure you keep it on at all times."

"Are you thinking of Daisie?"

"Yes—as long as you wear that, the soldiers will defend you. I don't think there's much cause for concern, but you never know . . . just as a precaution."

"Say you don't think Carl—?"

"I would have been notified had anything like that happened. He's fine, I'm sure.—And I'll leave your address at the front in the event he returns to the casino. In the meantime, be patient and rest." She steps into the doorway. "Now just *be cool.*"

Ella's room is also on the ground floor, roughly fifteen feet from the door to the window, and only seven or so from wall to wall; clean, with an old-house earwax smell. From her window all she can see at the moment are great leafy trees fondling the air in slow motion. She watches them as the sun sets . . . the sky's original azure color taken away in regular, gradational shadings of color too subtle for her eyes to make out . . . like a translucent blue marble panel lit from behind—no, no—iridescent and metallic like a butterfly wing . . . infinitely fine texture of the blue, harboring steadily more motes of black, a refuge as well for the lambent final particles of daylight.

Ella bursts out laughing at the thought that pops into her head—mental image of Dr. Belhoria saying "Now just *be cool.*"

*

The only other lodger is a medical student. Screen described him tersely as a serious young man of solitary habits. For all that, he generates a great deal of noise. Ella can hear him tromping up and down the stairs, pacing up and down in his room for hours. What's more, he talks to himself—giving practice lectures complete with a formalized system of jokes, judging from his tone. On occasion she will hear loud singing humming down from his room. Given her own medical associations, Ella avoids him in hopes of forestalling boring conversations, explanations, tiresome curiosities. Let him get his own cadavers. Not unlike the landlord, the medical student seems to do a lot of drinking in private; there are always empty bottles stacked in front of his door and on his fire escape, and on what she takes to be his windowsill . . . where she sees a yellow-white object that on closer inspection proves to be a human skull, wearing spectacles, jumbled in with the bottles. Well you might say they are all receptacles from which the spirits have been entirely drained; maybe he uses the skull as a cup like the vikings, but where would he put his lips to it—the eye sockets?

Exploring the house, she encounters some construction in the back hallway. There are strings, apparently approximating sight lines, running along its length through a number of different wire shapes suspended from the ceiling, and at the far end of the hall, where the walls open out into a funnel-shaped room, there are a number of lights in the doorway that evidently are shone through the wire shapes down the sight-lines. Looking into the funnel-shaped room, Ella can see all manner of beams set out to form partitions and a variety of what appear to be empty wood frame and lath forms, like molds or scaffolds. The back wall is partially demolished, and there is a huge heap of bricks lying in front of it. The roof is an extension from the side of the house and gives an impression of stability on its flimsy supports that doesn't seem possible. The whole room is an elaborate orchestration of space that has yet to come together, might already be irretrieveably botched, like a piece of music composed on out-of-tune instruments. Ella can't make head or tail of it. Construction, or composition, has apparently been on hiatus for some time now—dead leaves and bits of rubbish are scattered all over the floor, mostly blown in by the wind through the great gaps in the walls . . .

From time to time Ella would revisit this unfinished room—a portly orange cat tenants one of the empty lath forms, dozing there at all hours. Ella has sometimes observed it performing strange cat-gymnastics: squatting on its haunches, it pats and slaps the floor with its front paws, first to the right, then to the left, sometimes patting with both paws in unison, sometimes alternately, and always with touching concentration, following its own movements intently with its eyes the color of sapphires and turning its face this way and that. He really looks as if he's playing a pair of bongo drums.

Her room—plainly but neatly furnished with dead leaves on the floor, and a cool white-tiled bathroom where she treats herself to a lengthy bath with the latest copy of "The Cemetery Partisan". Night falls beyond the window as she bathes. She finds her dinner on a tray before her door . . . of all things, lamb tagine.

Screen sits on the roof of the unfinished room—silhouetted against the sky in a fantastically capacious fur coat—no it's a bear rug, she can see its great hollow head snarling at a tiny potted plant by his right foot. He is sitting there, smoking a cigar with evident relish. She calls out thank you for the dinner to him—but his mind is elsewhere, he doesn't seem to hear.

*

. . . Now it is later, Ella has put out the light.

She returns to the windows. Something about these views, these scenes come unmoored and swirl around her as though she were sitting in the center of a rotoscope. Now the trees she had seen before are somehow farther away and smaller, she can see more of the city. The wind has risen—what her father used to call "Witch Weather" . . . Layered like the waters of Tsalal, the wind is a skein of many different winds of varying textures and temperatures. Looking out into the booming night, she is thrilled and unnerved at the faint sound of a man's deep and sinister laughter. The moon has already set, the black sky appears to whorl, it seems both closer and deeper here . . . intermittently disturbed by some flickering, like flashes of transparent lightning. The crowded, plentiful stars give off a salty light that smarts the eyes. How terrible it would be to wander the streets in the open exposed to that sky, she thinks, she would fall to the ground and cling to it so as not to fall straight up . . .

How delicious to be safe inside. The house seems to dwindle around her forming a thin shell, a safe vantage point on the wild night outside. Across the street, she can see a blue-white draped figure carrying a will-o-the-wisp, drifting haltingly past the second-storey windows of a building she knows to be an empty shell, no floor there.

Abruptly, she turns her eyes to his dome. He's up there now in all the tumult, blazing like one of these stars. As she watches, she sees a lean black shadow or stripe slide steadily across the surface of the dome—what is that? Then she realizes it's the slit, the aperture in the dome through which he looks. His *gaze is sweeping the city now*—a needle in a haystack does he see *her*? The city stirs as the dome turns—a cry in the distance . . . some faint commotion . . . incipient panic—the slit in the dome turns past . . . and stops, just on the verge of disappearing behind the edge.

*

After her breakfast with Dr. Belhoria—leaving her with "Who would have thought things would go so far?" as she adjusts her hair—Ella finds herself alone on an immense balcony of stone overlooking an asterisk of streets. The bricks and stones of the walls look black and slimy with a nauseous effluvium of decay and fear. Now Ella is overwhelmed by a feeling she has had almost from the moment she set foot in Venefy, that she has refused to acknowledge or entertain. It is a creeping bitterness . . . despair . . . the sickening aura of death and putrefaction—the city oozes it. The horror of those dead grins . . . the triumph of death.

She believed and still wants to believe that he is all life, all alive, but she is beginning to have second thoughts. The black bricks, the merciless corners of the buildings and the relentlessly straight narrow alleys, they make her feel withered and frightened—more than threatened—doomed. Now she yearns to get away to someplace wholesome; she misses ordinary streets. And where is he now? —retired and inaccessible, as remote as a statue or a headstone. And lording like a monster over this necropolis, a city of murder.

"Murders happen everywhere my girl."

But then a wind bubbles up from the mountains, the air is clean and cold, the sun is brilliant, and the city sparkles beautifully before her. As swiftly as it arose, this painful fear and revulsion evaporates—yes he is inaccessible now, but sooner or later she will see him again. Her confidence is inexplicably tenacious, impossible to shake. Enormous carrion birds circle overhead, and she admires the great spans of their wings—and looking around her she sees the grinning pumpkins and, hanging from one of the street lights, a scarecrow witch with a faceless head of bundled straws, a crepe cape and a peaked hat made from black nylon and a wire hanger. And there is a pair of men all in white having a picnic on one of the opposing rooftops—they sit crosslegged on a little rug. One of them picks up a square, white sandwich from its wrapper of wax paper and holds it upright in both hands just above and before his face, holding it up to the Tyrant's observatory with a thanksgiving bow of his head. —And what's happening? Blue sparks are drifting down from the dome of the fort in long parabolas, and snowing down over the city . . .

*

"I could join his army," she thinks—"the sappers and soldiers here kill mortal visitors every day—one moment, like being knocked unconscious, and then——invincible joy . . . so—and Dr. Belhoria has not availed herself of their help, I notice. She doesn't seem ready to die into their ranks yet——

"——I can't see myself there either really——that's not what I came for I came for him——

"If I've come here to die," she is shocked to think this so frankly—"If I've come here to die, then let *him* kill me."

*

Sunlight shining on dusty courtyards without time, seen from a shaded doorway. It's only been a day or so, and yet she can't shake the feeling she's been here for . . . Everything that came before is starting to seem unreal. Ahead somehow she knows there is a complete change coming up. She's on its threshold now, any moment she could be precipitated through . . .

She catches sight of her landlord from time to time kneeling in the ruined basement of an adjoining building, performing what appears to be a rather mundane and unglamorous religious rite—he kneels davening back and forth as he drones aloud from a worse-for-wear *scroll*, while a cork smoulders in front of him on a little ad hoc altar made by laying a brick across two other bricks.

Why should he go on doing such a thing *here*? It seems utterly futile. That might be precisely why he does it, goes on doing it—

What am I waiting for?

Something I am certain is coming. I don't know why I am certain and I don't know what is coming.

*

General commotion—Ella is sitting with a bowl of soup when she notices people rushing by, a steadily growing mutter rising on all sides—what is it? People are running in the streets—claxons wail over the rooftops. Suddenly someone thrusts in at the doorway, silhouetted against the street his eyes and bared teeth glint and breathlessly he says

"*He's going to speak! He's going to give a speech!*"

Ella gets to her feet and a moment later she is lunging along with the others heading for Master Square, everywhere people trot in that direction.

The Square is already thronged with people, who have gathered in what appear to be designated areas at the rear of the Square, which is its lower part. The upper and more visible part is cordoned off somehow. Ella finds a spot without really choosing it but plants herself there as if to defy all comers. In a moment she is swamped by the crowd. The people around her are anxious and even visibly trembling, their eyes naked and wide, all bound up in one galvanic current. It binds her up as well and she feels the shock and ripple before the cavalry even appears, prancing out into the cordoned area bearing huge flapping black banners. The horses dance bound and bow, prance and nod, the riders brandish their heavy banners with effortless strength and circle round the crowd. Ella hears the banging hoofs, the people around her are cheering at the top of their lungs and she can feel hysteria building up around her and sweeping her up too with the howl of the claxons, as though she were topping over a roller coaster with that it's-going-to-happen it's-happening feeling. She shouts her love at the skull and crossbones.

At one end of the Square a stage appears—proceneum arch, golden fanlights, red velvet curtain with gold fringe. Lines of dead infantry gush into the Square skipping in formation and beaming. The dead cavalry ride through avenues in the crowd their horses nodding and bowing—all these dead performing and dancing for us . . . The crowd shudders and trembles and all around Ella she can see tears streaking down people's faces at the sight of sublime power, as though Power itself dances there for them that could utterly crush and destroy them but that will defend them and crush and humiliate all their enemies, trample the world that it has already brought to an end there for them. The throng ripples in unpredictable swells and Ella struggles to keep her feet.

The curtain rises on the stage and a cry goes up from the crowd. The stage is bare except for a prop tree sticking out of a little paper-mache hill on wheels. The footlights go up, and then a spotlight and the Tyrant—now the Oracle King—is there. The crowd explodes surges forward its roar rebounds from the mountainsides arms strain in the air past Ella's shoulders and she is borne up held erect without her crutches the faces all around her stretched shining with tears and howling. Ella is howling and weeping too. The Oracle King shines on the stage like a comet—he steps forward and sternly regards them their roar like a furnace blast in his face. He yet wears his lacerated uniform, and his brow is crowned with a wreath of perfectly-reproduced golden oak leaves with clusters of platinum acorns glinting with light. Without any fanfare or further ceremony, he stands in the footlights, and a boom-mike swings out from the wings stopping inches before his face.

The Oracle King opens his mouth to speak—his eyes will be a different color with every word—he open his mouth and begins to speak into the microphone Ella—Ella—Ella—

the ground up—her trees from powder and dark, light—burrow overhead—and onto the sky hair falls—gargoyle face—black and back frisks Mona Lisa's face—vitreous humor in braids of music—she looks from moon and feet—she which she horizon nearly now weak from dazzling sunbeams—now a dancer's wrist the earth sags—round she where she on the now she sees she a tossing she is orbiting rock—sea nothing attack her sails by foaming crests—she's drunk the sky midnight—still calmly tenth-century lanes—paralyzed there vibrating Ayer's alcove in Antarctica—sees jungle fibrous calloused—muse's face pine now palm—once, surveys the sun—sea floor from a face and clay river neck from blade of red lava—pair against the space wide his mouth . . .

—too much—

—too fast—

—a moment to close in on herself . . .

—a little kernel of herself collects itself and quickly sees that *this* is his speech—She is not hearing his words but he is speaking these images and speaking time and space travel—slow it down and decompress it, no let it wash over you without grabbing at it, go along . . .

The ground is white powder and the mountains overhead are starker and sharper than ever the sky is impossibly black and clear as vitreous humor. The horizon is bizarrely near and as she turns to see the blinding sun, she sees she is on the surface of the moon, and on the horizon nearly screened by dazzling sunbeams the earth—the earth—birds circle round the earth in space—

On the deck of a tossing ship in a black storm at sea nothing but foaming crests visible—it's midnight, the ship rises and falls on mountainous waves but in the distance there is another even more violently storm-tossed ship and somehow despite the distance she can see him on its deck speaking still calmly powerfully . . .

She is a tuning fork struck again and again vibrating Africa India China Antarctica—around her she sees jungle and now pine trees and now palm now desert—steppe—mountain—lake shore—meadow—marsh—sea floor—pack ice—clay river water—volcano, red lava bombs lobbed into the smoke—her skin is dark, light, freckled, dun, chocolate, hairier and less hairy and smooth her hair falls down her back frisks her back in braids her head is nearly bare is smooth is thin—she looks out from a height of eighteen inches—six feet—three feet—she is strong now weak now bent now straight her skin sags her skin is taut she is ill now she is well she is poisoned, cancerous, she's having a heart attack her arm tingles—she's drunk, she's stimulated opening her mouth to chatter—she flies and drives and stands still on the ocean floor on tenth-century lanes in London and Kiev the Great Wall and Mecca Egypt Greenland Peru Ayer's Rock—rings heavy on fingers now fibrous calloused and aching from slavery's work—wings, claws, fins, teeth, antennae, feathers and scales at once, surveys the earth from a fifty-foot neck from a swinging pair of shaggy arms in the trees from within a burrow a cave flies swims and runs and holds onto the stones—is stone, gargoyle face, muse's face, Mona Lisa's face, is wail of music singing reed brass skin stone bone wood gut organ brass and wood cry of a rook, look out from wooden frame, from the wall from which she half-emerges, from this inclination of a dancer's wrist and ankle, of course from this writing, from where she is she sees she is on some small orbiting rock spinning end over end as it were, the sun sails by momentarily turning the sky blue the day is only a second, in the strobe of passing days the muse is picking her slow jerky stop-motion way toward Ella across the rocky landscape while Ella lies still as though paralyzed there in an alcove in a jumble of rough black rocks . . . the muse's face inclined down enough so as to remain in shadow, inching closer with each flare of the sun, the Tyrant's face and the gleaming blade of his sabre geysering against the backdrop of space wide his mouth . . .

Ella is blinking at a badly-weathered poster on a wall—SE APROXIMA EL FIN DEL MUNDO—LAS PROFECIAS DEL CUMPLEN. The poster is illustrated with a woodcut depicting a city collapsing, people kneeling, repenting too late, fleeing in terror—one man is flying through the air, which bristles with lightning bolts. The poster rattles and floats lazily against the wall in the wind. Ella looks around. She is in Venefy, in an unfamiliar part of town . . . how did she get here? The last thing she recalls is the Tyrant's speech . . . Is it over—is this still his "speech"? Where is she? A plausible explanation: somehow in a trance she wandered off, either during or after the speech, and now comes to herself only here . . .

"Damn!" she shouts in wounded surprise. She had wanted to get close to him somehow, with no clear plan she had been counting on it, somehow getting close to him after the speech, and now—gone!

Now where is she?

*

Venefy changes as night falls. Some areas instantly withdraw into themselves quickly growing dark and silent. Others are slower to cool, and first take on a carnival quality, but these places will die down and empty out around midnight. From then until dawn, night populates the streets and uses them for its own purposes.

It is not long after sunset. Ella stands in a trash-strewn vacant lot. Foraging through a dense tangle of tall weeds, she makes her way to the pavement. The city has not just a secretive but a cold, hermetic air. She can hear music. A dog dashes up the street with clicking claws. Ella follows the sound with a vague notion of getting directions. Her lodgings are on Scythe Lane; Dr. Belhoria reminds her in her memory, "All the streets here have these joke names like Skull Boulevard and Carcass Crescent—sophomoric." Ella looks up at an enamel street sign bolted to a brick wall—"Death Drive" . . . well it figures.

Following the sound of music and crowds she presently finds her way into an area of gambling casinos nightclubs and saloons, punctuated with esophageal alleyways that bring to mind shades of Jack the Ripper. Muffled tunes waft from wide open fronts onto the street, mingled with the sound of a distant ship's horn or the groan of some very large machine perhaps under the street. Everyone she sees is plainly living, but mingled in with the obviously dissipated pleasure-seekers there are some others. They haven't got the air of *evil joy* that identifies the dead ones—these are familiar-looking souls that is they look like familiars—owls, cats, toads. Their purposive movements make them stand out from the idling crowd; if they are not sober, then they are taking stimulants. They seem to be scanning for occult signs. Magical procedures are evidently underway on all sides—blue and red lights twitch and gutter on rooftops and in the high windows of otherwise dark rooms.

Ella makes her way along a row of storefronts with glass shop windows like black lakes. Most of these are wholly obscure but in this shop with the narrow glass door she can see a group of persons holding hands around a table by candlelight. Their eyes are shut and a woman's lips writhe continuously as sentences inaudible from the street march out of her mouth. Ella wants to push forward—her idea of asking for directions is gone from her head, now she simply wants to keep moving, get out of this dark street that smells of perfume liquor rancid trash perspiration—but now Ella is trapped behind a small group of promenading men. The streets are too jammed and she can't manage to get around them. The men are talking animatedly in philosophical soliloquies like characters in a Dostoevsky novel. The one in the middle flings up his arms to the flanking facades.

"Any city, even a dead city—in fact, especially a dead city—is all dominated by desire. Wherever there is humanity there is desire, which is in each one of us, a complex that's poorly understood or not at all understood. Fickler than the wind, it operates in fits and starts. Almost all the buildings have outlived the desire that gave rise to them long before they are even completed, and the finishing touches are applied in a mortician's spirit. A lot like trying to prettify a cadaver for the final viewing, lots of futility and a dogged, habitual determination to make the best of things. Nobody wants to see or use these buildings any more, and no one really wants to see that corpse all rubbed with cosmetics. What they wanted in either case is something already gone. How people hate desire! They learn to distrust it—but deprive them of its convulsions for even one day and what will life look like to them then?

"Always—a first blush of enthusiasm and then, who cares? If only we could have a lasting enthusiasm. Perhaps that's why people resort to hoping and dreaming after objects that are so utterly unattainable . . . but then there's nothing upon which enthusiasm can sate itself. Nor is this mad strategy necessarily a bad one—even these observations are growing tiresome—all the same there is something beautiful, touching, in bearing witness as the heat and light fade out of these thoughts. That heat will leave behind a nostalgic residue, and maybe sometime, later, I'll pick up its contagion, and suddenly the whole sense impression will be there before me again. A desire remembered too late to do anything about it, to act on, to prompt action . . . like a desire out of a past life . . . suddenly becomes sort of infinite, and you can take pleasure in it, because it summons you without requiring you to do anything, summons you without asking anything of you. You are in a position to savor it freely, and you don't owe it anything.

"Those furtive and ill-formed fads of desire—you wouldn't even know what one of them looked like if you caught up with it finally, got a good look at it! How unfamiliar what we really want is to us. You don't even know what you want—and you don't want to know! You say 'Damn it let me sleep, I don't want to be *conscious* for this! Kindly let these blobs of smoke close over my head, and I will make my narcotized terror-train journey through clockwork dioramas of female anatomy. One by one the images rise up and brush by like wire and gauze ghosts on hydraulic arms, just brushing my face with perfumed hems as they drift by. 'Yes I like these artificially haunted houses the best.' You say to yourself, 'Why I've never felt so *free*!'"

At the word "free" Ella spots an opening and pushes past the men, crossing the street after a rickshaw and making for the opposite corner. A square is visible between a pair of old houses and she suddenly yearns for its open air. A small party of people pass her in the dark and she crosses their wake of alcoholic breath and vomit as she enters the square.

Ella wanders out into a small convex plaza covered with iron tables and chairs, blazing with candles. In the glare of livid housefronts, glassy-eyed citizens sit imbibing, their shoulders hunched, talking less and less and slower and slower. There are no young people in the city, no one Ella's age, or at least she hasn't seen anyone . . . nor has she wanted to. The city has in places that air of mysterious grown-up night life she recognizes from long ago when her parents would go out. Transformed into another sort of adult altogether, having nothing to do with being mothers and fathers, different clothes, her mother's make-up and perfume. Where they went and what they did she could never imagine, but it was somewhere like here.

At the plaza's center there is a fountain that jets turquoise flames instead of water. The flames travel in neat arcs from little nozzles around the basin of kerosene to play over the surface of a great suspended iron ball that smokes into the sky. Ella supposes everyone must crowd around it on cold nights. In addition to the citizens, the square is home to enormous owls the size of small children. One of them is butting a skull along the ground with its forehead —every now and then it stops, looks around, and seems to lick its beak. Overhead, bats in the night sky like fragments of black wind.

Ella crosses to a broad avenue with a planted divider running down the center. There are benches beneath the trees in the divider and Ella sits a while to rest her arms. This boulevard is lined with theatres—grand guignol shows everywhere, wrenching sentimental dramas, the facades open to the street, so that the avenue is lined with recessed stages visible over mobs of dark heads. The marquee directly before her reads "SISTER OF AN EVIL FAMILY & REVENGE OF THE HAND FROM SISTER'S GRAVE" . . . As she sits and rests, Ella switches from one theatre to another like changing channels (poisonous wind from the stars riffles her hair). On their stages are represented all manner of atrocities—a father ravishes and cannibalizes his crippled son—a pair of beautiful ghoulish twins kidnap infants for offerings on their homemade altar, render their victims' baby fat into tallow candles—posthumous incest: an idiot rapes the cadaver of his sister who has just poisoned herself, the grisly foam of her agony still on her lips . . . and an endless series of shows involving nuns: nuns ravished by Roman soldiers, Barbary pirates, Cossacks, werewolves, mummies; a nun raped and blinded by her own insane bastard son; pregnant nuns tortured to death by prurient Inquisitors—official torture, clandestine torture, family torture . . . autumn, spring, north, south, pagan, Christian, Muslim, Chinese, Aztec, tragic, or gloating, thirty-one flavors. Each stage is soaked with gore, and although the effects are crude, somehow when the heroine is dragged across the floor spilling sheep's intestines from a pouch in her costume the mere presence of the raw carrion even exceeds rather than vitiates the verisimilitude of the play.

Meanwhile, brigades of fiendish-looking young men in short red silk jackets and young women in skimpy outfits and pillbox hats circulate among the crowd with trays, selling bright red sour balls and little spun-sugar skulls, salt-water taffy in pink lumps veined with red or in white and blue eyeballs, chocolates with gushy centers colored a hideous vermillion, thickly-frosted cupcakes, and small tinkling bottles of gin, mandrake, and bitter anise.

One by one the shows end, the stages go dim, and the stage hands appear with mops and buckets to slop off the stages. The faces of those leaving the theatre are like deflated balloons, with here and there a knot of bright-eyed enthusiasts animatedly discussing with hand gestures the play's highlights and already searching for the next one. The actors emerge out the side doors to shouts of praise and bales of flowers. Their faces are dewy and sweetly fresh, relaxed, their bodies warm with wholesome fatigue. A woman whose screams only moments before were rending the air as her eyes were bloodily extracted from their sockets is now making eyes arm-in-arm with the Grand Inquisitor, who has peeled off his beetling eyebrows and wiped away the dark greasepaint creases that gave his face such a mercilessly stark appearance. Although the play is over these actors have lost none of their magnetism. Their appearance after the show is sort of the necessary counterpart to its atrocities.

Ella watches the stage hands mopping up in the aftermath of the sister's revenge, sees the locks of their white mops turn scarlet . . . and—

She remembers—

—there was a gap, like no-man's-land, between the crowd and the soldiers. When the Oracle King's "speech" had stopped, and he stood there before the crowd fallen silent themselves, suddenly a woman emerged, and ran trippingly across the gap toward the soldiers. Her arms were flung wide, and she wore an exulting expression. One of the cuirassiers drew, and fired, and she fell in a heap all at once, now completely still.

Ella saw her blood spilling onto the stones with a shock—although always deadly, there had never been blood or physical injuries before. But here in Venefy the soldiers draw blood when they kill. A man ran forward in much the same way as the woman had and an infantrywoman, hoisted onto her comrades' shoulders, aimed and fired her musket from that lofty place, and the ball caught the man in the side of his head spinning him around like a top. More dashed forward from the crowd the whole mob was surging this way and that some fleeing some still transfixed some stunned and many moving up to the front toward the gap. They dashed forward into the guns and were cut down by the dozens and unable to restrain themselves the cavalry pranced into the crowd bobbing over the darting heads stabbing on all sides.

The ground ran with smoking blood. Ella watched in shock to see those blades opening great scarlet rents in bodies the victims flung up their arms to the sky and collapsed under the eye of the Oracle King—but he withdrew. Confusion and cries of all descriptions—Ella was tossed and buffeted by the crowd. If she had tried to run with them she would have been instantly knocked down and trampled. She instead picked her way to the base of the central fountain which was fortuitously nearby and huddled against it.

From there she saw the victims rise shouting into the sky nearly levitating with explosive joy and they ran and pounced and clawed bit and tore with their bare hands at fleeing mobs catching up cobblestones—the square behind her was by then nearly empty—Ella fled the scene in terror . . .

*

". . . they must offer themselves—that's why the soldiers don't simply fall on them en masse . . . " she mutters aloud.

*

You call this the city of the dead and certainly the dead are here among us—but which is the city of the dead: this city, or the city that you come from? Which do *you* think is deader, Ella?

In the middle of the night when the stars blaze feverishly overhead and when the streets are deserted, seeing someone else appear in the distance is a terrible thing—as though that other person were an interloper in your dream. She passes down a dark lane lit only by starlight, between smooth white walls only two feet part. At the end, a white mausoleum with a modest little dome, all white and smooth like creamy soap, phantom buildings.

And here in the wider avenues dummies and mannikins walk the streets, although you almost never see them close up. It's only in hindsight that you realize a dummy took your ticket at the booth, all the while the bald head gazes unblinking off to the left . . . Sudden terror in the streets, like waking up in a nightmare, not knowing where you are . . . dark street . . . lost feeling . . .

Sense of pursuit . . . turn with mounting fear the worse for being inexplicable. Before her rushes up a cul-de-sac, standing there the Aged Doctor and the Veiled Nurse. She freezes—behind her the step-rap-step of an ivory leg knocks rattling tin cans aside, the tip of his cane pricking the stones. Ella turns . . . the Judge rumbles forward looming, and her body goes rigid . . .

He stops abruptly before her the points of two sabres indenting his cape at his chest—Ella glances behind her—two cuirassiers stand at her back their grins dim in the dark their arms extended holding the Judge at bay. She is under the Tyrant's protection. Beyond them, the cul-de-sac is empty, the Aged Doctor and the Veiled Nurse have somehow vanished.

"Oh all right," Daisie says. The Doctor and the Nurse emerge from his shadow as though sprouting from his shoulders, and stand abreast behind him.

Ella feels rage sneer on her features—"You can't have *him* so you come after me—"

A vile chuckle. "I come after you, as a route to him. You can't blame me for trying can you?"

"The hell I can't—"

"I'll never give up."

"*Why?*"

He grins wider his lips thin baring fangish yellow teeth.

"*I asked you why*"

There's a pause . . . now he chuckles . . . .

"*For the third time I ask you why*"

This time the answer is immediate: "You already . . . " he chuckles . . . and bows, "I am only a minor player, a functionary—and we are mad hallucinations, created at random like dreams, by-blows of insane convulsions. We act in accordance with the forms we are given . . . "

Something bare stark hideously plain about his explanations.

"You're no illusions—"

"We are *facts* . . . as much as you are anyway."

"You're part of him somehow—"

He nods and raises his chin.

"You are his self-destruction—"

Laughing—"We are *both* Mr. Hyde . . . "

"You you're nothing but a gargoyle you and your cronies misremembered stock characters—"

"We are *complete* fragments, I have an impairment of man. *You've* got one, too, my *dear—*" he pulls back his cape and raps his ivory leg with his cane.

Faster than sight Ella's crutch lashes out but he has already jerked back, the tip of her crutch strikes the wall by his head knocking out a divot of brick—"I'LL PIT MY LEGS AGAINST YOURS ANY DAY" she snarls. Ella lowers her head her shoulders and arms bunch menacingly as though she meant to spring forward and throw herself on him shatter his laughing teeth.

His body billows larger his face sizzles with hate "*I'll eat him alive!*" he snaps his glowing teeth bare slash the air his face thrust forward spraying saliva—the cuirassiers' blades push him back.

"All right . . . " his face fades like hollow flame . . . a drapery of smoke curls in the air, and disperses—she is alone in the alley.

*

Lost at night as the wind rises, Ella hastens as best she can through grim candle-lit neighborhoods. She comes across a sizeable intersection of three streets. The point at which they cross forms a large irregular open space, framed around by little shops. Here there are mobs, mostly young men dressed like Pamplonan bull runners all in white with red scarves. They stand anxiously along the edges of the intersection and in the adjoining alleys; their eyes dark. They are skittish, alert, gazelle-like, they are shining afraid. There are occasional defectors, slinking or rushing away; all but a handful are wavering, drawing away and then pausing, stepping back, and pausing, uncertain—but they stay.

Now on who knows what common impulse a detachment of about two dozen forms spontaneously and sprints across the open space into a narrow ascending lane. Their shirts flash white once and then dim down as they vanish in the shade of the lane. Ella can see the swelling silhouettes of riders in the lane, their swords held above their heads. Now the swords are rising and falling.

A moment later the riders erupt from the lane and streak across the open space dissipating into countless side streets in an instant. Now one of the men desperately pushes himself out from the sidewalk and dashes into the open space his arms akimbo his palms out his chest thrust forward and his head a little back his face all anguish or bizarre ecstasy and a rider bursts across the open space their paths intersect and the sabre slashes down slicing the man's chest nearly hacking him in half. The buttocks of the horse wink out against the shadow of the street opposite as the man crashes to the ground—Ella smells his blood.

Another man breaks from the rest into the open space a rider is there at once bringing his sabre up like a polo mallet the man is knocked backwards onto the ground his head strikes the cobbles with a terrible thump like a hollow gourd might make. As if this man were somehow magnetically joined to them, a knot of men all dash out after him and are all cut down and now like an avalanche more and more hurl themselves into the open space their legs pumping their breasts and necks exposed and the dragoons seem to bound out of the dark air and now they are simply wheeling round and round in the open space their swords rising and falling. Ella presses herself into the slimy wall her eyes are streaming she can't raise her hands from the crutches that support her to press them to her ears her eyes her nostrils. She sees the wounds smells the blood hears the blades chopping and the people dropping. She fights the urge to vomit or scream her teeth grind themselves painfully into her gums and her face is so contorted it is grinding shut her eyes. But despite her horror she also wants to toss herself forward with abandon, and be cut down—the waves of death tow at her, and she remains where she is only by repeating to herself with crazy endurance "Only he will kill me or I will not die," and keeping this fixed before her.

The soldiers are standing still all around the open space, making a ring around the massacre. From the narrow ascending lane the first group of runners suddenly dances out beaming, their bodies whole, and they skip into the open space like the first trickles of a stream in a dry riverbed. The miracle happens again—their presence causes the maimed bodies to stir, tremble and suddenly rise shuddering and vibrating with abounding vitality beaming and shouting . . . Ella staggers away.

*

. . .

A tenebrous figure slips from an open doorway in the deserted and shining street . . . Darkness fills the creases in her smile—her brow cheeks nose upper lip and chin are white islands half-emerging from dark water under the hood of her hair . . .

This part of town has the air of "The Turn of the Screw"—chilly rose gardens, dewy lawns, vibrantly green vines humped up atop wrought-iron fences, stately sphinxlike old trees, an air of repose on the brink of utter petrification . . . Vertinginous stasis, like falling forever in place . . . Croquet mallets, luminous fog too thick to play in, a sky that will never be disrupted by thunder and lightning, the rooftops of remote country homes and ruined abbeys that will never be silhouetted against the sky by lightning. A sinister calm, ebbingly lethal stillness . . . Phantom ladies like ice palaces, achingly beautiful and wan; they neither come nor go, nor do they talk . . .

Transfixing Medusa power flutters all around them like gauzy scarfs and a drizzle of fine ash. These ladies are native only to bleak mornings, dreamily oppressive afternoons, and bad nights. They are voiceless sirens, vampires of no appetite.

Now a narrow cobbled street that seems to rise into the starry heavens: hard-edged shadows, swept clean of every particle of dust by the constant sluicing of the wind, bordered by the sagging-roofed gabled houses with small-paned windows. In the blue-lit attics sit old women in rocking chairs their hands bundled in their shawls, and old men who paw thick, time-stained books whose pages puff out clouds of mold as they are turned. They both sit cackling crazily to themselves thinking of what mad things will drop from the pit of the sky onto the roofs over their heads. In the rooms below children toss and turn in ponderous nightmares in beds that are little more than crates padded with stale sodden bedding. Here the mother lies feverish in her bed with a single candle lit on the nightstand, tossing and turning, or lying dead, and the pale, bloodless sister who has been tending her is draped across the foot of the bed in an exhausted swoon. The father sits up in the front room by the window overlooking the street, blue light from the street playing over his features, his scalding eyes, orange and gold light from the fireplace dancing over his form. He turns, with simmering eyes burning deeper into his skull, and takes in the confines of the bare room all at once. Outside, perched on the chimney pot, a cricket the size of a german shepherd rubs its hind legs together with a low, woeful cello sound.

Ella creeps, with terror at the prospect of making the slightest sound. She yearns for the invisibility of those big carnival crowds . . . and now there are drunks all over the street and a smell of urine everywhere. The disarranged clothing of those who have passed out shows clearly that they have been robbed. More casinos . . . a static charge of sick excitement in the air . . . elongated women whose heads trail like balloons on their necks and who weave stoned slightly off balance on their high heels. They pass up and down among the tables, coming to rest here and there like birds pecking at a handful of seeds.

They are selected by this or that gambler and stand beside him, his arm encircles her naked waist as he plays and he gives her the dice to breathe on—and she signals the waiters to keep the expensive drinks coming. Here they are dressed in sumptuous evening gowns and scintillating golden veils, there they wear little more than their feathers and ropes of beads. The gold green blue and red flashing lights pulse over their exposed skin and seem to drug them; they are seemingly impervious to the cold. When their fellows win, they smile and applaud woozily.

A woman wearing long purple gloves and a headdress like drooping willow fronds and little else reels a step or two back from her place at the roulette table right by the entrance. Her eyes roll up showing two white crescents in black smears of kohl, and she collapses in a faint, half spilled out onto the sidewalk. None of her fellow employees or the other customers seem to notice. Three young street boys in castoff clothes rush up immediately and strip off her jewelry, her more expensive beads, her fine gloves and stockings.

And now Ella feels it too—an enfeebling vertigo. She looks around on all sides for a plain restaurant or a café. Increasingly unsteady, she selects the least ostentatious-looking place in her vicinity and makes her way in through knots of people. An empty table appears before her, and she makes for the chair as though it were a life preserver. The white tablecloth is stained, the seat is still unpleasantly warm. She is sitting in a nightclub; the golden stage thrums with remote dancing girls shrieking in a can-can. Ella thinks back to the cold lucidity of the Bly gardens or that stark street and wonders which is better, where is she safer—among this mob of pleasure-seeking goblins or in the frigid glare of those dead tableaux. Impulsively, she seizes up the half-empty bottle left behind by the couple who had just quitted the table and voraciously drains it. The contents have a faint plum taste, the liquor is surprisingly mellow, it pours into a hard ball of warm brass in her stomach . . . ghostly fingers of spirits press into her brain.

The atmosphere is stifling like a suffocating dream. The air sits on her as heavily as thick, sweat-soaked bedclothes, the repetitive oscillations of the dancers on the stage are just like the motionless, stale air above her bed, congealed there. Parade of legs rising and falling like the sabres of the cavaliers—and yet there's something so voluptuous in all this she isn't thinking about escape, she wants things to get if possible *more* oppressive *more* oppressive an atmosphere so oppressive you could *chew* it. She sits there panting and her body liquefies . . . she's not seeing more than an inch in front of her face, she's no longer aware of the dancers, their strange alarming display, her surroundings . . . Her mind is completely preoccupied and possessed by the bizarre physical change that is overwhelming her . . . Ella flattens deflates feels herself ooze down in the chair . . .

. . . and now the night is growing deeper here—the goblins are packing it in—even the passed-out drunks are sitting up and rubbing their eyes. They scurry away with bleary apprehension. In Ella's mind the thought appears as though engraved there YOU MUST RETURN TO YOUR LODGINGS.

Gropingly distantly weightless and in slow motion she rises, swims out the door . . . siphoning slithering boulevards and dark unfamiliar places one after another . . . Slower and slower gathering inertia from nightmares . . . But as she is beginning seriously to despair of making it, she catches sight of the park at the bottom of the city, and the shafts of colored light in the air playing on the foliage emitted by the hybrid orchid-whale in the park's central pool. At once she has her bearings, and retraces the route she took once before with Dr. Belhoria. Sense of the night's deepest part coming rapidly up upon her but holding back at the threshold. It can wait just so long and no longer and then the deep night that belongs only to the dead will begin, and she must not be caught on the street then or she will evaporate into freezing air . . .

It is purely by accident that Ella finds herself on her street again and she gasps with thankfulness on recognizing it. She is battered and worn thin, thinner and thinner . . . It takes twenty minutes for her to climb the steps onto the porch, each minute twice as long as the last. Remains of last night's dinner in the sink, her landlord turns to her with a mouth full of catsup. Somehow her door is swinging open and the quilt the pillow hurtle up . . .

*

Winds flap whipping black tatters of panic—Ella wakes the next morning to the sound of riot in the street and from her window she can see columns of black smoke rising all over the city. She can hear screams and the roar of mobs and shrill laughter everywhere—something has happened—the mainspring of Venefy is broken—Ella rushes downstairs and she can already feel it overtaking her, dread and worse—grief. Figures flash by the door. What's happening? What's happening? The mainspring is broken. A catastrophe blasted out the heart. The city is derailed crashing headlong; wrenched off balance; disintegrating in chunks.

Ella rushes out onto the front porch. She looks up and screams instantly violent, jarred. The Tyrant's observatory is a plume of fire. His fort is in flames. As she watches, one of the walls crashes down into the canyon, trailing smoke. The porch yaws and keels to the right like the deck of a sinking ship. Terror, nausea clutch at her stomach; in a thoughtless frenzy she goes into the street. A woman carrying a lapdog in her arms and looking over her shoulder instead of where's she's going turns a corner and sends Ella sprawling; Ella struggles but she can't regain her feet. She tries to edge to one side to avoid being trampled; a voice speaks her name in astonishment. A pair of hands reaches down and bears her upright again, she turns and finds Carl standing behind her.

"I was looking for you; we have to leave."

"Where's the car? I have to see Belhoria—where's the car? Where's the car?"

They bang over the rough cobbles in the street many of them already taken up by rioters, dodge people in flight many of them wounded streaming blood, swerve to avoid the larger pieces of debris. They won't have much chance to change a tire here if they damage one. Carl honks incessantly stopping and starting the car in jerks.

The casino is already empty. The tables and chairs are overturned. As Ella comes in, the heavy-looking manager emerges from behind the bar with an overstuffed briefcase and scrambles into his waiting limosine. In the interior of the casino the balance that once hung overhead lies in ruins, the two desks smashed wide open like cracked gourds. A smell of fresh blood and overpowering alcohol. In the back, Dr. Belhoria's door is standing open. Ella cautiously puts in her head afraid of what she might find fear acid in her stomach.

But Dr. Belhoria is there, hastily packing a large suitcase on the center table. Allan appears from the back room with a heavy box; he notices Ella and acknowledges her with a brief nod, then shoulders past her.

"What is it?"

"Ella, I don't know—I don't know. Daisie's done something to the Tyrant—assassinated, kidnapped, dined on him I don't know—"

"But—"

"I don't know how he did it but it's done—"

"—what about the army?"

Dr. Belhoria pauses, looks her fixedly in the eye, and says, "*What* army? You don't see—there is no army! They're all *free* now, to *do whatever they like* do you understand? It's time to *go*."

" . . . Free? Do you mean Daisie isn't in control?"

"No, he's not in control. Clearly he was able to eliminate the Tyrant, but it would seem he was not able to establish himself in his place. The army has dissolved—this is anarchy—not a coup. The soldiers burned the fort and the observatory and now they're tearing the city to pieces and all living persons present are in danger. Do you have your car here? Did Carl find you?"

"I can't go without—"

"Forget him!" Dr. Belhoria returns to her packing. ". . . I think this experiment is over, and I think this place is over too . . . Now you can draw your own conclusions, but you had better do it with dispatch."

" . . . How can we just be in the dark like this?"

Dr. Belhoria is shutting her last suitcase.

"What about Daisie? Will he come for us now?"

"I don't know. For now, I imagine the soldiers are holding him up. They might even be able to kill him. —I know they killed the old doctor and his nurse," she adds with a grim smirk, "I saw their bodies run up the flagpoles."

"And the army?"

"Who knows? Dispersed to the four winds, settle all over the world in dreams of their choice—how should I know?"

Allan stumbles in and seizes two bags sitting by the door, Dr. Belhoria hefts her suitcase.

"Goodbye, Ella."

In the street Carl is reproaching himself for not packing the car—his stuff and all of Ella's valuable instruments and irreplaceable research are in storage at his place, an apartment he had found on his own.

"It's just nearby; do you want to risk it?"

They bob and lurch through the streets now increasingly cluttered; smoke whirls in the air. Apparently Carl has been living in a section of an old slimy-looking brick dairy. He dashes inside leaving Ella by the car. Soon the Packard's trunk is full and he is heaping things up on the back seat. He has a heavy portmanteau from somewhere he needs to retrieve and he will need a few minutes to find a dolly and bring it out. Should he bother she says yes in a daze he rushes inside and she thoughtlessly wanders up the street.

She passes a wide alleyway between two brick buildings just a dozen or so feet up from the car. The roar of a huge truck at the opposite end of the short alley attracts her attention and she turns her head to look.

She looks—a scream is born and dies ravages unvoiced in her throat as her eyes fall on the Tyrant. He's naked, his head shaved. He's been castrated. His arms and legs have been hacked off, and his body has been bound up with twine like a parcel. He lies in bags of rubbish by the wall. A man in filthy coveralls and gloves picks up his torso by the twine bindings and carries him sideways. As she watches, the Tyrant's body is thrown into the hopper of the bellowing garbage truck, where it lands on its side . . .

The scene flashes—Daisie flies drunkenly at the Tyrant, teeth bared breathing in his face, lying in his face—"that angel broke you a long time ago"—the scalpel cutting in regular strokes teeth tear into the flesh of butchered arms legs genitals . . .

The man in coveralls is walking up to the front of the truck. Ella moves closer—the Tyrant is still alive, all the while talking, talking gently calmly to *her* . . .

* . . . it's all right Ella . . . I am not your strength . . . you will live . . . and outlive me . . . *you* are my immortality Ella . . . our experiment went very far . . . and will go on, impossible to check . . . I am not indispensable now . . . and you are our experiment's worthiest, and most loved witness . . . *

Ella stands by the hopper of the roaring truck and the engine suddenly groans louder, smoke gushes from the upright exhaust pipes, and any moment now the hopper will turn and crush him inside. Ella calls him frantically but he can't help himself—now their separation will be permanent. In a moment he will disappear forever and she can't raise her hands from the crutches that hold her upright to pull him out, or even to touch him. He is still reassuring her quietly . . . comforting *her*.

But now there's an idea—an idea that makes no sense or does it—out of the alley her crutches flying—no sign of Carl but she had seen in the jumble in the car's back seat there by the window the black-and-white plant she had grown from the poppet's excrement, now sprouting little black fruits. Hearing the grind of the truck she smashes the car window with her crutch and leaning in just manages to drag the plant forward by one leaf—she snaps off one of the fruits. She claws at its flesh tearing it open. She bends down and somehow manages to take one of its seeds between her teeth.

Back in the alley the truck is rumbling and the hopper is starting to turn. Trying not to crush the seed between her teeth she is gasping for breath rushing. Ella bends down to him where he is still talking and presses her lips to his speaking mouth, with her tongue she pushes the seed into his mouth and somehow slips it under his tongue. The truck jerks forward tearing their mouths apart . . . a thread of saliva links their lips and then breaks.

The truck grinds rumbles forward the hopper turning—gone.

CHAPTER THIRTEEN

Streets of rotting jack-o-lanterns—a weight bears her down to the earth . . . Blind gaze falls from her smarting eyes . . . lips solder to each other . . . in her breast, her voice keens in empty space—keening, keens and wails, keens, wails . . .

Graveyard: tombstones, obelisks, urns, grave angels, weeping willows, dewy green lawns, desiccated wreaths. Below, rank and file in the earth at a level of six feet, there are regular punctuated spaces in the earth. Here, the Tyrant's trunk lies in a full-sized coffin—retrieved and buried anonymously by strangers . . . (by court order, the cemetery donates a certain number of plots every year to John Does supplied by state and even federal authorities as a way of repaying the community for some shady dealings in the past involving the reuse of coffins and the unexpected reappearance of certain deceased improperly-buried persons during a spring shower, bodies slopped out in the mud onto the streets—the mayor's brother screeches to a halt at the sight of his lamented Aunt Clare sprawled with a fire hydrant between her legs—it seems some others were never buried at all just warehoused behind barrels of fertilizer in storage) . . .

Rows of still graves . . . The Tyrant's head rests on a white satin cushion—the only frill involved in his burial—surplus coffin—he was not even embalmed. They deposited him unceremoniously in the hole without a second look—no money in it. And so they missed the seed beneath his tongue.

Rows of still graves . . . the Tyrant's head rests on a white satin cushion. The back of his head pops open like a nut and a thick blunt white shoot like a brainstem screws out from the base of his skull. It grinds into the cushioning and through the bottom of the coffin. Contacting the rich black soil it sends out hairline roots in all directions and they swell and thicken as the root plunges deeper still.

Other shoots emerge from his eyes and nose and ears and soon the coffin is filled with a web of white roots the diameter of pencils. His slack mouth opens wide and a stalk pushes out and up into the coffin lid, corkscrewing through splintering wood and soft loosened earth the stalk claws its way to the surface breaking through into the light of the just risen full moon. The stalk breaks out in little stems that flex and wobble and unfold black leaves. The leaves open like pairs of hands to catch the moon light. The stalk thickens and jerks upwards further into the air sprouting more leaves. It twists and writhes and the sprouts lengthen and corkscrew in the air becoming branches, the stalk is six feet tall. Now it is ten feet tall a young white-trunked sapling with weird black leaves. By the time the moon is at its zenith directly overhead, the tree is forty feet tall pulsing and surging its spreading branches shadow nearly seven hundred square feet—near the top it has produced an enormous black bud.

The bud angles itself into the moon's light and bursts open—a sunflower-like blossom five feet across, a broad leathery pad fringed with white silky petals. The tree shudders and the pad distends filling with fluid. It grows into a great bilobed skin sac—the flower droops its head. When the moon is at the last quarter of its transit overhead the black sac turns translucent, and in the moon's light an x-ray shadow of a fully-developed human skeleton with a beating heart in his ribs is visible curled within the sac. The skeleton twitches now and again . . . and now the seam running the vertical circumference of the sac deepens and becomes an indentation—the sac ruptures spattering branches and grass with shreds of skin and clear fluid smelling of turpentine.

There is movement in the tree. The branches rustle, now high up, now lower, now lower still. A grimy booted foot plants itself atop a headstone standing by the base of the trunk, and using this intermediate step, a large pale full-grown man steps to the ground. He is huddled in a heavy black overcoat, and pauses a minute to finger the slimy lenses of his spectacles. Then he starts off picking his way jerkily through the graves.

He follows the paths, that are cut into the green now glowing blue breasts of rolling meadows dotted with stones. He walks swiftly with his head purposefully lowered swinging his right arm. Presently he comes to a tall wrought-iron fence with a two-foot brick base that separates the graveyard from an administrative area by the main gate. After a few clumsy attempts to clamber over the fence he resignedly takes a few steps back and hurls himself at it trying to hurdle it sideways through the air. He crashes through the bars which snap or break loose—lands with a heavy thud in a shower of iron bars. He gets to his feet uninjured, picks up a couple of the bars, and walks to the main gate. His gait is smoother now—it seems the fall knocked a few joints into place.

The gate is chained and padlocked. He reinforces the chain by twisting the iron bars around the gate's edge rods and by spiking the hinges. A groundskeeper's pickup truck is parked nearby; he pushes that in front of the gate and heaves it onto its side—a few dumpsters set behind that and he is satisfied with his barricade.

Why barricade? Now the tree is bristling with black buds they blossom one by one in the still-blazing light of the full moon. They bulge and droop and the tree is hung with dozens of fleshy fruits. They clear and reveal their contents like x-rays a fully grown human skeleton in each—and the seam sinks in becomes an indentation and now one ruptures, spattering the ground with shreds of skin and translucent gelatin. A pale figure in a worn shabby black overcoat clambers down the trunk, and here's another one who swings down from one of the boughs landing with a heavy thud. Another drops on top of him and they fall on each other punching and socking, screaming curses snarling and frothing. Sullen pallid skulking figures fan out from the tree in all directions. Joined by the first of their number they fall on tombstones urns obelisks and grave angels. One seizes a headstone by its edges at the base and breaks it off clean at ground level. Another grabs an obelisk, leans back and flexes his knees—the obelisk breaks off and crashes on top of him. He rolls it off his person staggers to his feet and pulls it onto his back. Unmoved by its fetching figure, another squats and wraps his arms around the feet of a grave angel and, lifting with his legs, hauls it from its pedestal.

Now they are everywhere a surly army of ogres plundering grave markers of all descriptions—snapping and grinding of stone fills the air. Fresh reinforcements arrive continually squabbling fighting grumbling. When they have acquired a prize they turn back to the hill on which the tree, now seventy feet tall, spreads it vast branches. Each of a group of four takes a corner of a mausoleum—they have procured tools from a groundskeeper's shed and they use them to pry the mausoleum up off its foundations. They work their fingers in and lift with their legs on a count of three, lift it entire from the ground perching it on their shoulders and they bear it ponderously up the hill grunting, bent double, saliva hanging in strings from their chins. Ad hoc chains of throwers form, stones of all kinds are tossed from one to another up the hill—those at the receiving end are placing the stones in a perimeter around the tree.

A security guard blunders across the scene during a drive-by and steps from his truck gaping at swarms of identical pale spectacled men in big black coats rambling through the cemetery tearing up the monuments with their bare hands and making off with them. Already meadows and hills lie bare dotted with broken-off butt-ends and stumps. A hand seizes him roughly by the shirt between his shoulders and hauls him off his feet before he can reach his radio. He only failingly catches a glimpse of the big overcoated man who drags him irresistibly along. The man's strength is astonishing—the beefy security guard struggles unavailingly against it. Now the figure forces his way into the mortuary offices and pulls open a locked door by the doorknob—the bolt flies out through splintering wood. He thrusts the security guard into the basement and slams the door to again. The guard rushes back up the stairs but a desk has already been shoved up against the door, and he can hear what sounds like a filing cabinet land with a crash atop the desk. He bangs on the door and shouts.

The next morning, cemetery administrators pull up alongside the guard's still-idling truck in astonishment. Daylight reveals a colossal fort has sprung up overnight in the heart of the cemetery, which is now completely denuded. A sharp-eyed young typist gasps, the fort is constructed entirely of tombstones obelisks grave angels . . . the turrets at each corner are mausoleums somehow transported intact to the top of a five-story wall. Troops of identical dark figures can be seen hard at work atop the wall and moving in little knots throughout the grounds. They toss headstones up from the base of the wall to their counterparts working atop them.

The fort is visible for miles around. By now, close inspection of the premises is not readily possible, owing to the construction of an earthwork trench ten feet deep and fifteen feet across, enclosing the fort in its perimeter. Further down the slope, work details are busily trying to convert the duck pond into a full-fledged moat. Reinforcements appear and begin lining the bottom of the trench with pongee sticks.

After a news helicopter is forced to land with a damaged tail rotor—these fort builders are deadly accurate with bricks and chunks of tombstone, and they can throw suprisingly hard and far—the press are requested to keep their distance. The barricade is broken and reporters are swarming in through hastily-cut holes in the fences—one team puts their man over the cemetery wall with a cherry picker and he jumps out into a tree and climbs to the ground. A police line is set up some distance from the moat, but a handful of gallant souls rush up and begin barking questions at the builders cross the rapidly-filling moat. One of the figures turns to them and says with possibly affected melancholy, "If you want anything done you gotta do it yourself." Further comments were forestalled by a hail of dirt clods that knock reporters to their feet and break their equipment. Police dash forward to defend the routed reporters and fire tear gas at the builders. The figures across the moat calmly pick up the smoking canisters and without batting an eye let alone shedding a tear they hurl them back over the heads of the police into the distant lines, where riot gear has not yet been donned. There is a stampede for the gate. The builders stand by the slimy water and shake their fists, then return to their labors.

Ella is passing a shop window filled with flickering televisions and as if a fishook had hooked the corner of her eye she jerks to a halt and turns her head her eyes practically suck a hole in the glass. It is a long helicopter shot of teeming heavy black coated figures . . . The shot shows the interior of the fort: it has been built around a massive tree in rising terraces and cloisters a little like a square coliseum, the ranks lined with grave angels—the tree has white boughs and black leaves. Black-coated figures in masks are welding obelisks to the roofs of the mausoleums—the cameras close in on a single figure carrying a one-ton stone obelisk on his shoulder, he tosses it to one of his doubles on the roof of a mausoleum, thrown and caught as though it were only a plank of balsa wood. Architectural experts reckon from the general shape of the upper part of the building that they are constructing an observatory dome over the tree. One of the builders rears back and pitches a brick which flashes through the air and breaks the camera two hundred yards away. Static on screen—but she saw his face and recognized it against a backdrop of white boughs and black leaves—"The seed! The seed!" she vibrates in place and spins accidentally breaking the shop window with her crutch. This brings the shop man from behind his counter but she is already away.

It's clear—the next strategy is proliferation. Daisie cannot reproduce himself, but the Tyrant is now many.

The police line around the cemetery is still forming—Ella is approaching the cemetery from the rear and she reaches the fence before the police arrive. Now how to get over? There is little time. The fence consists of old wrought-iron bars in a cement base arranged in panels between brick columns—she braces herself against one of the columns and uses it for leverage, thrusting a crutch through and up behind one of the bars at its base. Willing her crutch not to bend she pushes with all her might—the bar groans and warps, and snaps. Ella snaps two more bars. She can hear cars, engines, the police are on the way. She flings herself against the broken bars held in place by a horizontal rod near the top of the fence and pushes. The bars press into her flesh through her clothes bruising her but they bend forward and splay out to either side. Ella forces her way through and makes for the fort. Voices call after her—she plunges headlong into a screen of trees nearly toppling over the roots.

Now she's out in the open again—a voice off to the left—a lone police officer approaches calling "Miss! Miss!" and waving her back. She ignores him and keeps going. He comes up alongside her, "Miss you have to get back—" he doesn't know quite how to deal with this dogged teenage girl in legbraces, even a hand on her shoulder might send her tumbling to the ground. He rushes in front of her and holds up his hands. Ella bunches slightly with her head down and ploughs into him sending him sprawling on his back. Ella nearly keels over backwards but steadies herself quickly. The cop is bound to try again—she cracks him over the head with her crutch and he bellyflops on the ground, his legs curl like a dead bug's and he feebly covers his head with his hands. Ella is pretty certain she's concussed him.

Further in and no interference yet—she's come to the moat, into which they have incorporated a contemplating pool ringed with an artistic arrangement of large stones. Ella puts her back to the flat face of the biggest stone and plants her crutches, pushing. Sweat bristles on her brow and arms but the stone is slowly tilting backward. She slides down to give herself more leverage. As its equilibrium shifts she throws up her arms and allows herself to drop down instead of hurtling back with the stone, which plunges into the moat with an anticlimactic slapping sound. Breathing hard but not wanting to be arrested so close to her goal, Ella sort of ricochets herself back and forth on the flanking stones and so regains her feet. She inches out onto the large stone, which nearly spans the moat. At the very tip she is able to reach out and plant her crutches on the bank opposite—she can swing her feet onto the bank but her crutches have sunk into the ground—she couldn't pull them out without toppling backwards. So instead she crumples forwards and lands with a grunt lengthwise on the ground, crawls away from the bank.

Now the trench. Not far enough away to merit the trouble of getting back on her feet, she elbows her way forwards with her crutches sticking out on either side of her. She peers over the edge of the trench—no pongee sticks yet, that's good. She laboriously pivots around until she is lying lengthwise along the edge of the trench, she presses her arms to the ground and swings her legs over into space. Now she is hanging with her arms perpendicular to her body—nothing for it but to release the tension in her arms and drop the five or so remaining feet. Fortunately the trench wall is not plumb, but angles outward slightly; she slides more than she drops, and has time to bring her crutches down—nevertheless at the bottom she falls on her back.

Ella lies at the bottom of the trench looking up into the sky and breathing hard. After a moment's dazed rest, she turns on her belly and drags herself fifteen feet across the trench to the opposite wall. Catch her breath and then lever herself upright against the wall. When she is leaning belly up against it, she reaches behind herself and deftly unstraps her crutches. They have lanyards attached to them and she thrusts her right arm through the loops and awkwardly hefts them onto her back. Her braced legs slide a little bit. Ella claws at the soil wall and drives her hands in, begins to climb. The soil crumbles and gives but her hands dig in deeper and she is able to get a purchase and pull herself up. Sweat runs down her face plastering it with dirt, she has dirt in her mouth nose and eyes, and her shoulders burn. As with the other wall, this one is a little inclined, that's good. Near the top she flings one arm over, then the other, and hauls herself up and onto the grass exhausted.

Now on her feet . . . and through a thin curtain of trees—and suddenly, she is among them. In the lee of the walls, she is among them. Some ignore her, some glance, some stop and stare. A detachment passes her without looking up—they are going to remove that stone from the moat before the police can make use of it.

The fort here presents itself as a cross between a cloister and a classical facade, a high porch without steps rises several feet above the ground, flanked by a pair of stone sphinxes whose faces have been skillfully refashioned in the Tyrant's likeness. Likewise, the larger statues and grave angels stand among the pillars, figures chisel their own features onto the stone faces.

That same face . . . in every face, the identical flame of malice, the exalted vehemence, the sulking courage . . . Now, if *her* Tyrant is here at all, he's just one of the crowd . . . Not even Air Mail, not even a nameless test subject, maybe not anything . . . how much of his substance was sucked up by the roots of that tree, and to what degree was it dispersed amongst these? She is surrounded by Tyrants but where is *her* Tyrant . . . ? These Tyrants live, but does *her* Tyrant live?

She looks up at the figures among the pillars above her—and one of them stops and steps up to the edge—

* Hello, Ella. *

She looks at him . . . and he's her Tyrant, her Air Mail.

But does she *really know*?

She doesn't know.

But she *insists*. She calls him, "Lift me up!"

He reaches down and lifts her in his arms, bears her up with him.

Now they are together. Crutches still strapped to her arms, she embraces him and clings. For a moment, she clings, and then she feels herself enfolded in ponderously slow arms. She lunges at his face, vehemently pressing her lips gritted with dirt grains against his. Her kiss is slowly returned from ponderous, stony features. Does he return her embrace and kiss, or does he echo them? He *returns* them, because she insists. Ella throws back her head; he has carried her inside the walls. Above her, a tapestry of black leaves and white branches is outspread, speckled with livid blue in the gaps of its warp. She is one of them, too, and has been. She will fight to remain with them, and go on fighting, as she has always fought.

Now, these tyrants address you, from their murderous paradise.

LaVergne, TN USA
16 January 2011
212629LV00003B/173/A